A PLANET IN TURMOIL

Operation Stargate

Herbert Grosshans

CHARACTERS

Ethan Samuel Wolf, 43, Major with the ISS: Interstellar Secret Service. Born on Rion

Harry Turnbull, 43, Colonel with SPA (Solar Protection Agency) born on Rion

Alfred Swann, 43, Master Scout, born on Rion. He is a Major with Scouts Security.

Captain Wong. He picks up the three men with a shuttle and saves them from the Nulgarians.

Gorini. Anorian Female. A Captain in the Anorian Special Investigations Service

Troopers with the Solar Union Space Navy:

Brigit Harris, 29, Sergeant, Team Leader.

Beverly Thompson, 27, Specialist

Lena Nakamura, 28, Specialist

Sonia Lopez, 26, Specialist

Oliver Jones, Sergeant, Team leader

Arlo Garcia, Specialist

Cyrus Ahmed, Specialist

Ezra Hassan, Specialist

Jasper Bernard, Specialist

Ronen Lee, Specialist, temporarily promoted to Master Corporal, Team leader

Asher Whang, Specialist

Harrison Campbell, Specialist

Dakarai Abara. Pilot in small Spaceship. He was born on the asteroid Vesta.

Jonathan Malleway. Captain of Troop Carrier.

Doc Edward MacCulloch, Ship's Doctor, born in Old Edinburg, Scotland, Earth.

Other minor and major characters:

Colonel Terrex Stonewall. Head of Scouts Security and Scouts Special Forces

Admiral Swenson of the Solar Union Space Navy.

Sergeant Emil Slovinsky of Customs at the Spaceport in Greater York

Ltd Garcia. He picks up the team at the Customs office in Greater York.

General Edward Mitchell of the Freeland Army. He is also the Minister of Justice.

Ambassador Alexander Amsterdam. 8 years on Cerberus. He was born on Hyperion.

George McMahon. First Ambassador. He and wife got murdered after 7 years.

Paul Davenport. Second Ambassador. Left after 5 years.

Taria. Servant. Elderly. Worked for the Embassy 12 years. Born in Greater York. Cerberus.

Eugene. Driver for Ambassador Amsterdam. He is a Sartan.

Inspector Gifford. He is a major player and shareholder with Hyperion Cerberus Lirsium Group.

Malor. Supervisor at the mine. He is a Sartan.

Adriana Wilson. Wife of Dr. Benjamin Wilson. Amsterdam's sister. Lives in Windy Lake.

Dr. Benjamin Wilson. Surgeon in Windy Lake.

Albert Brownstone. Prime Minister of Freeland.

Corporal Horinder of the Windy Lake police department. Killed in the attack on the store.

Francis Dubois. Police Chief of the Windy Lake Police Department.

Linda Clark. Secretary for the Police Department. Killed by the alien raiders.

Sergeant Hermann Becker of the Windy Lake Police Department (friends with Scout Ikeda)

Scout Brian Ikeda (friends with Hermann Becker) He was taught by *Captain* Swann –Scout-Scout Anders Axelsson

Scout David Stavros. Red hair, cut military style

Scout Amos Hadad (mustache) –Master Scout-

Randor. Driver for Wolf and Swann driving in Tsacona.

Ramsy. Warrior for a Sartan King

Emril. Geologist for Hyperion Cerberus Lirsium Group (HCLG)

Mansfield. Geologist for HCLG

Berman. Geologist for HCLG

Captain Ranini. Leader of the Anorian team. She wears a black band around her left arm.

Soloniak, James. Lawyer for HCLG

Isaac Sanchez. Soloniak's secretary.

Steven Duron. Soldier in the HCLG Private Special Forces.

Francis Cornwall. Commander in the HCLG Private Special Forces.

Ltd. Vern Starling. Scout with Scouts Security.

Baranda. Catman on T'Par exploration vessel.

Raamur. Male Arani. Prisoner on T'Par exploration vessel.

THE UNIVERSE OF OPERATION STARGATE

Acura: 1/2 million colonists. Indigenous people: Sersani. Humanoids.

Agrar: A rugged planet with large regions of frozen tundra.

Apollo: Long cold winters. A strip around equator is livable. Healing waters. Near Spider territory. They love to go to Apollo to use the healing waters.

Apovi: Home planet of the Apovians. (Beyond the Star-portal)

Arbor: High Tech planet.

Arcadia: A transfer station from Star-Liners to smaller spaceships is located near the planet.

Aregon: A planet near the Crow Empire. Many different indigenous inhabitants. Has a Star-gate.

Archilles: An ice-planet circling a dying sun in the Horsehead Nebula, 1500 lightyears from the Solar System. Temperatures dip to minus 50F in temperate zone.

Artemis: A Sanctuary planet for animals. Earth-like in size and seasons. Named after a Greek Goddess. They discover a Stargate there.

Astralis: Low Tech Planet. They have vehicles that run on alcohol.

Athora: Populated by giant lizards.

Aurora: The 4th planet of seven in the Silica System. Earth-type, nearly as large as Earth. Has a Star-gate.

Belgona: Home of the Lurengi.

Breem: A planet next to the star system of the planet Swren.

Bloodvane: Earth-like, populated by kangaroo-like non-humans. They are primitive but they have a social structure.

Casaar: Alien planet, populated by Casaarians, Humanoid cat-like creatures. Advanced technology.

Chiron: An Earth-like planet. One of the first planets colonized. Two billion humans. No aliens. No indigenous people. 5th of seven planets circling Solaris.

Chirion XII. Advanced technology. 250 million inhabitants.

Cerberus: Earth-like. At the edge of the Galaxy in the Spinner-system. 4th planet of eight. Has a Star-gate

Devil's Nest. Most of the wildlife is avian. There are huge birds.

Erde. Second planet of Alpha Centauri. Air always smells fresh.

Easter. (Y25, the closest planet of Barnard's Star) is always red and not very bright. Rich people go there for their honeymoon. The gravity is less than one gee.

Epsilon. Jungle. Giant dinosaurs. Closed habitats. Ancient ruins from the Spider race and the Dragons.

Estrade. Two moons. 30 million people.

Exarion: Earth-like. Three moons. 20 million people. High Tech.

Fortune. In the Silica System.

Fury: (originally Poseido) Plagued by violent storms.

Glory: Earth-like

Goldstrike. In the Montello System. Close to Accilla occupied territory. Humans and Accilla colonists live peacefully side by side.

Grall. At the outer edge of the Crow Empire. It doesn't belong to any race or regulated territory.

Helios. Newly discovered and declared safe for colonization

Hyperion. Hich Tech.

Icarus. Earth-like.

Lazaar. Home planet of the Trevorians.

Lancelot. A planet in the Five-Suns-System.

Pallas: An asteroid in the asteroid belt in the Solar System. Diameter 400 km.

Perseus. Earth-type. Middle Ages stage. Humans and Tangari.

Rainbow: Third planet in the Alpha Centauri System. Seat of the Military Academy.

Radiant: Many deserts. Impenetrable jungles. High Mountains. Volcanos.

Rion: Commander Wolf, Colonel Turnbull, and Master Scout Swann were born there. Home of the Museum of Intergalactic Races.

Salamander: Planet Four in the Horsehead Nebula System. 270 Lightyears from Sol. Has a Star-gate

Savanna: Earth-like. 4th planet from its Primary. Blue Diamonds. Has a Star-gate

Sheffield's Planet: Home of Starshield Innovations, one of the largest and most influential companies on that planet.

Snowball. Ragged mountains. Ice storms. Continuous volcanic eruptions.

Starcross. A jungle planet. Intelligent plants.

Tellus: Not very suitable for colonization. Has lots of Allegrum. Mined by Starleaf Explorations.

Tulia: Advanced technology. One billion people. Headquarters of SAPG (Solar Animal Protection Guild) and of the GWA (Game Warden Academy).

Valhalla: Colonized by so-called Vikings. Their society sank back into savagery, but it flourished.

Valiant:

Virgil. Humans and Accilla live there.

DENIZENS OF SPACE

Humans.
Kraach. **The Spiders.** Ancient race. None-humanoid. Apparently originated from the red giant Arcturus star system. Oval black, hairy bodies
about three ft long. Six long, multi-jointed legs and two short front limbs
with long, bony fingers. Their spaceships are black with spidery stabiliz-
ers. Their ships are spidery and flowing. And menacing.
Accilla. Intelligent slugs that mimic other life forms. Shape shifters.
Telepaths. They cannot influence others. They suck blood.
Anorians. Reptilian race. Females are the dominant gender. Tiny, silvery
shimmering scales cover their body. Golden Eyes. Empaths. Pointy teeth.
Lisping voice. Slit pupils. Forked tongue. Vegetarians. Walk around
naked.
Apovians. Shapeshifters. Original form is a giant snake. Come from the
planet Apovi.
Arani: The counterpart of the Anorians on the other side of the Star-gate.
Males are dominant.
Crows. (Ventairians in the Crow language) Birdlike beings. Ancestry
birds. Spaceships have delicate, flowing lines. The Crows call their empire
'The **Ventairian Empire**'. It is controlled by twenty Supreme Councilors.
Dragons. All reptilian races. Ugly, square and bulky spaceships.

Mollard. A Dragon species. Bare Skulls. Brutish looking. Females no breasts. They have a short crest on their head. They are egg layers. Vertical slit pupils.

Lurengi: Humanoids. Mammals. Large eyes like Lemurs. Stubby nose. Thin lips. Small ears. Their body and head are covered with fine hair. From the planet Belgona.

Osirians. (Giant ants) Osirian Empire.

Sartans: Human-like. They came from the other side of the star-gate. They are living on Cerberus.

Sleer: Humanoids. Their ancestors were otter-like. They are slender and tall. Males are savage. The females have bald heads with a row of bristles at the top, running across the center of their head and down the neck. Their skin is purple. They have whiskers, like cats.

Sleevers: Bald scaly head. Formed like a dome, it sprouts a small feathery fin at the top. The ridged forehead covers two yellow, round eyes above a prominent snout. Bulging muscles on thick bare arms.

Snaar (small ears. Flat nose. Slit pupils.) Their Enforcers cover their faces with terrible masks to intimidate others.

Tangari. Humanoid people with wings. Young females are comely with humps (they hide their wings). Immature Tangari have humps. No wings. Purple eyes, no iris. They are linguists.

Trevorians Human-like with pointy ears. Home planet is Lazaar beyond the Star-gate)

T'Par. Spiders from beyond the Star-gate

Arani. The counterpart of the Anorians on the other side of the Star-gate. Males are dominant.

GLOSSARY

Solar Union: Earth, Mars, the moon, Ganymede, Titan. Planetary systems with non-human populations.

Human Federation. Only planets with human populations belong to the Federation.

Military High Command

Union Troopers

SPA: Solar Protection Agency

SIS: Solar Intelligence Service

ISS: Interstellar Secret Service (a secret branch of the SUSF)

SUSF: Solar Union Special Forces.

SUSN: Solar Union Space Navy

SUSS: Solar Union Secret Service

PIA: Planetary Intelligence Service (Secret Service of the **Belter's Consortium**).

SI: Scouts Investigation

SS: Scouts Security

SSP: Scouts Special Forces

SAPG: Solar Animal Protection Guild

GWIS: Game Warden Intelligence Service (Secret Service of SAPG)

SAI: Solar Animal Investigations (An investigative branch of SAPG)

The Belters live in artificial habitats on large asteroids. They also live in the tunnels of asteroids. They extract resources from asteroids. They are called Belt Miners.

High Senate: Members of the Solar Union, the Belters, the colonies of Bernard's Star and Alpha Centauri. Also a few non-Human races: Anorians, Spiders (Kraach), Accilla. Sleer.

Other minor information:
Tsakona: Name of the Sartan country
Freeland: Name of the Human country
Greater York. Capital of Freeland.
Windy Lake. Name of town where Amsterdam's sister Adriana lives. About 100 miles east of Greater York. The location of an attack by the raiders from the other side of the portal.
Stoneland. Country on another continent.
Freeland has what they call an army with about 2,000 soldiers, but they don't know how to fight. They have parades with juggling, dancing, baton swirling. In other words, they are entertainers. Guns and Sabers are only for show.
The Sartans are ruled by a Priesthood. They have warriors to serve only the Priesthood. They collect taxes for the Priesthood.
They have small kingdoms. The lesser kings are controlled by the Priesthood. The kings have their own warriors.

PROLOGUE

THERE WAS NOTHING BUT FROZEN TUNDRA AS FAR AS THE EYE COULD SEE. Ethan Wolf, Alfred Swann, and Harry Turnbull sat on their steeds studying the unforgiving land around them. Dressed in thick furs, their heads covered with furry hats, they were unaffected by the icy wind blowing from the east. The animals they rode were native to Agrar and didn't mind the nasty weather. They stomped their splayed feet impatiently and roared, as if telling their riders to either keep going or get off.

"We might as well camp here," Swann suggested. "We have these large rocks for cover to give us some measure of protection from the wind. No matter how far we travel today, we won't find a better place. What do you think, Ethan?"

Wolf didn't reply right away, trying to decide if he should agree. He didn't see much point in carrying on, either. "Alright, Alfred," he said. "You're the Scout. This is as good a place as any."

"Good. I'm glad you agree. I'm not sure about this, but it looks like a storm is coming," Swann said.

"In that case, I'd say we dig in. These storms can get quite violent."

"You've experienced one?" asked Turnbull.

Wolf turned to Turnbull. "No, I haven't. Not here on Agrar, but a few years back, I was on an assignment on Tellus, a planet much like this one.

1

Lots of open prairie and savannahs. And deserts. Those sandstorms were murder if you were caught in one without a place to hide. If it wouldn't have been for the native guides we hired, my team and I may have perished when we got surprised by one of those storms."

"I'm familiar with Tellus," Swann said. "I spent a year there on the Scouts Outpost. The original exploration team that mapped the planet gave it a low grade. Not an ideal planet for colonization."

Wolf chuckled. "Except for the rich deposits of Allegrum. The low grade you Scouts gave Tellus didn't stop Starleaf Explorations from establishing several mines in the mountains. They brought in hundreds of miners by offering them outrageous wages if they settled there. In fact, they spared no expense building whole towns with rows of residential units for the families of the miners."

He jumped to the ground, holding onto the reins of his steed. The Org shook itself, clearly happy to be rid of the weight on its broad back. "Easy." Wolf patted the massive animal's muscular neck. "Give me a chance to take off the saddle."

Swann and Turnbull followed his example. They piled the three saddles onto the ground and tied the reins of the animals together. They didn't have to worry about them running away. The Org were quite docile, despite giving the impression of being aggressive because of their immense size.

Wolf removed his facemask and took off his mittens, rubbing his hands together. "Damn cold," he cursed. "Whose idea was it anyway to take a trek across this wonderful landscape?"

"Yours." Turnbull also opened his facemask and smirked. "You always come up with these terrific ideas."

"I am questioning my sanity for allowing myself to always be talked into coming with you on these vacations," Swann said. Taking off his facemask, he sniffed the air.

"It isn't supposed to be a vacation. It is an adventure," Wolf informed them.

"You don't get enough of those on your assignments?" Turnbull queried.

"That is different." Wolf smiled. "I can't choose the places they send me, but I can damn well choose how I spend my free time."

"Next time we'll go on a real vacation," Swann said.

"What do you suggest?" Wolf was curious what Swann came up with.

"We should go to Easter. The sky is always red and not very bright. The gravity is less than one G. Rich people go there for their honeymoon."

"Are you planning to get married?"

Swann laughed. "I hope that was not meant to be a serious question. You know that Scouts don't get married—unless they retire."

"Well, neither does a Union Trooper." Wolf grinned and looked at Turnbull. "How about you, Harry?"

Turnbull grunted. "I wouldn't get married again. Once was enough. For your information, we didn't go to Easter on our honeymoon. That planet was a little bit too rich for us."

"I guess that settles that," Wolf stated with a chuckle. "Easter won't be happening." He studied the moon that appeared on the western horizon. "That moon is the biggest I've seen from the surface of all the planets I've been on. Perhaps that large moon is the reason for the violent storms they are having on this planet."

"It definitely will have something to do with that," Swann agreed.

They took shelter behind one of the large boulders nearby and broke out their rations. After eating, they got their sleeping bags and crawled into them.

The storm hit during the night. It was as Wolf had predicted. The howling wind came first and then came the ice pellets. Their sleeping bags were flexible but not soft. Their tough material protected them from the pounding of the pellets, but it could not protect them from the roaring sound of the fierce storm.

Wolf made sure his sleeping bag was closed tight. He was warm and dry inside his protective cocoon. As were Swann and Turnbull.

By morning, the storm was less severe than it had been at the onset. The wind had lost much of its velocity, and the ice pellets had changed to sleet, but it was still uncomfortable.

They decided not to wait out the storm and broke camp. The Org didn't seem to be inconvenienced, and Wolf and his companions were dressed for the nasty weather. They had known from the start this was not going to be a comfortable trek. The severe weather was expected, and so was the terrain. It was all part of the adventure.

At least that's what they told each other.

Wolf's face was completely covered. To protect his eyes, he wore goggles. He was not exactly uncomfortable, but he had to admit that moving around dressed in thick furs, wearing heavy boots, and large mittens was inconvenient. However, sitting on the back of a strong animal, they did not have to exert their bodies. Had they been forced to walk, it would have made this a strenuous, possibly deadly, activity.

As they rode across the dreary landscape, Wolf recalled other journeys he and his friends had taken over the years. He was forty-three years old and in top physical shape. Would he still be able to do this in ten years? How about Swann and Turnbull? Both were his age, and both were in decent shape. Would they want to join him still? If not, he would miss that.

"Company is coming. Ten o'clock." Swann, who had been in the lead, slowed down his Org. His voice sounded muffled behind his face covering.

Wolf looked in the indicated direction. Visibility was low because of the storm. He saw shadows coming toward them. As they came closer, they turned out to be a large group of riders on Org.

Nulgarians.

Most of the various indigenous races populating Agrar were peaceful. The Nulgarians on the other hand, were not. They were a nomadic race, traveling across the vast tundra following the herds of wild Org and shaggy One-horns on their migrations. When the herds settled down for a few months so did the Nulgarians. They did not welcome visitors with open arms, instead they attacked anyone coming too close to their tribe.

Their warriors were fierce and nasty and skilled with their diverse types of weapons, especially with the staff slings that they used to hurtle stones for long distances.

Wolf removed his laser rifle from its scabbard and melted a wide stretch of the frozen ground in front of the riders before they were close enough to use their slings. The riders brought their steeds to a halt and lined up in a wide half circle, watching the three intruders in their territory.

"What do you suggest we do?" Turnbull brought his Org to Wolf's side. "We could try to outrun them."

"Won't work. They know this part of the tundra, we don't. They could herd us into a trap." Wolf pushed up his goggles and looked around. "I must admit, we don't have many options. We could make a stand and burn them all, which clearly is not an option."

"It may be the only option we have," Swann said. "They won't negotiate."

"What do they want from us?" Turnbull asked.

Swann's laugh sounded ugly. "They want our Org, our clothing, and our weapons. Imagine what they could do with three lasers."

"They must know they'll never get close to us," Turnbull stated.

"Don't underestimate them. Time is on their side. They know we're trapped and only need to wait us out."

"Before that happens, we could kill them all, like Ethan mentioned."

"They know that won't happen, because we are not as ruthless as they are," Swann said.

"Sometimes it isn't a good thing if your enemies know too much about you. In primitive societies, warriors would pride themselves on being known as mean, fearless, and ruthless. Their enemies needed to shake with fear just at the mention of their name."

"Well, Harry, I don't believe the Nulgarians are shaking in their boots," Swann insisted. "Three years ago, they attacked and killed a team of six engineers and two Scouts from the Outpost. Ever since then, we always have at least three troopers accompany any of the scientific teams entering their territory."

"They are trying to completely surround us," Wolf observed. "They may even have the manpower to accomplish that."

"Does it really matter?" Turnbull asked. "Either way, we're fucked."

"We are the ones with superior weapons," Wolf reminded them. "If we have to kill most of them, we will."

"That may be considered cold-blooded murder," Swann argued. "It will be difficult to justify that in court. It was our choice to invade their territory. We knew the risks."

"I believe the decision has been taken out of our hands," Turnbull announced.

Wolf turned to see a large cigar-shaped object descending behind them and land. An opening appeared in its side, and four troopers dressed in battle gear, carrying laser rifles in their hands, jumped onto the frozen surface. They advanced toward the nearest natives and melted a sizable portion of the surface in front of them, causing the group to retreat.

Another trooper left the shuttle and walked toward Wolf and his friends. When he was close, he saluted and said, "Major Wolf?"

Wolf returned the salute and removed his mask. "Who wants to know?"

"I am Captain Song. I have orders to take you to the SUF Jupiter."

"When?"

"Immediately, Major."

"You mean *now*?"

"Those are my orders, sir."

"What can be so important to justify cutting short my deserved vacation?" Wolf glared at Captain Song.

"I can't say, Major."

"Damn!" Wolf cursed. "Alright." He dismounted and turned to Swann and Turnbull. "You heard. This is the end of our adventure. Seems we have no choice but to abandon our equipment and leave it for the Nulgarians."

"Just as I was beginning to enjoy myself," Turnbull complained.

"Sorry, sir," Captain Song said. "My orders are to bring back only Major Wolf. I wasn't informed of any civilians being present."

Turnbull pulled off his facemask. "Now listen, Captain Song. Obviously, you don't know who I am. I am not a civilian. I am Colonel Turnbull of the SPA, and I will be damned if I'm going to be left behind to become a victim of the most vicious group roaming this frozen nightmare. Forget about your orders. These are your new orders: You will let me and

Master Scout Swann board the shuttle, and then you will take us to the Scouts Outpost. Is that clear?"

Captain Song stood like a rigid statue. He had listened to Turnbull's outburst without flinching a muscle.

"Is that clear, Captain Song?" Turnbull barked.

"Crystal, Colonel Turnbull." Song saluted. "Please, follow me to the shuttle, Colonel. I will deliver you and Master Scout Swann safely to the Scouts Outpost."

[1]

EVEN SITTING IN THE CHAIR BEHIND HIS MASSIVE DESK, ADMIRAL SWENSON was still an imposing figure. However, Wolf was not intimidated, despite the Admiral's blustering tirade. Swenson finished with, "…what do you have to say about that, Major?"

"Not very much, sir. Harry Turnbull and I have been close friends since we were children. I'm sure you know that he is a colonel with the Solar Protection Agency. As far as Master Scout Swann goes, the story is the same. All three of us were born on Rion, and we've been friends since we started school."

"He is a Scout, a civilian!" the Admiral thundered, pulling his bushy eyebrows together, lending him the appearance of an angry bull about to charge. "The military and the Scouts do not fraternize. How many years have you three been going on these excursions?"

"About fifteen or so. I'm not sure about the exact number. I haven't been keeping score."

The Admiral leaned forward in his chair and glared at Wolf; his eyes were almost hidden by his bushy eyebrows. "I did some digging. Master Scout Alfred Swann has the rank of Major with Scouts Security. Were you aware of that?"

"I must admit, I wasn't." Wolf was surprised to hear that about Swann.

He thought he knew everything about both of his friends. As it turned out, he didn't. What else did Alfred keep from him?

"I try not to shudder when I think of all the military secrets you may have shared with Swann."

"We never talk about our work. It is an unspoken rule between us, but even if we would have, what difference would it have made? We are on the same side. The Scouts are not the enemy."

"How do you know, Major Wolf? Do you know what Scouts Security represents?"

Wolf shrugged. "I have no idea. Never heard of them until now."

"Scouts Security is a branch of Scouts Investigation. The head of Scouts Security is a Colonel Stonewall, a legend among the Scouts. He answers only to the High Senate, which makes him the most powerful man in this part of the Galaxy. When the Senate sends him to a trouble spot, his word is law. Even the military cannot interfere. They say he is incorruptible and cannot be bought."

"That is a good thing, isn't it?"

"Don't be so naïve, Major. Everyone has their price, even Stonewall. It is politics, that's all." Swenson's anger seemed to abate. "Your friend is a high-ranking member of Scouts Security. Anything you may have told him, even the smallest bit of information, in all likelihood reached the desk of Colonel Stonewall. Someday it could be used against you."

Wolf couldn't help but smirk. "I think now you're reaching, Admiral." He refrained from saying 'you're paranoid'.

"I can assure you that I am not reaching. Scouts Security under Colonel Stonewall have created their own Special Forces. They are not regular Scouts. They are a military branch of the Scouts Organization. Rumors are that they go through a much more intensive and rigorous training program than our troopers. Your friend Alfred Swann is a dangerous man and cannot be trusted."

Wolf found it difficult to absorb everything Admiral Swenson had said. He hadn't lied when he stated that he and his friends never talked about their jobs, even though they did keep up with their careers. Or so he thought. Why didn't Alfred tell him about the advancement in his career? If what Swenson told him was true, Swann wasn't even a real Scout anymore. He was far beyond that.

He became aware that Swenson was still talking and tried to recall his last words.

"Have you heard anything I said, Major Wolf?"

"I heard every word you said, sir. I'm just trying to come to grips with that information. One small tidbit I just remembered. I don't believe it is particularly important. I have heard the name Stonewall before."

"Where did you hear about him?"

"Major Falcon mentioned him briefly when we had a drink together a few weeks ago. He just came back from a mission on Aurora, where he was for nearly a year. He said he served with somebody by the name of Stonewall. I assumed it was some high-ranking officer in the Navy."

"Are you talking about Major Jeremy Falcon? He is also a member of the ISS, correct?"

"He is."

"I don't know him personally, but I hear he is a good man. Related to Commander Kennedy. He is one of the men that went through the enhancement program. Did he tell you anything about his mission?"

Wolf shook his head. "No. You know it is against regulations to exchange information about our missions with others, for security reasons."

Swenson nodded. "I know. I'm happy to hear that you adhere to that rule."

Wolf didn't tell Swenson that Falcon told him about a portal that opened the door to the other side of the Galaxy he and his partner discovered on Aurora. Wolf, of course, had never even heard of portals or stargates as some called them. According to Falcon, there were plenty of stories and rumors about an ancient race that built and used these portals to travel between star-systems. Apparently, in addition to the one on Aurora, there was one such portal on Salamander, one on Savanna, and another one on Aregon. When Wolf asked why nobody ever heard of them, Falcon said that the governments kept the information about them hush-hush and shared it only with certain people. He didn't know the reason.

He didn't tell Swenson anything about that. Neither did he mention that Falcon indicated that Stonewall was a Scout and a high-ranking member in the Scouts Organisation. He never mentioned anything about Scouts Security, though.

"Permission to change the subject, sir."

The Admiral made a face and gestured with one hand. "Permission granted. Go ahead."

"Is there a reason for me to be here, aside from getting a tongue-lashing?"

Swenson sighed as if he were about to make a difficult decision. "There is. It involves a planet in the Spinner System. The Spinner System is located in the Rim, near the edge of Human Space. It is far away from the regular trade routes that are frequented by us and other races, but it is still close enough for merchant ships and freighters to visit. There is not much beyond the Spinner System, except for a few rogue suns.

"The planet in question is called Cerberus, the fourth of eight. The number of colonists is estimated to be close to ten million; seven million Earth humans and about three million Sartans, human-like aliens that arrived on Cerberus about two thousand years ago. Nobody knows where they came from. Apparently, neither do the Sartans. Their society is much like that of the ancient Egyptians thousands of years ago on Earth."

"I don't know anything about the Egyptians, but I guess the Sartans are primitive?"

The Admiral moved his head from side to side. "Compared to our standards, yes. We don't have any details about their civilization. They do live in cities; they have some form of government, and, according to the information I have, they are quite peaceful."

"I suppose that is a good thing to know," Wolf admitted. "I'm just wondering why they didn't evolve in the two thousand years they've been on Cerberus. That is a long time to stay stagnant."

"I can't answer that question. If you know a little about the history of us humans, you may know that the original inhabitants of the North American continent on Earth lived there for thousands of years in primitive conditions without making much progress."

"Earth history is not taught in the schools on Rion, unless you are a student of interstellar history," Wolf confessed. "How about the humans on Cerberus?"

"They haven't abandoned technology. I also need to mention that the Sleer have established a few large colonies around the lakes and swamps. We don't know how many Sleer have made Cerberus their home."

"So, what is the problem with those colonists? Are they at war with each other?"

"On the contrary. They all get along fine. In fact, the humans are actively trading with the Sleer and the Sartans."

"Sounds like a peaceful place, which can't be said about many other colony planets. Are they having trouble with the Indigenous populations?" Wolf began to wonder what could be wrong with such an ideal planet.

"Nothing like that. The problem is much greater and much more dangerous. A new group of people have appeared on the planet. From where? Nobody knows. They look like Anorians. This group has modern vehicles and advanced weapons. There are reports of Sartan towns being raided and having their temples cleaned out of all their treasures. A human village was also attacked, and the local government building was destroyed. These people are cruel and ruthless. The curious thing is that instead of females committing these attacks, these are males."

"Male Anorians? That is curious. Have there been any casualties?"

"Sadly, yes," the Admiral confirmed. "One of the Sartan kings was killed when the invaders attacked his castle, and the priests in one of the temples were brutally slain when they tried to stop the invaders from stealing their treasures."

"Kings?" Wolf frowned. "They have kings?"

"They do. According to what we know. Don't ask me for more information on that."

"The Sartans must have weapons, even if they are primitive. Don't they have any soldiers or warriors?" Wolf wondered.

"There is nothing about that in the reports we have." Swenson lifted his hands in a defensive gesture. "Everything we have is pretty sketchy, but it is clear the people on Cerberus are in trouble and need help. The human colonists are scared."

"Surely, the colonists must have an army. How about peacekeepers or police? Can't they do anything about these invaders?" Wolf wondered.

"The colonists do have local police to keep law and order, but no other peacekeepers. Apparently, they do have an army. How large and effective that army is, is the question."

"What about the Anorians? Don't they have an explanation? Wouldn't they wonder who these people are? What planet the invaders come from?"

"They wonder and they deny any connection with the invaders."

"What are we going to do about the whole thing? It seems to me it wouldn't hurt to send a battle cruiser with a couple of platoons or a company of troopers to Cerberus," Wolf suggested. "It shouldn't take too long to clean up the place."

Admiral Swenson shook his head. "If it only were so easy. I can't justify the expense of sending in a cruiser and that many troopers. We aren't planning to start a war, you know. I've decided to send in a small team to find out what exactly is happening there. Once we know more, we can make an intelligent decision. A couple of people should be sufficient to do the job."

Wolf didn't think he heard right. "Did you say a couple of people? Like two people, sir? There are ten million lives at stake."

"Only seven million are true Earth-humans."

"Sir, you said the other three million are also human. Don't they count?"

"I'm sorry. That's all I can spare right now. I've been in contact with my Anorian counterpart, and she is willing to help."

Wolf tried to absorb the information. "How many teams are they sending?"

"Not a team. They'll send one agent."

"One. How generous. How about the Sleer?"

"They haven't committed yet."

"This is getting better and better." Wolf couldn't keep himself from making a sarcastic remark. "Who are we sending?"

His suspicion was confirmed when he heard the Admiral say, "You,

Major Wolf. However, you are the only human. Your teammate will be Anorian."

"Wonderful. Now I'm really excited. I hope it isn't a female."

Swenson pulled his bushy eyebrows together. It made him look like an angry cat. "I must admit when it was suggested you be one of the investigators, I had my reservations. I read your file, and everything looked good at first, but when I dug a little deeper, I found things about you that didn't impress me at all. For one thing, you don't get along with your partners. You are reckless and defy orders. You have a habit of ignoring rules. Should I go on, Major?"

Wolf lifted his shoulders. "I can't stop you, sir."

Swenson glared at him, anger clearly clouding his face. "Remarks like this make me wonder if I shouldn't override the recommendation to send you and demote you to a desk job for a while to teach you respect for your superiors."

Wolf stayed silent, not wanting to antagonize the Admiral more, but then he said, "You still haven't answered my question, sir."

"Unbelievable." Shaking his head, Swenson said, "Of course it will be a female Anorian. You know as well as I do that the Anorian males are the weaker sex in their society."

The information didn't make Wolf happy. "I hope she doesn't run around naked as is their custom."

"I have no control over the way she dresses, Major." Admiral Swenson actually smirked, clearly enjoying himself. "I hear the Anorian females have perfectly formed bodies. That shouldn't bother you, or will it?"

Wolf pulled himself erect. "A naked female has never bothered me, sir. Neither will this one."

"Good. That'll be all. You will get your marching orders and all the information you need shortly." Swenson saluted. "Dismissed."

———

HER NAME WAS GORINI. SHE WAS TALL AND SLIM. THE TINY SCALES ON HER skin shimmered silvery when she moved. Her golden reptilian eyes studied him with curiosity. She had the habit of flicking her forked tongue across her sharp, pointy teeth. According to the information he received, she held the rank of Captain.

He breathed a deep sigh of relief when they were introduced to each other, and he saw that she was wearing a uniform. Not exactly what he had hoped for, but better than anticipated.

It was green and formfitting like a second skin, exposing every tiny detail of her trim body. Fortunately, the uniform did have plenty of pockets. It helped to confirm the fact that she was not nude but actually wore clothing. Without those pockets, she might as well have been naked.

"Why do I get the impression that you don't like me, Major?" She spoke with a slight lisp, but her Inglis was flawless.

Listening to her soft voice and looking at her sensuous body, he couldn't help but think that she would not be out of place in a house of pleasure in any port city. It was difficult for him to think of her as a capable agent.

"Why would you think that? We don't even know each other," he said.

Her laugh teased him. "I shouldn't tell you this, but since we'll be working together, we shouldn't keep secrets. Anorians are not telepaths, unlike the Accilla. We can't read the thoughts of other entities, but I am an empath, which means I am able to read emotions and feelings. Your stance, the tone of your voice, the words you say, your facial expressions, and the way you move your hands all tell a story. Right now, I can read you as easily as an open file. Just because I'm a female doesn't make me any less capable. If you know anything about my species, you will know that in my society, we females are the dominant gender. Accept that."

"I already have."

"No, you haven't. I may not be of your species, but I have studied humans. Human males are different from Anorian males. Our males don't think about us females the way you human men do about yours. Don't look at me with the eyes of a typical human male calculating how long it will take me to spread my legs for you. It won't happen. Just think of me as your partner and nothing else." She chuckled. "You can count yourself lucky that I am wearing a uniform. I'm sure you know about our habit of not covering our bodies with clothing."

"I know all about that. Perhaps it would be better if you were naked. It wouldn't leave me wondering what you look like without clothes," he rumbled.

"That can be arranged once we are alone in our cabin." She tilted her head. "You didn't know?"

"Know what?"

"That we'll be sharing living quarters on the ship."

He stared at her. "Another thing I wasn't aware of. Please, don't tell me we will be sleeping in one bed."

Any other time he would have enjoyed her silvery laugh, now it just irritated him. Still laughing, she said, "We can do that, too, if it will make you happy." She became serious. "Don't worry, we will have separate beds."

"I am not worried. Just so you know, I was not trying to figure out how long it would take you to spread your legs for me. I wondered if I could get used to an alien female partner. I prefer to work with males. Preferably a human one. Less problems."

———

THE GOLDEN COMET USED TO BE A LUXURY CRUISER. NOW IT WAS NOTHING more than an old rundown vessel, missing all those amenities. It had jump capabilities, but it didn't have the range larger ships had. It took close to three weeks, and a dozen jumps to get to Cerberus instead of the one week it would have taken in a troop transporter. Even a freighter would have been faster.

The pilot was an old Union trooper the navy should have retired years ago. He was also the cook and steward. One thing Wolf had to admit, the meals he prepared and served were better than anything they would have had on a military ship.

His name was Dakarai Abara. Even though his rank was Captain, he insisted on not being called 'Captain' Abara. Just Abara was good enough. He was tall and thin, and his wrinkled skin was the color of coal. Aside from being a charming storyteller, he was also a skilled interrogator.

At first, Wolf assumed it was just his way of having a conversation, but it didn't take him long to realize that there was more to Abara's questions.

He began to wonder why the pilot was interested in a detailed account of Wolf's last assignment or other aspects of his life.

It was on the third day after the first jump when Abara joined them at the table, as he usually did. Wolf waited until everyone was comfortable when he confronted him. "Who are you working for, Abara?"

The pilot gave him an astonished look. "What kind of question is that, Major Wolf? You know I'm working for the SUSF."

"I don't know that. Are you sure you're not working for someone in the secret spy department?"

"What if I am?" Abara sounded defiant.

"Then I would say from now on my lips are sealed. Don't ask me any questions because you won't get any more information out of me." Wolf glanced at Gorini. "Or from her." He turned to look at her when she laughed. "I don't see any humor in this. Do you have any idea what he was doing?"

Before she could answer, Abara asked, "What was I doing? I'm curious to find that out."

"You know damn well what you were doing, grilling me ever since we boarded your ship. I finally caught on."

Abara sat silent for a moment, staring at his plate. When he looked up, he said, "You must forgive an old man's habits. You see, I'm a Belter. I was born on Vesta, one of the asteroids between Mars and Jupiter. In my younger years I used to work for the PIA. The Planetary Intelligence Service of the Belter's Consortium. I was an interrogator, trying to squeeze as much information out of a prisoner as I could. You do that long enough it becomes second nature. The job came easy to me because I'm curious to begin with. Years later, I was recruited by the SUSF to do essentially the same job." He sighed. "I finally decided to become a pilot, but as much as I try to change, I am still an interrogator."

"And a good one from what I can see," Wolf admitted. "You almost fooled me."

"I wasn't trying to. My interest in your career is genuine. You see, I live a pretty boring life these days, piloting this ancient derelict, jumping between star systems, and transporting teams like yours to wherever they are sent, among other boring jobs the navy gives me."

"Shouldn't you be retired by now?" Wolf made a gesture of apology. "I don't mean anything by that. I'm just wondering why you still do it. You could be enjoying your retirement on one of the more peaceful planets like Glory, lying on the beach, breathing fresh air, surrounded by pretty girls instead of spending your time in a tin-can and inhaling artificial air and cooking for guys like me."

"You are right. I could do that. It sounds wonderful and exciting." Abara sighed. "Even those pretty girls sound tempting but take a good look at me. What pretty girl would want a used-up old man like me? I should have done that twenty years ago. To be honest, lying on a beach and do nothing all day long doesn't appeal to me. This is what I'm good at and what I enjoy. I still feel useful, and I get to meet interesting people like you two."

"I never thought of myself as interesting," Wolf said.

"But you are. When I listen to the stories and adventures of people like you, I can transport my mind to the places you and the others have been and let my imagination go wild." Abara chuckled. "So, if I sound like an interrogator, it isn't because I have an ulterior motive or a sinister plan to use the information against you." He looked at Gorini. "Or against you."

She smiled. "I know that. I am not as paranoid as Major Wolf."

"I'd like to put on record that I am not paranoid, but that I am a cautious man, never blindly trusting a stranger I meet. It is part of my training. Like interrogating people has become second nature to you, Abara, being suspicious of everything and everyone has become part of me."

"Sometimes you have to trust people," Gorini said.

"Easy for you," Wolf pointed out. "I am not an empath. I may be able to read people by their gestures and expressions, but never the way you can."

She gave him a little smile. "I shouldn't give away all of my secrets, but my gift isn't foolproof. I've been misled when I was certain I read all of the signs correctly."

It was his turn to smile. "As you did with me."

"Perhaps I did or perhaps I didn't. It doesn't really matter." She turned to the pilot. "Captain Abara. You mentioned that you were born on an asteroid called Vesta. I'm curious to find out more about that. I never met anyone who was born on an asteroid. How large is it?"

"Vesta's diameter is about 330 miles which makes it one of the largest objects in the asteroid belt. It is really nothing more than a dead piece of rock with no atmosphere. People live in giant domes, artificial habitats, as they do on the other large asteroid in the Belt. My parents were miners. It is a hell-of-a-way to make a living. I didn't see a future in following my father's footsteps. That's how I ended up as a pilot." He grinned. "Now, instead of living in the tunnels of Vesta breathing artificial air I live in this tin-can, as the Major called it, still breathing artificial air."

"Some improvement," Wolf remarked with a little smirk. "Do you ever spend time on the surface of a planet?"

"I do. Not often, but it happens. In fact, I am supposed to stay on Cerberus until further notice. I hope they'll have a bit of nightlife near the spaceport."

"It looks like the same people that planned our mission also had a hand in yours," Wolf commented with a grin. "My hope is that somebody laid out some kind of strategy for us on how to proceed after we get to Cerberus."

They had no reason to complain about the cabin. It was roomy with two large beds and its own private lavatory. No tub, but a shower that worked. By all likelihood it had been the bedroom of the cruiser's former owner.

It was the only such cabin on the ship. Abara's cabin was not as luxurious but much more comfortable than cabins on freighters or military ships usually tended to be.

Everything would have been fine, if it hadn't been for Gorini's habit of walking around in the nude and sleeping without a cover. Wolf was certain she did that only to irritate him.

[2]

THE SPACEPORT WAS AT THE OUTSKIRTS OF GREATER YORK, THE OLDEST human city on Cerberus, also the capital of Freeland. It was not as busy as spaceports on planets closer to the more populated sectors of the Human Federation. It could almost be considered abandoned. There were a couple of merchant ships and three freighters sitting on the tarmac when the Golden Comet landed. No pleasure cruisers.

"This is the strangest assignment I've ever been on," Wolf remarked before they left the ship. "We have no contact. There is nobody waiting for us with either new instructions or more information." With a look at Gorini, he asked, "How about you? Any secret orders I don't know about?"

She shook her head. "No. I was under the impression you had everything under control since you are supposed to be the team leader."

He laughed. "What team? There is just you and me. I must admit, I am totally lost as what to do. All the information I received is sketchy at best."

"How about we three go into town, look for a tavern, and get drunk," Abara suggested.

"I can't think of a better idea," Wolf said. "However, it is still too early for that."

"First, I have to register with the port authorities, anyway," Abara informed them.

"We'll go with you. Might as well get all formalities behind us with the custom's people. We might even get some information on the latest news." Wolf didn't have a high opinion of the people who worked at spaceports. Most of them thought of themselves as gods who had the power to allow or deny entry to new arrivals. So far, he had never run across anyone who had been denied entry, but he wondered where they would go should that happen. There was a good chance it could happen this time since he had nobody on Cerberus who would vouch for him.

"One good thing. My passenger list is not exceedingly long," Abara joked. "I should be in and out in no time."

"I hope so will we," Wolf said.

The customs office was in the same building as the port authority's office. They planned to meet in front of the building once they completed their formalities.

After Wolf walked through the scanner, the customs officer gave him a curious look. "When I was notified about your arrival, Major Wolf, I expected you to wear a uniform."

"I apologize for disappointing you, but I'm not much for uniforms," Wolf said drily. "Especially when I'm undercover."

"It seems it is my turn to apologize for blowing your cover."

Wolf chortled good-humoredly. "No harm done since you, my partner, and I are the only people in the room. Unless you announced it all over Greater York that the famous Major Ethan Wolf is coming to your planet on a secret mission. Tell me, what is your name?"

"I am Sergeant Slovinsky. I have a message for you, Major."

"A message?" Wolf turned to Gorini. "Maybe our mission has been scrapped."

Slovinsky handed him an envelope with the words, "The print-out of your orders are in this envelope."

Wolf turned that envelope in his hands. "I can't remember the last time I saw an envelope and a letter made from real paper." He gave Slovinsky a piercing look. "Did you read it?"

"Of course, I did. How could I not? You don't have to worry, Major. I am under oath. Your secret is safe with me."

Wolf opened the envelope and pulled out a sheet of paper. There was only one line printed on it: *Proceed to the Military Base immediately after arrival for further instructions.* He looked up at the Sergeant who had been watching him silently. "Do you know where the Military Base is located?"

"I do."

"How do we get there?"

"I can send them a message to let them know you are here. They will pick you up."

Wolf let out a sigh of relief. "And here I worried we might have to wander around in Greater York for days searching for that place." He turned to talk to Gorini. "I wonder why this cloak and dagger game?"

She just smiled. "Aren't we supposed to be undercover?" The sarcasm in her voice was not to be missed.

"Would it be alright for me to make an observation?" Slovinsky wondered.

"Go ahead," Wolf told him.

"Your partner. She isn't human. May I ask what species she belongs to?"

"Why don't you ask her yourself?" Wolf chuckled. "She may even tell you, unless she shoots you first."

Slovinsky took a step backward. "I am sorry if I made a blunder."

Gorini laughed. "Don't listen to him. My species is quite civilized. I am an Anorian, and a peaceful person. I am surprised you have never seen a member of my race before."

"I haven't. The only alien species I am familiar with are the Sleer. They live mostly near lakes and swamps. None of them live in Greater York, but they come to the market to trade."

She stepped up to him and looked him in the eyes. "You're a handsome young human male. If there were an opportunity, I would show you how gentle Anorian females are."

Wolf almost choked. Anorian females were neither peaceful nor gentle. They were the dominating gender and could be fierce and even cruel. "Don't give him the wrong impression about your species," he said. "And don't tell him about your peculiar habit."

"I'd better go and make that call." Slovinsky took the opportunity and hurried away.

"Civilized species?" Wolf accused her. "Don't make me laugh. If I didn't know anything about the Anorian race, spending the last three weeks with you in such close quarters taught me plenty. You are neither gentle nor peaceful. You can be bitchy and irritating."

"Anything else?" she challenged him.

"Yes, you are a big tease."

She came closer and touched his cheek. "Did seeing me in the nude bother you?" she asked with a soft voice.

"Don't act so innocent," he said harshly. "I am a soldier and trained to suppress my urges and desires, but I am also a normal male. My body reacts involuntarily to the sight of a naked female with a sensual, attractive body like yours."

"You find me attractive and desirable, even though I am not of your species?"

"Of course, I find you attractive. The only difference between you and a human woman is your skin and your lack of hair. In the dark, nobody can tell the difference."

"Don't be so grouchy because I didn't sleep with you." Her smile mocked him. "I know you wanted to. That is one more thing you know about me now. You can't hide your feelings and desires from me because you and I have formed a certain bond with each other. Admit it or not, but that is a fact." She stepped away from him when the customs agent came back.

"Someone will be here shortly," Slovinsky announced. "Oh, I almost forgot. Welcome to Cerberus."

"I'd like to say I'm happy to be here, but I can't lie. Tell me something. I am curious. How long have you lived on Cerberus?"

"I was born here," Slovinsky said proudly. "I can trace my ancestry back quite far. I know that my ancestors were among the first wave of colonists."

"How did Cerberus get its name?"

"I am not sure, but the story goes when the first colonists looked into the night sky and studied the alien constellations, one caught their interest. It looks like a large dog with three heads. Old legends talk about a three-headed beast that guards the gate to Hell. That beast is called Cerberus. You should look at the sky tonight."

"Interesting story. I'll make sure I do that. Every planet is different."

"Must be exciting to look at all the different constellations on other planets." Slovinsky heaved a deep sigh. "That is something I'll never be able to do."

Wolf smiled. "The excitement wears off after a while. Well, I guess we'll go. We'll wait outside." Wolf picked up the duffel bag that carried his meager belongings.

Abara sat on the stone steps, already waiting for them. "I began to worry about you, wondering if they wouldn't allow you into their country." He pulled his thick brows together. "They did, didn't they?"

"They did," Wolf assured him with a smile. "You don't have to worry about us going back home with you."

"That would have been fine. I rather enjoyed your company." He rose. "Are you ready to join me looking for a seedy bar and getting drunk out of our minds?"

Wolf chuckled. "It sounds tempting, but we actually made contact. Somebody is picking us up shortly. It seems our ways part here." He held out a hand. "It was an honor to get to know you, Captain Abara. Who knows? Our roads may cross again someday."

Abara took his hand and shook it. "Good luck, Major. I hope your mission is a success." He switched his attention toward Gorini. "I enjoyed your company also, Captain Gorini. I don't mind admitting this, but in my younger days, I would have tried to get to know you more intimately, if you know what I mean." He grinned. "Seeing you parade around in that tight-fitting uniform made these old loins of mine flutter, reminding me that there is still life down there, albeit not enough to look for an opportunity to still the desire it caused."

She laughed. "If you know anything about us Anorian females, you know that we usually don't wear any clothing. Would it have caused you any anxiety had I walked around without clothing all the time?"

"I didn't need any more anxiety, but I think I could have managed that." He winked. "That uniform didn't hide anything anyway."

She gave him a playful slap on the shoulder. "You human males are all the same, but it is refreshing. Sometimes I wish our males would be more aggressive when it comes to mating."

Wolf wanted to make a remark, but he didn't get the chance. A black, sleek vehicle came silently around the street corner and came to a halt in front of the customs building. The door on the driver's side slid open and the driver climbed out. He wore a dark-blue uniform and a hat with a wide brim. His high leather boots were black and shiny. A holster holding a pistol hung from his wide belt. When he came closer, Wolf noticed the thin, black moustache adorning his upper lip. The rest of his face was clean-shaven.

Wolf didn't have to guess that this was a military man, especially, when he tipped the rim of his hat in a smart salute. "I am Ltd Garcia. Are you Major Wolf?"

Wolf didn't bother returning the salute. "That's who I am," he said. He pointed at Gorini. "And this is my partner, Captain Gorini."

Garcia gave Gorini a short nod. Then he turned his attention back to Wolf. "I am here to take you to see General Mitchell. Please follow me." He turned and marched back to the vehicle.

Wolf and Gorini barely slid into the backseat when the vehicle began moving.

"Are we in a hurry, Ltd Garcia?"

"No. Why do you ask?"

"Your speed. You are racing."

"Sorry, Major. Do you want me to slow down?"

"I would appreciate that. We are new to this city. Actually, to your planet. I wouldn't mind seeing a little of the scenery. The buildings look old. I find them interesting."

"The majority of buildings in Greater York are old. Ours is the oldest city in Freeland." Wolf detected a feeling of pride in Garcia's voice. "It was the first city built by the colonists when they arrived on Cerberus five hundred years ago."

"I was informed that Cerberus was colonized about nine hundred years ago," Wolf interrupted Garcia.

"You are not wrong, Major," Garcia agreed. "You are talking about Standard years. These are local years. It takes close to two Standard years for Cerberus to finish one revolution around Ibirius Prime."

"I wasn't aware of that. This means that your seasons are much longer than on many Earth-like planets. On Rion, the planet where I was born and raised, one year and, of course, the seasons, were almost identical to Earth's."

"I was born on Cerberus, and I think I would find it difficult to get used to a shorter year and shorter seasons," Garcia said.

"How about time? How long are your days?"

"One full day has twenty-four hours." Garcia pointed with his thumb to the screen on the dashboard. "It is nearly eleven o'clock. An hour before noon. Are you counting time like that, too, Major Wolf?"

"We are, but one hour on Rion may be longer or shorter than your hour. I'm not sure about Captain Gorini."

"We don't use hours or minutes, but our system does use numbers. While I am with you, I am using a watch, just like you. I have learned to adapt. It is of foremost importance for communication to work as one unit," she explained.

Wolf noticed that, while not busy, there was quite a bit of traffic on the road. The majority of vehicles they encountered were of the same basic design. None as large as theirs. All drove in complete silence.

The vehicle slowed down and came to a stop.

"We have arrived at headquarters," Garcia announced.

The door on the side of the curb slid open. Garcia waited until Wolf and Gorini exited the car before coming out.

Expecting a modern structure of steel and glass, Wolf was surprised to see a building of weathered stone, like all the other old buildings on the street. The steps leading up to the front entrance were chipped, grey concrete.

Ltd Garcia opened the massive wooden door and held it open for them. They entered a large vestibule with another door at the end. Stepping through that door, they walked into a large, surprisingly well-lit room. It held a few desks. All were occupied by women and men in plain uniforms.

"They are civilians," Garcia explained.

He led them through the room to another door. There was a sign on the door that read: General Mitchell. Entry only by permission. He knocked on the door and waited until a voice on the other side invited them to come in.

General Mitchell was not an imposing man. Tall and thin with a narrow face and a bushy moustache, he did not fit the image of a man commanding thousands of soldiers.

He looked up from the file he was studying and got up from his chair. Coming around the desk, he stood still for a moment as if deciding how to proceed before saying with an unexpected deep and resonant voice, "Welcome to Cerberus, Major Wolf. I've been looking forward to meeting you." Then he took a few more steps toward Wolf and held out his hand.

Wolf shook it, noting the General's strong grip. "If I would say I've been looking forward to this moment as well, it would not be the truth," he said with a little smile, letting go of the General's hand. "I don't mean about meeting you, but everything about this whole mission is odd. All my information is vague. It appears to me the upper ranks in the military are not taking your problem seriously."

When Gorini cleared her throat beside him, reminding him of her presence, he said, "My apologies, this is Captain Gorini, my partner."

General Mitchell turned to her. "Perhaps it is I who needs to apologize for ignoring you, but I must admit, I am a little perplexed why the Solar Union sends a female Anorian, especially since the invading plunderers are Anorian males."

"That is precisely the reason I am here. If you are familiar with my species, you know that we females are the dominating gender. Our males are, how should I put it?"

"The weaker sex?" Mitchell suggested.

Gorini laughed. "Actually, our males are physically quite strong. However, they are better suited for domestic chores. For instance, their parental instincts are much stronger than those of a female. They lack aggression and even interest in going exploring or being adventurous. My mission is to find out where these males are coming from."

"Supposedly, that is also my reason for being here," Wolf added.

"We are not as much interested in where they come from as stopping them from their rampage," Mitchell explained. "So far, they've invaded only a couple of human villages and vandalized one of the buildings, with most of the killing and plundering happening to the Sartans. Possibly, because they are less advanced than us humans. It is just a matter of time before they focus on us. They need to be stopped."

"That is the part that puzzles me," Wolf ventured. "You have an army. Why can't your army take care of these invaders?"

The General chuckled. "You are correct. We have an army of about two thousand soldiers. If you are familiar with our history, you will know that we've never been at war with anyone. From the beginning of colonizing this planet we tried to get along with the Sleer and the Sartans. None of them have ever displayed any aggressive behavior. We trade with each other, and we live in peace and harmony."

"So I've heard. It is very unusual and not the norm on most planets. Even the humans can't get along with each other. Why then the need for an army?"

Mitchell shrugged. "The only reason we have an army is out of tradition. From our history we know that the early colonists created a small army in case it was needed. It never was, but they wanted to make sure just in case. To give some purpose to having one, they started to have a parade a couple of times a year, and we kept it that way."

"A parade?" Wolf's eyebrows lifted involuntarily. "I find that peculiar. Don't you have drills and other military exercises just to keep in shape?"

"I wouldn't call it drills exactly. The soldiers practice and hone their skills, swirling batons and throwing sabers into the air. They practice playing the drums and trumpets; they sing and march in precise unison and learn many other entertaining skills."

"How about practising shooting a rifle and a gun, unarmed combat, or instead of throwing the sabers into the air, learn how to use them to kill a man? How about strategy and maneuvers using live ammunition? There is no end to what a soldier needs to be proficient in."

The General's expression was almost one of distaste. "Why? Those are unnecessary skills here on Cerberus."

"Until now." Wolf stared at Mitchell. "Didn't it ever occur to anyone that there was a possibility for needing professional men and women who know how to defend this country? This world and your way of life? Like a real army and not a bunch of entertainers?"

Mitchell absently rubbed his chin. "Humans have been on Cerberus for five hundred years and lived in peace with the others. There was no reason for anyone to assume that this peace may be shattered someday."

"But it has." Wolf knew he sounded condescending. As a military man, he had a problem accepting that people could be so naive to assume that everyone everywhere was peaceful and loving. believing that evil didn't exist. "Do you have any weapons? I notice you are wearing a pistol. I also saw one on Ltd Garcia's hip."

"Just show. They are not even loaded." The General looked uncomfortable. "I don't think we have any bullets for them."

"Bullets?"

"Yes, bullets. What else would you use?"

Wolf drew his own weapon out of its holster. "This, General, is what is called a laser. When I pull this trigger, it releases a bundle of energy that will drill a hole into an enemy's skull. It will melt metal. We have rifles that fire a proton beam that will destroy an aircraft with one shot."

"Now you know why we asked for help." Mitchell sounded apologetic. "We are completely helpless and without any means to defend our people."

"How about the Sleer? Are they as complacent as the humans?"

"I don't know about them being complacent, but their history here on Cerberus coincides with ours. They have no use for an army, either. However, so far, they haven't been attacked by these invaders. Probably, because their habitats are surrounded by swamps and lakes. Plundering them is too much trouble. It doesn't mean they will be left alone for good."

"That makes sense. This means it probably is left to us humans to clear up this mess," Wolf mused. His gaze moved to Gorini. "I don't believe we can count on assistance from the Anorians. Or am I wrong?"

"Probably not," she agreed. "The only interest we have is to find out who these invaders are and where they come from. We don't want to be blamed for these attacks."

"There it is. The Human Federation will have to take care of the problem." Wolf looked at the General. "One more thing, General Mitchell. I must admit I didn't expect things to be the way they are. I assumed to find the usual army base, with soldiers staying and living in barracks. I had hoped to be able to stay in a suite reserved for visiting top brass."

Mitchell's expression was again one of embarrassment. "I'm sorry, we don't have such facilities. Our soldiers live at home with their families."

"Unbelievable," Wolf murmured to himself. Aloud he asked, "What do you suggest we do now?"

"We have wonderful hotels. Or you could find a private residence that rents out rooms."

"Sounds great. How are you settling debts in Freeland? By that I mean how are you paying for merchandise or services you buy? I'm sure you have banks that control the money. Are you paying by electronic means, or do you use physical money?"

"We use physical money. We have metal coins and paper money. You are right, the banks control the flow of currency. The bank is also the one that prints the paper money and creates the coins. We pay with Dockats, by the way."

"That is the problem," Wolf said. "We don't have any Dockats."

Mitchell gave him a surprised look. "No Dockats? How did you plan to pay for anything?"

"We didn't. Remember, I'm a military man. We expected the local military to take care of us. That includes lodging and food. You didn't really think our services are free?"

"We never thought about that." Mitchell scratched his head. "It seems we have a problem."

"We certainly have." Wolf turned to Gorini. "It appears our mission ends before it begins. We'd better head back to the spaceport and hope our pilot is still there."

"Are you planning to abandon us?" The General couldn't hide the panic in his voice.

"What choice do we have? Without any funds, we can't accomplish anything here. I'm curious about something. How did you contact the Solar Union's military? Do you by any chance own a proton transmitter?"

"We don't, but we have access to one."

"Who on Cerberus is rich enough to own one of those?"

"It is not in private hands. They have one at the Solar Union Embassy."

It was Wolf's turn to be surprised. "The Solar Union has an Embassy here?"

"You didn't know?"

Wolf glared at Mitchell and then at Gorini. "Fuck it all. This is the tip of the mountain. I am wondering what else they didn't tell us. No, General, I didn't know. Where is the Embassy?"

"Not far from here. Ltd Garcia can drive you there."

"That is the first sensible thing anyone said today. I would appreciate that very much. Perhaps, they will be able to shed some light on this mess."

"I hope so. I am sorry we have disappointed you. I would like to mend things between us. You must be hungry and thirsty. I know I am. Let's go up to our cafeteria and let me treat you to lunch. That is the least I can do for you."

"I won't say no. I'm sure Captain Gorini will appreciate that also."

"I hope I don't offend you by asking this," Mitchell said to Gorini. "Do you eat human food?"

She gave him a little smile. "I eat anything humans eat, except meat."

"That should be no problem. Quite a few of my staff don't eat meat, either."

"I have one more question, General," Wolf said. "Since the members of the army don't contribute anything to society other than a couple of parades and entertaining the people, who pays you?"

"The State pays us." He noticed Wolf's frown. "Perhaps I need to clear this up. Being a member of the army isn't a full-time job. For instance, I am the Minister of Justice. Ltd Garcia is a chauffeur driving dignitaries around. Most of the military personnel have some kind of job in the government."

"I see. I was wrong in judging you too soon and assuming you had two thousand non-productive individuals in your country. It seems they are useful after all."

"I'm glad you approve."

Wolf didn't know if the General meant it in a sarcastic way or not. He didn't really care. In his book being the Minister of Justice didn't mean that he earned the high salary he probably enjoyed. It was a cushy job and overvalued.

[3]

AFTER LUNCH, THEY SAID THEIR GOODBYES TO THE GENERAL, PROMISING they would be dropping by for a visit, if time allowed. They slid into the backseat of the limo, and Wolf leaned back to enjoy the ride.

The houses on each side of the street were smaller and not as well-kept. Wolf also noted that the area looked dirtier with garbage lying on the streets. He wasn't surprised. The cities and towns on every planet had districts that were populated by people of a different class. Areas with a high crime rate. Most of them were run by gangs.

"This doesn't look like one of the better neighborhoods," Gorini remarked.

"That can't be denied, but there are worse places than this one," Garcia said.

"Worse? I'm not sure if I want to drive through one of those."

Garcia chuckled. "Oh, don't worry. We will."

He was right. After about another half hour, many of the houses lining the street needed to be repaired. A new paint job was the least of the problems. Some had windows missing, and some had their windows boarded up. The street was empty. Wolf didn't see any pedestrians, no children playing games only they understood. It was like driving through a ghost town.

"Does anyone actually live here?" he asked.

"Yes. This is where the downtrodden live, the ones with no jobs, no funds. The ones that are at the end of a rope."

"How do they live?" Gorini wondered.

"Good question. They steal, they rob and kill people. Any way to make a living."

"Where are the police and the social workers? Where are the people that run the city?"

"Nobody dares to come here. Not the police and not the officials. They've given up on these people." He cursed loudly and slammed on the brakes.

Wolf saw two men wearing long coats standing in the middle of the road. More stepped onto the street from the dark places between the houses.

Garcia drove slowly toward the group of men and stopped the car. "Stay calm," he advised Wolf and Gorini. "These are the toll-collectors. As long as I pay them, there won't be any trouble. They may look harmless, but they carry weapons under their coats, and they are not afraid to use them."

"You are not actually paying them? Does this sort of thing happen a lot?" Wolf wondered.

"All the time. This is how these people survive."

"By robbing people and by using extortion? What about the police? Why are they tolerating this?"

"Because the police are just as corrupt." He stopped talking when someone banged his fist against the side-window. "I'd better pay them now." He rolled down the window.

"What is the holdup," the man by the window demanded. "You want to be shot?"

"No need to threaten," Garcia said. "I have the money right here." He reached into a compartment on the dashboard and pulled out an envelope. Handing it to the rogue outside with the words, "It's all there. You can count it if you will."

"Oh, I will." The man stated and looked into the car. Spotting Wolf in the backseat, he said, "Who are you?"

"None of your business," Wolf told him.

"What if I make it my business?"

"I would tell you to fuck off."

The man glared at him. "I think we have us a comedian with a big mouth here." He pulled a gun from under his coat and poked it through the window, aiming it at Wolf. "How about you come out of the car so I can teach you some manners?"

Wolf gave him a little smile. "How about if I come out of the car and teach *you* some manners? Sadly, most likely it won't end well for you."

Before Wolf opened the car door, he saw another man coming up to the rear window on Gorini's side. He heard him say, "Hey, there is a woman in there. I don't think she is human." He knocked against the window. "Come out of there and let me have a good look at you. I've never fucked an alien bitch."

Gorini opened the door at the same time Wolf did. "And you never will," she said. "For your information, I am not an alien. I'm an Anorian."

"Who cares? You're a female, and that is good enough for me." He reached for her. Wolf only heard his surprised shout and knew Gorini had reacted.

The rogue with the gun had come around the car. He had shoved the gun back into his coat. "Hey, big mouth, go ahead and teach me." He put up his fists in a classic boxing position.

Wolf shook his head, amused by the rogue's dramatic gesture. "If you think you are a fighter, you will find out you're nothing but a common thug. I will demonstrate to you what it means to be a fighter. But first things first. Give me back the envelope with the money. No toll payments today."

The man gaped at him, obviously not believing what Wolf just said. Then he burst into loud laughter. He turned around to look at his companions. "Did you hear that? This guy is a real comedian. He wants his money back. What should I do with him?"

"Beat the crap out of him first and then let us have some fun with him," one of the guys in the small crowd yelled. Everyone laughed at that. "Go, Randall, go! Go, Randall, go!" they chanted.

"I have a better idea," Randall said. "I'm going to carve up his face first.

He looks too handsome." He pulled a long knife out of a sheath hanging on his belt.

Wolf didn't give him a chance to use it. Hand-to-hand combat without a weapon was one thing, bringing a knife into the picture was another. He kicked the man hard in the groin, making him cry out in surprise and drop the knife. As he buckled, Wolf brought his fist down on his neck, hard. He collapsed and lay on the street, unmoving. Wolf bent down and pulled the envelope with the money out of his pocket.

There was complete silence from the other members of the gang for a moment, but only for a moment until they realized their leader lay unconscious or even dead in the dirt. All of them began shouting, while two reached into their coats and pulled out guns. Wolf registered that without conscious thought. His laser was already in his hand. He shot both men before they even got the opportunity to aim their guns at him.

He was among them within moments, kicking with his fists and legs. He had no desire to shoot more of them. Gorini was beside him, and in a short time all ten either stood bent over or lay on the ground, moaning.

Wolf grabbed one of them by the collar and held him steady. Putting his laser to the man's head, he bellowed, "Now listen. This ends now. Two of your friends are dead. They made a huge mistake by planning to shoot me. I am a professional soldier, and I reacted the only way I know how."

"You murdered them in cold blood. We will report you to the police. The law will take care of you," the one he held by the collar accused him.

"You've got that wrong. You attacked us. We were driving on the road, minding our own business."

"We have an agreement. Anyone who uses our street has to pay a toll. It is our right."

"By whose authority?"

"The city and the police," the man said in a defiant tone.

"Well, not this time. You picked the wrong vehicle. I have this strange feeling that changes are on the horizon. This city is all fucked up." He gave the man a shove. "Now, you all crawl back under the rocks where you came from."

Once he was back in the car, he threw the envelope with the money onto the front seat and ordered Garcia to start driving.

"You may think you did a good thing," Garcia said. "I have to tell you what you did was wrong. Not good. There will be repercussions."

"They are thugs, bandits, criminals. They deserved everything they got. What do you think would have happened to Gorini had she not defended herself? Or me? Their leader Randall was ready to stab me with his knife. He was lucky I didn't kill him. It would have been easy. The two I did kill gave me no choice. As I told them; I'm a soldier, a trained killer. That is my reality. When my life is threatened, I defend myself the way I was taught."

"I am a soldier, but I have never killed anyone," Garcia seemed shaken by what he had witnessed. "I've never seen somebody die like that."

Wolf chuckled grimly. "You are not a soldier, Garcia. You are an entertainer. What I saw today tells me that you people are living a lie. Just because you've never had a war doesn't mean that this is a peaceful planet. If your police can't stop people from being murdered, extorted, robbed, and intimidated, then you have a huge problem. You need an army, a real army; soldiers who are trained and not afraid to kill. You do have a war on Cerberus. Not with another nation but with your own people, people that don't respect the law and the rights of their fellow citizens to be safe in their own homes, on the streets, and wherever they go."

Garcia drove on in silence, obviously mulling over what Wolf had said. "I still don't know if what happened here was right. It just seems so wrong, but deep down I know that there is truth in what you told me," he finally admitted.

"Things need to change among your people. It will take time, but it must change. I haven't spoken to anyone other than to you and General Mitchell, and I don't know how people feel, but I suspect if things don't change, eventually you may end up with chaos, a lawless society where brother will kill brother. A civil war is the worst kind of war that can happen to a society."

"You are painting a scary future for this planet," Garcia confessed.

"I don't mean to, but it will happen. The only ones that can prevent that are the people on this planet. Change is always scary, and people will suffer, no question about it." Wolf looked out of the window. He saw fewer houses. Smaller and of assorted styles.

"This area is populated by colonists who came later," Garcia explained. "They came from diverse cultures and had other ideas. Perhaps they were not as ambitious as the earlier colonists."

"That happens on other planets, also. By the way, how long until we get there?"

"We are almost there," Garcia assured him.

Wolf received another surprise when Ltd Garcia pulled up in front of the Embassy. It was a fenced-in area. The entrance was guarded by two guards armed with rifles. One of the guards stopped their vehicle by stepping in front of it, laser rifle ready.

Ltd Garcia got out and walked up to the guardhouse to talk to the other guard. When he came back, he said, "I am not allowed in the compound, but you can go ahead. If you have any weapons, you must leave them with the guard in the guardhouse."

Wolf looked at Gorini. "I find this whole thing quite peculiar. What are they afraid of? I guess they found out the truth about the way things are on Cerberus. They discovered it isn't the peaceful planet everyone says it is."

"Let's get in there and find out," she said.

Garcia got their duffel bags out of the trunk. Before he got back into his car again, Wolf said to their driver, "Thank you, Ltd Garcia. Perhaps we'll run into you again."

Garcia gave him a smart salute, and Wolf returned it, perhaps not as smartly as Garcia.

When the guard by the gate saw Gorini, he bellowed, "I can't let you into the compound. Please, step back."

"What is your reason for refusing me entry into your Embassy?" Gorini spoke with a level voice.

"Only humans are allowed in the Embassy," he informed her harshly. "Now, move back. I am not afraid to use my rifle."

"Aren't you?" Her voice mocked him. Putting down her duffle bag, she asked, "Have you ever fired that laser? I mean at a living person?"

"That is none of your concern."

"Maybe not. I'm..." She moved without warning, disarming the guard with such ease it made Wolf chuckle. Then she threw him to the ground and stood over him, aiming his own rifle at his head. "Had I been so inclined, you'd be dead now, but I am a peaceful person. Just to prove that to you, I will let you get up, and I will even give you back your rifle, but I keep my laser pistol. Understood?"

He nodded and got up when she stepped back.

"Just for your information, my name is Gorini. I am a captain with the Anorian Special Investigations Service, and I am a temporary member of the Solar Union Space Navy. That allows me all the all the rights and duties the SUSN gives its members. Let me give you some advice. If you aim your weapon at someone, be prepared to use it. Your life may depend on it."

Wolf had kept a watchful eye on the other guard in case he decided to interfere, but he had been watching the whole incident standing as rigid as a statue. It was probably the first time they had to deal with an aggressive visitor.

Gorini scowled at the guard. "Do you have any objections against me entering your Embassy?"

The guard shook his head. "Not at all. You made a valid point."

He didn't even ask Wolf if he had a weapon, and Wolf didn't tell him.

He opened the gate, letting them walk through, and closed it after them. Looking around the courtyard, Wolf saw a small pool with a fountain in the center. On one side, there was a flagpole with a flag flapping in the breeze. There were several small buildings and one large one, which they entered.

The building was nothing at all like the houses and apartment buildings they had seen so far. It was plain to see that it was built only recently. After seeing all those old buildings adorned with statues fashioned from stone this building looked plain and ugly. Wolf had seen plenty of their kind on most technically advanced planets. They were built for practicality, not for their aesthetic appearance. The smaller buildings looked as cold and plain.

The foyer was impressive, with a large chandelier hanging from the high ceiling.

Out of one of the doors walked a man wearing a dark suit. "May I be of service?"

"You sure can," Wolf said. "Which way to the Ambassador's office?"

"Right through this door is the office of his personal secretary. She will have to announce you if you want to speak to the Ambassador."

When they entered her office, she gave them a questioning look. "Can I help you?"

"We came to see the Ambassador?"

"Do you have an appointment?"

"No. We came here on a whim. Why? Is he busy?"

"Ambassador Amsterdam is always busy," she said in a haughty tone. "You need an appointment to see him. How did you get past the guards, anyway?"

"We showed them our lasers, and then we walked right past them." Wolf stepped up to her desk. "We are making an appointment right now. Please be so kind and announce us."

She leaned back in her chair. "It doesn't work that way. You have to follow certain protocols to get an appointment. Did you pick up and fill out the forms by the guardhouse?"

Wolf was getting impatient. Bending over the desk, he said, "We have no forms, and we have no intension of getting any. We are here now, and we will see the Ambassador. Tell him Major Wolf of the Solar Union Space Navy and Captain Gorini, also of the SUSN, are here to talk to him." He snapped his fingers. "Let's go. We don't have much time."

"No need to get hostile," she said, all flustered. She touched a plate on her desk. "A Major Wolf here to see you, Ambassador."

Wolf didn't wait. "Come on," he said to Gorini and headed for the door to the Ambassador's office, ignoring the secretary's protesting words.

Amsterdam's office was plush, with a couch, upholstered chairs, and pictures on the walls. The tall statue of a nude woman emerging from a large half-shell stood in one corner.

The ambassador sat behind a massive desk, watching a hologram. When he heard them coming in, he turned his attention toward the opening door.

"Who gave you permission to come into my office?" he said with a loud and demanding voice.

Wolf didn't say anything until he stood in front of the desk. "I apologize for barging in without being properly announced, but we just spent three weeks in an old relic on a mission that seems so poorly planned nobody has any idea what we are actually supposed to do. My patience is wearing quite thin, and I would appreciate a little sympathy. When I found out the Solar Union actually has an Embassy here, I was hoping to find someone who may have more knowledge of what is happening on this planet than the useless general of the local army."

Ambassador Amsterdam looked him up and down. "You are an angry man. Who are you really?"

Wolf's expression was not friendly. "I am also tired of constantly having to introduce myself. I am Major Ethan Samuel Wolf of the Solar Union Special Forces, and I am here to investigate the possible invasion of this planet by an alien species. And to find out what needs to be done to stop it from happening. General Mitchell informed us that he used your proton transmitter to alert the Solar Union's military and to send help. Well, here we are."

"I can see that. To be honest, I don't blame you for being angry. May I inquire who your partner is?"

"I am Captain Gorini. I was sent here by the Anorian Special Investigations Service," she answered his question before Wolf could say anything. "My purpose here is to find out where the invaders come from. They are not Anorians."

Amsterdam got up and sank into one of the plush chairs. "Please, make yourselves comfortable."

Wolf sat down in another chair, but Gorini chose the couch. Wolf took a look around the room. "I am puzzled by a few things. I was not aware of an Embassy here in Freeland or anywhere on Cerberus. From what I see, you seem to live well, Ambassador. What do you actually do here? How long has there been an Embassy on Cerberus?"

Amsterdam chuckled. "So many questions all at once. This Embassy was built nearly twenty standard years ago. As you most likely know, the only alien species on this planet are the Sleer. Certain people in the Union want us to keep an eye on the Sleer, and to watch out for other alien species that may try to get a foothold on Cerberus."

"How long have you been here?"

"Eight standard years. The first Ambassador was here seven years, and his replacement lasted five years before he asked for a transfer."

"I don't blame him," Wolf said. "It seems to me you are nothing but watchdogs."

"You are not completely wrong," The Ambassador said with a deep sigh. "You talked with General Mitchell. He probably filled you in about a few things on Cerberus. The inhabitants are extremely peaceful. They all get along, according to General Mitchell. The Sleer, the Sartans, and the humans. This is something unique and unusual."

"Very unique. It is also something I find hard to believe. We humans have a history of violence. We don't even get along with each other, never mind with non-humans. Humans have always been prejudiced." Wolf gave Amsterdam a hard look. "Something is not quite right here. Why, for instance, do you need a high fence around the Embassy and armed guards by the gate if this is such a peaceful planet?"

Amsterdam took a long time to answer. "Alright," he finally said. "As usual, appearances are deceiving. Yes, humans, the Sleer, and the Sartans get along with each other. It is also true that there has never been a war on Cerberus, however, the report that there is nothing but peace and happiness on this planet is completely wrong. Crime is rampant. Gangs are ruling the neighborhoods. Houses get broken into, and people get murdered. George McMahon, the first Ambassador, didn't ask to be transferred. He and his wife were murdered in a home invasion. Paul Davenport, his replacement, left suddenly one day without an explanation. Does that answer your question about the armed guards?"

"It does. I am glad you are honest with me about the situation on Cerberus. On the way here, we had our first taste how bad things are. I can tell you one thing. Those two guards are completely useless. Just an observation. I am wondering why you decided to become the Ambassador for the Solar Union if things are so dangerous. Why did you?"

"They didn't tell me anything. I found all that out after I arrived here. There is something else I need to clear up. I don't represent the Solar Union. Didn't you wonder about the flag on the flagpole in the courtyard?"

"It did cross my mind."

The Ambassador scowled. "It is the flag of my home planet, Hyperion. Many wealthy families live on Hyperion. They are the ones who built this place. They pay for all of this, my salary and any expenses that occur. I want for nothing. You were correct when you said I live well."

"I am totally confused now. Why would these wealthy families invest so much money on another planet? What are they getting out of it?"

"More wealth. Cerberus has an abundance of Lirsium Crystals. You may know or not, Lirsium Crystals are essential components of the jump drives. Without those jump drives we wouldn't be traveling the long distances between star systems in such a short time. Colonists would still be transported in huge colony ships in cryonic suspension for years to get to their new homes."

"These wealthy families, are they part of one huge company on Hyperion? If so, what is the name of this company? Are they part of the Hyperion government?" Wolf didn't really have to ask that question. He already knew what the answer would be.

"The name of the company is Hyperion Mineral Explorations. It is strictly private and above board. Before I signed any contract with them, I did some research. I found out that HME is part of Interstellar Research and Investment Conglomerate, an umbrella organization that has connections to many powerful companies on other planets. In other words, it is a solid and legal business."

"Are there any other companies operating mines on Cerberus?"

Amsterdam shook his head. "I am not aware of any."

"In other words, HDLA is the only one. They have the monopoly." Wolf turned to Gorini. "A few things are beginning to make a lot of sense. This is the reason why nobody mentioned anything about an Embassy on Cerberus. The Solar Union does not know about it. It seems we've stumbled into an illegal operation."

"Not illegal," Amsterdam protested. "The Solar Union has never shown an interest in Cerberus. There are no laws that prevent private companies from setting up an operation on another planet."

"No, but there are intergalactic laws that forbid cartels to operate illegal businesses like mining and factories producing uncontrolled substances on another planet, which is the case here."

The Ambassador lifted both hands in a gesture of defence. "There is nothing illegal about operating a mine."

"You are only partially right, Ambassador. Lirsium crystals are considered a controlled mineral because of their rarity and importance to space travel. The planets where the crystals exist are registered and numbered. Only the High Senate can issue permits to mine them. It will do so only to companies from planets that are part of the High Senate. I don't believe Hyperion is one of them, which means the company is here illegally."

Amsterdam looked at him with a doubtful expression. "How do you know this?"

"I am an agent of the ISS, and it is my business to know things like that."

"Forgive me, but what does ISS stand for?"

"It stands for Interstellar Secret Service."

"Didn't you say you are a member of the Solar Union Special Forces?" Amsterdam gave Wolf a bewildered look.

Wolf chuckled. "That is no lie. Interstellar Secret Service is just another branch of Special Forces. The reason I don't mention it is because I have to keep my identity a secret. After all, it is the Secret Service. As a member of the ISS, I answer to the High Senate. Part of my job is to investigate possible invasions of a planet, be it by an alien species or a terrorist organization within the Solar Union."

"The only invasion happening on Cerberus is by an alien species. I assumed that is why you are here. Was that also only a cover?"

"No. It is our true mission. That has not changed. Of course, now we have the extra job of clearing up this business with the HDLA." He gazed at Amsterdam with a thoughtful expression. "All this means that you are not an ambassador representing the Solar Union."

"What is the difference?" Amsterdam said defiantly. "I am still an ambassador. Instead of the Union, I represent my home planet Hyperion." He bent forward, questions in his eyes. "What is happening now? Are you reporting what you found out to the High Senate?"

Wolf nodded. "I have no choice."

"Will that mean the mines will be shut down? What about me? What is happening to this operation and to me?"

"Nothing so far. Right now, I have more important things to do than wasting my time with this mess. It may take a long time until I get around to it. Years. Maybe never."

There was a look of gratitude in Amsterdam's eyes. "Thank you," he said softly. "How about your partner? What will she do?"

"Well?" Wolf was quite sure of her answer but let her say it.

"Me? Nothing. We have no interest in the Solar Union's problems. We have our own."

Amsterdam took a deep breath and exhaled it loudly, as if a heavy weight had been lifted off his shoulders. "I won't forget this. I am in your debt forever. How can I make it up to you?"

Wolf saw an opportunity and jumped right in. "Actually, there is something you can do for us. We have a big problem. We have no funds and no place to stay. The local army turned out a huge disappointment. In fact, General Mitchell sent us to you to see if you could arrange something, since you, as we assumed, represent the Solar Union."

Wolf wasn't the only one who recognized an opportunity. Amsterdam's expression turned from that of a man in despair to one with hope. "You came to the right place. As a representative of Hyperion, I invite both of you to be my guests for as long as you want. We have a suite we use for visiting dignitaries." He paused. "I'm afraid, though, you will both have to share it. I hope that won't present a problem."

"We've been sharing a room for the last three weeks," Gorini said, glancing at Wolf with an amused smile. "I see no problem with that."

"Neither do I," Wolf said without joy. He had been looking forward to spending some time alone.

Amsterdam rubbed his hands together. "Wonderful. I can't wait to have a few discussions with you and catch up with what is happening in the rest of the Galaxy. To be honest, life has not been very exciting lately. I will tell my secretary to instruct the kitchen staff to prepare meals for two extra people. In the meantime, one of my servants will take you to your suite, where you can freshen up."

The servant turned out to be a man dressed in a dark suit. They followed him up a flight of stairs and then down a corridor. He stopped in front of one of the four doors and opened it for them. "Please, make yourselves comfortable. I'll send somebody up to make sure everything is alright."

When Wolf and Gorini stepped into the guest suite, they looked at each other. "So this is how private citizens live," Gorini commented.

"Not all, to be sure," Wolf said. "This is how the superrich private citizens live."

The room was spacious, with four upholstered chairs, one huge couch, and a couple of wooden tables with carved legs. On one wall was a bar. The shelves were stacked with bottles filled with light and dark liquids. A hologram projector stood on a small table, in case they wanted to spend time entering worlds of fantasy and adventure.

Through an open door, Wolf could see a bed in the next room. "That looks like the bedroom. I'm going to stash away my duffel bag."

When he walked through the door, he saw there was only one bed in the room. Even though it was a huge bed, he was not impressed.

Gorini, who had been close behind him, chuckled when she saw his expression. "Look at it this way," she joked, "we can always snuggle if either one of us gets cold."

"Very funny," he growled. "I hope you are not a bedcover-hog."

"Bedcover-hog? I have no idea what you are talking about."

"It means to roll yourself into the bedcover without any concern for the other person on the bed with you."

She laughed. "You can have the cover all to yourself. Did you forget? I usually sleep in the nude."

"I haven't forgotten, but this time you'll be lying right beside me."

Her golden reptilian eyes studied him thoughtfully. "Do you have some kind of hang-up when it comes to the female gender? Do you have this problem with naked human women, or is it only naked alien females that bother you?"

"I've never been bothered by a naked human or a naked alien female. I am a normal, virile male with a healthy appetite for women, human or alien. I am talking about my private life, which I separate from my job. I have never had to deal with a female partner on my missions. Yes, I am attracted to you, and I have a hard time dealing with that. Does that answer satisfy you?" He gave her an angry stare.

She took her time to answer him. When she spoke, she talked with a serious expression and tone. "I did not know that my presence had that effect on you. You must realize our males are not like human males. They don't initiate intimacy like human men do. They don't get sexually aroused when they see a female walking around in the nude. We are the aggressive gender, and we control what happens when we want to mate. I apologize if I caused you this aggravation. In fact, to me, this was nothing but a titillating game to see how far I could get. I don't have any actual experience with human males."

"I appreciate what you are saying. It isn't your problem. It is mine, and I have to come to grips with it." He grinned to ease the sudden tension between them. "Just make sure you stay on your side of the bed."

"If I decide to come over to your side, will you reject me?" She did not smile when she said it.

"Should I?"

"I don't know how to answer that. I have a confession to make. I shared with you that I can read your feelings and emotions. Being exposed to them for these last three weeks is having an effect on me, and I am confused. I have developed feelings within me which are not familiar. Your masculinity makes me want to give in to those feelings."

"What exactly are you saying?"

Her eyes were veiled behind her long lashes when she spoke. "I am saying if you would want to have sex with me, I may not reject you."

He didn't know how to react to this unexpected revelation. "Is this another one of your games you are playing with me?" he finally said.

Her smile teased him. "There is only one way to find out."

Their bantering was interrupted by the arrival of an older woman in a black dress. "Sorry to disturb you, but I just want to make sure you have everything you need. There are fresh towels in the bathroom if you want to take a bath or shower. My name is Taria. Ask for me if you need something."

"Thank you, Taria. I'm curious. Were you born in Freeland?"

"Yes, I was. Right here in Greater York." She seemed proud of that fact.

"How long have you been in the employ of Ambassador Amsterdam?"

"I've worked for the Embassy now for twelve years. Ambassador Paul Davenport was the one who hired me."

"Do you like working here?" Wolf made a movement with his hand to negate the question. "You don't have to answer that if you don't want to. I am just curious, that's all."

"I don't mind. Yes, I am happy. Ambassador Amsterdam is a very generous man. He compensates me adequately. I wouldn't get paid this well anywhere else."

"How many servants does he have?"

She lifted her thin shoulders. "I'm not sure. I would guess about twenty-five."

"All of them locals?"

She nodded. "Yes. All are happy."

Wolf regarded Gorini with a little smile. "It seems the Ambassador is a wonderful man and quite popular."

"It seems that way." She turned to the servant. "If you will excuse me, I am going to take a bath now."

Wolf watched her walking away, still mulling around in his head what she told him. "Thank you, Taria. What time is dinner?"

"Somebody will let you know." She gave him a polite smile and left.

Wolf went into the bedroom and pulled a shirt and a pair of pants out of his duffel bag. "I think I'll take a shower," he said to himself. "I wonder if I can have my clothes laundered here."

He knocked on the door to the bathroom. "How long will you be?"

"I just stepped into the tub," Gorini called. "The door is open."

He opened the door and walked into the bathroom. Gorini lay half-submerged in the tub. He could see her breasts quite clearly, but she made no move to cover them. "I'm thinking of taking a shower after you're done."

"You can take one right now. I won't mind."

He went back into the bedroom and stripped. Gorini watched him coming into the bathroom again, naked this time. "You have a great physique," she commented.

"You never said so before."

"I didn't want you to take it the wrong way. This is just an observation, that's all. It means nothing."

"I know, but it still is nice to hear you say something complimentary." With one last look at her exposed upper body, he entered the shower stall. Standing under the warm spray of water, he went over their conversation and realized that she had offered herself to him. There was nothing stopping him from taking advantage of her offer, and yet, he knew he wouldn't. He found her extremely attractive, and not giving in to the desire to have sex with her was a struggle, especially since she didn't seem to find anything wrong with parading around in the nude when they were alone. She was Anorian, not human. She came from a culture where the females walked around naked all the time. It was second nature to her.

Deep down, he knew that getting involved with a member of his team was wrong and not advisable.

[4]

"I MUST SAY, I COULD ALMOST GET USED TO THIS KIND OF LIFE. ALMOST. I'M afraid I'd get bored after a while," Wolf mused.

"Not only bored but also flabby and fat." Gorini laughed softly.

"I can't argue that. I didn't have a pampered life when I grew up. I've never experienced such luxury. Once I joined the military, even that little bit of comfort was gone. A soldier's life is a harsh life, but that is all I am used to." He made a circular movement with his hand. "This pool, the garden with colorful flowers, and this huge house with all the servants, they make me feel uncomfortable in many ways. It is too overwhelming."

"Living like this wouldn't be for me, either."

"What about you? What kind of life did you have when you grew up? I know nothing about your race. Do you have family units where the parents raise their children, or are the children raised by the government?"

"That is a question difficult to answer. Just like you humans, we have a diversity of cultures. However, there is one constant that doesn't change. Anorian males are the weaker sex. The females form the government, they make the laws, and they are the ones exploring space and fighting the wars. That's how it's been as far back as our records show. We have family units, just like you humans, except it is the males that raise the

51

children and take care of domestic chores. To answer your question, I was raised in a government facility. My parents were killed in an accident when I was still young."

"I am sorry to hear that." Wolf didn't just say it, he meant it. "In other words, you didn't grow up surrounded by luxury and comfort."

"I've never experienced luxurious surroundings, nor do I know how it feels to live with parents or siblings."

"At least I had those. I have one brother and one sister. We were not rich, but we enjoyed a relatively comfortable life. My father is in law enforcement, and my mother is a scientist."

"It looks like you had a pretty normal childhood." She gave him a questioning look. "What made you join the military? You could have gone into law enforcement, like your father, and spent the rest of your life fighting criminals on Rion. Why the Space Navy?"

"Why does any young man or woman leave the comfortable nest?" He shrugged. "You tell me."

"That's easy. I didn't have much choice. When I reached adulthood, I had to leave the facility. Not by choice, either. To become a member of the military provided me with a home, with a family. It also gave me an opportunity to see other worlds. There was nothing for me on my home planet. I didn't have any ties to anyone." She smiled. "To be honest, traveling between the stars and visiting other planets had a certain magic to it. Something pulled me out there. It is difficult to explain."

"Did things turn out the way you imagined?"

She chuckled. "Does it ever?"

The arrival of one of the servants interrupted their conversation. "Sorry to disturb you," the man said, "but the Ambassador is wondering if you are interested in joining him on a trip to one of the mines."

"I certainly would be," Wolf sat up from his comfortable position. "When?"

"He wants to leave in half an hour."

"Tell him we'll be there." He turned to Gorini. "You are coming, aren't you?"

"Of course. Anything to break this boredom."

They were on their way an hour later. The road they traveled on looked neglected. Overgrown by vegetation, it sometimes was nearly impossible to see. It didn't really matter. The armoured truck they rode in floated on a cushion of air, powered by antigravity.

"I guess the company that pays for all of this is not suffering financially," Wolf commented.

"The trading of Lirsium Crystals is a lucrative business. Those crystals are in high demand," the Ambassador agreed. "Cerberus has an abundance of them, and they are not difficult to mine. I don't know much about them, but from what I understand, on other planets that have them, they are not easily accessible and mining them is costly and dangerous."

"And the HME has no competition here on Cerberus you said?"

"That's correct. Nobody else seems to know about their existence." Amsterdam regarded Wolf with a serious expression. "I am violating company policy by telling you about them. And now I am even taking you to one of the mines. I know we've discussed all of this, and I am grateful for the decision you made, but I am still counting on your discretion not to discuss the Lirsium Crystals with anyone, here on Cerberus and anywhere else."

"If it doesn't come up, I have no reason to mention it. Let me caution you, though. Even though I said I have no interest in pursuing this matter at present, what is happening here is still illegal. I cannot guarantee what may happen in the future. For now, your position is safe, but that won't last forever."

"I appreciate your candor." Amsterdam looked out of the window as if he were studying the bleak countryside. "You know I'm not a fool. When I took on this job, I did so with some misgivings. It all sounded just too good to be true, and you know what they say about that. My employers assured me it was all above board. Cerberus was not an important planet, and nobody was really interested in it. The people on Cerberus were peaceful, and living here would almost be like living in Paradise. I found out that was not the case, as you already discovered firsthand. I ignored the warnings and became complacent." He gazed at his hands. "I've had eight good years. Perhaps it is time to move on."

"I wouldn't throw in the towel yet. Your comfortable life is not in danger yet," Wolf assured him. "My advice is to keep an eye on the signs around you. Things are rotten on this planet, and changes will come. Not because of you, but events have been put in motion, and they will escalate from now on. It is inevitable. It all started with that report of an invasion you sent to the Solar Union. Now that the Union has been alerted, nothing can stop the tsunami that will roll over Cerberus."

Amsterdam's chuckle was not one of amusement. "You sound like a doomsday prophet. I'm not sure if I want to be around when that happens. Perhaps, I should pack my things now and get the hell off this planet before it is too late."

"I wouldn't panic yet, Ambassador. Changes don't happen overnight. You just have to make sure you don't miss the last ship, that's all." Wolf looked over to Gorini. She seemed to be uninterested in their conversation. Her eyes were closed, and her chest moved gently up and down, but she was an alien and judging her by human standards could be a mistake. Even in a relaxed state she still might be able to hear and understand everything that went on around her.

Amsterdam noted Wolf's glance at her. "Can she be trusted?" he wondered.

"You guess is as good as mine," Wolf said. "I've only known her for about four weeks now. We've been living in close proximity during that time, and we got along fairly well. She seems honest and loyal once she gets to know you, but she is an Anorian, an alien species. She and I are a team. We've bonded in an unspoken way and, personally, I trust her with my life. She trusts me the same way. I cannot vouch for her when it comes to everyone and everything else. If she says she has no interest in your affairs, I believe her."

"That's good. I trust your judgement. By the way, it won't be long now until we get to our destination."

"A question, Ambassador. I noticed we've been following a sort of road. Was this an actual road at one time?"

"It was. There used to be a Sartan village not far from here, and the villagers used this road to take their trading goods to Greater York, but that was many years ago. They moved the whole village farther down south. I don't know the history of that. The Sartans, as you may have been told in your briefing, live in a completely different time. Their society is still primitive. They use wagons with wheels and animals to pull them. They are not stupid, by the way. Far from it. They are quite intelligent, but they prefer to live the way they do."

"It probably is a much simpler life, possibly with less stress," Wolf agreed.

The road took them through a forest. On each side of the road grew tall conifer trees with wide-spreading branches. When they emerged on the other side, they looked into a deep valley surrounded by a mountain ridge.

Amsterdam watched Wolf with an amused expression. "Beautiful, isn't it?"

"Yes, it is. What's down there?"

"This used to be the location of the old Sartan village. At the bottom of this valley is also one of the mines."

They followed the road down into the valley. Halfway down, they drove through another forest. Coming out of it, Wolf stared at the sight that greeted them.

"Is that what I think it is?" he asked.

"It is." Amsterdam nodded smugly. "That is a private spaceport belonging exclusively to the Hyperion Mineral Explorations company."

"I can see a large shuttle on the tarmac."

"It appears the company decided to make a surprise inspection." Amsterdam didn't sound happy about that. "I wonder why."

"Will that present a problem?" Wolf wondered.

"I hope not. Please, do me a favor. Do not tell the inspector that you're with the Solar Union Special Forces. He will want to know why you are here. Both of your lives might be in danger. The agent won't be alone. A squad of troopers will accompany him."

"Surely not Union troopers," Wolf stated.

"No. Renegades. The most dangerous and brutal soldiers you can hire. They are loyal only to the company."

Gorini, who had been silent until now, said, "This whole thing is taking on a different aspect. They are making this planet their own. The Solar Union will want to take a closer look at this."

"That cannot happen." The Ambassador sounded desperate. "If you reveal that you are agents you may be signing your and my death warrant. You two won't stand a chance against them."

"Don't worry. They won't find out about us." Wolf assured him. "Not from us." He indicated the driver. "What about him?"

"Eugene is my most loyal servant. He can be trusted to stay silent."

"Good. Then we should have no problem."

"By the way, Eugene is a Sartan."

"I would have never guessed," Wolf said, taken by surprise.

Amsterdam chuckled softly. "What did you think a Sartan man looked like?"

"From the information I got, I knew he would look like an Earth-human. However, I admit I thought I might spot something different, like bigger or smaller ears. Perhaps a differently shaped nose. I don't know."

"There is no difference, believe me. Eugene has been my driver for over five years now. I would have spotted some difference by now if it existed."

"I hope I didn't hurt your feelings, Eugene," Wolf addressed the driver.

"I am not offended, sir. When I saw my first Earth-human, I was just as surprised as you are. I am used to you people now."

Wolf couldn't help but laugh at that. "Your sense of humor proves that there is no difference."

"Thank you, sir."

The road led straight to the spaceport. As they came closer, they saw one large building and a few smaller ones. They also saw a huge hole in the ground not far away. As if expecting Wolf's question, Amsterdam said, "The Lirsium is mined in an open pit. That's what makes mining the crystals on Cerberus so convenient. Apparently, on some planets, they have to blast their way into deep rock to get to them."

Wolf spotted a row of small buildings on one side of the hole. "I assume those are the living quarters for the workers?" he ventured.

"You are correct. By the way, just for your information, all of the workers are Sartans."

"Why Sartans? Couldn't you get any humans to do the job?" Wolf wondered.

"The Sartans are humans, except that technologically they are not as advanced as we are. Why am I using them instead of Earth-humans? They work hard and don't mind living out here."

"How do you pay them? I assume you are."

"Of course. I pay them with Dockats, our local currency."

"Are the Sartans using the same currency?"

The Ambassador shook his head. "They don't, but my workers use the money to buy things from our stores, things they cannot get in their country."

Eugene maneuvered the vehicle onto the tarmac and stopped in front of the large building. After getting out of the car, Amsterdam, Wolf, and Gorini entered the building. Eugene stayed with the car. Wolf didn't know what to expect and was surprised when he saw comfortable couches and chairs. On one wall was a shelf stocked with bottles, obviously filled with alcohol.

Amsterdam pointed to a staircase at the far end of the room. "Those stairs lead to the third floor where the living quarters of the men and women working here are located. All of them are humans, and none of them are locals. I have nothing to do with them. They are employees of HME. The offices are on the second floor."

While he was talking, three men flanked by two men in uniforms, obviously their bodyguards, came down the stairs. They stopped for a moment, and then they started walking toward them.

"Remember what we discussed," Amsterdam said in a low voice.

The three men stopped in front of Amsterdam, while the two body-guards hung back, studying Wolf and Gorini with suspicion in their eyes.

"Inspector Gifford, I am surprised to see you. I didn't expect anyone for another couple of weeks. Everything alright at the home office?" Amsterdam sounded jovial, but Wolf detected the tension in his words.

"Why wouldn't it be, Ambassador Amsterdam?" Gifford spoke in an arrogant tone. Wolf disliked him instantly. Here was a man with power and no regard for anyone except himself.

"I'm not suggesting there is," Amsterdam hastened to assure him that he meant no disrespect. "I'm just wondering, that's all. I am here to see if everything is running smoothly in the mine and to make sure that the next shipment will be ready in time."

"I see you brought company. I'm not sure if that is wise. You are acting against company policies. I hope you haven't forgotten that company rules don't allow strangers snooping around here. Who are these two? The female is Anorian, an alien." Gifford didn't hide his displeasure.

"They are friends of mine and guests on my estate," Amsterdam informed him. "They have no interest in this place, I can assure you of that."

"Clearly, they are not citizens of Freeland." Gifford looked at Wolf with narrow eyes. "Who the hell are you, and what are you doing here on Cerberus? Be careful how you answer my question. I'll know if you are trying to mislead me."

Wolf gave him his most sincere smile. "I have no reason to mislead anyone, sir. My name is Samuel Wolf, and I am what you might call an independent traveler."

"A traveler? What does that mean?"

"I travel wherever destiny leads me. My home is the universe, and I desire neither fortune nor fame. I own very little, but the universe always provides for my needs."

Gifford snorted. "In other words, you are a misfit, a parasite living off other people's hard work. What about the Anorian? Where does she fit in?"

"We are kindred spirits."

"Are you fucking her?"

"Such crude words, sir. We are joining our bodies to become one with the universe."

"Alright, I've heard enough. I don't have much use for your kind. I notice you both carry lasers. Why?"

"Just for protection. The universe is a violent place."

"Have you ever had to shoot anyone?" It was an innocent question, but Wolf knew it wasn't.

"We try not to get dragged into situations where that is necessary," he said.

Gifford turned his attention back to Amsterdam. "I am not happy with this, and I will keep an eye on these two. Make sure you don't spill any sensitive information. It may not end up well for either of you. Just a word of advice."

"As I mentioned before, they are not interested in politics or anything else. Right now, they are enjoying the comforts of my home, but I will take your advice and be careful. Thank you, Inspector. By the way, when did you arrive?"

"We landed a couple of days ago. I'm planning to stay the week and take a look around to make sure our investments are showing profits. I may have to ask you to increase production. The demand for Lirsium Crystals is great, and we want to make sure we keep our position as the largest supplier in the Union."

"I understand, sir, but the men are already working as much as they can and to their fullest capability. It may be difficult to increase production."

"Then hire more workers. I understand the people you employ are not real humans. They have no rights as far as the Union is concerned. Putting them under a little more pressure won't do any harm."

"That may be true, Inspector, but they are as human as you and I. Because they don't have any rights doesn't make them less human." Amsterdam sounded defiant.

Gifford glared at him. "If you are unable to manage it, I can have you replaced within a few weeks. I think you've become too comfortable in your position, Ambassador Amsterdam."

"May I remind you that I have a contract, sir?" Amsterdam spoke up. "You can't just fire me."

Gifford laughed. "That contract means nothing to me. I can fire you just for the fun of it. Who is going to challenge me?" He turned to the two men with him. "I've had enough of this chit-chat. I'm getting thirsty. Let's go and see what we can find in the liqueur cabinet."

They walked away and left Amsterdam, Wolf, and Gorini standing there.

"What a pompous ass," Wolf said when they were out of hearing.

Amsterdam didn't comment. He seemed subdued. Wolf didn't blame him.

"Let's get back into the car. I want to drive down to the mine," Amsterdam suggested.

"Gladly," Wolf said. "I was afraid we might have to spend some time with that moron."

The road leading down into the pit was not steep, which wouldn't have mattered, because the truck didn't have any wheels. It floated silently down the hole until it reached the bottom.

The floor of the pit was not flat or nice and clean. Piles of large and small rocks were scattered all around. To one side stood two trucks with large loading boxes. Half a dozen small trucks with buckets in the front were either standing or moving about.

A number of smaller holes dotted the bottom of the large pit.

"Feel free to look around," Amsterdam said. "I'm going to talk to the supervisor of the project." He pointed to a small building. "He should be in there."

Wolf and Gorini headed for one of the holes. Once they reached it, they saw several men in coveralls digging up the ground with picks and hammer drills. One truck with a bucket kept scraping along the ground, either loosening the soil or transporting loose rocks and sand to another truck with a small box in the back.

A couple of the men stopped working when they became aware of the visitors and watched as they came closer. They looked human. When one of them removed his hardhat to wipe his forehead he exposed a mass of black hair.

"They sure look human to me," Gorini remarked.

"Apparently, there is no discernible difference between the Sartans and Earth-humans," Wolf said.

"Do you speak Freeland?" Wolf addressed the two workers.

"We do," one of them answered. He stared at Gorini. "You are not human."

"You are right. I am not human. I am an Anorian. All of my people look like me."

"Are you male or female," the other one inquired, not hiding his curiosity as he studied her.

She laughed. "I am a female. Isn't it obvious?" She turned to Wolf.

"Perhaps I should take off my clothes to make them believe," she said with a little smirk.

"I don't think that is necessary," he advised her. "These poor men probably haven't seen a female in a long time."

"You seem to enjoy looking at my naked body."

"I do, but I've hardened myself to seeing you parade around, trying to tease me. Don't torture these men."

"I wasn't serious," she said.

"You could have fooled me. I can never tell if you're serious or not." He turned his attention back to the two Sartans. "Are you being treated well?"

Both men shrugged. "We can't complain. The work is hard, but we get compensated for it. The Dockets we receive make it possible for us to buy wondrous things we can't get in Tsakona."

"Tsakona?" Wolf wondered. "Is that what you call your country?"

"Yes." The man gave him a curious look. "You don't know?"

"I am not a native of this world." Wolf pointed into the sky. "We come from another world."

"Did you come with that metal vessel that is parked near the big building?"

"No." Wolf shook his head. "We have nothing to do with the men that came in that vessel. Have you met them?"

The man nodded. "We have." He paused as if deciding what to say next. "They are not nice men," he said finally. "Is everyone who lives on these other worlds like that?"

"No. Not everyone. The worlds out there are all different. Not only humans live on those worlds. There are many different kinds of people living there. Some look like us, some look like Gorini here. That is her name by the way. There are some that look like giant spiders, and others look like giant birds. All are intelligent. A few are nice, and many are hostile. Have you never seen any visitors to your world that look different?"

"The only different people we know are the people that live in the swamps and the lakes. We trade with them."

"You are talking about the Sleer."

"I am. They are good people."

"My people are good, too." Gorini smiled. "But we can also be bad if we have to."

"Why are you here?" the second man asked.

"Out of curiosity," Wolf said. "I cannot tell you more. We need to go. We don't want to get you in trouble because we are keeping you from working."

"Yes, you are," the first man admitted. "It was interesting to talk to you. Nobody ever comes down here to do that. Not even the Ambassador."

"I find that strange. Maybe he thinks you are not interested in talking to him. I will mention it to him."

Wolf watched the two men going back to their work. "They seem to be quite intelligent," he said to Gorini. "I would like to find out more about their people."

They spotted the Ambassador coming out of the building he had been in. He wasn't alone. Another man was with him. He didn't wear coveralls. Wolf assumed he was the supervisor.

When they came closer, Wolf couldn't tell if he was Sartan or not.

"This is Malor, my supervisor," Amsterdam introduced him. "These are my guests, Wolf and Gorini."

"Good to be in your presence, Wolf and Gorini," Malor said. "I hope you enjoy your stay."

[5]

"Usually, I have lunch with the staff, enjoying conversations with some non-locals, but I am not looking forward to spending time with Inspector Gifford. Unfortunately, I have no choice. You are not obligated to put yourself through that."

"Don't worry about us, Ambassador," Wolf assured him. "I am interested in what the Inspector has to say."

They met Gifford and the other two men in the dining room. It was not the same room where the rest of the staff ate. It was private, reserved for visiting members of the company's executive.

Gifford voiced his displeasure of having Wolf and Gorini joining them for lunch. "I want to have a private talk with you after lunch, Ambassador. We need to discuss a few things meant only for your ears."

"Don't mind me, Gifford," Wolf said in a jovial tone. "You can discuss anything you want with the Ambassador. I am not even vaguely interested in the politics of some company I've never heard of before today. It is too confusing and interferes with the tranquility of my being. By the way, this fish I am eating is delicious. Did you know that fish have a conscience?"

"I did not know, and I don't care to know, Mister Wolf. In fact, I don't even like fish." Gifford shook his head in annoyance. He took a sip from his wineglass. Putting it back onto the table, he said, "How did your meeting with the supervisor go, Amsterdam? Everything on schedule?"

"Things are great, Inspector Gifford. Almost better than great." Amsterdam coughed delicately. "About that meeting after lunch. I'm afraid I won't be able to stay. The Prime Minister of Freeland has invited me to a small function at his residence. As Ambassador representing Hyperion I am obliged to be there. After all, we want to stay in the good will of the Prime Minister and his country to make sure nothing interferes with the mining of the Lirsium Crystals."

Gifford put down his glass. "Fuck the Prime Minister! What's his name again?"

"Albert Brownstone."

"Fuck Albert Brownstone! I don't think you understand the situation here, Ambassador. We don't need his good will or permission to mine the crystals. If he or any of his cabinet ever give us trouble, we will get rid of them and take over. Who will stand in our way? They have no army to defend their country. The police are as corrupt as the criminals they are supposed to arrest and put away. You don't need to worry about that. For now, just play ball and pretend everything is fine. Enjoy your dinners and dances." He chuckled. "Things can change in a very short time. There are developments underway that will shake up things a bit."

"What kind of things?"

"Big things. Sorry to say, but you are not privileged to that kind of information. Let's face it, you are just an employee like all the other low-level executives. Actually, you're not even in the executive." He lifted his glass. "Cheers, Mister Ambassador."

———

AMBASSADOR AMSTERDAM WAS IN A DOWNCAST MOOD WHEN THEY DROVE home. "I don't trust him," he finally said. "I can see big problems on the horizon. I get this feeling my peaceful life is coming to an end."

"A man like him can create a lot of chaos and do much damage," Gorini agreed. "He has no respect for anything."

"I wouldn't panic just yet," Wolf cautioned. "An operation of this scope cannot be re-organized that quickly. They won't shut it down completely. It is too important. As long as they mine the crystals, they will need somebody on this planet to oversee the operation."

"He threatened to overthrow the government of Freeland. He is a madman, drunk with power. I wouldn't put it past him to do that if he suddenly feels like it," Amsterdam voiced his fear.

"If for some reason that would happen, it would draw the attention of the Union. Somebody would wonder about the reason for such a bold move and the secret about the Lirsium Crystals would be exposed. It would be the end of the company. He knows that. He can't be that stupid."

"I guess not," Amsterdam agreed. "I still don't trust him."

"Are you really going to a small gathering at the Prime Minister's place?" Wolf wondered.

"I made that up. I just wanted to get away from that madman," Amsterdam admitted. He heaved a deep sigh. "I always knew that this dream I am living would not last and come to an end someday."

"I don't want to pry, Mister Ambassador, but have you prepared for such an eventuality? I mean financially?"

Amsterdam threw Wolf a quick look and nodded slowly. "I am trusting you with this information. I anticipated a few years ago that things may change. Call it premonition or just coincidence. I purchased a moderate home in Windy Lake, a quiet, peaceful town about a hundred miles east of Greater York."

"I am happy to hear that. Anyone looking after it?"

"Yes, my sister and her husband." He chuckled when he saw Wolf's surprised expression.

"Your sister? I would have never guessed you had a sister here."

"She came for a visit a few years ago, met a local man and fell in love. He was a resident of Windy Lake, and she moved in with him. They got married a year later. A couple of years ago, the house next to them became vacant, so I decided to buy it. It seems it was the best decision I made in my life."

Wolf couldn't agree more. "Life sometimes throws us a few opportunities. It is up to us to take advantage of them."

"If it comes to the crunch, my servants will be the ones with most to lose. They are good people, and they will lose their jobs. Unfortunately, I won't be able to help them."

"You can't worry about them, Ambassador. If they are smart, they will also plan for their future. People have to do that no matter in which country or on what planet they live."

"On my planet it is the young that take care of the old and feeble," Gorini said.

"How about on the other planets where your people live?" Amsterdam asked.

"The same. Nobody gets neglected or pushed aside. It has always been like that with the Anorians."

The guards back at the Embassy saluted and opened the gate when their vehicle pulled up.

"Are those two members of the local army?" Wolf inquired as they drove into the compound.

"They are. Why do you ask?"

"Maybe Gorini and I should teach them how to use a rifle and how to fight. They might thank us some day when they have to defend their families against the enemies that already lurk among the people of Freeland."

"Why do you believe that will happen?"

"It is inevitable. You talked about the premonition you may have had a few years ago? This is my premonition," Wolf said.

———

"WINDY LAKE HAS BEEN HIT BY THE INVADERS YESTERDAY." AMSTERDAM looked upset and worried. "I have to drive there immediately to see if my sister is alright."

"What exactly happened?" Wolf inquired.

"We have no details, but we know from the information we received that they raided a store and burned it down along with two houses. They killed the owner of the store and five customers. Apparently, there are many injured people. That's all we know."

"We will come with you."

Just because the vehicle had no wheels didn't mean they didn't need a road. They could get away without a road had the terrain been smooth and flat, but it wasn't. Rocks and shrubs and other debris would have made for rough and probably dangerous traveling. The surface was not as smooth as a paved road, either, but smooth enough to keep the vehicle from jumping up and down while traveling at high speed. Small obstacles were not even registered by the vehicles detection system.

It took less than one hour to get to Windy Lake and about ten minutes to arrive at the home of the Ambassador's sister.

"You didn't have to come," she said. "You could have called."

"I needed to see you to make sure you are fine."

"I am good. We are all good." With a glance at Wolf, she asked, "Who are these people?"

"They are my guests. This are Major Wolf and Captain Gorini."

"You are not human," she said to Gorini, giving her a piercing look. "You look like the raiders that burned down the store and killed all those people."

"She may look like them, but she has nothing to do with that," Amsterdam hastened to explain.

Gorini smiled. "Pardon me, Ambassador, but I can speak for myself. I am an Anorian, but you may notice I am a female. Those raiders are all males. They do not come from my people."

"My brother introduced you as 'Captain Gorini'. Why are you here? I mean on Cerberus?"

"Major Wolf and I are here to investigate these raids. That's all I can tell you." She tilted her head. "You know my name. What is yours?"

"Oh, I am sorry. I am Adrianna. Welcome to my home." Her eyes focused on Wolf. "Major Wolf. Major of what?"

"I am a major with the Solar Union's military."

"You're a soldier. I hope you brought an army with you. Our army is completely useless."

"That's what I've heard. I hate to disappoint you, but for now it is only Captain Gorini and me. We are here to evaluate the situation, but I can assure you as soon as we know what is going on here, we will call for military action."

"It better happen fast, because the attacks are more frequent, and now they have made our town a target. They may be back."

"Where is Benjamin?" the Ambassador inquired.

"He is at the hospital. A lot of people have been injured; many are burn victims. He'll be late."

"My brother-in-law is a surgeon," Amsterdam explained.

"I'd like to visit the site," Wolf said. "Perhaps talk to some witnesses."

"We can go right away." Amsterdam gave his sister a hug. "I'm so relieved you are not injured or..." he left the sentence hanging.

"No need to worry anymore," she assured him with a smile. She took a few steps backwards and did a little pirouette. "Notice anything?"

"I do, but I didn't want to assume. Are you with child?"

She laughed. "In my third month."

"Congratulations. I am so happy for you." Amsterdam gave her another hug. Beaming, he burst out, "I'm going to be an uncle. Wow! Benjamin must ecstatic. We'll have to have a drink together when I come back."

There wasn't much left of the store except for a metal skeleton. Inside were small mountains of smoldering pieces of wood and other materials. The same was true of the two houses. On one side on the street lay the burned-out shell of a car. At closer look Wolf saw that it was a police car.

Two police cars were parked in front of the still smoking charred walls of the two houses. Wolf saw three uniformed men standing beside the cars.

"I want to talk to those police men," Wolf announced.

Eugene parked their car a short distance from the two police cruisers.

"I hope they don't freak out when they see me." Gorini seemed worried.

"Don't worry about that," Wolf said. "Once they know who you are they will understand."

The three police officers looked in their direction when they left their car. When they saw Gorini all three tensed and watched them coming closer with obvious apprehension. One of them recognized the Ambassador and said something to his colleagues.

"Ambassador Amsterdam," he greeted them, "it looks like the news travels fast."

"Hello, Chief Dubois." Amsterdam shook his hand. "It is all over Greater York."

"Your two companions? Who are they?"

"Major Wolf of the Solar Union military and Captain Gorini of the Anorian Special Investigation Service," Amsterdam introduced them.

"We are here because of this," Wolf explained, indicating the smoldering ruins.

"Before you try to connect the Anorians with this attack, let me assure you that we have nothing to do with these raids. I'm here to put those rumors to rest," Gorini told them.

"What happened here?" Wolf pointed at the turned-over car.

"Corporal Horinder was the first one here. He watched them entering their flying machine and take off. They shot at his car once they were in the air and killed him," one of the officers told him.

"Damn shame," another one said. He was a good man and still so young. We'll miss him."

"He managed to record everything on his body camera. It transmitted the recordings back to the Station. That's how we got all those live images."

"I'm going to take a closer look at the ruins," Wolf advised them. "Come on," he said to Gorini. "Four eyes are better than two."

They couldn't get close. The heat was still too intense.

"There really isn't much to see," Wolf speculated. "This isn't like a murder case or accident where you can find evidence of the crime. Sure, we have plenty of evidence of what happened here, but it won't tell us how to find the criminals. One thing we know. They have aircraft and advanced weapons. Of course, we already knew what they look like. Still, not much to go on."

"It is a little more than we knew. The reports only said modern vehicles, but they never mentioned aircraft. That puts a new angle on it. Perhaps we can watch the whole thing at the Police Station," Gorini suggested.

"Good idea."

Chief Dubois had no objections to that. He suggested they follow him to the Station.

The recordings were quite clear. They started with the images of the store and one of the houses in flames. Then seven figures came running out of the last house, carrying sacks filled with something. Moments later, the last house exploded with debris being thrown into the air. There were other people on the street, some running away from the burning store and some stumbling around; a few collapsed to lie motionless on the ground.

There was no doubt that the raiders were Anorian males. They wore some kind of dark green uniform that left their muscular arms bare. The weapons they had slung across their shoulders were of unfamiliar design, but it was obvious they did not fire bullets. They climbed into a disk-shaped vehicle. Before it lifted into the air, a spear of light appeared from its belly. The images abruptly stopped as the screen exploded into a sheet of bright whiteness.

"That was the moment Corporal Horinder lost his life," Chief Dubois said with a grave voice. He looked at Gorini. "The raiders surely looked like members of your race. Are you quite certain they are not Anorians?"

"I admit they look like Anorians, but our males are not as big as these here and not as aggressive. In fact, our males are quite timid and not adventurous at all. They are perfectly happy to stay home and take care of all the domestic chores and raise the children. I can assure you that these are not Anorians. That is the reason my government sent me here to find out where they come from. We are not aware of any Anorian planet or colony where they could originate from."

Chief Dubois glanced at Wolf. "Is it possible that the Solar Union military may have records about Anorian males attacking colonists on other planets?"

Wolf shook his head. "None. Their planet of origin must be from outside Known Space. Of course, we haven't been in contact with any of the other races. There is a possibility that at least one of them has records about Anorian males invading or raiding a planet. I will have to contact my superiors and make my first report. Until now we had only rumors to go by. Let's face it, Cerberus is not really at the top of the list of important planets or colonies. We are only one team out there investigating the many incidents that happen on other colonies. Perhaps, after I make my report, what is happening here on Cerberus will move it up the ladder of important issues."

"That doesn't help us now," Chief Dubois said. "What prevents them from coming back again? We can't defend ourselves. Not against their weapons or way of traveling through the air. Having no real army is biting us in the backside now. I'm sure by now you know about our army, a bunch of useless entertainers. The police are the only ones carrying lethal weapons, but ours are outdated, and we are only a few. We can't even manage the criminals."

"How is the crime situation here in Windy Lake?"

"Not nearly as bad as it is in Greater York. We have roughly about eight thousand people living in Windy Lake. In small towns like this one, people tend to get to know their neighbors. They visit each other, form interest groups, and organize functions for the adults and the young people. Criminals will be found out quickly and not tolerated. I'm not saying we are crime-free, but close to it. Criminal organization won't be able to take over a part of the town like in Greater York. Anyone caught committing a crime, is arrested and thrown in jail. I see to it, and the judge sees to it. We are fortunate to have a judge that is fair but tough and not corrupt. He won't be intimidated by any group trying to put pressure on him."

"I am happy to hear that. As a lawman, I have no sympathy with criminals and zero tolerance."

Dubois chuckled. "You talk just like my deputy. He would execute anyone who commits a capital offense. I think you'll like him."

"Sounds like my kind of man." Wolf smiled." I'd like to get back to what we just witnessed." Wolf turned to the Ambassador. "I need to contact Military High Command. We have to get back to the Embassy as soon as possible."

"Surely it can wait one day, Major," Amsterdam said. "I was hoping to spend a day with my sister."

"I sympathize with you, but this is urgent. Besides, it would mean staying here overnight. I'm sure your sister would not be overly excited entertaining us as her guests. Where would we sleep anyway?"

"We have good hotels in Windy Lake," Dubois suggested.

"I'm sure you have. The problem is we don't have any funds to pay for anything. We have been guests of the Ambassador. He's been kind enough to take us in."

Dubois scratched his chin. "That is a problem. I have an idea. You could stay at Scouts Base. In fact, you may even be able to contact your headquarters from there. It is worth a try."

Wolf frowned. "There is a Scouts Base in Windy Lake?"

"You didn't know?"

"Scouts and Troopers do not get along. We stay out of each other's way if at all possible."

"Sergeant Becker can drive you there. He is friends with one of the Scouts, and he can introduce you." He smiled. "Just be civil and pleasant, they'll look after you. In Windy Lake everyone gets along."

"What do you say?" Wolf turned to Gorini.

"I'd say it is worth a shot." She laughed. "I'm a friendly person. I've been getting along with you, haven't I?"

"I don't like the sound of that," he grumbled, but softened it with a smile. "Alright. We have nothing to lose."

"Good. I'll call the Sergeant. You can leave as soon as you are ready to go."

"We are ready now."

[6]

SCOUTS BASE WAS ONLY TWENTY MINUTES AWAY. FROM THE OUTSIDE, IT WAS just another old two-storey building. The front door opened before Sergeant Becker had a chance to bang on the door or ring a doorbell to announce their presence.

The man that stepped out did not look like a Scout, dressed as he was in local civilian clothes. "Hermann, what brings you here? Everything alright? Do you have the day off?"

"I wish. I just came from investigating the store that was destroyed in that attack. What a mess. So many people dead and injured. Sorry, to barge unannounced, but I bring guests." He turned to Wolf. "This is my friend Scout Brian Ikeda. He will help you."

"I will?" Ikeda looked surprised. "Who are these two?" He seemed to notice Gorini for the first time. "She is an Anorian. What is she doing here?"

Wolf stepped forward. "I apologize for bothering you, Scout Ikeda. I am Major Wolf. My companion is Captain Gorini. We are in Windy Lake to investigate the attack Sergeant Becker mentioned. However, we are stranded here and in need of a place to stay for one night. We were hoping you could help us."

"What makes you think we can help you?"

"Chief Dubois suggested it."

"You are a trooper, Major Wolf?"

"Correct. I am with Special Forces." While he said that, he had a sudden flash of inspiration. "I know Scouts and troopers are not socializing, usually, but my best friend is Major Alfred Swann of Scouts Security. It proves, Scouts and troopers can get along."

"You know Major Swann?"

"We grew up together and we've been friends since we were in preschool. That is the honest truth."

"That is quite interesting and curious." Ikeda's demeanor changed from hostile to exciting. "Come in. We have a few things to discuss."

"It looks like everything is in order," Becker said. "I'd better be going. Will I see you this Saturday, Brian?"

"Sure thing, Hermann. See you then."

Even though the house was old and weathered on the outside, the inside was well kept and clean. They followed Ikeda down a corridor to a door at the end. When they walked through the door, they stepped into a large brightly lit room. There were four desks in the room. Three were occupied. All three people looked up when Ikeda walked through the door with Wolf and Gorini in tow.

"Who are these people?" an elderly dark-skinned man with a goatee asked.

Another, a younger man, looked up from the computer screen he was studying. "We are not expecting anyone yet."

"You won't believe this," Ikeda announced. "This is Major Wolf. He is here to investigate the attacks that have been happening. I know he is military, but he claims to be a good friend of Major Swann." He let that sink in. "What are the chances? Tell me! What are the odds of this happening?"

All three men stared at Wolf. "Are you really a good friend of Major Swann?" The dark-skinned man voiced his doubts. "Or is this just a ruse?"

"No ruse," Wolf said. "Alfred and I have been friends forever. In fact, a little over a month ago, he, Harry Turnbull, another friend, and I spent a short time on Agrar. I was called away from that trip and sent here. By the way, all three of us were born the same year on Rion. We've been getting together once a year for a couple of weeks challenging the universe to try and kill us." He smiled, remembering it almost did happen on Agrar.

"I know about those adventures," Ikeda said. "Major Swann talked about them with fondness."

"May I ask you a question, Scout Ikeda?"

"Sure. Go ahead."

"Do you have a personal connection with Major Swann?"

"He was my teacher when he was still Master Scout Swann. I was just a rookie then." He chuckled. "He was a wonderful teacher and a great storyteller."

"He is coming here," one of other Scouts blurted out.

Wolf gave him a sharp look. "What do you mean?"

"About a week ago, we received a message announcing that he is coming here to investigate these incidents that are happening so frequently now on Cerberus."

"Coming here? When?"

"He should be here within a week," Ikeda told him.

Wolf turned to Gorini. "It took us three weeks to get here. It seems he has more influence than I have."

"He is the right-hand man of Colonel Stonewall," Ikeda said proudly. "I'm sure you know who Colonel Stonewall is?"

"Until about five weeks ago I had never heard of him. However, I don't know anything about him except what I was told by my superior."

"Colonel Stonewall is a legend in the Scouts organization. He is a hero." Ikeda sounded as if he were talking about a god. "I still can't believe Major Swann is coming here."

"Neither can I. What could be the real reason for him to be sent to Cerberus?" Wolf wondered. "My superiors didn't seem to take these attacks seriously. It is of utmost importance that I meet with Major Swann."

"There is no reason you can't," the Scout with the goatee told him. "By the way, let me introduce my brothers. You already met Scout Ikeda. I am

Master Scout Amos Hadad, and these two are Scouts David Stavros and Anders Axelsson."

"Wolf gave them a little nod. "It is an honor to get to know all of you. You already know my name. My partner is Captain Gorini."

"She is Anorian. How did you two end up as partners?"

"Luck." Wolf smirked. "We are two lost souls thrown together by fate."

"The only lost soul is Major Wolf," Gorini said with a little smile, letting her forked tongue play across her lips. "It wasn't fate. It was all organized by my superiors. I am a member of the Anorian Special Investigation Service, and we need to find out where those invaders come from. They are not Anorians, even though they appear to be."

The Scout nodded. "The whole thing is a mystery. The question is where do they come from? Why are they doing what they are doing? How are we going to stop these attacks? All of us have been wondering why the Solar Union has not sent at least a platoon of troopers and a couple of battle cruisers to wipe out these invaders."

"I suggested pretty much the same thing to my superior. Apparently, he can't justify the expense."

"I can't say I am surprised," Hadad commented. "The military is not famous for jumping in when they are called upon." He lifted a hand. "No offense, Major, but why do you think we Scouts don't think much of the military system? We've been thrown into many situations on planets we mapped where we needed military protection. We hardly got it. That is one of the reasons the Scouts Organisation created its own Special Forces."

"I wasn't aware of any of that until a short time ago. It certainly makes me wonder about much of the stuff going on within the military and the Scouts."

"In a way it is too bad Scouts and troopers aren't friendlier with each other," Hadad mused. Then he exclaimed, "Where are my manners? You two are our guests here. Take a seat and get comfortable."

"Thank you. I won't say no to that." Wolf sank into one of the three easy chairs, while Gorini chose a wooden chair.

"Why use that hard chair when you can use the couch?" Hadad wondered.

76

"I am a soldier. Comfort is not something that I'm used to," she explained.

"Well. Suit yourself." Hadad shrugged and then went back to the discussion he had with Wolf. "Since you and Major Swann were such good friends, you must have had discussions about certain things."

"We had a policy never to talk about our careers. The Scouts and military brass frown about stuff like that. They almost look upon exchanging ideas as treason. We decided long time ago we would not jeopardise our careers by being careless and tell each other *secrets*."

"It makes sense. I know what you are talking about. However, when lives are at stake, rules and laws have to be broken. After all, we are supposed to be on the same side."

"I agree, Master Scout Hadad." Wolf's smile was almost sardonic. "I've done my share of breaking regulations whenever I saw the need for it. It didn't always sit well with my superiors."

"You made it to major. Someone must have seen something in you."

"I suppose, but I'd like to think that I earned my rank by showing initiative and being true to the military and the Solar Union." He paused. "Now for the main reason we are here. We came to Cerberus hoping to be able to stay at one of the army bases. Of course, the Freeland army is non-existent. There are no bases. That put us into an embarrassing situation and a dilemma. We have no funds to sustain ourselves. Ambassador Amsterdam was kind enough to take us in. When this attack happened, he was eager to drive to Windy Lake to check up on his sister who lives here. He wants to stay a couple of days and that creates another problem for us. We have no place to stay. Sergeant Becker suggested we give the Scouts a try." He smiled. "Here we are. Like a couple of beggars thanks to the Solar Union military."

"We are not the military," Hadad said with a little chuckle. "We are the Scouts. Our number one mission is to get a planet ready for colonization, but that is not where we stop. We also help people in trouble. It seems you are in trouble, and you came to the right place. We happen to have four guestrooms. You are welcome to use two of them. The rooms are not luxurious. After all we are the Scouts. Both rooms have a bed and a toilet, but you will have to share a shower."

"Two rooms?" Wolf looked at Gorini. "Did you hear that? Two rooms."

"I heard," she said, a smile playing around her lips. "You can finally sleep without bumping into me during the night. You should be happy unless you got used to sleeping with me."

Wolf didn't miss Hadad's eyebrows going up.

"I'll just be fine without you in my bed. Don't give them the wrong impression. I never get involved with a member of my team," Wolf said stiffly, mainly for the benefit of the Scouts.

Gorini just smiled. "Because you never had a female partner, especially one like me."

"I feel really blessed right now." Wolf gave her an annoyed look. "It wouldn't have changed anything."

"I don't care about your relationship," Hadad assured them. "You can both sleep in one room if you want, but I'm afraid the bed is not wide enough."

"It will be wide enough because I'm going to be the only one in it. I will sleep like a baby in his mother's arms."

"You'll miss seeing me naked in the morning," she teased him. Then she laughed. "Oh, I forgot. We have to share the shower."

"I'll make sure to ignore you," he said gruffly. "Now let's drop the subject." He looked at the four Scouts. "That's what I had to deal with all this time. She loves to tease, but that's all there is to it. I can't really blame her. We've been inactive for weeks now. To be honest, we both are bored. We need some action."

The action came three days later.

It was just before noon, when the communicator lit up to display the face of Chief Dubois. "There has been another attack."

Scout Stavros answered the call. "When and where?"

"Right here in town. This time they hit one of the churches. In fact, they are still there, looting the ancient treasures. It looks like they are thumbing their noses at us, since the last time they encountered no resistance."

"Which church, Chief Dubois?"

"The Church of Redemption."

"Where are you now, Chief?" Wolf cut in.

"I am in my car watching them. They are totally ignoring us."

"Do nothing heroic, Chief Dubois. Don't risk your or your men's life," Wolf advised him. "We will be there as quickly as we can." He turned to Gorini. "You heard. If we're lucky and get there quickly enough, we may be able to stop them."

Scout Stavros obviously had his doubts. "How can you stop them? Just the two of you?"

"No time to explain. Can you or anyone else get us there?"

"I can drive you."

"Go and get the car ready. We'll be out in a moment."

While he was talking with the Chief, Gorini got their rifles. Wolf appreciated her quick reaction. She knew exactly what they had to do. He grabbed one of the rifles and rushed outside. Gorini was right behind him.

Stavros just pulled in front of the building, and they jumped into the back.

It took them less than ten minutes to get to the church. The three police cars were standing a safe distance away. Wolf saw the Chief standing beside his car. Three other police officers stood behind their cars, watching the church.

On the street, a number of people stood, also watching.

Wolf left their car and walked up to the Chief. "How many did you see?"

"Seven. They are most likely the same ones that burned down the store."

As he spoke, two of the raiders came out of the church and walked calmly toward their disk-shaped vehicle, their arms full of things they took from the church. It was obvious they were in no hurry.

"They certainly are arrogant," Gorini said behind Wolf. "I wish our males would possess a little of that arrogance. This proves beyond any doubt that they are not of my race."

"What are you planning to do?" Chief Dubois asked.

"We will make sure they don't leave here," Wolf told him. "Please, tell your men to move the people on the sidewalk behind us. It is for their protection."

The Chief bellowed some orders. He even yelled to the nearest watchers to get 'The Hell out of the Way', as far back as possible.

"You know what to do," Wolf told Gorini. "Between the two of us we should be able to get the job done. On the count of three."

He lifted his rifle and started counting. They both fired their rifles at the same time, the combined energy of both weapons creating an inferno that melted rock and metal.

The sound of an explosion echoed from the nearby buildings. Where moments before the disk-shaped vehicle of the raiders stood there was nothing left but large puddles of boiling liquid inside a shallow crater.

"What in the name of the three-headed hell-dogs kind of weapon is that?" Dubois cursed, staring at the spot where the aircraft had been.

"These are Proton Beam rifles," Wolf explained. "The newest weapon the Union's military has to offer. So far only Special Forces have them. Let's not waste time chattering. I suggest you all take cover behind the cars with your guns ready. Those raiders will be coming out any moment to see what caused the racket. They'll be enraged when they discover their aircraft gone and will want revenge. When they realize they are stuck here, they will behave like cornered rats. They will kill everyone blocking the way to their means of escape, which are your cars."

No sooner did he finish talking when the first two raiders appeared. It took them only seconds to discover what caused the explosion. They sprinted back and disappeared into the church.

"They'll be coming out with weapons blazing," Wolf warned. While he talked, Gorini ran at full speed toward the church to hide behind one of the thick pillars.

All seven came out, but instead of running toward the cars firing their rifles as Wolf had predicted, they walked calmly into the street. They threw down their weapons and took a few more steps forward and stood, their arms spread and their hands open.

"They are giving themselves up," Dubois exclaimed. "I'll be damned."

"I didn't expect that," Wolf admitted. "I don't trust them. They have something in mind. I advise extreme caution when approaching them.

Let me go first before any of you come. Stay alert with your weapons ready."

Walking toward the seven raiders, he saw Gorini leave her post behind the pillar and also head for the raiders. She carried her rifle loosely in her hands, ready to be used in an instant if necessary.

Wolf watched the raiders, his senses alert. In a way it made sense for them to give themselves up. Unless they wore bullet-proof suits, there was a good chance they could either be killed or wounded in a hail of bullets from the primitive guns the police officers were using. Of course, the complete destruction of their craft would give them a reason to wonder what type of weapon the locals had used. Obviously, not a primitive projectile weapon. They still felt confident in having the superior weapons.

When the raiders saw Gorini, their surprise was easy to see. One of them said something in a language foreign to Wolf. Having heard samples of most of the main languages spoken by other races, this one didn't sound familiar.

He activated the translator chip behind his ear. Gorini had obviously activated hers already.

"You look like one of us," the same raider said, this time looking at Gorini. "You are a female and should not be here. What are you doing on this primitive world?"

"I may look like you, but I am not one of you," she answered. "I am Anorian. What are you and where to you come from?"

"We come from the other side of the portal. Don't you?"

"The portal?" Gorini paused for a moment. "What is a portal?"

"It is the door that lets us move from one world to another. You don't know?" He turned to his companions. "She is from this world. Be careful what you say."

"Perhaps she is here on a secret mission," another one speculated. "Apparently, females are best suited to be spies."

"I don't know what portal means," Gorini admitted. "Tell me about it."

"We'd rather not discuss it here," the first speaker said. "Some things are better left unsaid."

"Alright, we'll leave it at that for now. Answer me this: Why are you destroying properties, robbing, and killing people on this planet?"

"We are only following orders."

"Who is giving you these orders?"

The speaker hesitated for a moment, but then he said, "The Overlords. We don't question them."

"Who are the Overlords?"

One of the other raiders gave her an odd look. "The T'Par. They are one of the old races. Their technology is far beyond anything the younger races possess."

"What do they look like?"

"Their oval bodies are covered with hair, and they move on six long legs. They have two, short front limbs with long, bony fingers. They could cut your body in half with their sharp mandibles."

Gorini turned to Wolf. "He just described a Kraach."

Wolf deactivated his translator. "The information we just received is monumental. It explains why we don't know where they come from. They came to Cerberus through a star-gate from the far side of the Galaxy."

"I have absolutely no idea what you are talking about. I've never heard of such a thing."

"Because it isn't widely known. The knowledge about the star-gates is kept a secret by the military and the government agencies that participate in the research. We can talk about it later." He switched on his translator again. Addressing the raiders, he said, "On this side of the portal, they call their race Kraach, but here they are not Overlords."

"What reasons do the Overlords have to tell you to kill and plunder the peaceful people on this world?" Gorini asked.

"We don't know or care. They have their reasons."

"Perhaps you should care," Wolf suggested. "How many teams are operating on this planet?"

The raider shrugged. "That is not known to us. We do not communicate with the other teams."

"What are you doing with the things you plunder?"

"We take them through the portal where they are picked up by another team."

"Seems simple enough," Gorini commented. "Too simple."

"What is going to happen to us?"

Wolf gave all seven of them a thoughtful look. "I don't know what to do with you," he admitted. "You have destroyed valuable property in this city and killed a number of people in cold blood without cause. I have in mind to kill all seven of you."

A few of the raiders looked back at their discarded weapons, obviously calculating their chances.

"You won't reach your weapons in time," Wolf warned them.

"We have never encountered any resistance before," the leader of them said. "What changed?"

"We are here," Wolf told him. "That's what changed."

"You are only two."

"That is correct, but we are different from the other people. We are soldiers and not afraid of you."

"What if we promise never to come back here, would you let us leave?"

Wolf laughed. "You don't really believe I would trust you, do you? Even if you'd never come back to this city, you would plunder other places. We are here to stop you and the other teams from committing more carnage and from ever coming to this planet again. If we have to kill you all, we will do so."

"Is that what you have in mind for us? To kill us?"

"I will have to think about it. For now, you are safe. You will be our prisoners until we decide what to do with you." He looked back at the police officers standing by their car. He waved toward Chief Dubois and motioned for him to come nearer.

"What is happening?" the Chief asked when he was close.

"Arrest these seven and put them behind bars," Wolf told him.

Dubois scratched his head. "There is a slight problem. We only have three cells and two are occupied."

"I guess you'll have to set those prisoners free and put these seven into the cells."

"How long will we have to keep them?"

Wolf shook his head. "I don't know. We'll have to play it by ear. For now, I'm just happy to take them out of circulation."

"I feel like shooting all seven of them for the murder of all those good people and for destroying the store," Dubois burst out.

"We still might do that, Chief," Wolf said.

Dubois gave his men a signal. "Cuff these guys and put them into the cars. They're going to jail."

"I suggest you don't keep their weapons at the station in case they manage to break out of jail. I will take them with me to Scouts Base."

[7]

Nobody at Scouts Base had ever heard of star-portals or star-gates, except for Master Scout Hadad, but his knowledge was even more limited than Wolf's.

"There are rumors and theories circulating about an ancient race that existed long before any of the races now populating the Galaxy. Even long before the Spiders. Apparently, that ancient race seeded all the planets. Nobody knows what they looked like, but they created all the different races in our Galaxy. They were gods. They didn't travel through space in spaceships. The belief is that they traveled between the planets through holes in the fabric of space. Some call these holes portals, gates or even doors. That is all I know. Sorry. As I said—rumors, legends."

"You are correct about the legends of the star-gates, but they are not legends anymore," Wolf said. "They exist."

"How do you know?" Stavros almost challenged him.

"Can you prove it?" Ikeda demanded. "Have you ever seen one?"

Wolf chuckled. "I have never personally seen one. The existence of the star-gates is a well-guarded secret among the people that participate in the research and the protection of them. Only a few people know about the portals. The knowledge about them is shared on a need-to-know basis. There are more than one, by the way. The last one to be discovered is on a planet called Aurora. How do I know? Only through coincidence, because I am not in that small inner circle of people who are privileged to even know about them."

"In other words, your knowledge comes from hearing other people talk about the legends of the ancient race rumored to have existed," Gorini said. "You don't know anything concrete, either."

"I have it from a trustworthy source. What I am going to share with you, may land me in trouble if it gets out. So, you must promise not to mention my name when you talk about the gates with others." Wolf smiled. "Just call me a trustworthy source."

"You may be trustworthy, but what you will tell us is for us already second-hand information," Stavros commented.

"I realize it is, but the man who told me was directly involved with the discovery of the star-gate on Aurora. His name is Major Jeremy Falcon, and he is an agent with Interstellar Secret Service, just like me. He and an Accilla female, his partner, discovered the existence of the gate during their mission on Aurora." He looked at the sceptical faces of the Scouts. "You may find this interesting. He told me that a high-ranking Scouts leader took command of the project, and he served under him for a year, protecting the star-portal. The Scouts leader's name was Stonewall, and he had been involved in the research of the other portals. He never told me that Stonewall was a Colonel and actually the creator of Scouts Security. That is news to me."

They stayed silent for a while.

"That is curious and interesting as well," Master Scout Hadad mused. "I would consider that information as first-hand and not just hearsay."

"I really didn't think much of it at the time, but now I am almost a bit angry to find out that my good friend Swann probably knew all about the star-gates and the dangers we may be facing from other races on the other side of the gates. Sometimes I really hate all the classified secrets in the military, the 'above-your-paygrade', the 'clearance' and this 'need-to-know' crap."

"Don't forget Major Swann is not military. He is a Scout. Military people and Scouts don't exchange information," Scout Axelsson reminded Wolf. "Aside from not getting along." He smiled when he said that.

"I know that, but we have been friends since we were children. The best of friends. Brothers. We share a deep bond few people ever do. That changes things, you know." Wolf knew he sounded bitter and disappointed, but deep down he knew Axelsson was right.

"You'll be able to talk about that with him when you see him," Hadad said.

"I suppose you are right. Something else I've been wondering about this Colonel Stonewall. Since he is such a legendary hero, why didn't any of you know about the star-gates? What made him such a legend?"

"Let me answer that," Hadad said. "Colonel Stonewall was instrumental in preventing a war with the Spiders after he became a Master Scout. On Savanna, he stopped one of the Cartels from taking over the planet. He also participated in an important secret mission on Salamander. That was never publicised. On Aurora, he again foiled a plan of the Cartels to take control of the planet's resources. He signed peace treaties with a few of the Spider factions. You mentioned Aurora. It was Colonel Stonewall who prevented a war with the Ant-Empire. Those were just a few of the things he did."

"That's quite some roster of achievements for one man," Wolf admitted.

"It is," Hadad said, "but after hearing you tell us about Aurora, I am suspecting that Colonel Stonewall was involved with all these other star-gates. Wow! He really is a hero. I hope Major Swann can tell us more stories about the Colonel. I am really looking forward to meeting the Major."

"So am I," Wolf said, the beginning of a smile playing around his lips. "For a different reason, though." He knew Swann would be just as surprised as he to see him here at Scouts Base.

———

CHIEF DUBOIS CALLED A COUPLE OF DAYS AFTER THE DISCUSSION. "THE prisoners are gone. Early this morning, another crew came and blasted them out of jail. There was nothing we could do to stop them."

"Anyone killed or injured?" Wolf asked.

"Linda Clark, our secretary. They shot her dead. She was the only one in the station at the time."

"Sorry to hear that, Chief. Is there anything we can do?"

"Go and find those bastards," Dubois almost shouted it. "Find them and kill them all. We should have done that with this bunch."

"I know," Wolf said. "Hindsight is a wonderful thing, but it fixes nothing. We won't be so charitable the next time, I promise you that."

"Have you found out what planet they come from?"

"We have leads but nothing concrete." There was no reason to tell the Chief about the star-gates. He could do nothing with that information. It would only cause confusion or panic, aside from the fact that the upper echelons in the military would not be happy about that.

"There is one thing I am wondering about," Dubois mused. "How did that other gang know where to find them?"

"That's what I'm wondering, also. Before you put them into the cells, did you check them for hidden weapons or communication devices?"

"I guess we didn't. They left their weapons on the street, and you took them with you. As far as any devices they may have had on them?" He shrugged. "It never occurred to us. It's our fault."

"Well. Too late to rectify that. Thanks for letting us know. Our condolences to the family of your secretary."

The Chief sighed. "I will let them know. I'm not looking forward to telling them the horrible news. She was a good woman. We will miss her." His image faded away.

Scout Ikeda was the only other person in the room.

"I have to take the blame for trusting someone else," Wolf told him. "I should have thought about searching them for anything that could be used to help them escape. Damn it! We need to find the location of that portal. The only chance we had slipped through our fingers."

"Yes, that is unfortunate, but crying over it is not going to solve anything."

———

SWANN ARRIVED THE NEXT DAY. STAVROS DROVE TO THE SPACEPORT IN Greater York to pick him up.

Wolf decided not to be in the room when the Scouts welcomed Swann. He gave them thirty minutes before he made his appearance.

All four Scouts had smiles on their faces when Wolf walked into the room. Gorini chose not to be there. She didn't want to spoil the moment by drawing attention to her person.

As expected, Swann was more than just surprised to see Wolf.

"Where are you coming from?" Swann blurted out.

Wolf laughed. "Is that how you greet an old friend, Major Swann?"

Swann stared at Wolf. "You know."

"Yes, I do. I found out when I got reprimanded by my superior for consorting with the enemy. The enemy being a certain Major Alfred Swann of Scouts Security. Imagine my surprise to find out that my best friend kept such an important piece of news to himself all these years."

"I wanted to tell you many times, Ethan, but you know the rules. In fact, the military has even stricter rules than the Scouts. I didn't want to get you into trouble." He walked up to Wolf and embraced him. "Let's not have a little thing like that mar our friendship."

Wolf patted Swann on the back. "I wouldn't call being a Major a little thing. You must have done something to earn that rank. As for myself, I am proud of mine."

Swann stepped back and shook a finger at Wolf. "Now, let us talk about that, Major Wolf. I knew you were a major, but you never told us in which service branch." He pulled his brows together and looked at Wolf with narrow eyes. "You know my station, now tell me yours."

"I am with the ISS."

Swann's eyebrows went up a little. "The Interstellar Secret Service. Very impressive."

Wolf chuckled. "No more impressive than yours. I heard you are practically the right-hand-man of Colonel Stonewall. I'd say that is quite a remarkable achievement."

"Then you know about Colonel Stonewall?"

"Not that much, but enough to know that he is a legend among Scouts and deeply involved with the star-gates."

"You know about the star-gates." It was a statement not a question.

"My information is second-hand, but I know about them." Wolf acknowledged. "I know they exist, and I know on which planets they are. I don't know your roll in the study of these star-gates, but there is one here on Cerberus."

Swann walked over to one of the empty chairs and sat down. "I didn't know about a portal being here, but we suspected it when we found out about a large group of humans living here for a couple of thousand years and nobody knows where they came from. Then we heard about the raiders. Everything pointed to a portal." He seemed suddenly quite excited. "That is why I am here. To find out how all this connects. I never asked you, but why are you here?"

"My mission is to stop the raiders from doing more damage and to prevent them from killing people. I didn't expect to find out that there is a star-gate on Cerberus."

"Where is the rest of your team?"

Wolf laughed. "Good question. The rest of my team is in the next room waiting for me to call her and introduce her to you. A word of advice. She is Anorian and she represents her people in this investigation. You may know or not that the raiders are Anorian males."

"In other words, you are a one-man team to stop an invasion. Incredulous. Typical military."

"I was told that the expense of sending in a cruiser and a platoon was too high. Cerberus doesn't seem to be on the list of important planets." Wolf didn't keep the bitterness he felt out of his voice.

"That really sucks," Swann said. "Have you sent in your report about the gate? That should bring a battlecruiser and a whole battalion to Cerberus."

"Not yet. The discovery of the star-gate changes everything, of course. My superior would be the last one to find out about the gate. As a major in the ISS, I can go over his head and report my findings directly to the High Senate. Unfortunately, there is only one major stumbling block keeping me from going over his head. I don't know the location of the gate, and therefore its existence is still only speculation. Until then, it will still be Admiral Swenson who will see my report. He will do nothing."

Swann nodded. "I understand your dilemma. I don't have such restrictions. After I find out a little more about this, I will send in my preliminary report. That will start rolling a number of things. For one thing, Scouts Security will send a team of at least twenty trained special agents to help me with this investigation. When we discover the location of the gate, that's when the action begins. That's when Colonel Stonewall may get involved."

"I understand he is on Aurora right now or did I get the wrong info?"

"He is, but things are running smoothly there and since this will be the newest discovery, he will be here to take over." Swann smiled thinly. "No matter how the military is involved by then, it doesn't matter. Scouts Security under Colonel Stonewall will be the ultimate authority then and the military will be here only as backup. Whoever the top soldier is at that time will report to Colonel Stonewall. It is all sanctioned by the High Senate."

"What if we get into an all-out war with the invaders, who will fight the war?" Wolf wondered.

"That's a completely different animal. If it comes to that it will be the Union who fights the war. Obviously, we Scouts don't have the manpower, but let's not worry about that now."

There was a knock on the door and moments later Gorini walked in. "I couldn't help but overhear," she said, "but should we discover the location of the gate, we Anorians will have something to say about how things will continue. I also have the suspicion that the Kraach will arrive on the scene, especially since the raiders told us that they follow orders from their Overlords. They described the Overlords looking like the Kraach." She looked at Swann. "I am Captain Gorini of the Anorian Special Investigations Service. I understand you are Major Swann of Scouts Security."

Swann looked her up and down. Then he said, "I am surprised to see you dressed."

"I would prefer not to, but you humans, especially you men, seem to have a problem with naked women. At least Major Wolf has." She smiled, obviously to take the edge out of her statement.

"I've known Major Wolf all of my life and I don't believe he has a problem with naked women. Neither do I. We don't mind looking at a naked woman, but at the proper place and the proper time." Swann shrugged. "We are just normal human males. Nothing odd about that." He got up from his chair and held out a hand to her. "I didn't mean anything by my remark. I apologize if I offended you in some way."

She looked at his outstretched hand. Then, with a little smile, she shook it. "No offence taken."

"You'll have to get used to her," Wolf said. "She enjoys teasing. What can you expect from an Anorian female?"

"Perhaps someday I'll let you find out," she said, giving him a look from under lowered lashes. Fortunately, none of the others in the room seemed to notice it.

"I'd like to hear a little about Colonel Stonewall," Scout Stavros said.

"How much do you know about him?"

"Only what Master Scout Hadad told us, but he didn't mention anything about the Colonel and his involvement with the star-gates."

"To begin with, he and a crew from different species were the first ones to walk through a star-gate on Salamander. They arrived on the other side of the Galaxy where they went through a punishing series of events. On Savanna, he stopped the Cartel from taking over the portal. He did the same thing on Aurora. I wish you could meet him in person and listen to him reminiscing about his adventures. He is a gifted storyteller. He can transport your mind to the places he's been." He moved in his chair and lifted a hand to cover a yawn. "Forgive me, but I am tired from my long trip here. Besides, I wouldn't mind a drink."

"It is almost supper time," Hadad said. "I'll have a look to see how the cook is coming along."

———

AFTER SUPPER, THEY SAT AGAIN IN THE COMMON ROOM. THE SCOUTS WERE eager to hear Swann talk about his missions, but he told them to wait for a more proper time. He was more interested in finding out more about the raiders, especially about what happened in the few days before he arrived.

"That is unfortunate," he remarked when he heard about the escape of the captured aliens. "That should never have happened."

He was also not overly impressed when Wolf told him about the local army. "They are entertainers, not soldiers," Wolf said. "If they would have a real army, things may never have progressed this far."

"That is too bad. Perhaps living in a peaceful society for so long is in the long run not a good thing. People get complacent and are not prepared when violence finally finds them. Eventually it always will. It proves that even when everything is peaceful, it doesn't hurt to be prepared just in case." Swann scanned the faces of the Scouts. He gave Ikeda a closer look. "I've seen you before, but I can't recall where and when."

"I was one of your students." Ikeda smiled.

"What's your name again?"

"Ikeda. Brian Ikeda."

Swann drummed his fingers against the armchair. "Ikeda. I remember you now. That was ten years ago. It was my last year teaching rookies. That was also the year I joined Scouts Security. I'm glad you didn't give up and became a full-fledged Scout." He smiled. "To be honest, I didn't think you'd make it. You were one of the youngest in that group."

"I was aware of that, but that didn't stop me from trying to keep up with the others. That wasn't the only reason. I don't mind admitting, I was a little intimidated by you and I tried not to disappoint you."

"Well, you didn't." Swann chuckled softly. "I know, sometimes I came on a little strong, but only because I wanted you all to succeed. As you probably found out already, being a Scout is not a walk in the park. You have to be tough and willing to go where no other human has been before." With a glance at Wolf, he continued, "even though some people think Scouts do nothing else but follow a path in the forest looking for tracks."

"If you're hinting that I'm one of those people, you are wrong," Wolf protested. "I always knew you were a tough guy, even though you were a

Scout and didn't have the same survival training troopers have to go through."

Swann looked around the small circle of Scouts, pointing a finger at Wolf. "You all heard what this tough military man just said about us. Are you going to sit there and take that?"

Wolf laughed. "You know I was only kidding, Alfred. I never looked down on you. You were probably the toughest one from the three of us. I've always had nothing but respect for you, more so now than before. You know, Admiral Swenson called you a dangerous man and I shouldn't trust you."

"What do *you* think about that remark, Ethan? Do you think I shouldn't be trusted?"

"I trust you with my life, and you know that, my friend. Four decades of being best friends fused us together in a unique way seldom matched. I am looking forward to collaborating with you."

"I am touched by this declaration of affection," Gorini said. "I hope at least one of you wants to work with me."

"I don't foresee a problem, and I don't think Wolf does. After all, from what I heard you to two have been sleeping together in one bed and both of you are still alive."

Wolf noticed the mischievous grin. "I don't know what exactly you heard, but there was nothing going on between us. Although, it wasn't because she didn't try."

Before Gorini could respond, Swann said, "Captain Gorini, you may be interested in this. When Colonel Stonewall crossed the star-gate on Salamander, his team included a couple of Kraach, a human looking woman by the name of Salabet. She appeared human but her brain was a Kraach. Another team member was Anorian. Her name was Gorana. They all got along just fine. We'll make a great team, the three of us. I have no doubts."

"Thank you." She glanced at Wolf. "And it won't be because I'm not going to try."

Wolf shook his head. 'She just won't give up. This female has a sharp tongue. I wonder if all Anorian females are like her. I pity their males.'

"Don't lose sleep over it, Gorini." Swann smiled. "If he gives you trouble, he will have to deal with me." He rose. "I think it's time for me to retire. I can hardly keep my eyes open."

[8]

THE NEXT DAY THEY DROVE TO THE POLICE STATION. SWANN WANTED TO SEE the videos.

"They do look like male Anorians," he commented after watching the videos.

"They may look like Anorians, but I can assure you they are not," Gorini said. "I am not aware of any planet populated by Anorians or where Anorian colonists live side by side with other races where the males are the dominant sex. Seeing these aggressive males is almost shocking. Learning about star-gates that connect all the star-systems in this galaxy suddenly explains this phenomenon. It makes a lot of sense now."

"I am surprised you didn't know about the star-gates."

"Humans are not so different from us Anorians. Our governments keep the rest of the population in the dark about many things. They have the same principle: Need to know. You may or may not believe this, but I did not know until the last minute that my mission would take place on a planet called Cerberus. All in the name of 'security'."

Swann chuckled. "I believe it." Addressing Chief Dubois, he said, "I am sorry to hear about the death of Corporal Horinder and your secre-

96

tary at the hands of these plunderers. We will try our best to bring them to justice."

"Is there a chance you will be able to stop these raids altogether?"

"We won't give up until we do, that I can promise, but what I can't promise is how long it will take."

"Do you have any idea where they come from?"

"To be honest, we don't. We have a suspicion but no proof." Swann obviously didn't want to create any false hope, but it was also obvious he needed to tell the Chief something. "I've only been here a couple of days now, and I need to get more information before I can justify bringing in more investigators."

"Something I don't quite understand." Dubois looked from Swann to Wolf and back again to Swann. "You are a Scout. What is the reason for the Scouts to get involved? Why is the military not doing anything?"

"Perhaps you should ask Major Wolf," Swann suggested.

"I cannot give you a satisfying answer," Wolf told him. "Call it politics or whatever. I would like nothing better than bringing in a whole battalion of troopers and scour the planet until we find their hideout and put an end to the problem."

"So why don't you?"

"Why don't I?" Wolf sighed. "I am only a small cog in the military wheel, but when it comes to Cerberus it doesn't matter. My superiors think that Freeland's military should take care of this. I agreed. We didn't know that the two thousand soldiers that make up the Freeland army only play drums and trumpets; they sing and swirl batons. They don't know how to fight or use weapons. They are not soldiers, they are entertainers."

"Entertainers?" Swann lifted an eyebrow. "I don't understand."

"I can explain that." Chief Dubois spoke up. "We are a peaceful planet. We get along with everybody. Sure, we have criminal elements in our cities, but that's where the police come in. We take care of crime. There never was a need for a real army."

"It seems to me that now would have been a good time to have one." Swann shook his head in plain disbelief. "I've never run across a planet that was so peaceful it didn't need at least a few peacekeepers. It almost sounds like a fairy tale."

"Our world is that fairy tale. At least it was until now." Dubois sounded almost apologetic.

"This planet is like a ripe plum," Swann said. "Ready to be plucked by anyone who wants it and can back that up with a large enough force. And there is nobody around to defend it."

"I have to confess to something I did," Gorini spoke up. "Right now, is as good a time as any. You'll find out eventually."

Wolf and Swann looked at her. Wolf wondered what important news she had to tell them.

"Last night I took the liberty to contact my people. I filed my report as I was ordered to. They know about the possible existence of a portal here on Cerberus."

"Damn! You should have discussed that with me before you did." Wolf felt betrayed. "I know you are not bound to do anything, since you are here on behalf of your government, but it would have been just common courtesy. After all, we are supposed to be partners. Partners work together."

"I don't believe there is a reason to get all worked up over this," Swann said, obviously trying to downplay it. "After all, what harm is that report going to create? She only reported the possible existence of a gate."

"I didn't mean anything by it. I apologize if I offended you in some way. It is just that I need to report something useful. My position in Special Investigations is somewhat precarious right now." She gave Wolf a rueful smile. "Call it politics or a disagreement with my superiors."

Wolf's anger subsided. "If you have a problem, you can always confide in me. I will not judge you in any way. Sometimes it is good to talk about things to avoid a misunderstanding. That's what it means to be partners."

"There is nothing to stop you from sending in your report."

"It isn't that simple. You are not the only one with problems. I have nothing to report, that is my dilemma. My superior and I are not exactly bosom buddies. It seems to me he is undermining this mission, and he wants me to fail. I need something concrete. You and I need to work together and make sure we report the same thing."

"We can do that when we have something." She paused as if to decide if she should say more. "If I may, I'd like to explain the other reason I did it. It seems your military is not going to send any help. You know as well as I that you and I can't do much alone. We need more people. We need soldiers that can fight this war with the invaders. My people will be willing to send as many soldiers as we ask for. They would be a great asset."

At first, Wolf was going to retort with a sharp remark, but then he thought about it. "You know, your idea may have some merits. I will get in touch with my people and tell them about your suggestion. If they promise to send troopers, I will agree to your plan."

"That sounds like blackmail to me," Swann said.

"It will be worth it when we get what we ask for."

"There is something I don't quite understand." It was Chief Dubois who made that remark. "What kind of portal are you talking about?"

Wolf looked at Gorini. "I hate to say this, but here is the first consequence of your report." Turning to Dubois. "What I am going to tell you cannot be repeated. This is top-secret information only allowed to be known by certain people. If it becomes common knowledge, it could create a panic among the population. Even I have only basic knowledge about it."

"Now you're making me very curious. Possibly even a little worried."

"You might have reason to be. The threat Cerberus is facing is not something to be taken lightly. These invaders don't come from any planet we know. They come from the far side of the Galaxy. They didn't arrive in spaceships. How did they get here? Well, there are legends of an ancient race that roamed the stars long before any of the races populating the Galaxy existed. That ancient race did not use ships to travel from planet to planet. They used what we call star-gates or portals. We suspect that one such portal exists on Cerberus." When Dubois opened his mouth to comment, Wolf held up a hand. "I cannot answer any questions you may have, because I don't know the answers."

"How about the Scouts? Do they know more?"

"We do, but my knowledge is also limited, because I've never been close or even inside a portal, but I know people who have. The danger we are facing is real and not to be underestimated. My reason for being here is to find this portal."

"Now more than ever, I wish the military would send at least a thousand troopers with a dozen fighter planes and wipe these invaders off the map," Dubois almost shouted it.

Wolf could not help but smile over the Chief's outburst. "Chief Dubois. Please relax. This is exactly the reason why we don't broadcast the existence of the portals. We won't abandon you. Now that we know what we are dealing with, we will do our best to find the location of the portal and then go from there. And we will find it, I can assure you of that."

Dubois wiped his forehead. "I hope so."

"We are not alone in this fight. After the gate has been found, we will request the help of the other races. The Anorians are already on alert now. There is nothing to fear." Swann tried to take the sting out of the bad news.

"Unfortunately, locating this portal comes with a caveat," Wolf said. "Once it is known that a portal exists on Cerberus, things on this planet will change. Gone will be the anonymity you've enjoyed all these centuries. We might be drawn into a war with powerful enemies. Should that happen, we will need the help of the other major races, and Cerberus will turn into a battleground."

"Don't scare the Chief," Swann advised. "There is no need to do so. Whatever happens, we will deal with it. So far, nothing has happened on any of the planets where we discovered a portal." He paused. "Actually, I shouldn't say that because we did have to deal with threats. However, mostly from enemies from within."

"That reminds me of something," Wolf said, addressing Dubois. "Is Ambassador Amsterdam still in the city?"

"As far as I know, he is. In fact, he called here and wanted to know about you. I gave him the contact number of the Scouts. He is probably going to get in touch with you," Dubois told him.

"I was not aware of an Embassy on Cerberus." Swann gave Wolf an inquiring look.

"Neither was I until I got here. I will give you more information when we get back to the base."

Swann turned his attention back to the Chief. "Thank you for showing me those videos, Chief Dubois. That is just the kind of information we need to make progress in this investigation. And don't worry yourself sick over the news we gave you."

"What if they come back and want revenge?"

Swann shook his head. "I don't believe they will. They suffered a great loss here, and they know they will be facing opposition in your city. Major Wolf and Gorini brought down one of their aircraft. They won't want to lose another one. Just relax and trust that we will find them and stop them."

———

THERE ACTUALLY WAS NEWS FROM THE AMBASSADOR WAITING FOR THEM AT Scouts Base. Amsterdam had left a number asking for Wolf to call him back.

"I have a feeling that you wanted to tell me something about this Ambassador, but not in front of the Chief," Swann said.

"You are correct. You will find this quite interesting. The Union does not have an Embassy here. Alexander Amsterdam is the ambassador for a planet called Hyperion."

"That is interesting. Why would Hyperion have an Embassy here?"

"Lirsium Crystals."

"Are you saying they mine Lirsium Crystals here on Cerberus?" Swann looked perplexed. "Isn't the mining of Lirsium Crystals controlled and regulated by the High Senate?"

"Yes, it is."

"What about this Amsterdam character? Is he for real, or is that all a scam with him parading around pretending to be an ambassador?"

"As far as he is concerned, it isn't a scam. He is the ambassador for Hyperion. I don't believe he is a bad person. He got caught up in a political game. There is no law that forbids any planet or country to have an ambassador in another country or on another planet. If Freeland recognizes him as the ambassador and representative of Hyperion that makes it legal. The problem with this case is that Amsterdam has no connection to the Hyperion government. He was installed as ambassador by Hyperion Mineral Explorations."

"I see. In other words, he is not representing the planet Hyperion but a private company, which doesn't make him an ambassador," Swann pondered.

"That pretty much sums it up," Wolf agreed. "Apparently, Amsterdam did some digging and found out that the H. C. L. Alliance is part of Interstellar Research and Investment Conglomerate, a company with many connections to companies on other planets."

Swann looked surprised. "Did you say Interstellar Research and Investments?"

"That's what I said. Why? You are familiar with that company?"

"Sure am. Interstellar Research and Investments Conglomerate is controlled by the Vanderley Cartel, one of the most ruthless and powerful crime syndicates. Even the High Senate is reluctant to tangle with them because nobody knows who sits on the Board of Directors. It could be anyone, even your Admiral Swenson."

The look Wolf gave Swann was one of disbelief. "Surely you're reaching now?"

"Maybe I am. I'm only saying it is a possibility. Like I said—anyone."

"Even you?"

Swann broke into loud laughter. "Now you are the one reaching. I don't have the money or influence, or even the connections. Would I have been hanging around with you or Turnbull all these years?"

"I don't know. It could have been your cover."

Still laughing, Swann said, "I'd say you know me better than that."

Wolf's expression was serious. "Do I? Until a few weeks ago I thought I did, but now I don't know anymore. You kept one secret from us. Are there more?"

"Don't get paranoid now, my friend." Swann spoke solemnly. "My rank and deeper involvement with the Scouts is the only thing I didn't share with you. There was never a good time. You know yourself we never discussed our work. When we got together, we wanted to leave our daily life behind for a few weeks and spend time with each other without all the problems we had to deal with at work. There was no sinister reason involved in not telling you."

Wolf smiled. "I believe you. Does Harry know? If he doesn't, you must tell him next time we get together. Of course, only if you want to. I'm not telling you what to do. I just think it would be proper and a sign of trust."

"I agree, and I promise you that I will."

"I'd better return the call from the Ambassador. He probably wants to tell me he is driving back to the Embassy."

Ambassador Amsterdam's image formed only a short moment after Wolf initiated the call.

"Ambassador, good to see you. Everything alright with your sister and her family?"

"They are fine. Thanks for being concerned. I'll be heading back to the Embassy tomorrow morning. I suppose you are staying?"

"I am," Wolf confirmed. "I assume you are aware of the second attack?"

"How can I not be? The whole city is buzzing with how you destroyed their aircraft. People are filled with hope knowing that the invaders can be beaten back. Too bad the prisoners escaped."

"Yes, that was unfortunate. I will let you go, Ambassador. Have a safe trip back. I hope everything goes well with Inspector Gifford."

Amsterdam made a motion with his hand. "I'm trying not to think about him. He was going to stay only a week. Hopefully, he'll be gone by now." He paused, and then he said, "I wish you well, Major Wolf. I've been thinking about what you said. I have a feeling there will be changes coming to Cerberus, and I will have to make a drastic decision in the near future. The experience with Inspector Gifford made me open my eyes, and my career may be coming to an end shortly." He smiled. "It is possible that I'll be a citizen of Windy Lake sooner than planned."

"Probably a wise decision," Wolf agreed. "My advice: Don't wait too long. I wish you good luck."

Amsterdam's image faded away as both men broke the connection.

"So that is the ambassador for Hyperion," Swann commented. "He seems like a decent man."

"He is. We discussed his position here, and he told me that he planned ahead in case something went wrong. He confided in me that he bought a house here in Windy Lake near his sister's place."

"He has a sister who lives here?" Swann sounded surprised.

"She married a local man and decided to stay."

"In other words, he has family here. Buying property as a way to protect himself is a smart move," Swann approved. "It also means there is a good chance he is only an employee of Hyperion Mineral Explorations and has nothing to lose if he quits his position."

"That is exactly my thinking," Wolf agreed.

"You are aware that you have to notify the High Senate about the illegal mining of Lirsium Crystals here on Cerberus, right?"

"I am aware. I promised Amsterdam to turn a blind eye for a little while, but the way things are developing here, I have to break my promise to cover my rear-end."

"I'm glad you are sensible about this situation. You don't want to risk your career to protect someone you don't really know."

Wolf knew Swann was right. He was a law enforcement officer. His sworn duty was to uphold the law and bring criminals to justice. He couldn't let sentimental feelings get in the way of doing his job. After all, Amsterdam was still a stranger to him. He didn't think Amsterdam was a criminal, but he couldn't say without the shadow of a doubt that the man wasn't.

As if reading his thoughts, Swann said, "Are you one hundred percent sure this Amsterdam doesn't have a clue that his company engages in an illegal activity?"

"If he didn't know before, he knows now, because I told him. My feeling is that he is just an innocent victim. Unfortunately, if the company goes down, he won't be spared."

"True. He will be caught up in the sweep. I hope he is smart and follows your advice."

———

THAT NIGHT AT SUPPER, WOLF SAID TO SWANN, "I DON'T KNOW HOW extensive your knowledge is about this planet, but I assume you know about the Sartans?"

"I was briefed, but not very much is known about Cerberus," Swann told him. "This planetary system is not listed as one of the important ones. I didn't find much in the archives. All I know about the Sartans is that they seem to be a lost tribe of humans. They came to Cerberus a couple of thousand years ago, seemingly out of nowhere. They flourished, but they don't have any modern technology. They seem to be stuck in time, never evolved to the next stage of evolution."

"You are correct, but they are not stupid. In fact, they are quite smart and had no problem learning how to operate the big modern construction machinery. I was at one of the Lirsium Crystal mines and had a good conversation with the miners. All of them were Sartans. Apparently, they are industrious workers, and they are not against living in the mining camp."

"I wouldn't mind visiting their country. Possibly, one of the places that was plundered by the aliens."

"They call their country 'Tsakona'," Hadad said.

"Tsakona? Sounds interesting. I wonder how they arrived at that name. Can you tell me more about the Sartans?"

"They live in cities. The houses they live in are made from clay bricks, and their family structure is similar to ours. They farm and raise animals for food. They grow vegetables. In short, they are not much different from us."

"I'm curious. Do they have an army?"

"No army, but they do have a warrior cast and use weapons made from metal."

"What kind of weapons?"

Ikeda chuckled. "Swords and spears."

"Not much use against lasers or even guns that fire bullets," Swann said.

"Their society is, of course, different from ours. They have Kings and Lords. It is a feudal system but not overly strict. I don't know what kind of religion they practice, but they do have priests. Again, it is not a theocracy."

"Sounds almost like paradise," Swann speculated. "Can such a system actually exist?"

"It seems to exist in Tsakona. As long as I've been here, I have never heard anything about suppression or unrest in that country. We humans get along with them just fine. So do the Sleer."

"It seems to me there is more violence and unrest here in Freeland," Wolf said. "Apparently, crime is rampant in this country. I've had a confrontation with a vicious gang in Greater York and killed two people. They have an understanding with the local police and the city to extort and rob people."

"That doesn't sound like an ideal situation," Swann remarked. "I have a feeling they have bigger problems on Cerberus than this invasion by the aliens."

"You've got that right, my friend. There also is the illegal mining of Lirsium Crystals by this Hyperion Company that needs to be investigated." He shrugged. "Of course, that is another story and not really part of our mission."

"It still needs to be brought to the attention of the High Senate, Ethan. We cannot ignore this."

"I know, I know." Wolf smiled. "As usual, you are correct. That ethical streak in you always comes to the surface."

"It is the Scout in me. To come back to our original conversation. I really think we should take that trip to Tsakona." He looked at Ikeda. "Can you arrange for transportation and a driver? Ideally a Sartan, if possible."

"I'll see what I can do. Actually, I wouldn't mind coming along."

"Have you been there before?"

"I have. The first year, after I had been transferred to this place, I did a little exploring to become familiar with the conditions on this planet. Master Scout Hadad gave me the tour. One of the places we visited was a small village not far from the border between Freeland and Tsakona."

"Do you or anyone here speak their language?"

"We don't. Many Sartans speak Inglis, especially the ones that want to trade with us or want to sell their wares at our Marketplaces."

"I have a translator chip behind my ear," Wolf informed them. He glanced at Gorini. "As far as I know, Gorini has one also. Somewhere on her body."

"I have," Gorini acknowledged.

Swann smiled faintly. "It isn't only the military with all the gadgets. The translators may be an aid, but they are not infallible, especially with a new language. It would be helpful if we could scan the brain of a Sartan who speaks Inglis and transfer that knowledge into a CI. It would take only seconds for it to become fluent in the Sartan language, but I'm afraid we don't have access to one here on Cerberus." He looked at Ikeda. "Or am I wrong?"

"No, you are not wrong. The people on Cerberus may be more advanced than many colonists on other planets, but they have not kept pace with the rest of the Galaxy."

"Like I said, it would be good to have a Sartan driver and guide," Swann insisted.

"I'll see what I can do."

[9]

It took Ikeda only a day to find a driver. His name was Randor. He was older and familiar with vehicles. He and his family were selling trinkets at the market. At first, he was reluctant to leave his son and wife to take care of the business, but when Ikeda offered him a large amount of Dockets, he agreed to be their guide and driver.

Ikeda picked him up three days later.

"How far from the border do you live?" Swann asked him.

"About three hours with my wagon. On horseback, I could probably make it in less time." He chuckled softly. "When I say horseback, I don't mean a horse like the ones you have in Freeland. We call them Burras. They bear little resemblance to your horses. You must have seen them at the market."

"Yes, I saw those long-legged sleek animals with their long necks. They appeared strong and fast."

"They are, and they make great companions because of their gentle nature. Without them, it would be difficult for us to get around and transport heavy items."

"I can see that," Swann agreed. "Without the help from strong animals a society would stay stagnant, never developing wagons, wheels, and all the other things needed to move from one place to another. Of course, the next step is machines, although primitive at first. Do you live in a town or village?"

"In a village of about a thousand people."

"Sounds cozy. Where did you learn how to drive a vehicle?"

"In my younger days, I worked for one of the repair shops in Greater York. That's how I learned to drive one of these machines and how to fix them."

"How long until we get to your village?" Wolf asked.

"In this machine? We'll be there in less than one hour. It depends on how fast we drive and how long it takes at the border."

"What's at the border?" Wolf asked.

"That's where we pay the taxes."

"Taxes?"

"Yes, everyone entering Tsakona has to pay a tax."

"Really?" Wolf found that intriguing. "Who collects this tax?"

"The Priest-guild."

"How much is this tax?"

Randor shrugged. "It depends what mood the collectors are in. Each person has to pay the tax."

"Everyone? Even non-citizens of Tsakona?" Wolf wondered.

"It doesn't matter. Citizen or not."

Wolf looked at Swann. "No matter where you go," he said with a little smile. "The taxman has his fingers everywhere."

Swann chuckled. "Let's hope the fingers of these guys are not too long, otherwise we may have to shorten them a little."

The vehicle moved easily and smoothly on the hard-packed surface of the road. There were ruts from the wagons that moved between Tsakona and Freeland, but it didn't matter to their vehicle because it floated about a foot above the ground.

The only sign they had arrived at the border was a stone building surrounded by a few trees. They could easily have passed it without stopping, but Wolf didn't suggest it, even though the thought had occurred to him.

When their vehicle came to a halt, it settled on the hard ground.

"Open the doors," Wolf told Randor. "I'd like to stretch my legs a little." Actually, he wanted to be outside should there be a problem with the four guards that came out of the building, wearing leather armour, their muscular arms bare. Metal helmets protected their heads. They carried spears, but Wolf saw the swords strapped across their broad backs.

Gorini and Ikeda stayed in the vehicle, but Swann joined Wolf outside. Both men were watching the four guards walking toward them with arrogant steps, looking stern and grim.

"They don't look very friendly," Swann remarked.

"It's all part of the intimidation technique they are using."

Swann chuckled. "They don't know that we are immune to that kind of stuff. In fact, they have no idea what real intimidation is."

One of the guards went to talk to Randor, the other three approached Wolf and Swann. Two of them confronted them while the third stood watching, his spear planted into the ground. The one standing in front of Wolf said something in a demanding loud voice.

Wolf had activated his translator, but it needed to hear a few words and sentences to give an accurate translation. He pointed with his thumb at Randor. "He's the guy you want to talk to."

"...you...he...now...pay..." the translator translated. Most words were garbled. In the meantime, the translator also listened to the conversation between the guards and Randor, evaluating the words.

"We are not citizens of your country. I don't think we should pay," Swann said to the one confronting him.

"You pay," his opponent said in a harsh voice.

The translator automatically also translated Swann's voice into the language of Tsakona.

"I agree with my friend," Wolf said. "We don't have to pay you anything."

The guard talking to Wolf took another step forward and stared at Wolf. He was as tall and big as Wolf, possibly even a little wider in the shoulders. "Everybody pays." His words came clearer now. "You refuse, and we will take you prisoner!"

"You have that backward. You insist, and we will make you our prisoner," Wolf growled.

"Don't threaten a guard of the Priesthood!"

"Please, don't make trouble," Randor said in Inglis from the other side of the vehicle. "My family will be on the bad list."

"How much do they want?" Swann asked.

"Twenty-five Dockets from each of you," the one with Swann answered the question.

Wolf addressed Randor. "Is that a lot?"

"It is reasonable."

"Alright," Wolf agreed. "We'll pay you one hundred Dockets. I still think it is robbery."

"Don't argue, please," Randor pleaded in Inglis. "They may just change their mind and ask for more."

Wolf looked at Ikeda who had stayed inside the vehicle. "Give these guys one hundred Dockets. Randor says it is reasonable."

"It is a bit excessive, but still within reason," Ikeda commented. "Give me a moment." He pulled out a box from under the seat in front of him and removed a few coins. He handed them to Randor. "Here, you give these to them. It will look better coming from you."

Randor took the money and gave it to the guard.

They were on their way again shortly after.

As they traveled further into Tsakona, the landscape changed. Gone were the high-tech farm machines. They saw farmers working their fields with simple tools. Plows were pulled by Burras, guided by men.

"Since you travel to Freeland on a regular basis and you see how the Freelanders live, are you and the other Sartans happy living the primitive way you do?" It was Swann who put the question to Randor.

"I can't speak for everyone, but I am still quite happy with my way of life. Living in Tsakona maybe harder, but it is also less hectic. Probably much safer, also. Crime is rampant in Freeland, especially in the larger cities. That is not to say we have no criminals in Tsakona, but anyone caught committing a crime in my country is severely punished. Not so in Freeland."

"It cannot be that bad," Swann questioned Randor's statement.

"Gorini and I have firsthand experience with crime in Freeland," Wolf said. "It was pretty bad."

"I find it fascinating how you people farm," Swann commented as he watched a number of farmers cutting tall grass with a scythe and spreading it with pitchforks to make hay.

Randor chuckled. "They don't think it is primitive. They've been doing this for centuries. We bond with the spirits of Cerberus and with the animals. It is rewarding. If you are interested, we can stop at my parents' farm. You can talk to my father. He will explain our ways to you."

"As long as it isn't too much out of the way." Wolf expressed his concern. "I was hoping to get to the next larger city where we can spend the night."

"It is actually on the way," Randor assured him.

It didn't take more than half an hour to get there. As they came closer to the small buildings, Randor became suddenly agitated. "Something is wrong."

"Why do you think that?" Swann asked.

"Do you see those Burras in the yard?" He pointed ahead. "They belong to the King's warriors. That is not a good sign."

He increased the speed of their vehicle. Wolf worried he may crash into one of the buildings. He stopped so suddenly had it not been for the antigravity device controlling the vehicle, they would have smashed their heads into the windshield.

Wolf counted six Burras standing in the yard. "Don't get out," he warned. "They may have sentries posted."

"Highly unlikely," Randor said. "They are conceded and arrogant. Nobody ever stands up against them."

"They haven't met us." Wolf smiled grimly. "What kind of weapons are they using?"

"Spears, swords, knives."

"Like the Priesthood-guards?"

"Yes, but they also carry bows with metal arrows."

"In other words, there is a good chance one or two of them may be hiding somewhere."

"It is not impossible," Randor agreed.

"A good enough reason to be cautious. I've been in situations where being careless cost lives."

"What do you suggest we do?" Ikeda inquired.

"I will take a scan. It will detect anything hiding outside the house." Gorini rummaged in her backpack and removed a small gadget. "I have to go outside for that. I should be safe."

"We are far enough away. No arrow will reach us," Swann assured her.

Gorini left the vehicle and pointed her gadget at the house. After a few moments, she nodded. "It is safe. Nobody is hiding anywhere. I detected eight bodies inside the house," she told them through the open door.

"That's six warriors and the two occupants of the house," Wolf observed.

"My parents," Randor informed them. "Can you tell if they have been harmed?"

Gorini shook her head. "No, I can't."

"Let's go in," Wolf said. "I don't have to tell you to be cautious and alert."

All five got out of the vehicle and slowly walked toward the house. Only Wolf, Swann, and Gorini were armed. The front door of the house stood open, so they boldly walked in. There was nobody in the corridor.

"Sloppy," Wolf commented.

The first room they approached was large, obviously a sitting room. Wolf saw six warriors in that room. Four of them were standing around, leaning on their spears, watching the other two. They were bending over two people slumped forward on a couple of wooden chairs. An old man and a woman, most likely Randor's parents. Just as Wolf walked through the door, one warrior smashed his flat hand across the face of the man. The man's clothing was stained with blood.

Randor, who was behind Wolf, yelled something Wolf didn't understand and rushed toward the people on the chairs. He grabbed the warrior by the arm and swung him around.

"Be alert," Wolf called out sharply, warning the others.

Swann was the next one to come into the room, his laser ready, as was Gorini who came right after him.

The warrior Randor clutched by the arm, shook off Randor's hand and gripped him by the throat with one hand. His other hand went to his belt to pull out a knife.

"Stop right there!" Wolf roared. Three steps took him behind the warrior who froze momentarily. He threw his arm around the warrior's neck and took him into a strangle hold. Pulling the knife out of its sheath, he put it against the warrior's throat.

He heard more than saw some commotion beside him and heard the thump of a body being slammed to the floor. The hissing of a laser being discharged, made him turn his head to see another body crashing to the floor. It was one of the guards. Not far from him, stood Swann with his laser in his hand.

Ikeda was grappling with another warrior who tried to run his spear through his belly.

With Wolf's attention on Ikeda, the warrior in his grip, kicked back and managed to free himself. He was fast and agile and pulled his sword from its sheath. Waving it in front of Wolf, he snarled, "You dare to threaten a warrior of the king? You will pay for that with your life."

Wolf was in no mood to play games. Drawing his laser, he drilled a hole into the warrior's forehead. When Randor shouted, "Watch out!" he swung around just in time to throw himself out of the way as one of the other warriors lunged at him with his spear. His laser still in his hand, he killed his attacker with one shot into the chest.

Only one warrior was still standing. He threw down his spear and sword and spread his arms. "I have sworn an oath to the king, but I will not die for his taxes."

"Smart decision," Wolf growled. Perusing the room, he saw Gorini standing over the one she had wrestled with. He was on his side, his hands in a magnetic hold behind him. Swann had shot and killed the one Ikeda had engaged.

Four dead and two alive.

"This is a bad thing," Randor said. He was holding his mother in his arms. "We killed four of the King's warriors."

"We had no choice. They would have beaten your father and most likely your mother to death." Wolf looked at the warrior who gave himself up. "Why did you beat up these people?"

"They refused to pay their taxes."

Randor's father looked up. He was sitting in the chair, his face covered in blood, as was his clothing. "Because we can't afford to pay more. The harvest was poor. Another group of the King's warriors were here only a short time ago." He coughed and wiped his mouth. "They left us little. We can't give you the seeds we need for next year. Without those seeds we will starve." He coughed again.

"We only follow the orders of the King," the young warrior defended himself.

"Then the King is wrong," Randor exclaimed vehemently.

"What should we do with these two?" Swann asked, bringing up a touchy subject. "We can't just kill them in cold blood, which would be the smart thing to do."

"It would be, but it would be a violation of our laws." Ikeda protested. "I wouldn't feel right."

"The King will send more warriors. They will surely kill my parents," Randor said.

"He won't unless he finds out about what happened here." Wolf contemplated.

"I won't say anything," the young warrior spoke up. "This gives me a chance to escape the servitude of the King."

"What's your name?"

"Ramsy."

"Alright, Ramsy. Where would you go?"

"I will flee to Stoneland. Many of our people have escaped there."

"Where is Stoneland?"

"On the other side of the ocean."

"Stoneland is the next continent. A small population of humans and Sartans live there. Apparently, many different tribes of Indigenous people call Stoneland home," Ikeda explained.

Wolf nodded. "I can accept that." With a thoughtful expression, he studied the warrior Gorini had fought with. He sat on the floor, his hands still tied behind him. "What about you?"

The warrior stared at him with hateful eyes. "You killed four of my friends," he spat. "The King will punish you for that."

"Like I said before: Not if nobody tells him," Wolf said.

"I will tell him." He spoke in a loud and defiant tone.

Wolf knew this man would be trouble and there was no way to change his mind. He was loyal to his king and that was admirable, but it was also his downfall. Wolf drew his laser again and fired a beam into the warrior's head, killing him instantly. "No, you won't."

He heard Randor gasp.

"That was cold-blooded murder," Ikeda accused him. "Under the laws of Freeland, you could be arrested for murder."

"It may look like that to you, Scout Ikeda, but it was justified. I just saved lives. Randor and his parents, his wife, and children, and possibly many of his kin. You forget that I am a soldier, a trained killer. I do what must be done, and this needed to be done. You might do well to remember I do not answer to any of the laws on Freeland. I am an agent of the ISS, the Interstellar Secret Service, and I answer only to the High Senate. The only laws I follow are the laws of the High Senate. They supersede any other laws anywhere in the Solar Union. On any planet."

"I would have done the same thing, had these been my people," Gorini came to Wolf's defence.

"Wolf did the only thing open to us," Swann said. "Randor's parents would have been punished for this. There is no doubt about that." His expression was serious when he looked at Ikeda. "Scouts are not soldiers and are not trained in warfare. Our motto is to help people, not kill them. We are peacekeepers, guides, sworn to hold up the peace whenever possible. Unfortunately, the universe is a cruel and violent place. Sometimes, we have to resort to violence to keep the peace. That is why we created a separate branch of Scouts. We call it Scouts Security. I am an agent of Scouts Security. I am also a Major in Scouts Special Forces. Peace is still our goal, but we will resort to violence if necessary. All agents of Scout's Special Forces are trained in warfare. Our training is possibly even more intense than that of the Union soldiers. Like Wolf, we answer only to the High Senate, and we don't have to justify our actions to anyone."

"That is a dangerous thing and a great responsibility," Ikeda said.

"It is," Swann agreed. "That is why only a few ever get accepted to Scouts Special Forces."

"The same goes for the ISS," Wolf added.

Ikeda gave Wolf and Swann a curious look. "You are like gods."

Wolf chuckled, but his expression was serious. "We are not superior beings, if that's what you mean. Deep down we are just regular men with all the faults and desires humans suffer from. We are not robots without a conscience, killing indiscriminately. Do I have regrets for killing this man? Of course, I do. However, we cannot let feelings like that sway us. One man's life means nothing when it comes to the lives of many. Cruel and unfair? No, just common sense."

"I have nothing to add to that except for Wolf is right," Swann said. "Men like us live in a different world. We are agents of death. That is our reality."

"I've always admired you, Major Swann, but after listening to you and Major Wolf I don't envy either of you."

Swann laughed. "I don't blame you, Ikeda. I don't envy myself sometimes. I carry a heavy load on my shoulders."

They all turned around when Randor coughed delicately. "Now that you justified what happened, can we please get to the problem we still face?"

"Which is?"

"What to do with the bodies of these men. We must get rid of them."

"There is only one way, and that is to bury them," Wolf suggested.

"We will do that," Randor's father said. "We'll take them into the field and bury them deep. Nobody will ever know they were here."

"What about their Burras?"

"We'll burn their saddles and other gear and then we will set them free."

"Can I have two Burras, one bow and all the arrows?" It was Ramsy, the young warrior, who asked the question.

"Sure, you can," Swann told him. "I see no reason why not." He looked at Wolf, who nodded in agreement.

"Thank you. With your permission, I will take my leave now."

"You have our permission. I hope you keep your promise."

Wolf suspected that Swann had doubts about letting the young warrior go free. Should he break his promise, it would have dire consequences for Randor and his family. He didn't worry much about himself and the others. The King and all his warriors had no chance of winning against the superior weapons they would be able to use against him.

Wolf breathed a sigh of relief when Ramsy walked out of the door. Hopefully, this chapter was closed.

"How are your parents?" Wolf asked Randor.

"We'll live," Randor's father answered instead. "They never touched my wife. I may be bruised and bleeding a little, but it is all superficial. I will heal." He smiled, but it was obvious he supressed the pain he must be suffering. His cheek was swollen, and one eye shut. A long ugly-looking bruise ran along his left jaw. "Thanks to you we are alive. We won't be able to repay your kindness, but the least we can do is invite you to have supper with us."

"If it isn't too much trouble for you, we will gladly accept your offer." Wolf didn't ask his companions for approval. It was an easy decision. He was hungry and knew it was too late to travel on. "How long would it take us to get to the next city where we can spend the night?" He looked at Randor.

"There are plenty of smaller towns and villages on the way, but the next larger city would be Briem, about three hours in your vehicle."

"I see. We may have to spend the night here. Is it possible?"

"Randor can sleep in his old room," Randor's mother said. She chuckled. "I'm sure he can find a spot among the things we are storing in there now. You are welcome to sleep in the loft. The nights are not cold at this time of year. We can give you a few blankets if you want."

"That is no problem," Swann said. "We've slept under worse conditions."

"Perhaps before we sit down and relax, we take these bodies outside. There is still time before dark to bury them," Gorini suggested.

"I think that is a good idea," Wolf agreed. "The quicker they are out of sight the better for anyone."

They carried the bodies out of the house and loaded them onto one of the wagons. Randor produced a few shovels and hooked a couple of Burras to the wagon. He drove the wagon into the field. They took turns digging a deep pit.

"It has to be deep to prevent animals from digging them up again," Randor said.

Once he was satisfied, they threw the bodies into the pit and filled the hole again with the dirt. Then they smoothed out the surface until there was no evidence left that under the smooth surface the dirt was hiding the remains of four once living men with hopes and dreams, warriors that were loyal to their king literally until the end of their life.

Randor stood at the grave for a moment, his eyes closed. They didn't ask him what he did. It was clear, he followed some ceremony, and they honored that.

"I asked the gods to let them enter the Sacred Garden," he explained. "They were not evil. They only obeyed the orders of their King." He bowed one last time and then climbed back onto the wagon.

None of them made any comments. Even though the warriors had threatened and tortured his parents, it was obvious he didn't bear them any ill will. He was a simple man, but he had integrity and honor. Wolf for one, appreciated that and he had respect for him. Men like Randor were not common, even on a planet like Cerberus.

When they got back to the house, Randor's mother had prepared supper. The food was simple but tasty. His father produced some home-made wine. It was not the best but drinkable, and they enjoyed even that.

When it was time to retire for the night, they spread the blankets on the wooden floor of the loft.

Wolf slept, but it was an uneasy sleep. He was used to sleeping on hard surfaces under austere conditions, but lately he'd been spoiled. One could easily get used to sleeping in a bed on a soft mattress. His last thoughts before he fell asleep were 'I should have become a research scientist like my brother'.

[10]

They left early the next morning. Their destination was Briem. Randor called it a city, but in reality, it was nothing but a large town. It was also the seat of the local Priesthood. On the way, they drove through small villages. It was plain to see Tsakona was not far advanced when it came to technology. In fact, it was still quite primitive. There were no cars, only wagons drawn by Burras, those long-necked sleek animals. The Sartans really lived in what humans considered the Dark Ages.

Since their vehicle floated on a cushion of air, they were never held up when they came across an obstruction on the road. Once they were forced to drive around a large flock of woolly animals a farmer herded through one of the villages.

"They look like the sheep I've seen on many of the colonized planets," Wolf remarked.

"We call them Burrees. They may look like sheep, but they are not sheep," Randor explained. "The farmers raise them for food and wool. They are quite popular because they are not fussy about what they eat. You can raise them even in areas with sparse vegetation, like on mountain hills or in the tundra. Their resistance to cold and hot temperatures makes them ideal domestic animals."

"Are they native to Cerberus?" Swann wondered.

"I believe they are. If I'm not wrong, even the human farmers raise them." Randor looked at Ikeda.

"You are not wrong. Some farmers do, but many also raise real sheep. They were introduced to Cerberus by the first colonists. In the mountain areas, they raise Llamas, also for their wool and for food. They lend themselves well as pack animals on the mountain trails. Most animals the early colonists brought with them adapted to the environment on our planet and are thriving."

The people they passed didn't act surprised or awed seeing their vehicle. According to Randor, the majority of Sartans were used to seeing the magical contraptions that floated a foot above the ground without any visible wheels.

Randor's estimate was right. It took them about three hours to reach Briem. The houses that lined the streets were of the same type as the houses in the smaller towns and villages. Most of the streets were hard-packed dirt and clay, but closer to the center they were paved with flat stones. It didn't matter to their vehicle, but for anything with wheels it wouldn't be a smooth ride. The buildings were getting taller toward the city center, and they were closer together.

There was traffic on the streets. Just like in the villages, the traffic consisted of wagons and carts pulled by Lupas, goat-like animals with four horns. As large as small horses, they were strong and could easily pull a farm-wagon filled with fruit and vegetables.

Wolf spotted a large wagon loaded high with what seemed to be dirt, but he didn't think it was just dirt. The two draft-animals hitched to the wagon looked like the huge buffaloes he had seen on other planets.

"What do you call those big, shaggy beasts?" he asked Randor.

"Those are Wypees. Used mostly, as you can see, to pull heavy loads, but the farmers raise them also for food and for their fur. Their hide is tough and makes good and strong leather. The horns also have many uses. For instance, they can be used for making tools and even jewelry."

The Temple of the High Priest was located in the center of a large open area. A sprawling building surrounded by tall trees and large shrubs, it was an architectural marvel, as far as Wolf was concerned. As with many religions, the places of worship always stood for the wealthiest organizations in a country.

It was obvious, Tsakona was no exception.

"It is easy to see where all the money ends up," Swann voiced Wolf's thoughts.

"Where do you want me to park?"

"Just drive around the corner of the building and park it on the side," Wolf suggested.

As Randor passed the corner, they saw something none of them expected—another vehicle.

All of them climbed out of their car and walked to the other car to get a closer look. There was a crest painted onto both sides.

Wolf stared at it. "I know that crest. This vehicle belongs to Hyperion Mineral Explorations, the company Ambassador Amsterdam is working for, the same company that is mining Lirsium illegally on this planet. I wonder what they are doing here."

"Nothing that is good; of that I'm sure," Swann wagered.

"Well, let's go and find out." He turned to Randor. "This is obviously a place of worship for your people. A holy place. I'm wondering if it is safe to go unarmed into the building."

"You will be safe. No violence ever happens inside this Temple. The gods would rain death and destruction upon this land if we should ignore the warnings edged into the walls."

"I hope the owners of this vehicle follow those rules. I'd hate to become a victim of our own carelessness," Gorini voiced her doubts.

"Don't worry," Wolf soothed her fears. "I have a small but powerful pencil-laser attached to each of my boots. They look like decorations."

"So have I," Swann admitted.

"Good." Gorini showed her pointy teeth in a smile. "Then I won't feel so guilty with the laser inside my belt buckle."

Randor didn't comment, even though he seemed to appear a bit worried by these confessions.

As they approached the huge entrance doors, two armed guards stepped out of an alcove on either side of the doors, blocking their way.

"You are not Sartans," one stated, while the other one stared menacingly at them, his spear ready.

"They are with me," Randor told them. "They want to get the blessing of the High Priest and ask for permission to explore Tsakona. I will vouch for them."

"Are they aware that they have to pay a toll if they want to enter the Holy Temple?"

"They are and they are willing to pay."

Apparently satisfied, the guards stepped aside and let them enter.

They walked through a small vestibule and then through another set of large doors into a huge chamber, obviously the place where the congregation gathered to worship. The walls were decorated with carvings and life-sized statues. Some depicted mortal men and women in long gowns, while larger statues featured gods and goddesses. There were also statues of human-like beings with the heads of animals.

All statues and carvings glittered golden in the light of the many candles high up on the walls and in the golden chandeliers hanging from the high ceiling.

Otherwise, the room was bare, except for a few benches scattered along the walls. Even the benches were golden. The floor was covered with shiny, smooth tiles, most likely made from precious stones.

"There is a lot of wealth in this room," Swann whispered.

"No wonder the invaders loot these places," Wolf whispered back.

At the far end of the room was one massive chair flanked by a dozen smaller chairs. All made out of gold.

The large chair was occupied. Behind him, in each corner, stood two warriors. They wore armor of silver, and their spears were tipped with blue-shimmering spearheads.

They followed Randor as he walked toward the figure in the chair.

As Randor got closer, the figure rose. They saw a tall man, wearing a cloak around his thin shoulders. The cloak shimmered in rainbow colors as he moved his frail body. His face looked old and weathered, like the face of a man who has spent years in the desert, exposing his body to the rays of the burning sun. Something one would not expect of the High Priest.

Randor fell to one knee in front of the Priest, touching his left shoulder with his right hand.

The Priest ignored him, looking instead at Wolf and his companions. "You brought strangers into the Holy Temple." As frail as he appeared, his voice was strong and carried a note of authority. "One of them looks like the aliens that have been plundering our people and holy places."

"She may look like them, but she is not one of them. These strangers came to our world to stop the invaders."

The Priest stood for a while, regarding them silently. "The others. Are these four with them?"

"I know nothing about any others," Randor replied. "Whoever they are, my friends have nothing to do with them."

"I apologize for interrupting," Wolf said. "Those others you mentioned, who are they and what are they doing here?"

The Priest didn't seem surprised to hear Wolf speak Spartan. "They came to us many suns ago to make us an offer. They have been generous."

"What kind of offer?"

"They asked if they could dig in the mines for the rocks infused with the silvery metal. We have great quantities of it and are happy to trade it for other things. It is worth nothing."

"What are you using that silvery metal for?"

"Many things. We melt it and coat spearheads, swords, and knives with the liquid when it is hot. It lends strength to the swords and spearheads."

"Unless I'm wrong, he is talking about Rhodium," Swann said in a quiet voice.

"What is Rhodium?"

"It is an extremely hard metal and quite rare on most planets. And it is very pricy," Swann explained.

"Those other men. Are they somewhere in the temple?" Wolf asked the Priest.

"Yes, they are."

"Is it possible to talk to them?"

The Priest hesitated for a moment. Then he said, "It is possible, but there is a price to be paid."

"We are willing to pay," Swann told him. "I notice that you have an abundance of gold, which we usually use for payments, but we can give you Dockets. It is used in Freeland to buy things. I hope you can use them."

The Priest smiled. "We are quite familiar with Dockets. We will gladly take them from you. My acolyte will take you to our treasurer. He manages those matters."

A young boy rushed out from behind a hidden doorway in the back and stood waiting.

"You go with him," Swann told Ikeda. "Don't let them cheat you," he added in a quiet voice.

While they waited for Ikeda to return, they looked around the room. The Priest watched but didn't say anything.

"You have a beautiful temple," Swann remarked. "I've been to many other worlds, but few are as beautiful as yours. I have never seen so much gold in one place."

"Thank you." The Priest beamed, visibly proud. "Gold is in abundance on this world, and we have many gifted artisans that create these statues and reliefs."

"Can I ask you a question about those other men?"

"You can ask, but I may not be willing to answer you."

"The dealings you have with them. Are they done freely?"

"What do you mean?"

"Did they force or threaten you in any way?"

The Priest chuckled. "Nobody forces us to anything, ever. We know how to protect ourselves."

"That is good." Swann nodded. "Because if anyone ever threatens you, we can and will protect you. That is my promise to you."

The Priest's look was full of doubt. "You have the power to do that?"

"I have. We have."

At that moment Ikeda came back. "It is done," he said. "That's a shrewd and skilful negotiator. You couldn't pull a fast one over him."

"Why? Do you feel cheated?" Wolf queried.

"Not at all. He is fair and reasonable, but unwavering."

They were interrupted when another acolyte came up to them and said, "Come with me. I will take you to the viewing chamber."

Wolf and Swann made a little bow to the Priest. Wolf said, "It was an honor to meet you. Perhaps we will meet again."

The old Priest smiled. "I have a feeling we will." He turned to Randor. "I would like to give you a special blessing, my son. I sense a feeling of unrest and division inside you."

The acolyte took Wolf and his companions through a door in one of the corners, down a narrow corridor and then down a set of stairs. They headed for a door in the back that opened into a garden. They walked on a winding path paved with colorful stone tiles. Tall shrubs and flowers grew on either side of the path. At the end of the path was another building, that they entered. The short corridor they found themselves in led into a large, long room. There were shelves along the walls loaded with rocks.

Three men were standing in front of one of the shelves, studying the rocks.

They turned when they heard Wolf and his companions and watched them coming closer.

"Who are you?" an older man with a beard asked them.

"We could ask you the same thing," Wolf said. "In fact, what are you doing here?"

"We are studying these rocks."

"What are you hoping to find?"

"What do you care?" One of the other men challenged Wolf. "Besides, who are you anyway and what business do you have with these people?"

"None whatsoever. We are friends with this man here," Wolf pointed at Randor. "He is on a pilgrimage to visit different temples in Tsakona. We are historians and are studying the history of the Sartans on this planet." As he said this, he wondered what made him say that.

"Historians. Right." The other man smirked. "Somebody must be paying for that. What company you said you're working for?"

"I didn't."

"The Anorian female with you. Who's fucking her?" He sneered. "All of you, maybe?"

"I don't appreciate such vulgar language." Wolf acted indignant. "I'm a religious man, as is my brother. We use words that praise. As a historian I would be very much interested to know what you are searching for in those rocks."

"What harm can it do to tell him?" the bearded man spoke up. Without waiting for an answer, he said, "We are geologists. We discovered that this planet is rich in Rhodium and Iridium. We've never seen anything like it on other planets. Both metals are quite rare, and any company lucky to mine it is or will be wealthy indeed."

"And who is this lucky company?" Swann asked.

The bearded man shrugged. "If you must know, we are employees of Hyperion Mineral Explorations. The company has acquired exclusive rights to dig for minerals on Cerberus."

"Who granted them exclusive rights?"

"The Sartan priests."

"That means you are allowed to dig only in Tsakona," Wolf pointed out.

"Not really. The Company is already mining Lirsium in Freeland. So far, we have only one mine here in Tsakona, but we are on the verge of opening another one."

"We know about the one in Freeland. It was Ambassador Amsterdam who took me to one of the Lirsium mines to show me around." Wolf didn't see any harm in telling them that. "He never mentioned anything about mining Rhodium."

"So, you are the friend Amsterdam was talking about. Inspector Gifford also talked about you. He doesn't like you. You told him you are a traveler. I'm beginning to wonder about you now. You said you are historians. What are you? A traveler or an historian?"

"To be honest, I disliked Inspector Gifford from the moment we met. He seems arrogant and taken in with himself. I had no reason to tell him the truth."

One of the other two men chuckled. "You may be correct, but Gifford is a man with many friends in high places. He wields great power. To be on his wrong side is not healthy. By the way, Amsterdam knows nothing about what is happening here in Tsakona. He has lost Gifford's confidence. It is no secret in the company that Amsterdam may be replaced in the near future."

"The Ambassador confided in me that he is worried about that happening," Wolf disclosed. "He is a good man, you know. I had the impression the company is important to him."

"Of course it is." The bearded man laughed. "With the salary he gets, who wouldn't be? Some of the executives are not happy with this whole arrangement. It cost too much money to keep the Embassy going. We don't need an Embassy on this planet. We don't need the good will of the people in Freeland. Their army is a joke. We could send a small army of trained soldiers and take over this whole fucking planet with ease. It may even happen. There are things going on right now that will bring about a lot of changes on Cerberus."

"You are talking too much, Emril," the third man, who had been silent until now, warned him.

"I say whatever I want, Mansfield," Emril snapped. "You're not my boss. Who are they going to tell? And if they do? HME is much too powerful to worry about any company trying to muscle in." He looked at Wolf. "You never told us who finances your research."

"The Museum of Intergalactic Races on Rion," Swann answered for Wolf. "It is the largest and richest museum on Rion. The work they do is very important. Researchers from all over the Galaxy are relying on the museum's records."

"I guess you are doing important work, then. You must excuse us; we'd better get back to our work."

Wolf thought he detected a hint of sarcasm in the bearded man's voice.

They had been dismissed.

"I believe it is time to go," Wolf said to the others.

Once outside, Gorini, who had been silent as usual, spoke up, "They are hiding something they don't want us to know. I suggest, we check out that mine."

"We don't know where it is," Swann reminded her.

"No, we don't, but it should not be too difficult to find that mine. We could do a search with a seeker," Gorini suggested. "If it is within range, we'll find it."

"I agree," Wolf said. "One problem. We don't have one. I never thought of bringing one."

"Neither did I." Swann smiled remorsefully. "As a Scout I should be aware of their usefulness. A gross oversight."

"It doesn't matter," Gorini said. "I brought a tracker and a few seeker eyes. Ours is possibly more advanced than yours."

They watched Gorini unpack a small box from her backpack. "I thought it may come in handy," she explained with a little smile. She inserted a small pebble into a port on her tracker. A small screen appeared in front of her. She let her fingers fly across what looked like a keyboard. After a few moments, the seeker separated from the tracker and shot into the air. It was gone in seconds. "Now we wait," she said. "Everything the eye transmits will be recorded, but I don't have to tell you that. Hopefully, it will find what we are looking for."

Randor was already waiting for them by their vehicle. He seemed calm and happy.

"Your session with the Priest went well?" Wolf asked.

Randor nodded. "He knew something was troubling me, even though I didn't tell him anything about what happened at my parents' place. He told me to forget what happened in the past and look forward to the future. The past cannot be changed. He told me to accept it. Whatever happened has been planned for me by the gods and I should not question the plans of the gods. I am at peace now."

"That's good to know." Wolf was happy to hear that Randor had not confided in the Priest. In most religions the clergy were sworn to secrecy when it came to confessions, but Wolf didn't trust them. Priests were only mortal men and women with all the weaknesses and desires humans suffer from. Not all were trustworthy. It was no secret that the clergy in every religion seek to control the members of their congregation. If they know about a secret someone is harboring, they will use it to their advantage. They will use extortion should they find it necessary. All in the name of their god.

"If we had a more advanced vehicle, we'd have a tracking device built into the vehicle's computer," Swann complained.

Wolf chuckled. "If we had a more advanced vehicle, we'd be flying instead of crawling on the ground."

"That is one of the drawbacks with trying to do anything on these backward planets. You can't take full advantage of technology."

"Agreed, even though Cerberus cannot be considered a primitive planet," Wolf said.

"Primitive enough to hinder our investigation. Sure, they have ground vehicles but none that fly. We can't even match the technology of these invaders." Swann looked into the sky as if expecting to see something in the air. "They do have the advantage over us."

Ikeda cleared his throat to get their attention. "I'd hate to interrupt these interesting speculations, but since we can't take to the air, what should we do now?"

"We could wait here until we find out something from the searcher or we could go and have something to eat. I heard my belly growling," Wolf said. "There must be an eatery somewhere in this city." He looked at Randor.

"I'm sure there is, but I have no idea where it even could be." He chuckled. "Don't forget, I don't live in this city. I'm a visitor just like you. We'll have to look around. It shouldn't take long to find something suitable."

"Alright, let's start looking."

———

"WELL, THAT WAS NOT SO BAD," SWANN SAID ONCE THEY WERE BACK IN their vehicle. "In fact, the food was quite tasty, even though it was different from what I'm used to eating."

"What animal did the meat come from?" Wolf turned to look at Randor.

"Most likely Burrees. It is the most popular food animal. Their meat is tenderer than meat from Wypees or Llamas."

"I can't keep track of the animals that flourish here. Which ones are the Burrees?" Swann asked.

"They are like the sheep the human farmers raise," Randor explained.

Gorini had been busy studying the screen of the tracker. "I believe I found something quite interesting."

Wolf, who sat in the front, swiveled his seat around. The three-dimensional screen on top of the tracker could be seen from all sides. Gorini had slowed down the images she found interesting. She zoomed in on the scene below. It showed a machine going into a hole in the mountain side and one coming out. There were two buildings near the mountain, but what caught their attention was one of the vehicles parked in front of the building.

"What the Hell!" Wolf cursed. "Is that what I think it is?"

"It is," Swann growled. "I did not expect this. Can you bring the image of that vehicle closer?"

The image of their interest grew and then they all stared at it.

"What kind of vehicle is that?" Randor inquired.

"It is a flying machine that should not be there," Ikeda said.

"Why not?"

"Because it belongs to the invaders of your planet," Wolf explained. "It means that Hyperion Mineral Explorations either has teamed up with the invaders or the company has been taken over by the enemy."

"Neither one is desirable. We need to drive there and investigate to make sure," Swann suggested. "How far is it?" The question was addressed to Gorini.

"Let's see. With driving conditions as the eye recorded them and according to the computer, we could make in under three hours."

"Then let's get going as long we still have daylight," Wolf urged. "We'll probably have to drive back in the dark."

They all agreed and a few moments later they were on their way.

"I'm sure glad they introduced vehicles that float on a cushion of air to Cerberus," Wolf said. "We would never make it operating a vehicle with wheels on this rough terrain, especially with no roads."

"You are right," Randor agreed. "But even with the air cushion I still have to watch out for these large boulders dotting the landscape."

"I hope they don't have an alarm system set up," Swann voiced his concern. "If they don't, we should be able to sneak up on them. I noticed on the screen that the mine is in a valley. There is no reason we can't get close without being detected by a watcher."

"They will detect us if they have an alarm system, but we'll have to take the chance, hoping they don't have one." Wolf had been thinking along the same lines. They could easily find cover behind the tall, jagged rock formations growing out of the ground everywhere. However, they'd be sitting ducks if the aliens took to the air to search for vehicles approaching their position. He didn't see a reason why they would unless they were paranoid about unwanted visitors.

Gorini had been watching the screen of the tracker and given Randor instruction which way to drive. They had been following the route the eye had been mapping.

"We are close," she said suddenly. "Keep watching. When we are getting our first glimpse of the buildings, stop and back up at once."

It was about ten minutes later when they saw one of the buildings. Randor brought the vehicle to a halt and backed up. Once they were out of sight, he stopped.

All of them got out and approached the top of the hill on foot. As they got closer, they crept on their bellies to get a better look.

Wolf and Swann studied the building and the surrounding area through their binoculars. On the virtual screen it seemed to Wolf as if he was standing beside the foreign vehicle.

"Yes, that definitely is one of theirs, unless HME has developed a vehicle just like the invaders have, but I don't see that even as a possibility," Wolf speculated.

"Neither do I," Swann agreed. "I wouldn't mind getting closer and looking inside that building, possibly even inside the mine. Maybe we can grab one of the invaders and interrogate him. I really would like to know what is going on. Why would HME associate with these invaders? What are they hoping to gain?"

"My question is what reason do the invaders have to get into an association with HME?" Wolf wondered. "By the way, we can't just wander up to the building and not be seen. We'll have to wait until dark."

They took turns watching through the binoculars as they waited for darkness. There was not much action except a couple of times a machine with a bucket in the front came out of the mine and dumped the contents of the bucket into the huge box of a truck. Wolf found it quite interesting to see that the truck was of foreign design and did not have any wheels.

"I wonder what kind of deal the invaders made with HME. It looks like they are transporting the mined rocks to a planet on the other side of the portal," Wolf guessed after telling them what he saw.

"It seems to me that HME is the middleman between the Invaders and the Priesthood," Swann said. "The Priests would never agree to let them dig anywhere after they destroyed property, killed one of the kings, and looted temples."

Ikeda chuckled. "I don't believe they would ask anyone for permission if they wanted to dig anywhere on this planet."

"I'm afraid you are right." Wolf handed him the binoculars. "I've seen enough for a while."

"Even though we don't know anything concrete yet, it is safe to say that the invaders and HME have made a pact with each other," Ikeda said. "I think we should let Scouts Base know where we are right now and what we found so far."

"We don't really know what exactly is happening here. Perhaps we should wait with that report until tomorrow," Swann suggested.

"I side with Ikeda," Gorini said. "It won't hurt to send a preliminary report and tell them what happened so far. As added insurance, I will use one of the seeker eyes to record our conversations from now on. Should anything happen to us, the tracker will send a distress call to the base if we don't contact them within twenty-four hours and send everything the eye recorded."

"Good idea," Wolf agreed with Gorini. "Go ahead, Ikeda. Send your report. We have plenty of time before we can do anything."

Not everything went according to plan. The side of the mountain where the mine was found was thrown into darkness earlier than the more open areas. It still wasn't dark enough to set their plan in motion when the building and the surrounding area was lit up by bright floodlights.

"So much for sneaking up on them undetected, damn it," Wolf cursed.

"Perhaps we have to change our tactics," Gorini suggested.

"What do you have in mind?"

"Why don't we just drive a little closer and then walk boldly up to them? According to the number of vehicles parked by the building, the humans there will be in the majority. We should be quite safe from the aliens. Besides, we won't go unarmed."

"What do we tell them why we are paying them a visit?" Ikeda wondered.

She smiled. "Don't you remember we are archaeologists? We are exploring this part of the country and just by pure accident we came across this site. We figured we shouldn't be strangers and decided to say hello. Besides, we are curious what this place is all about."

Swann nodded. "Sounds plausible to me."

Wolf didn't care much for that plan. "What, if by pure chance, the aliens are the same bunch we ran into in Windy Lake?"

"The chances of that happening are pretty slim," Swann argued.

"I admit, they are, but it is possible."

"I think we should take that chance," Gorini said. "I agree with Major Swann. What other choice do we have except for leaving without investigating?"

Pursing his lips, Wolf mulled it over in his mind. "I have misgivings, but you are right. What else can we do other than leaving? We don't really have any choice in the matter." With one last look at the building in the valley, he said, "Alright, let's get moving."

They climbed back into their vehicle and Randor drove slowly down into the valley. He parked what they considered a safe distance away and then they walked on at a slow pace. They left their Proton Beam Rifles in the trunk. Archaeologists didn't have rifles like that. However, they still wore their sidearms.

Before they reached the building, a man came out and stood there, watching them coming closer. He held a rifle in his hands but didn't show any aggression.

"Good evening," Wolf said when they were close enough. He smiled. "We didn't expect a living soul in this part of the country. What a surprise when we saw your building." He pointed at one of the flood lamps. "To keep the animals away? We were warned to look out for Mountain Skarks. Apparently, they are huge and unpredictable."

"I couldn't say. We've never seen any around here. Who are you people and what are you doing here?"

"We are archaeologists searching for ancient artefacts. We've been told this area would be a good spot to find evidence of earlier civilizations on this planet." Wolf pretended to peer around the building. "It seems you people are digging for something, judging by the huge hole in the side of the mountain. I guess you already have a working mine going. What are you mining if you don't mind me asking?"

"Actually, I mind." The man seemed nervous about something. He was holding his rifle in a tight grip. "This is private property, and visitors are not allowed even near this area. I suggest you people turn around and leave this area as quickly as possible."

Wolf held up a hand. "Now hold it there, my man. We didn't see any posted signs. If what you are doing here is legal, there should be no problem letting us look around a little. We're just a group of scientists trying to explore an alien planet. We've got permission from the local priest. He never mentioned a private company operating a mine here."

"We've been here for the better part of a fucking year; and a year on this planet is a long time. And as far as legal goes? I know nothing about that. I'm just a guard on a fucking alien planet in a desolate area trying to keep nosy people from snooping around and finding I don't know what. So, please, don't make my job any harder and just go away. I've never shot anyone, and you don't want to be the first ones."

"Isn't that a little bit too dramatic?" Wolf smiled disarmingly. At least he thought it was disarming. "What horrible secret could you be guarding that justifies shooting innocent people?" He took a couple of steps, bringing him closer to the guard.

The guard brought up his rifle. "Not a step closer. I will shoot."

Wolf had been looking around during their discussion and spotted the other building behind the first one. It was smaller and of a strange design. While the larger building had been built from logs, it blended into the landscape as if it belonged but that second one clearly did not belong.

Even in the dark, he could tell it was not built from local materials. Shiny and smooth, it sat there like an intrusion, like an ugly pimple on flawless white skin.

Out of the darkness appeared a tall, broad-shouldered figure wearing a sleeveless shirt. It took Wolf only one look to realize this was one of the invaders.

"I don't think your friends will like it if you shoot me," Wolf said to the guard.

"My friends?" The guard turned to look behind him. Spotting the three aliens, he lowered his rifle with the words, "They are not my friends." He spoke with clenched teeth.

One of the aliens stepped into the light. His expression was neutral and the look in his reptilian eyes cold. "What do you want?" His words came out harsh and demanding.

"Like I explained to your guard, we are archaeologists searching for ancient artifacts."

"You won't find any here."

"I told them to leave," the guard spoke up.

"That was a mistake. They've seen us and we can't let them leave." He looked at Wolf and his companions. "Throw down any weapons and communication devices you may have and kneel with your hands behind your backs. You are our prisoners."

"Are you afraid we will discover that you are trying to hide what you are doing in that mountain? We already know. We've talked to three geologists from HME back at the temple and they told us that the company is mining Rhodium and Iridium. They didn't tell us about you. We know who you are. It is no secret that you are plundering and destroying property and murdering people in Freeland and in Tsakona. It comes as a surprise that HME has teamed up with you." Wolf spoke calmly and for the benefit of the seeker Gorini carried, hoping everything that happened here was transmitted to Scouts Base.

"It seems you know too much already. More reason to take you as our prisoners."

"What are you going to do to us?"

The alien chuckled. "You'll find out." He walked up to Gorini. "You are one of us. What is a female Arani doing in the company of these humans?"

Gorini gave him a haughty look. "I am not one of you. We call our race Anorian on this side of the portal. We don't invade other planets and slaughter innocent sentient beings."

The alien didn't act surprised. "I should have guessed that you are not one of us. An Arani female would never dare to talk to a male in such an arrogant tone."

"Our males are weak and obedient. They don't swagger around and pretend to be intelligent." Even though the male towered over her, she stared at him. "I am not afraid of you."

He laughed. "You will be after you've been trained. I will make it my personal goal to break you and teach you obedience."

"Touch me and it will be the last thing you will ever do!"

———

Master Scout Hadad looked at Scout Stavros and Axelsson with a grim expression. "They are hostages of these aliens. We've learned something new. They call their race Arani. We also know that they have formed an alliance with Hyperion Mineral Explorations, and they are mining Rhodium and Iridium in Tsakona."

"What can we do?" Axelsson looked at Stavros and then at Hadad.

"We have to send this information to Scouts Headquarters," Hadad said. "They will decide what to do. Most likely, they will pass it on to the Solar Union Space Navy. It is out of our hands now. All we can do is wait."

Colonel Harry Turnbull of the Solar Protection Agency knew something was up when he received an urgent call from Admiral Swenson of the Solar Union Space Navy.

The Admiral was a big man, square-chinned with bushy eyebrows. He had the habit of pulling them together. It made him look like an angry man.

"You are probably wondering why I've summoned you to my office with such urgency, Colonel."

"The thought has occurred to me, Admiral." Turnbull stood at attention, wondering if the Admiral was angry at him or if it was something else.

"I understand you are a good friend of Major Wolf of the ISS. Correct?"

"That is correct, sir."

"Good, good. At ease, Colonel. You are not under investigation for something you may or may not have done. I've heard nothing but good things about you." He smiled jovially, but to Turnbull he looked like an angry bull ready to charge.

"I am happy to hear that, sir. I wasn't really concerned."

"Good. That's good. Now to the reason I sent for you. Have you ever heard of the planet Cerberus?"

"No, I have not, sir."

Swenson folded his hands in front of him as if he were about to pray. "Cerberus is the fourth planet of Ibirius Prime. It is located in the Spinner System near the Rim, far away from the regular trade routes. That doesn't mean it is a forgotten planet. It gets its fair share of visits from freighters and other merchant ships; even a few passenger liners once in awhile."

"How about the population?"

"We don't know the exact numbers, but it is estimated that there are about seven million Earth humans and around three million human-like colonists, origin unknown, living on Cerberus."

"Is that where I'm going?" Turnbull wondered. "If so, why?"

"We received a message from Scouts Security..."

"From where?" Turnbull interrupted the Admiral.

Swenson ignored his breaking of protocol and continued, "Scouts Security. Don't ask me to explain, just take my word for it. You will get more information in your briefing. Just in a nutshell, Cerberus is being invaded by an alien species. We already have an agent on Cerberus. He and his partner, an Anorian, have been kidnapped by this enemy. It will be you and your team's mission to rescue them."

When Swenson took a breath, Turnbull used the opportunity to ask a question. "What is this agent's name?"

The Admiral gave him a look that could easily be interpreted as 'You won't believe this'. After a short pause, he said, "It is your friend Major Ethan Wolf."

"Ethan?" Turnbull blurted out. "Is he alright?"

"As far as we know. The last news we have of him is that he and his partner were taken prisoners by these invaders. That's all we know."

An icy hand touched Turnbull's brain. His best friend was in trouble. Suddenly, he felt an urgency to get to Cerberus. "How old is this news?"

"The Scouts sent the message a week ago. They never said how long ago they got it."

"Damn! It could be a couple of weeks old. I don't want to criticize, Admiral, but why did it take another week to plan this mission?"

"We started at once. The team is ready to be deployed, but we couldn't decide who would lead the mission. Your name came up as the most capable candidate. You'll have your briefing tomorrow and you will leave the day after."

"What do we know about the invaders?"

"They may look like Anorians, but they insist they are Arani."

"I've never heard of this race. What planet do they come from?"

The Admiral looked at Turnbull with a somber expression. "What I'm about to tell you will not leave this room, Colonel Turnbull. Understood?"

Turnbull wondered what Swenson was going to tell him. "Understood, sir."

"This information is way above your paygrade, but it is essential that you understand what you are up against. Have you ever heard anything about star-gates or star-portals?"

"I've heard rumors about an ancient race that existed long before any of the races inhabiting this Galaxy now. Apparently, they had portals on all the inhabited planets which they used to travel the Galaxy. They didn't have starships, because the portals allowed them to cross the void between star systems in an instant. In a sense, they were teleportation stations. However, there is no evidence that these doors, if you will, ever existed. They are just rumors, legends."

"What if I tell you, they do exist?"

Turnbull stood silent for a moment, before he answered. "It is obvious to me that you will tell me exactly that. If it's true, then I am lost for words, but I am wondering why such a discovery is kept a secret."

"The rumors are true, Colonel. The star-portals exist. I won't go into details about them, but there is one thing I can tell you and that is the fact that there is most likely such a portal on Cerberus. We don't know yet where it is, but the Arani came through such a portal to Cerberus. To find and rescue Major Wolf is only one part of your mission. Your job is to find this portal and when you do you will make sure its location will stay a secret with the military."

"I assume that there are a number of portals known to the military already and nobody else knows about them?"

"Not quite. The location of most of them are known to the military and governments of other races. Everyone is still trying to figure out how to work them. That's why it is important that the existence and location of the one on Cerberus is kept a secret."

"I am a soldier. I swore an oath, and I am not in the habit of blabbing military secrets to anyone, Admiral," Turnbull said stiffly.

"Good. Very good. I didn't expect anything else from you." The Admiral paused, pulling his eyebrows together, reminding Turnbull of the primates he had seen in the zoo. "I've only told you part of the problem we are facing on Cerberus. There is more, but you will receive more details at your briefing." He pulled something out of a drawer in his. It was an information rod. He handed it to Turnbull. "Everything you need to know is on this chip. The information is encrypted. Only you will be able to read it. The code will be downloaded into your personal data-base on your wrist computer at your briefing."

Turnbull knew the interview was over. "Thank you for opportunity to save my friend, Admiral."

"There is a reason you were chosen, Colonel Turnbull. Good luck with the mission. That is all."

When he reached the bottom of the steps that led to the main entry of the Military High Command building, Turnbull paused and stared at the huge fountain in the center of the tiled terrace without actually seeing it. His thoughts were on the mission ahead.

His lifelong friend Ethan was in trouble, abducted by an alien race. He was glad High Command had chosen him for this mission. If it meant entering the inferno of hell itself and fight an army of three-headed beasts to rescue his best friend, he would not hesitate to do that.

"Colonel Turnbull?"

Pulled out of reverie, he turned to look at the man who had spoken to him. He was tall and bulky, dressed in a brown uniform and wearing a Scouts hat.

Turnbull looked him up and down, wondering what a Scout would want from him. "Yes, can I help you?"

The Scout smiled. "Sorry to bother you, Colonel. I am Lieutenant Vern Starling. As you probably deduced already, I am a Scout. We know about your mission to Cerberus and there is important information we have. Please, kindly accompany me to Scouts Headquarters where you will be briefed."

Turnbull stiffened and took a step backward. "How can you know about my mission? It is supposed to be secret."

"It still is, but you'd be surprised how much we Scouts know about so-called secret missions the military is conducting." He chuckled. "Just so you know, we have our own secret missions of which the military is completely in the dark. Scouts and the military are not always sharing information. Actually, seldom." He became serious. "It is important you meet with my superior. The information you will receive concerns Major Swann. We understand he is your friend."

"He is my friend, but he is no major."

Starling smiled again. "You will be told everything at headquarters. Please, follow me to my car."

Cautious and suspicious, Turnbull walked with the Scout to his vehicle. It was white with the emblem of the Scouts on both sides. Getting into the vehicle, he was still apprehensive.

It took about thirty minutes for them to get to Scouts Headquarters. The building was not as impressive and large as the Military High Command building. Above the double doors leading into the building a sign said 'Scouts Investigations'.

"This isn't Scouts Headquarters," Turnbull commented.

"No, it isn't. Our headquarters are not even on this planet. This is, as it says on the sign, the Bureau of Scouts Investigations."

"I wasn't aware one even existed."

"Oh, yes, it does. There is a lot you don't know, Colonel Turnbull."

More suspicious than even before, Turnbull walked beside the Scout toward the entrance. The vestibule they entered was not flashy or impressive. He had to remind himself, this was a building belonging to the Scouts.

They walked down a long corridor, through a door, and then they entered another larger room. He saw four elevator doors. They headed to one and after pushing the button beside the doors, they slid open. After entering the elevator, the doors closed with a soft rushing sound and the elevator began its journey up. When they opened again, it said Level Fifteen on a small, bright sign.

"After you," Starling said.

Another room with several doors leading into other rooms or corridors. A small sign on one door declared the room behind it as Scouts Security.

More secrets. It was getting better and better.

He followed Starling into the room with the sign. There were a couple of round tables with chairs and a small couch. Two doors on opposite walls. One of the doors was decorated with a small sign.

Colonel Stonewall.

Starling knocked on the door and opened it. "Please, go inside."

Turnbull followed his request. The room was quite large, with a bright, big window offering a view of other tall buildings.

The man sitting behind the huge desk was a little past middle-aged. He had a full head of graying hair, cut military style. Even sitting, he presented a formidable figure.

He looked up from a screen he had been studying. Turnbull registered his steel-gray eyes. "Colonel Turnbull," the man said with a deep, resonant, and pleasant voice. "I am Colonel Stonewall." He got up from his chair and walked around his desk, offering his hand. "I am pleased to meet one of Major Swann's good friends. I've heard a lot about you."

Turnbull took the offered hand and shook it. "I am a little confused, Colonel Stonewall. It is true, I am a friend of Alfred Swann, but he is not a major. He is a Master Scout. He never mentioned anything about being a major. I did not know that the Scouts even had ranks like the military."

Stonewall smiled. "It is not commonly known, Colonel. Have a seat, and I will try to make a few things clear to you." He pointed to one of the two upholstered chairs in front of the desk.

After both were seated, Stonewall said, "Let me explain about Scouts Investigation and Scouts Security. The High Senate created them. Why? The military has grown into a monster that is difficult to control. There are too many factions with their own agenda. There is too much politics and too much rivalry. The different sections don't communicate with each other. It takes too long for any group to act. That's where the Scouts come in. The Scouts organization is not affiliated with any interest groups. We are not military men or politicians. The Scouts do not swear any allegiance to any planet or country. Members of Scouts Security are what Special Forces are in the military. They undergo rigorous training just like Union troopers, even more intense. We are sent into situations the military cannot solve. When we arrive on a problem planet we take over. We are the highest authority. Our law supersedes any other law, even that of the military. We report directly to the High Senate."

"That's a lot of power," Turnbull remarked.

Stonewall nodded solemnly. "Yes, it is. I am quite aware of that. It would be easy to abuse such power."

"I suppose it would be. Who is the top man in Scouts Security?"

"I am."

Turnbull was overwhelmed by a feeling of awe when he looked at Stonewall. "That makes you the most powerful man in this part of the Galaxy. One could say you're the Emperor of the Human Federation."

Stonewall's laugh was more than amused. "You could also call me the poorest man in the Human Federation. Remember, even with all that power, I am still a Scout."

"How does Alfred Swann fit into all of this?"

"Major Swann is my second in command. He is a man of integrity and honor and more than capable to fill that position."

Turnbull was stunned to hear that. The man who had been one of his best friends since childhood, a man he thought he knew, was suddenly a stranger to him. "Is he around?"

Stonewall didn't answer for a long moment before he dropped the bombshell. "I'm afraid he is not. He has been abducted along with Major Wolf on the planet Cerberus."

———

TURNBULL HAD NOT EXPECTED A BATTLECRUISER, BUT HE WAS STILL impressed with the size of the ship. The name on the hull proclaimed it as the SUSN Nemesis. It was not a new ship, neither was it some old heap ready to be retired.

After boarding the ship, he inspected the cargo hold and was surprised to find six corvettes, one Shark, and one personal transport vehicle. The corvettes were two-seaters for a pilot and a gunner but with extra space for equipment. The Shark had the capacity to carry up to a dozen troopers. None of the vehicles were space-worthy, meant only for operating on the surface of a planet.

There were twelve members in his team.

The personnel of the carrier were made up of eight crew. All of them, including the captain, were seasoned veterans and capable of defending the carrier in the event pirates should attack it. If needed, they were also assigned to become part of Turnbull's team.

After liftoff, he had his team assemble in the cargo hold. He knew from looking at the roster that four of the twelve troopers were women. They all stood at attention when he walked in. He told them, "Stand Easy."

After they took on a more relaxed position, he said, "I'm sure you all know who I am, but I'll introduce myself anyway. I am Colonel Harry Turnbull. I'll be your CO on this mission. Our destination is the planet Cerberus in the Spinner System near the Rim. We should reach it in about seven days. Cerberus is being invaded by an alien species we know next to nothing about. This mission is to discover their military capabilities and their strengths, but it is also a rescue mission. One of our agents has been kidnapped by the enemy. His name is Major Ethan Samuel Wolf. He is a personal friend of mine, and we won't rest until we find and extract him from the clutches of this enemy. Let me make this clear. It won't be a picnic. From what we know, these aliens are brutal and ruthless. On a lighter note, as long as we are in flight, we will dispense with rigid military rules, but I expect all of you to conduct yourself properly. Do I make myself clear?"

"Loud and clear, sir," they said in unison, standing at attention and saluting.

Turnbull returned the salute and said, "Dismissed."

Most of the men left the cargo hold. There was only one other place they could gather and that was the mess hall. As an officer he couldn't join the enlisted men and women in the mess hall, but that didn't mean he couldn't talk to any.

The four women were still in the hold. He had studied their pictures and knew them all by name. One of them, Brigit Harris, was a sergeant. He decided to have a talk with her.

The women looked at him when he approached them. "I don't mean to break up your conversation," he apologized. "I'd like a word, Sergeant Harris."

She seemed surprised and said, "No problem, sir."

Before she went with him, she turned back to the other three women and shrugged her shoulders.

"You're not in any trouble, Sergeant," he assured her. "I just wanted to talk to you."

"What about?"

He smiled. "Nothing in particular. You sure are suspicious, aren't you?"

"It doesn't hurt."

"I don't have an ulterior motive, if that's what you're wondering."

They had arrived in front of the door that led into the officer's lounge. A couple of the tables were already occupied. He recognized the ship's captain Malleway and Doc MacCulloch at one table. He didn't know the three men sitting at the other table. Obviously, they were crew.

He steered her to the only empty table. When she took her seat, he had to impression she was not quite comfortable with the situation. "You're my guest," he told her. "Besides, this may be a troop carrier, but the atmosphere on this ship is more relaxed than on a regular carrier. So, please, relax and have a drink with me. It is not against regulations."

"I'm not so sure about this." Her eyes were large when she looked at him. "I'm trying to fit in with the others, and having a drink with the CO is not exactly the proper way of doing so."

"You're a sergeant, aren't you?"

She nodded.

"Well, that already sets you apart from the rest. In fact, I want you to lead the three other females in this outfit. You will oversee their conduct and plan their activities and duties."

While he talked, he studied her. She had her hair cut short, with strong feminine features. Normally, he didn't find women with men's hair-cuts attractive.

She also had a nice smile. "What activities and duties here on the ship do you want me to plan?"

"You've got me there." He returned her smile. "I'm sure you'll find something. You're a sergeant, familiar with daily exercises to keep in shape. Make your team the top team. Don't slack, stay sharp. I said we'll dispense with military rules, but don't take it literally. I think you know what I mean."

"What about the men?"

"Oliver Jones is a sergeant. All the others are specialists. I will give Sergeant Jones three men to lead. I will promote Ronen Lee to the rank of Master Corporal and give him three men. I studied his file, and he seems the best choice." The look Turnbull gave Harris was solemn. "I hope I can count on your discretion to keep this information to yourself until I have made up my mind."

Her expression mirrored his. "I am not in the habit of blabbing every-thing I'm told or everything I hear," she challenged him.

"I wasn't insinuating you do. Just making sure we understand each other." He leaned back in his chair. "I think it is time for a drink. What can I get you?"

"Just a glass of wine. Red, preferably."

"You've got it." He got up to go to the bar and ordered a beer and a Scotch for himself and a glass of red wine.

"I prefer Scotch myself," the man beside him said. He turned to look at the man. It was MacCulloch, the ship's doctor.

"I was introduced to it by my father." Turnbull chuckled. "I guess one could say I'm keeping the tradition going."

MacCulloch lifted his glass. "To traditions. Slainte Mhath."

"Cheers." Turnbull emptied his glass, savoring the taste of the Scotch. "You're a Scotsman?"

MacCulloch laughed cheerfully. "Can't hide it with a name like mine. Born and raised in Old Edinburgh on Earth. And you?"

"I was born on Rion. Apparently, I do have Scottish blood in my veins. According to my father, anyway." He chuckled. "How much or how little is anyone's guess. Lost in the mist of time." He grabbed his beer and the glass of wine. "I'd better get back to my companion."

"I couldn't help but notice when you walked in with her. Beautiful woman. You're an item?"

"No. She's a sergeant in my team. I've just gone over a few things with her."

MacCulloch chortled and lifted his glass again. "You might get lucky with her. She'd be hard to resist. One never knows."

"No chance of that happening. I don't get involved with a member of my team." He smiled. "Tradition."

Harris didn't say anything when he returned to the table, but he could see in her face that she was slightly displeased with him for leaving her alone, even if it was just to get her a glass of wine. He put the glass in front of her. "I hope you like it. They don't have much choice."

"I'm sure it will be fine. I don't get many opportunities to enjoy a glass of wine these days." She favored him with a little smile and reached for the glass. Taking a small sip, she swirled the wine in her mouth before swallowing it. "Not bad," she said, "I guess officers do get the better stuff."

He examined the bottle of beer in front of him. "Maybe they do. I never thought of it."

When he looked up, he noticed the gaze of her bright, blue eyes on his face, scrutinizing him openly. "I am curious. How long have you been in the military?"

"Twenty-three years."

"Family tradition?"

He shook his head. "I'm the first and only one. My father is Chief of Police, and my mother is a lawyer."

"Any siblings?"

"One brother. He's a lawyer, like my mother. My two sisters are married and are staying home, raising a family. Their husbands are in the food business." He frowned. "I am their poor brother-in-law. They make more money in a week than I make all year."

"Look on the bright side. You are roaming the universe, living exciting adventures, while they are stuck on their ball of dirt, bored out of their minds." She smiled and sipped her wine, still studying him.

"I think you haven't been in the military long enough to realize that all that is just wishful thinking." He looked into her eyes. "How long since you joined the military?"

"Eleven years. I joined when I turned eighteen."

"That makes you twenty-nine. What made you join? Don't tell me because of your sense of adventure."

"Don't worry, I won't. Nothing so glorious. I ran away from an abusive father and a broken home."

"Sorry to hear that. Where is your home?"

"I was born on Chiron."

"I've never been there, but I know all about it. One of the early planets to be colonized. Almost Earth-like. The fifth planet circling a primary known as Solaris. Strangely, only humans live there. High tech. Population nearly two billion." He chuckled. "Do I have that right?"

"Very good. I'm impressed. What makes you so knowledgeable about my home world?"

"It is one of the history lessons we were taught in School. It stuck in my mind because Chiron seems to be so much like Rion."

"That's where you were born?"

"Born and raised. Married our neighbor's daughter at eighteen, got divorced when I was twenty. Joined the military soon after." His smile came out a little lopsided. "That's my boring life in a nutshell."

"I don't believe for one minute that you had a boring life. I'll bet you could entertain someone many evenings with the exciting adventures you've lived through." Her face took on a dreamy look. "Adventures I always dreamed of. Ever since I was a little girl, I wished I could fly away in a spaceship and get lost in the vastness of space."

"And here you are. Your dream came true."

"Yes, I am, except I dreamed about landing on a planet covered with flowers and populated with beautiful people living in harmony, never arguing and never fighting over stupid things." Her chuckle almost sounded like a sob. "Silly dream, I know. It was my way of trying to cope with an ugly environment." She reached for her glass and emptied it. Putting it carefully back onto the table, she said, "Sorry to bore you with my wretched childhood. Joining the military was the best thing I did in my life. Here I found order and camaraderie. I was taught discipline and how to deal with difficult situations."

"That's all that counts. Any brothers and sisters?"

"Two brothers. No sister. My older brother left home when he turned eighteen. I don't know what happened to him and where he is. My younger brother?" She lifted her shoulders. "Who knows? I haven't been back home since I moved out."

"What about your mother?"

"She left us when I was sixteen." She stared into her empty glass. "Can we talk about something else?"

"Certainly. I didn't really plan to grill you about your life. I just wanted to get to know you a little better. Sorry."

"That's alright. Can I ask you about our mission?"

"Go ahead."

"This agent we are supposed to rescue. You said he was your friend. Who is he and what exactly happened to him? Why was he on that planet in the first place? What makes this planet so important?"

Turnbull rubbed his chin, wondering how much he could tell her. "Many questions. His name is Ethan Wolf. Major Wolf. He was sent there on the request of the inhabitants to investigate the apparent invasion of an alien species."

"The inhabitants are humans?"

"Approximately seven million of them, in addition to another three million of humans nobody knows where they came from. They were there already when Earth began sending colonists to Cerberus. There is also a large number of Sleer living there. How many is not known."

"Sleer? My knowledge about them is not very extensive. I know they are humanoids. Their ancestors were otter-like, and their males are quite savage."

"That's about it. Their males may be considered savage, but the Sleer are highly advanced when it comes to technology. They were already roaming space when we humans were still planet-bound."

"How do the Sleer fit into the picture?"

Turnbull frowned. "I don't really know. They were only mentioned as just another piece of info in my briefing. It seems they are not important."

"Another question. What planet do these aliens come from?"

Turnbull didn't answer right away. Harris was coming dangerously close to information she didn't have clearance for. He could not tell her about the portals. "We don't know. Apparently, they look like male Anorians, but the Anorians claim they have nothing to with them." He spread his hands. "They are part of the mystery." He sighed. "There is much more to this. It would take too long to fill you in on everything. Some of the information I am not allowed to discuss with you. Sorry."

"Typical military crap." She stared at him. "The brass sends us into danger, possibly to our death, but we are not qualified to know why we put our lives on the line."

He saw the anger in her face and eyes, and he couldn't blame her. "I agree with you. It is not just the lower ranks that are kept in the dark. Even we officers are on a 'need-to-know' basis. As a colonel I am not privileged to share certain information an admiral is allowed to have. It is above my paygrade." He chuckled. "As if money has something to do with it."

"Then what does it have to do with?"

"Politics. Planetary Security. Solar Security. For instance, we have the ISS, which stands for Interstellar Secret Service. SIS, Solar Intelligence Service. SUSS, Solar Union Secret Service. The PIA, Planetary Intelligence Service. SPA, Solar Protection Agency, to name just a few. One Agency does not know what the others are doing. Nobody shares information unless they have to. And then it is like wading through a swamp. It is frustrating and confusing. There are so many undercover agents out there, even the agencies are losing track." He gave her a questioning look. "How do I know you're not an agent?"

"You don't and I won't tell you." Her laugh teased him. She bent forward, looking into his eyes. "I can assure you I am not an agent. I am a sergeant in the Solar Union Forces. That's all. What about you? I know you are a Colonel. In what branch of the military?"

"Solar Protection Agency. No secret there."

"What about Major Wolf?"

"He is with Solar Union Special Forces." It was not a total lie. He just didn't tell her that Wolf was with the ISS, which was a branch of SUSF.

Wolf had confided in him, but only because he and Wolf were good friends. "There is one other thing I want to tell you. It isn't only Major Wolf who has been kidnapped. With him was another friend of mine. His name is Alfred Swann. He is not a military man. He is a Scout."

"What makes him so important?"

"He has a high position in the Scout's hierarchy. I really can't tell you more."

"Any other people with them?"

"Yes, there are. An Anorian female, another Scout, and a civilian. It doesn't matter how many there are. Our mission is to free all of them."

"I understand."

Turnbull looked at the large clock on one wall, realizing they had spent over an hour talking. "It is almost time for supper. We'll end this session. Perhaps, we can do this again. I enjoyed getting to know you better."

She rose. "This meeting was quite informative. Thank you, for trusting me with all that information."

"That was only the beginning. I want to meet with all the team leaders every day for more briefings. There is a lot you don't know yet."

[12]

SEVEN DAYS LATER, THEY ARRIVED AT THE SPACEPORT OF GREATER YORK. Right on schedule. Their ship sat down on the tarmac without any difficulties, even though there was nobody there to guide them in. Something that wasn't actually necessary because there was no other traffic of incoming or outgoing ships.

Turnbull took Harris with him to report to the spaceport authorities. There wasn't much there. Just one lonely desk Sergeant by the name of Slovinsky. His name was on a nameplate on his desk.

When Turnbull and Harris walked in, he looked surprised.

"We didn't expect any military vessels," he said to Turnbull.

"A surprise visit," Turnbull commented.

"You are wearing a uniform."

"Why is that so unusual?"

"Because the last military officer that landed here didn't wear one. Neither did his companion. I remember her. She was an Anorian." He lowered his voice, even though there was nobody else in the room. "He told me in confidence that he was undercover."

"Are you talking about Major Wolf?"

Slovinsky's eyebrows went up. "Do you know him?"

Turnbull smiled. "Yes, I do."

"Are you also an undercover agent?"

"Actually, I am not. I'm the real thing. Let me introduce myself. I am Colonel Turnbull. I am officially taking command of this spaceport. This spaceport will be my command post. Starting right now, you will be my eyes and ears, and you will report to me personally anything that happens on this spaceport, Sergeant Slovinsky."

Slovinsky saluted. "Yes, sir, Colonel. I am honored to be under your command."

Registering the eagerness in the Sergeant's voice, Turnbull couldn't help but chuckle. "I don't mean every small thing that happens here. I'm talking about important things. Anything that involves security."

"I understand, Colonel Turnbull. I won't disappoint you."

"I'm sure you won't. I trust you. Dismissed."

Slovinsky saluted but kept standing like a rigid statue.

"Relax, Sergeant. At ease."

The Sergeant lost his rigid stance. "Thank you, sir. I mean Colonel. I must confess I'm not quite used to this military etiquette. The Freeland military is not very big on protocol."

"I am surprised to hear that. The military is all about rules and discipline. What are you big on?"

"Marching, singing, big band music, things like that. For instance, I am very good with my baton."

Turnbull frowned. "Are you using batons in combat?"

"I never got into a combat situation. It just doesn't happen. I swirl my baton. You know, throw it into the air and stuff like that." His pride could not be missed.

"How good are you with a real weapon? A rifle, for instance. Can you hit a target?"

Slovinsky shrugged. "I don't know. I'm good at swirling a rifle around, but I've never fired one. You need bullets for that."

"I don't think I understand. Are you saying you still use obsolete guns that fire bullets?"

"We use them, but like I said, we don't put bullets into them. First, we don't have any bullets and second there is no reason to do that. We are not feuding with the Sartans or the Sleer. We trade with them and that's all."

"Do you actually have an army in Freeland?"

"Oh, yes. There are about two thousand soldiers in our army. You should see the parades. They usually are a celebration the whole country enjoys. We sing, we dance, and we have wonderful feasts."

Turnbull looked at Harris. "Did you get all that, Sergeant?"

She nodded. "I did, but I have a problem processing it. If he is telling the truth, there are no wars on this planet. The army is made up of entertainers not soldiers. No wonder they can't defend their country. The way I see it, this planet is ripe for a takeover by anyone who wants it."

Turnbull nodded. "Your analysis hits the situation dead on. It seems we have a bigger job ahead of us than we expected." He turned back to Slovinsky. "How far is Windy Lake from here?"

"About one hour. It depends how fast you drive."

"You are talking about a ground-bound vehicle, I suppose?"

"Of course. What else is there?" Slovinsky smirked. "Unless you are using a horse-drawn wagon."

"Don't be an ass. I mean with one that travels in the air."

"Sorry. We don't have those."

Turnbull swallowed a curse word. "We do. You didn't really think we use vehicles that crawl on the ground?"

"I didn't think anything. The only ones that can fly here on Cerberus belong to the invaders."

Turnbull gave Slovinsky a hard look. "Prepare yourself for changes on this planet. I'm afraid the peace you've been enjoying is about to come to an end. Your army will have to trade batons, drums, and musical instruments for rifles and guns. Instead of dancing and singing, you will train in warfare and the use of real weapons that kill."

"Who would I want to kill?"

"Your enemies, Sergeant. You kill them before they kill you."

"But we don't have any enemies."

Turnbull sighed. "The enemy is at your doorstep, Sergeant Slovinsky. You just aren't aware of it. It's not only the aliens that have been plundering your cities. I'm talking about the ones that are stealing your natural resources and are planning to overthrow your government and taking over your country. But don't worry. We are here to stop them. It will come at a cost, but changes are inevitable."

Slovinsky's expression was a blank. It was obvious he had no idea what Turnbull was talking about. Turnbull almost felt sorry for him. For him and everyone on this planet. A storm would hit them with full force, and their lives were going to be thrown into turmoil.

"We'll be in touch, Sergeant Slovinsky." Turnbull tipped his hat.

"Weren't you a little tough with the man?" Harris commented when they were outside the building again. "You scared him half to death. He'll have nightmares."

Turnbull smiled grimly. "I meant what I said to him about changes. You and the other team leaders know what is waiting for us. Our first trip is to Scouts Base in Windy Lake to let them know about our arrival and our plans. They may have more information for us. More detailed information."

While Turnbull and Harris were at the customs office, the rest of the team had unloaded the six corvettes, the Shark, and the personal transport vehicle. All of them carried the symbol of the Solar Union. Turnbull meant to make their presence on Cerberus known.

A builder ship was scheduled to arrive within the week to erect a secure building with sleeping quarters, a kitchen, a mess hall, a communications center, and a common room for everyone to relax. Until then, they would live on the ship.

———

IT TOOK ABOUT TWENTY MINUTES FROM THE TIME THEY LEFT THE SPACEPORT until they landed in front of Scouts Base in Windy Lake.

Looking at the old two-storey house, Turnbull remarked, "Not very impressive. But then again, you can't expect much more from a Scouts' building. They enjoy the austere lifestyle."

After ringing the doorbell, the shabby-looking door opened and a man, dressed in the brown outfit of the Scouts, came out. Looking at Turnbull, who was wearing his uniform, he smiled and said, "You must be Colonel Turnbull. We received communication from Headquarters just a couple of days ago with details about your arrival on Cerberus." He held out his hand, "Welcome to our base. I am Scout Anderson."

Turnbull shook the offered hand. "Happy to be here. By the way, this is Sergeant Harris. She is my second in command."

Anderson gave Harris a friendly nod. "Please, come in, Sergeant Harris."

As they walked down a dimly lit corridor, Anderson chuckled and said, "We even put on our Scouts' uniforms today to make a better impression. We know how the military is obsessed with rank and uniforms."

He opened a door and invited them to enter. The room they stepped into was large, and brightly lit. Two of the four desks in the room were occupied. Both men wore their Scouts uniforms. The younger of the two even wore his hat.

The Scouts rose and came around their desks. "Welcome to our humble office, Colonel Turnbull," the dark-skinned man with the goatee said. "I am Master Scout Hadad."

"Honored to make your acquaintance," Turnbull said. "My companion is Sergeant Harris." He looked at the younger Scout and smiled. "You didn't really have to get all dressed up for us. Contrary to what you think about us, we don't always wear our uniforms. Basically, we are no different from the Scouts. I didn't catch your name."

"It's David Stavros." He smiled and took off his hat, revealing red hair cut in typical military style. "I didn't want you to think I'm a trooper who deserted his post and joined the Scouts."

Turnbull's laugh seemed to break the ice. Everyone relaxed. The older Scout took his seat again behind his desk. "Please, take a load of your legs and sit down."

"Thank you. I don't mind doing that." Turnbull sat down in one of the three chairs. Looking around, he said, "Judging by this chair, you do like to live in comfort."

Hadad chuckled behind his desk. "There seems to be some misconception about us Scouts. We are used to living in Spartan conditions, but we won't turn down comfort, either, if available." His dark eyes were full of mischief when he looked at Turnbull. "I've heard military men bragging too many times how tough they are and that they don't mind sleeping outside on the bare ground without a sleeping bag. Comforts of home are a luxury they easily can do without."

"Don't believe everything you hear. Troopers and Scouts alike will brag a little sometimes." Turnbull grinned and looked at Harris. "I have a feeling you might be corrupted by some of the things you will hear while we are in the company of these Scouts, Harris. I'm used to them. My best friend was a Scout."

"You're talking about Major Swann." Hadad's expression was suddenly serious. "He and Major Wolf have been kidnapped by the Arani, as you know. You also know that one of ours, Scout Ikeda, was with them. I assume you are here to find them."

"It is part of our mission, but only a part. We are here to turn things upside down on Cerberus. There is a lot we have to discuss. I was briefed with all the information we had about the situation here, but I am sure there is much more we need to know."

"You are right about that." Hadad gave Turnbull a grave look. "We have to set aside our differences, Colonel Turnbull. Let's forget about secrets and banned subjects. That's why it is important to share everything we know. There can be no holding back."

"I agree. We are here not only to rescue four humans and one Anorian. We are here to save a planet from being invaded by an enemy from the far side of the Galaxy and from being taken over by an enemy from within."

"You are talking about Hyperion Mineral Explorations." Hadad nodded solemnly. "Major Wolf gave us all the information needed to understand how grim the situation is. He told us about Alexander Amsterdam, the Ambassador from Hyperion. The Freelanders think he is a representative of Earth and the Solar Union. He also told us about the mines and the Lirsium Crystals they are mining. The last and final report we received from him and his group was many hours long. They recorded their conversations until the moment they were abducted. That's how we knew what happened to them. We know exactly where they were abducted and by whom. It wasn't HME but the aliens. Apparently, HME either have an alliance with the Arani or the Arani have taken over HME."

"Hyperion Mineral Explorations is merely a branch of Interstellar Research and Investment Conglomerate. However, that is not where it ends. IRIC is controlled by one of the most powerful Cartels," Turnbull said. "I can't imagine that the Arani have taken control of the Cartel."

"It wouldn't be an impossible assumption," Hadad mused, stroking his goatee. "What are your plans in the way of finding and rescuing the missing men? What about HME? Will you close down the mines? In a way, it would be a shame. From what Major Wolf told us, they mainly employ Tsakonians, or Sartans, as they call their race. They would be out of a job."

"Closing the mines won't be the first job on our agenda. That can wait. It would give away our plan. No, first we will visit the mine in Tsakona, where the team was abducted and take it from there."

Hadad nodded his approval. "That makes sense."

"Another thing I want to watch is the recording of the destruction the Arani caused here in Windy Lake. I want to get a good look at their aircraft and weapons."

"You will have to visit the local police station for that."

"That's what we'll do this afternoon. You're welcome to accompany us." Turnbull glanced at his companion. "There is something else before we do that. I believe I also speak for Sergeant Harris if I say I wouldn't mind having a bite to eat. Can you recommend I good eatery close by."

Hadad chuckled jovially. "I can. You are there already. We have a good cook. She can whip up a delicious meal in no time. Remember, we talked about comforts? Well, eating well is one of them. All of us enjoy good food. There is no better place for that than right here on the Base." He laughed. "It is one of our secrets we keep to ourselves. No need to broadcast it or, heavens forbid, report it to our Headquarters. After all, we're supposed to be Scouts and live simply. Eating only basic foods with no taste, or maybe just enough taste to keep us from throwing it out, is one of those simple things."

Turnbull grinned and winked with one eye. "Same goes for us troopers, but I've never turned down a good meal."

"I have a feeling we'll all get along just fine," Hadad said with a laugh.

He looked at Harris. "You've been awfully silent, Sergeant. Is the Major keeping you from talking?"

She shook her head and gave him a cautious smile. Glancing at Turnbull, she said, "Major Turnbull is not the kind of man who would give me such orders, unless security is at stake. That is not the case here. I've never been a big talker. I prefer to silently observe."

"It seems to me you are a perfect candidate for the Secret Service."

Her eyes were again on Turnbull. "I wouldn't turn it down if I should get the opportunity to join."

"Anything can happen in the military," Turnbull said. "Sometimes, an opportunity comes along out of the blue. Perhaps, I should phrase that differently. Nothing ever happens out of the blue. If someone in the top ranks has his or her focus on you, such an opportunity may arise. If it does and you really want it badly, you'll jump at it."

Hadad chuckled. "Is that some kind of prediction? A hint, maybe?"

With a glance at Harris, Turnbull just shook his head. "Don't read anything into that statement. It is only an observation. Possibly, because it happened to me."

"Are you among the upper brass?"

Turnbull laughed. "I'm a Colonel with the SPA."

"Sorry, I'm not familiar with all the different branches of the military. SPA stands for what?"

"Solar Protection Agency."

"Your friend, Major Wolf, told us in confidence that he is an agent with the Interstellar Secret Service. I'm sure you are aware of that."

Turnbull acknowledged it with a short nod. "The ISS. I know."

"All these different agencies in the military. Totally confusing. I couldn't keep up."

"I don't think anyone can," Turnbull agreed with Hadad's observation.

"It isn't any wonder that it always takes so long for the military to act. Too many agencies, branches, departments, and ranks. It is much simpler with the Scouts. We are just that—Scouts."

"Except for Scouts Security," Turnbull said.

"You know about that?"

"Yes, I do. In fact, I received most of my information from Colonel Stonewall, the head of Scouts Security."

Hadad slapped his hand onto his forehead. "Of course, you would know that. After all, your friend, Major Swann, is a member of Scouts Security."

"I did not know that about him until I had the talk with Colonel Stonewall. Major Swann and I are good friends, but he never confided in me about that." Turnbull smiled. "Even the Scouts don't tell all."

"Touché." Hadad sighed. "Sad, in a way. To keep secrets and to hide your true identity is almost a form of lying." He looked at Harris. "So, think about that, young lady, should you get invited to join one of these secret branches. You may have to give up part of your soul as collateral."

"So far, I haven't had the opportunity to choose my future career." She lifted her shoulders. "I won't worry about that until it happens. If it ever does."

"I'm sure it will." Hadad clapped his hands together. "Now, let's see about that food."

———

NOBODY SAID MUCH AS THEY WATCHED THE EVENTS UNFOLDING ON THE screen. When the screen went dark, Turnbull just grunted.

"That bright light you saw was the moment Corporal Horinder died," Chief Dubois said.

"I'm sorry to hear that. Many people died in that explosion. These invaders sure are ruthless. By the way, they call themselves Arani, in case you didn't know."

"I didn't," the Chief admitted.

"What I can deduce from this recording is important. They definitely are males, and they do look uncannily like Anorians. They are technologically highly advanced. They use laser rifles, and they have vessels capable of flying at high speeds. We cannot underestimate them."

"We made that mistake. I'm sure you know that we had them in our jail, but they escaped with the help of another group of Arani. They killed our secretary at that time."

"I read the report, Chief Dubois. From what I saw on this recording, these people show no mercy. We'll remember that when we run across them. I'll promise you that." Turnbull clenched his fists. "Watching this recording makes me angry and anxious to start my investigation. The lives of our friends and colleagues are at stake."

"Are you sure they are still alive?"

"Nothing is for sure. We just have to hope. If they are dead..." Turnbull didn't finish the sentence. He didn't want to think about that possibility. Should the unimaginable have happened, there would be hell to pay. Those Arani would regret the day they stepped out of the portal onto this planet. If he had to blow up that whole damn portal, he would. He would hunt down every last one of them until there was no trace left of them on Cerberus.

Of course, first they had to find the location of that portal.

"They are alive, Colonel," Harris said beside him. "You just have to believe that."

Turnbull relaxed. "You are right, of course," he growled. "We won't accept anything else. Let's go, Sergeant, and map out our next steps. We'll say our good-byes to the Scouts and then we'll head on back to the base."

[13]

TURNBULL DECIDED TO TAKE THE SHARK WITH SERGEANT HARRIS AND three women from her team to accompany him in the Shark. There was no special reason he chose Specialist Beverly Thompson and Specialist Lena Nakamura to take control of the guns. He chose the fourth member of the team, Specialist Sonia Lopez, to be the pilot. It seemed natural to take the women, since Sergeant Harris was also a woman and she and the three women in her team had already formed a bond.

For this first mission, he paired Sergeant Jones and Specialist Hassan for one Corvette and Specialist Garcia with Specialist Ahmed for the second Corvette.

The other four members of the squad were left on standby back at the base, which, for now still was the ship.

They had the co-ordinates of the mine where Wolf and his group had been abducted.

Turnbull wasn't worried about being spotted by the enemy as they approached the mine. Until now there had been no air travel on Cerberus, and the Arani might wonder about the sudden traffic in the air, but there was a good chance they would not be overly concerned. Wolf and the others had been captured so easily. Another nosy visitor would be dealt with in the same manner.

Turnbull was determined to prove them wrong. This time, he would be the one taking prisoners.

Should they be spotted and attacked, nothing could penetrate the thick and armored shell of the Shark, unless the enemy was in possession of weapons more advanced than what any race in this part of the Galaxy could throw at each other.

Finding the mine was fairly easy. Whoever owned it now hadn't tried to hide it from prying eyes that may approach from the air. A good omen.

The Shark circled the mine area a couple of times, while the two Corvettes hung back, ready to appear should the need arise. Lopez set down the Shark a safe distance from the two buildings near the entrance to the mine.

"Sergeant Harris and Lopez, you will come with me. Thompson and Nakamura, you stay in the Shark. Don't leave your positions behind the guns. Do nothing on your own but be ready to follow any command I give you, even if I tell you to level the buildings. No matter what."

"Understood, sir," both women said at the same time.

Turnbull knew he could trust them.

Harris and Lopez walked on either side of him. They carried their weapons openly as they approached the bigger building. Before they reached it, the door opened, and a man came out. He wore a uniform with a shiny metal shield on his chest. He was armed with a laser rifle, a weapon banned on Cerberus.

"Don't come any closer," he warned them.

Turnbull gave him his best smile. "Or what? Are you going to shoot us?"

"I didn't say that. You are the second bunch of intruders. This is private property. Best turn around and leave as quickly as you can. I cannot guarantee your safety."

"Neither can we guarantee yours should we be attacked by anyone."

"There is nobody else here. I'm alone."

"You're sure? There is nobody in that sleek building behind yours? That building doesn't appear to be something built by humans. Who owns this mine?"

"I didn't say this is a mine."

"No, you didn't. We know it is a mine. An illegal mine, at that. Owned by Hyperion Mineral Explorations. We are here to close it down. But first, something else. You said we are the second group coming here. What happened to the other group?"

"They were taken prisoner. Unless you want the same thing to happen to you, I urge you to leave before it's too late. I have no control over this."

"Are there others in the guardhouse?"

"No, I'm alone."

Before Turnbull could say more, two large figures, carrying rifles, came out of the other building. Turnbull noted that they were larger in life than they appeared to be on the hologram they had watched. It was easy to see how they could be mistaken for male Anorians. When they saw Turnbull and the two women, they lifted their weapons. "You are trespassing," one of them said in accent-free Inglis.

"We are here to free the five people you are keeping prisoner," Turnbull said.

"They are not here."

"Then you'd better tell us where they are."

The second Arani laughed. "You are not in a position to make any demands. You might as well drop your weapons. You are our prisoners."

It was Turnbull's turn to laugh. "You have that wrong. Do you see that aircraft parked behind us? I have two troopers aiming their guns at you. We are taking you prisoner."

The Arani pointed at the sky. "I don't believe so. Watch."

Turnbull turned just in time to see a blinding bolt of lightning from the alien craft hit their vessel.

"Corvette One and Two. We are under attack," Turnbull barked.

"We are on it," came the answer.

Moments later the two corvettes came streaking from behind the monoliths they'd been hiding. They shot into the air, circling the alien vessel like a couple of hornets, firing one bolt each. Both bolts hit their target. The alien vessel imploded, leaving only a fading bright after-image in the air.

Turnbull had not wasted the time. While the two aliens were preoccupied watching the display in the air, he drew his stun gun and fired it. The two Arani toppled unconscious to the ground where they stood.

"I told them we'd be taking them prisoner, but they didn't believe me," he said to the human guard, who seemed frozen to his spot.

"There will be hell to pay for what you are doing. You won't get away with this, whoever you are," the guard warned them.

"This is just the beginning. The only ones paying for what is happening on this planet will be your new friends and the company you work for. We are the force that will set things right on this planet." Turnbull said. "By the way, you are also under arrest."

"I did nothing wrong," the guard protested. "I only work for the company."

"Yes, you do, but you should be aware that it is illegal to mine Lirsium Crystals, Rhodium, and Iridium on any planet without the permission of the High Senate. Your company doesn't have that permission."

"I have nothing to do with permits and permissions. I am a citizen of Hyperion and I only have to follow the laws of my home planet."

"You are correct, but that only applies when you live on your home planet. You are on Cerberus, which means, you have to follow the laws of Cerberus. The law of Cerberus is clear in that it states no mining or other activity is allowed without the special permission of either Freeland or Tsakona. Your company doesn't have that. In reality, you are breaking two separate laws. The law of Tsacona and the law of the High Senate." Turnbull was watching the guard. He may just be stupid enough to do something foolish. "Throw down your rifle, which by the way is also illegal on Cerberus, and give yourself up. I'm warning you, don't do anything you surely will regret."

The guard threw a glance at the two unmoving aliens lying on the ground. "Are they dead?"

"No, only unconscious, because we need to interrogate them. However, it is different with you. We don't need you and we will surely kill you, should you give us a reason." He turned to Lopez. "Disarm him and cuff him. I'll check up on those two."

He knew he didn't have to worry about the human guard. He also knew that they would let him go free after getting back to base. He was just a small fish, and they couldn't be bothered with him. Walking over to the two unconscious Arani, he tied their wrists behind their backs and put their legs into a magnetic hold. Then he wrapped a band around their heads that would keep them unconscious until the band was removed. They weren't going anywhere for some time.

"We have company," Harris called behind him.

He swung around, bringing up his rifle, just in time to see an aircraft landing not far away from them. Before it touched the uneven ground, four telescopic rods unfolded under its belly, like the thin legs of a large insect.

The Solar Union craft were egg-shaped and smooth-looking, with flat bottoms. They floated on an energy field, making support struts unnecessary. The Anorian ships on the other hand were designed to look like large bugs. Not streamlined at all. Probably to intimidate a potential enemy. Obviously, Turnbull didn't have a clue.

Lowering his rifle, he said into his communicator, "Take no action. That's an Anorian war craft."

An opening appeared in the side of the aircraft and half a dozen figures spilled out. Dressed in green army fatigues, they were armed with long rifles, but of different design than the ones the humans used. No less lethal, though.

He knew they would all be females. In Anorian society, the females were the dominant gender. Usually, they walked around naked, but not when on a mission.

He watched them coming closer. In a way, he was not surprised to see them. In fact, he had expected to find them already on Cerberus when he and his team landed at the spaceport.

When they were close, one of them walked up to Turnbull. He noticed a black band around her left upper arm, a band the others were missing. "I am Captain Ranini of the Anorian Space Force. We came here to assist you in the search for your missing team. As you surely know, one of ours is among the team that has been kidnapped by the Arani." Her Inglis was impeccable.

Turnbull nodded. "I am Colonel Turnbull of the Solar Protection

Agency. We don't really need any help, but we won't refuse it either. As long as you are willing to collaborate with us."

"We will, up to a point." She looked at the two unconscious Arani. "I see you have captured two of the enemy. What are your plans for them?"

"We will interrogate them. How did you know where to find us?"

"Our agent sent us a distress call. In fact, it is still broadcasting."

Turnbull gave her a perplexed look. "From where?"

She smiled. Then she pointed at one of the ground vehicles parked against the mountain. "From the inside of one of those."

Turnbull followed her pointing arm. He had seen those vehicles, but never gave them a second look or thought. One of them must be the one Wolf and the others had used to drive to this mine. "I admit, I was not aware of that. We had the coordinates to this mine, of course, but had not been informed that the distress signal was still alive."

"You couldn't have known about it, because it broadcasts on a frequency you probably are not monitoring." She looked to the entrance to the mountain. "Have you been inside the mine?"

"No, we haven't. That was our next task."

"We will come with you. There may be more of the enemy inside."

"You are welcome to join us, but before we leave, I have to contact my team."

"Of course. We wait."

He turned and spoke into his communicator. "Thompson and Naka-mura, leave your stations and join me. Corvette One and Two, stay alert and watch for company."

"Aye, aye, sir."

Moments later, the two women left the Shark and rushed toward them. Both carried their rifles.

With one last look at their human prisoner lying on the ground, complaining about being tied up, Turnbull, his team of four troopers, and the six Anorians walked into the entrance to the mine.

The tunnel was high and wide enough for trucks and other equip-ment to drive in. The width of the tunnel allowed them to walk four abreast.

Turnbull sent Specialist Thompson and one Anorian ahead to scout the way and alert the group of any possible danger.

He and Harris and two Anorians walked in the first full line. Behind them humans and Anorians walked in loose formation. They left plenty of room between each other to be an effective force.

Artificial suns mounted on the ceiling at certain intervals lit up the tunnel. The floor of the tunnel was littered with crushed rocks, which made it somewhat treacherous to walk on.

They didn't know how deep the tunnel was before they would come across any miners and, surely, their supervisors. They could be human or Arani. Most likely both. All five humans and the six Anorians walked in silence, watchful for any movement, their weapons ready to be used in an instant should danger threaten them.

As they walked, Turnbull realized that he was the only male in the group. All others were females.

The Anorians appeared to be relaxed, but he knew it to be a false impression. He didn't miss the way they scanned their surroundings and the way they held their weapons. However, he was secure in his knowledge that his team of four was in no way less competent. He had watched all of the teams going through their exercises and he was satisfied that all of them were proficient in the use of weapons and combat.

They had almost reached a sharp bend in the tunnel, when the Anorian ahead of Turnbull froze and lifted one arm. They all stopped moving and listened. Turnbull became aware of sounds coming from around the corner.

Ranini, the captain of the Anorian, team turned to Turnbull. "We should stay back and let the two scouts go ahead to investigate."

"I fully agree," Turnbull said. He nodded to Thompson, who looked at him expectantly. "Be careful and take no chances," he told her. "And don't engage. Come back to report."

He heard Ranini giving similar instructions to her team member.

Moments later, Thompson spoke to him over the communicator behind his ear. "There is a huge cave with lots of equipment. Further down is a row of what appears to be small houses. To the right, not too far from us, is a guardhouse and on the left side of the cave is an alien-looking contraption, fairly large. It could be living quarters for the Arani. Beside it stands one of their airships. It is smaller than the one we shot down, but clearly an airship."

"Do you see anyone? Human or alien?"

"No. All seems quiet."

Turnbull walked over to Ranini. "What do you suggest we do?" It was just a curtesy question. There was only one thing to do and that was going into the cave and flushing out either the humans or the aliens. Most likely both. There was no way to know how many they would come across. They had the element of surprise on their side, but they had to move fast.

"We'll have to split up," he suggested to the Anorian leader. "Each of us can either take our own team or we can mix them up. What do you want to do?"

She didn't take long to make up her mind. A good sign of her leadership. "We'll split up and exchange soldiers. It will be more effective, especially if we meet either humans or Arani."

"I agree." He spoke into his communicator. "Lopez and Nakamura. You stay with the Anorian team."

He watched as three Anorian troopers came over to his side, while Lopez and Nakamura went to the other side.

Both groups began to move ahead.

The first thing Turnbull registered as they rounded the corner was the building on the left wall. Thompson had described it as an alien-looking contraption. Her description was dead on. This had not been designed by a human architect, but it was obviously some kind of habitat, which meant the Arani were here to stay for the long haul. A plan Turnbull was going to cancel.

In the center of the cave were a number of huge machines connected by wide, moving belts. Obviously, machines crushing the ore and extracting the minerals being mined. The noises coming from them were quite loud, leaving no doubt that they were in service.

The guardhouse on the right side was fairly large. Not just a guardhouse, Turnbull deducted. It looked more like a housing complex, most likely where the guards and supervisors lived when they didn't work.

Looking straight ahead at the row of smaller units, he was willing to guess that those were living quarters for the miners. They would not be Earth humans but citizens of Tsakona. He knew from the report Wolf had provided that the Hyperion Mineral Explorations employed Sartans. They, in all likelihood, were cheap labour.

Even though darkness was the natural condition in the cave, with the artificial lights they would follow the rhythm outside. The living units should be unoccupied right now.

He and his team were heading for the guardhouse while the Ranini and her team were going to check out the alien building. There was a good chance it would be empty as well, but they still needed to be cautious.

As Turnbull's team closed in on the guardhouse, a door opened, and a man stepped out. Like the guard outside the cave, he wore a uniform. He also was armed with a rifle, which he pointed at Turnbull. "Stop right there!" he shouted. "You are invading private property."

"You've got that wrong," Turnbull said in an equally loud voice. "It is you and your company that is trespassing on private property. Now, lower that weapon of yours and put it on the ground. Do you really think you will survive a firefight with us? We are trained soldiers, which means you have as much chance as an ice cube in a hot oven to walk away alive."

"What gives you the right to do this?" he challenged them without lowering his laser rifle.

"I am Colonel Turnbull of the Solar Protection Agency, which means I am the law, and I have every right to do this. Now, I have no time to waste on chit-chat. Throw down your weapon or get fried. Your choice," he said sharply.

With visible reluctance, the guard laid his rifle down carefully, as if he were afraid it might break if he mishandled it. "If you put it that way," he grumbled. "I never meant to use it in the first place."

"Then you shouldn't have aimed it at us, you moron. You're lucky none of us is trigger-happy. How many guards are in the house?"

"I'm the only one." The guard shrugged. "We've never had reason to even post a watch. I mean, who comes here but the bosses?"

"Well, you never know. We came. How many workers are servicing the machines over there?"

"None. Everything is automatic."

"How many guards or supervisors are in the mine watching the workers?"

"Eight altogether."

"What about those aliens?"

The guard made a face. "Right now, there are only six of them. Usually, there are more. They just showed up one day and told us that they'll be taking over. To tell you the truth, none of us are happy with having them around. They act as if they own the place."

"What did your bosses say?"

"They told us that the aliens are partners in the company, and we should treat them as such."

Turnbull turned to Harris. "As we suspected. They've infiltrated that company. We don't know how far up their reach is. Time to put an end to this cozy arrangement."

Ranini's team had joined them in the meantime.

"We found nothing in that building. It clearly is used as living quarters," the Anorian captain reported. "The noisy machines in the center of the cave are processing the ore they are mining. Nobody is there. I wouldn't mind checking out the units ahead."

"Same here," Turnbull agreed. "I'm quite positive that's where the workers live."

The group made their way to the row of units at the other end of the cave. They were near the entrance to another tunnel. As Turnbull had stated, the units were living quarters. When they entered one it was obvious each unit was just large enough to hold four beds. They saw one larger building. When they checked that one out, it was easy to see that it was the dining area. The aroma of food being prepared wafted into the dining room, and it wasn't difficult to find the kitchen. The two people working in the kitchen didn't even see Turnbull and his team until all five of them had entered it. The Anorian troopers were still in the dining room.

One of the cooks looked up from what he was doing, saw Turnbull and froze.

"Don't mind us," Turnbull said with a smile. "We are just checking out things. What's for supper?"

"Boiled tubers and fried fungus," the cook answered without thinking. Then he looked past Turnbull and saw two Anorians coming into the kitchen. "What are they doing in here?"

"They will join us for supper." Turnbull grinned jovially, almost feeling sorry for the man, knowing he would be responsible for the cook losing his job. He became sombre. "You are the only two in the kitchen?"

The cook nodded, suddenly realizing that this was not a social call. "Those soldiers don't look like the others. Are you another interested group to take over this mine?"

"Actually, we are not. I am Colonel Turnbull with the Solar Protection Agency, and we are here to shut down this place."

"Why? What's wrong with it?"

"Everything. The company you are working for is mining minerals that are on the prohibited list. They can only be mined with the approval of the High Senate. Your company doesn't have the permits for that and therefor it is here illegally. You are here illegally."

"I...I didn't know that." He spoke haltingly. "What is going to happen to me?" He looked at the other cook. He was just a young man, and he looked scared. "What about my son? He is innocent, too."

"We are not after you. I'm sure things will work out. If you cooperate, we might just be able to put in a good word for you."

"Anything. What do you need?"

"There are two tunnels on this side of the cave. Which one leads to the mines?"

"Don't bother with the far one. It won't lead anywhere. At least, that's not the one they are using. Use the closest one. It'll take you to the next cave." The cook spread his fingers. "I'm just the cook here and not too familiar with the location of all the mines. If you follow the tunnel, it will lead you to the mines."

"Alright." Turnbull turned to address the other members of his team but looked at Ranini, the Anorian leader. "You heard him. We'll follow that tunnel. It'll lead us to the mines. We don't know how long the miners work. I'd like to surprise them before they quit and come back here. If the guard told us the truth, we should expect eight other guards, possibly supervisors, and six Arani. We don't have to worry about the workers, the Sartans. The human guards won't give us any trouble, either. From what we saw, they are not soldiers and won't risk their lives to fight us. The aliens are another matter. I'm inclined to suggest we kill them on sight."

"I don't agree," Ranini objected. "I want to take at least one of them prisoner. We need to get information from them, like what happened to the other team. Where did they take them? Are they still alive? And most importantly, we need to find out where this portal is located."

"Alright, even though we already have two prisoners," Turnbull remarked.

"Yes, you do, but they are yours, not ours." Ranini's smile was almost feral. "Our interrogation tactics differ from yours. Humans are much too soft when it comes to gather information from prisoners."

"How do you know?"

Her reptilian eyes were cold when she looked at him. "From personal experience. I was taken prisoner once by a human criminal gang that tried to raid a village on one of our colonies. They tortured me, even raped me, during their interrogation. They got nothing from me except false information, which led to them being captured. None of them survived."

"I'm sorry to hear about your ordeal, but your captors were criminals, and from what you are telling me not even good ones. I am a special kind of soldier. I am trained to withstand torture and at the same time, I have no problem putting the squeeze on a prisoner to get information."

Her smile mocked him. "I doubt that you'd get any information from me."

"Don't be so sure." He looked at the entrance to the tunnel. "I think we should get going."

[14]

THE NEW TUNNEL WAS EVEN HIGHER AND WIDER THAN THE ONE THAT LED outside. The evidence of rock being mined was everywhere. Small and large rocks covered the floor. Turnbull bent to examine one of the rocks. There were streaks of some kind of mineral embedded in the rock, but he didn't know what to look for.

"Find anything interesting?" Harris asked.

He flung the rock away with the words, "I don't know. I'm not a geologist."

They walked again in loose formation, leaving enough space between them to move if the need should arise. The sound of machines, explosions, and falling rocks came down the tunnel from ahead. Turnbull knew it wouldn't be long before they would come across miners and their equipment.

He was surprised they hadn't met any guards or lookouts. It was obvious that whoever was in charge of security didn't worry about anyone coming down the tunnel. No living person intercepted them. He doubted that they had installed electronic surveillance cameras or alarms.

When they finally ran across someone, it was one lonely guard sitting on a chair in front of a small guardhouse, playing some kind of electronic game he had on his lap. He was concentrating so much on his game he didn't notice Turnbull until it was too late. Turnbull poked him in the shoulder with the barrel of his rifle to get his attention.

The guard looked up from his game and stared at Turnbull, an annoyed expression on his bored face. Then he saw the rest of the soldiers. He tried to jump up and reach for the rifle on the floor beside him, but Turnbull had his hand on his shoulder and kept him in his seat.

"What is the meaning of this?" the guard croaked, clearly not quite comprehending the situation.

"What does it look like?" Turnbull was amused by the guard's reaction. This guy was in the wrong profession. Being a guard wasn't one of them. Hopefully, the rest of them were like him. This mission would be over in a short time.

"You're not supposed to be here. Even employees of the company can't come here without proper clearance. If I let you pass, I'll get fired."

Turnbull had to give him credit for standing his ground. He was stubborn and wasn't going to cave in without a complaint. "We don't need clearance. If I were you, I wouldn't worry about being fired. Your cushy job ends right now because there won't be anybody around to fire you. We're closing this mine, and Hyperion Mineral Explorations won't exist once we are done on this planet."

The guard actually laughed. "You'll never leave this mine alive. We have powerful friends. They'll crush you like a bunch of annoying beetles."

"Talking about your powerful friends. How many Arani are in here? Where are they hiding?"

"I'm not telling. Just keep on going and you'll find them."

Turnbull was getting impatient. He had underestimated this guy. He yanked him out of the seat and, holding him by his collar, pulled him close. "If you think we are playing a game here, think again. I'll give you thirty seconds to give me the information I want."

"Or else?" the guard sneered and spit into Turnbull's face.

Losing his patience, Turnbull kneed him between his legs. The guard gave a loud shout, surprised by Turnbull's reaction, and collapsed. Pulling him up, Turnbull held him in a tight grip and snarled, "Another stunt like that and I'll break your neck. Don't believe for one minute that this an empty threat. I'm a trained killer and so is every member of my squad. Now—talk!"

Supressing a moan, the guard said, "This tunnel leads into another, smaller cave. They are in one of the side tunnels by the Rhodium mine. There are six of them. All six are heavily armed and they are as mean as can be." He moaned deeply. "I'm hurt badly. I think you crushed my balls."

Turnbull gave him a push that landed him on the floor. "You're lucky that's all I crushed. Usually, I am not that gentle. How many human guards are there? And don't tell me you are the only one."

"There are eight of us, only three are actual guards. The other five are supervisors. I am here. Another guard and three supervisors are in the tunnel to the right. That's where we mine Iridium deposits. Heller, Manny, and Ron are in the tunnel in the middle. Ron is the guard. That cave is a little further away. We mine Lirsium crystals there."

"Are they armed?"

"Yes."

"All of them? Even the supervisors?"

"Yes, even the supervisors, but they only have stun guns."

"The guards?" Turnbull wasn't taking any chances.

The guard gave him a questioning look. "Rifles, of course."

"Lasers?"

"No. The Arani have them, but we don't. Our rifles fire projectiles." He sat up and moaned. "I'm hurting, you know. Did you have to kick me so hard?"

"You have only yourself to blame. Be thankful you are alive. You might not be or, possibly, hurt worse had I let the Anorians deal with you. By the way, what is your name? Even though we had a misunderstanding in the beginning, you've been helpful in the end. I'll make sure you'll get a fair trial."

"A trial?"

"Yes, a trial. You're under arrest, but that is only a formality. I need your name to make sure you'll be treated fairly."

"It's Ryan. I still don't understand about a trial." He moaned again. "I think I need a doctor."

"The pain will pass. Just give it some time." Turnbull gave him an encouraging smile. He turned away and looked at Ranini. "We have three tunnels. Do you want to take the ones with the human guards? Or do you want to tackle the Arani?"

"There is no question. I'll take the one with the Arani. We'll show them what Anorian females can do," she said savagely. "They are putting our whole race into a position we do not appreciate. We are trying hard to live in harmony with everyone. We do not want to create strife or resentment toward us in other races, especially not with the humans."

"Never fear, we know that. We value our association with the Anorians. Humans feel exactly the way you do. We strive to avoid any conflict, not only with the Anorians but with all the other races. War has never resolved anything. Unfortunately, sometimes war is unavoidable. There always is somebody who stirs up trouble."

"Let's hope we can deal with these troublemakers and put them in their place as quickly as possible. Oh, before we leave, I want my three soldiers back in my team." She smiled. "I'm not saying that your soldiers are not capable. I would just feel more confident with my own." Ranini seemed impatient to get going.

"Alright, you can have them. Let's just get on with it. Be careful and don't take any chances," he warned her. "Don't underestimate them. It seems to me you are feeling overconfident."

Her laugh was without humor. "We are not afraid of them just because they are males. They may call themselves Arani. We have the same ancestors, and they went a different route on the far side of the Galaxy. Basically, we share the same genes. In our species, the females are the more savage gender. We will prove that today."

"Overconfident, as I said," Turnbull insisted. "Perhaps, we should be the ones facing them and you deal with the humans."

"Out of the question!" She seemed offended. "We will deal with those males. Don't worry. We will be victorious. You just make sure you don't run into any trouble with your group."

"I don't expect any problems. The supervisors carry stunners only, and they are not soldiers. The guards have only primitive weapons, which they may not even know how to use. The Arani, on the other hand, have energy weapons, and they are fighters and therefor dangerous. Be careful, please."

Her face softened. "I will. You worry too much." She lifted an arm and gave her team the signal to get moving.

Shaking his head, Turnbull watched them disappear in the tunnel. "Good luck," he murmured. Then he turned to his own team. "Same advice I gave her goes for you. I don't want heroes. Stay alert and alive and don't underestimate the enemy. Let's go."

They chose the tunnel that would lead to the Iridium mine. According to the information, there should be only one guard and three supervisors. If the information was correct. Turnbull never took anything for granted. He didn't expect any trouble, but to be careless and overconfident could be a deadly mistake.

As it turned out, Ryan had told them the truth. This time, the guard saw them coming. He raised his rifle and fired a warning shot. The sound of the shot echoed through the tunnel. "Not one step closer, whoever you are. Nobody gets past me. There is danger ahead, and I'm responsible for the safety of everyone in this mine."

Turnbull detected the quaver in the guard's voice and signaled his team to stand down. There was no reason for bloodshed. Not yet anyway. "You are a brave man, but don't be stupid. You are one man with a primitive rifle. We are five soldiers with energy rifles. How long do you think you will last if we attack?"

"Why are you here and how did you get past Ryan?"

"We are the new law on this planet. I am Colonel Turnbull, and this is my team of trained soldiers. We are here to shut down this mine. Anyone standing in our way will be terminated. As for getting past Ryan? He tried to play the tough guy. Next time you see him, ask him about his balls." Turnbull chuckled. "Unless you want to find out firsthand how we deal with tough guys. It might be the last thing you do in your life. We are not on a charity drive. The choice is yours."

The guard lowered his rifle. "They don't pay me enough to deal with this crap. I give up."

"Smart decision. Click on the safety on your rifle and put it onto the ground. Gently. We don't want it to discharge accidently and kill someone. These primitive weapons are dangerous that way."

Turnbull sent one of his team to pick up the discarded rifle. Just another small part of being on the cautious side. It was remotely possible the guard might change his mind and try to use his weapon.

Even though, he didn't expect any resistance from the three supervisors, he and his team walked on, alert, and watchful. The cave at the end of the tunnel was larger than Turnbull had expected. From the high ceiling hung stalactites that glistened in the light of the artificial suns. The noise from the machines processing the excavated rocks was deafening and made conversing difficult. All along the outside perimeter of the cave, men wearing yellow coveralls were attacking the walls with picks and jackhammers, which added to the racket.

Fortunately, Turnbull and the members of his team were outfitted with communication devices.

"Locate the three supervisors," he ordered the others. "Approach with caution. Remember, they carry stun-guns."

It didn't take long, before all three were subdued and restrained. Because of the noisy environment, they never realized they were being invaded until it was too late. They complained fiercely, but Turnbull didn't feel like wasting time listening to their objections.

He estimated there had to be at least thirty Sartans spread along the walls. Some worked solo and some worked in small groups.

There was no easy way to make the Sartans aware of their presence because of the noise the machines made, so Turnbull decided to free one of the supervisors and get him to shut down the machines. It took a few minutes to get all the machines to stop working. The sudden silence must have startled the Sartans. They probably wondered if something was wrong. All of them stopped working and looked around.

When they saw five people in uniforms different from the uniforms the guards and supervisors wore, they surely realized that something was happening.

Turnbull approached the largest group of Sartans while his four troopers stood watching. The Sartans shouldn't present any danger, but military people are trained to be suspicious of everyone and everything. One mistake can make the difference between life and death.

"Do you speak Inglis?" he asked.

"I do," one of them said.

"I speak a little but understand most," another one revealed.

"Okay. Then you can translate to the others. I am Colonel Turnbull, and this is my team of troopers. We represent the Solar Union. We are here to shut down this mine because the company that extracts these minerals is doing so illegally. This mine, with everything it contains, belongs to your people. The company that is removing the minerals is stealing them from you."

At first, he was met with silence. Then one man held up his hand. "Does this mean we a losing our job?"

"I'm afraid so. You are free to go."

"Where would we go now?"

"You can go home to your families, to the jobs you held before you started working for Hyperion Mineral Explorations."

More of the workers had gathered around, curious what this was all about. One of the newcomers shouted, "They gave us an opportunity to earn a living for ourselves and our families. I have a farm, but my land is not producing enough to feed my family. The priest's warriors come and take most of what we grow. I can hide the money I get paid and use it to buy things from Freeland. My family lives well. What do you suggest we do after you close the mine?"

Turnbull didn't know how to answer the man. His question was a valid one. Obviously, this was something that needed to be worked out. Sergeant Harris stood suddenly beside Turnbull.

"I have an idea, Colonel," she said.

"Go ahead, Sergeant."

"This is a working mine, and it produces valuable minerals that are urgently needed. Why doesn't the High Senate work something out with the Kings or Priests that rule Tsakona and gives the contract to a legitimate company? This way these people wouldn't lose their livelihood. They could even hire the guards and supervisors that run this mine. It would make it legal and there would be no losers."

"Except for Hyperion Mineral Explorations and the Cartels that rob Cerberus now," Turnbull said. "I like the idea. You might just have something valid to think about."

"Thank you, Colonel."

He turned back to the miners. "Don't give up hope. I have the authority to decide what will happen. None of you will be abandoned, I promise you that. You will be compensated generously for the time you will be waiting until what is going to happen to this mine has been resolved."

"How long will that take and where will we stay in the meantime while we wait?"

"You will stay right here. You have living quarters, and we'll make sure you have enough food. How long will it take? I don't know, but I will do my best to make it happen quickly."

There was a pause while the ones that understood him explained it to the others.

"What about the Arani? Won't they be a problem? They have claimed this mine, and they will fight. Can you defeat them? Do you have better weapons?"

"We can and will defeat them. That is one of the reasons we are here. We are not alone in this fight. There are other races out there, and they will help us."

"We should check on the Anorians," Harris advised him. "They may need our help."

"Alright. We're done here. Let's go and see how our new allies are doing."

They hadn't walked far into the tunnel that led to the other mine, when they saw the bright flashes of energy weapons being discharged. "As I warned Ranini," Turnbull said, "they are facing professional fighters. They won't give up easily. It is six against six. The odds are even."

They approached the battle scene cautiously. It was dark in the tunnel. Somebody had taken out the artificial suns on the ceiling. The only illumination came from the streaks of lightening. Turnbull switched on his headlamps. His team did the same.

They found the Anorians crouching behind large boulders and hiding in the protection of deep fissures in the tunnel walls, barely wide enough to provide enough cover. He saw a lifeless body lying on the ground. One of the Anorians. It was obvious to Turnbull the Arani had the Anorian team boxed in.

Turnbull spotted Ranini hunkered down behind one of the boulders. He shut off his headlamp to prevent making himself a visible target. It seemed there was a temporary lull in the barrage of lightning bolts the Arani threw at the Anorians. Covered by the blanket of sudden darkness, Turnbull sprinted to the boulder Ranini used to hide behind. He barely made it before the Arani began their bombardment again.

"What's your status?" he inquired.

"Poor," Ranini responded. I've lost two of my soldiers. They took us by surprise. They must have had a warning system installed at the entrance of the tunnel. How about you?"

"As expected, we didn't run into any problems. The human guards and supervisors had no reason to put their lives on the line for a company that was on the way out."

"Glad to hear." She chuckled. "Perhaps I should have chosen the mine with the human guards and let you deal with the Arani."

Even though he knew she could not see his face, he smiled grimly. "I gave you the choice."

"I know you did, but I still believe I made the right choice. There really was no other choice. I admit, we were careless. I should have heeded your warning. What do you suggest we do next?"

"Obviously, they have us pinned down. They have the advantage. We can't get any closer without any casualties. I won't take that chance. What kind of weapons do you have?"

"Rifles and personal weapons for close combat."

"Useless in this case, but not all is lost. We have come prepared." He shrugged out of his backpack and turned on his headlamp, switching it to low. Rummaging around in his pack, he removed a couple of oval objects. "These are stun-eggs. They have two functions. They will light up the area like two mini suns, blinding anyone not taking proper precautions. They'll also explode at the same time. Everybody within range will be stunned into unconsciousness and stay that way for quite a while. All we have to do is pick them up."

"Sounds simple enough."

"It is." He chuckled. "Or it should be. We only have to make sure we are not too close. Otherwise, we'll be joining the enemy in their unconscious state."

"Not desirable," she agreed. "Are you sure we are far enough away?"

"I'm sure. I'll have to notify my team to be prepared. I suggest you do the same. I will let you know before I throw the eggs."

She nodded. "Go ahead."

"Attention, Alpha One. We have no other choice but to stun the enemy. Be ready for my warning. Acknowledge."

After the four troopers replied, he put on his goggles. Taking one of the eggs, he called, "Now," and threw the egg as far as he could.

Even though he wore protective goggles, he still didn't look directly in the direction he had thrown. The tunnel was suddenly brighter than any mini sun could achieve. It was like looking into the heart of a sun. There was no sound. There was no way of knowing if the enemy had been rendered unconscious. The stun-rays were silent and undetectable.

"Get ready for the second one," he announced. Then he threw the other egg. The tunnel lit up again. He waited a few moments before he said, "Keep your stations. I will go and check on the status of the enemy. Cover me." Not waiting for anyone to acknowledge, he got up and proceeded to walk ahead. The light was not as bright as it had been, but bright enough to illuminate every crevice in the tunnel walls.

He didn't have far to walk to find out if the stun-rays had been effective. The first unconscious body sat slumped over behind one of the boulders, his fingers gripping his rifle. The second body lay in a crumpled heap inside a gap in the tunnel wall.

Standing still, he perused the tunnel in front of him but didn't see any movement. The only sound he heard was the noise the miners made in the cavern that lay ahead. He lifted one arm. "Target secured and area safe," he announced.

He waited for his team and the Anorian team to join him. "I don't expect any trouble but stay alert."

They found all six Arani unconscious. Everyone relaxed. They knew the battle had been won.

"What should we do with the prisoners?" Ranini pondered.

"You wanted prisoners. You can have them all. We have our two and that's enough for an interrogation," Turnbull told her. "You can execute all six of them. I don't care. We have no use for them."

"Neither have I," She walked over to the first body and fired a bolt of energy into the head. She did the same with three more. Coming back, she said, "All I need is two."

Cold Turnbull thought, regretting his suggestion, but he didn't say anything. They killed two of her soldiers and would have killed all of them, even him and his team, had they gotten the chance. He might have done the same thing. War has no rules, even though some people believe there should be.

The Anorians secured the two surviving Arani with magnetic restraints and made sure they couldn't get away once they regained consciousness.

There were only about ten or twelve miners in this cavern. They were unaware of the battle that had taken place in the tunnel. Turnbull sent one of his team to announce their presence, not wanting to scare them. After the miners stopped working, Turnbull, and the others, including the Anorians, entered the cavern. When the miners were told about the closing of the mine, their reaction was similar to the way the others had acted. They calmed down when Turnbull explained the situation to them and promised they would not be left in the cold.

They used one of the vehicles that was meant to transport the ore to carry the two living Arani and the two dead Anorians out of the cave.

The Anorians left to get back to the spaceport, while Turnbull and his team stayed to get things organized. Turnbull didn't bother arresting any of the human supervisors and guards. They were only small cogs in the wheel of the giant organization that was robbing this planet. He didn't have time to waste with them. There were much bigger problems ahead.

THE ANORIAN SPACESHIP SAT NOT FAR AWAY FROM THE SUSN NEMESIS. IT was larger than the Nemesis and, judging by the number of turrets, it was plain to see that it was a battleship. They had parked their aircraft near the ship right beside another aircraft, which meant there was at least another team of soldiers on the battleship.

More than a week had passed since Turnbull and his team came back from the mine. The builder ship had landed three days earlier and started to build the military base. Within a few days the base would be ready for occupation. Robots did all the work. They worked without taking any breaks. Every part and component of the base was stored on the huge ship, and it was just a matter for everything to be assembled.

Once the base was finished, they'd be moving from the cramped confines of the spaceship into a more comfortable environment.

The long-term plan was the make the military base permanent on Cerberus. In the coming weeks, more troopers and personnel intended to be stationed for a longer term would arrive. It would not be feasible or cost-effective to ship supplies from a planet far away, which meant supplies would have to be bought locally. They may even have to hire Freelanders to fill open positions, but that was still in the future. Not his responsibility.

One thing he did, and that was making sure the Sartans and the human supervisors at the mine were taken care of. He sent a team to buy provisions and delivered them to the mine with one of the Sharks. Other details about what to do in the future would have to wait until the base was finished and he had more personnel to deal with it. There was much work ahead.

Turnbull's thoughts drifted to their two captives. They were not talking. They sat in the hold of the ship, withdrawn and unresponsive. Refusing to eat, they seemed to be losing weight. They were starving themselves to death. That was obvious.

He wasn't sure what to do. They injected them with truth serum, but it seemed ineffective. Either their metabolism was different from humans, or they were conditioned. Sergeant Harris suggested they use torture to draw the information out of them, but Turnbull didn't believe in using physical 'encouragement' to make a prisoner talk.

He wondered how successful the Anorians were with the interrogation of their two captives. There was no doubt in his mind that they used physical torture, but if the Arani were conditioned to withstand pain to the point of dying when tortured, anything the Anorians did was as useless as the humane way Turnbull and his interrogators used to, hopefully, extract information.

Turnbull sighed as he stood watching the progress of the base. He couldn't make out details from this far away, but it was growing larger every day. Once the buildings were finished, they'd be erecting a metal fence around it to keep out intruders or nosy locals.

Looking up into the blue sky, he closed his eyes and enjoyed the warm rays of the alien sun on his face. Everything looked so peaceful, and he wished, like so often, he had chosen a different path in his life. He should have become a lawyer, like his brother, or a merchant, like his two brothers-in-law. He probably would be married today to a beautiful woman, have two beautiful children. A boy and a girl. Live in a nice house with a yard for flowers. Even grow vegetables.

He had been married once. His marriage had lasted two years. They both had been too young. Had it lasted, he may have stayed on Rion.

Opening his eyes, he squinted against the sun. Hearing voices, he turned and looked at the Anorian battle cruiser. When he saw Ranini and two members of her team walking toward him, reality settled over him like a dark blanket, destroying his daydream mercilessly. He was a soldier, married to a ruthless mistress. Instead of carrying a briefcase filled with letters and contracts, he carried an instrument of death. An energy rifle that could destroy an aircraft in the blink of an eye with the gentle squeeze of a trigger.

He watched them coming closer, wondering if they had been lucky after all. He was surprised to see them without their uniforms. All three were naked.

Before they reached Turnbull, they stopped and Ranini spoke a few words to the two soldiers. They nodded and walked away, back to their ship.

"I saw you standing here, looking forlorn," she said with a little smile. "Something wrong?"

He shook his head and chuckled. "No. I was just lost in my thoughts for a moment, wishing I were somewhere else."

"Daydreaming?" She didn't wait for him to respond before she continued. "You look surprised. I do that too, sometimes. We Anorians are not cold beings without feelings and longings. I know humans seem to think that about us. We have desires and needs, just like you humans."

While she spoke, her golden eyes seemed to study him from behind lowered lids. The fine scales covering her body shimmered silvery in the bright rays of the sun. He realized how beautiful she was, like all the females of the Anorian race. Her body was slim and well-formed, her breasts small but beautifully shaped.

He felt himself react to the sight of her naked body.

Her forked tongue brushed across her lips. Her smile seemed to mock him. "Does my naked state bother you?"

"Bother me? No, it doesn't bother me." He felt suddenly uncomfortable. "I admit it's been a while since I saw a naked woman. That's all. I may be a soldier, but I have desires like any healthy male."

"I'll remember that. Next time I'll put on my clothes. By the way, unless you know that already about our species, you should know that

Anorian females are empaths. We can read emotions." She chuckled softly. "Your face and eyes give you away."

"Sorry. I don't mean to offend you."

"I'm not offended. Any other place and time I might even feel the same way, but this is the wrong place. Tell me, how are the interrogations coming along?"

"Not very well. We can't get anything out of the prisoners. They are clammed up tight. How about you?"

She hesitated for a moment. "One is dead. The other one refuses to talk. We've tried everything. There seems to be a barrier around his brain we can't penetrate."

"That's unfortunate." Turnbull wondered how that prisoner died but didn't ask.

Ranini looked at the construction going up. "You're planning to have a permanent military base here in Cerberus?"

"Yes, we are," Turnbull agreed. "After all, this is basically a human colony."

"Except for the Sartans. They may look human but are not. What about the Sleer? Won't they object if the Solar Union makes this planet part of the Human Empire?"

Turnbull shrugged. "I am not a politician. What I think doesn't matter. Have you been in touch with the Sleer?"

She answered with a shake of her head. "We haven't talked to anyone since we landed here. I was wondering if you could fill me in on the situation on Cerberus. I know that there are two countries on this side of the planet. Freeland and Tsakona. Before we landed, we circled Cerberus once to become familiar with the continents. From what we saw, there isn't much to speak of on the other side. Everything seems to happen on this one. Have you done any reconnaissance flights at all?"

"No. Our first mission was to find the mine and, hopefully, gather information on what exactly happened to our team. Sadly, we found out nothing." He studied Ranini thoughtfully, pondering how much he could and should tell her. "The rescue of our team is only part of our mission. This planet seems to be peaceful, but there is a lot going on under the surface that needs to be fixed. Perhaps, you and I can get together and exchange information. You must know more about conditions here than you let on?"

"I don't, but there is one you should talk to. She is on our ship."

"Who is she?"

"Our Matriarch. She instructed me to get you for an informal discussion. Please, do not refuse."

Turnbull wasn't quite sure what to make of it. He was not familiar with the class structure of the Anorians. He doubted if any human actually knew much about their species. "Now?"

She nodded. "Yes, please. Don't worry. You are in no danger." She smiled, almost impishly. "She doesn't eat humans. None of us do. We are vegetarians."

"That's good to know." He laughed to cover his trepidation, almost said, "Into the mouth of the dragon," but suppressed it at the last moment. Just because the Anorians were descended from reptiles didn't mean they were carnivores. Many humans assumed they were.

He had never been on an Anorian ship and was a little surprised to notice that the design of the interior wasn't much different from the inside of a human spaceship, but he was not surprised to see all the soldiers naked. After all, it was their custom and their natural state in familiar surroundings.

The Matriarch was, as expected, an older female. When he and Ranini entered her cabin, she was sitting cross-legged in front of a large screen, studying it. Turnbull recognized the displayed image as the continent on this side of Cerberus.

She turned around when the cabin door slid open to look at the intruders into her domain. Seeing Turnbull and Ranini, she rose with graceful movements and looked expectantly at both at them. She was as naked as the others. Even though she was not young, her body was trim and her scaly skin smooth and without any apparent wrinkles.

Ranini made a deep bow and said, "As instructed, I brought Colonel Turnbull from the Solar Protection Agency."

The Matriarch made a dismissing motion with her hand. "You did well, Captain, but now leave us alone."

"As you wish." Ranini bowed again, turned around and left.

The Matriarch's reptilian golden eyes seemed cold as she looked at Turnbull. Her expression was unreadable. She motioned with her hand, pointing to a small mountain of pillows on the floor. "Make yourself comfortable."

He followed her invitation and looked expectantly at her, wondering what she wanted to talk about.

She sank into another pile of cushions and reached for a small bowl standing on a low stool. Taking something out of it, she put it into her mouth and began chewing, still studying him. "Colonel Turnbull, have you wondered why we came to this planet with such a large ship?"

Her question came unexpected. "Actually, I have not, but now that you bring it up, yes, I wonder."

"Why?"

"It seems overkill to bring so many soldiers to search for one missing agent."

"You've only lost one agent and one Scout, and yet, here you are, establishing a military base on an insignificant planet as Cerberus. My question should be why, but it isn't." She shifted her position, pulled up her knees, covering her breasts.

She suddenly looked small and vulnerable, like an innocent little child, as she sat there hugging her knees, not at all looking like a powerful matriarch, but he wasn't fooled by that picture. Her eyes were hidden behind long lashes.

"You know more than you let on," he said.

"I know about the gate."

It took a moment for her blunt words to sink in. "The gate? It is not common knowledge. What do you know about the gate? And how do you know about it?"

Shifting her position again, she leaned back into the cushions. "The gates or star-portals were rumored to be built by an ancient and long vanished race of beings nobody knows anything about. We don't know what they looked like and on which planets they lived, but they must have been numerous and populated a huge number of planets in this galaxy. They did not use ships to travel from one planet system to another. They used gates to connect all the populated planets with an invisible net. I'm sure you are aware of that, Colonel Turnbull."

"It's only been a short time that I was told about the star-gates. Our government seems to keep a tight lid on the knowledge about this old race of beings and the gates. How much do you know about them?"

Her smile was almost condescending. "It seems all governments are alike. It isn't much different with our species. I am fortunate to be one of the privileged who knows more than most. One of my nieces was a member of the scientific team led by a high human official on Sala-mander that went through a gate. Her name was Gorana. The knowledge she brought back was instrumental in creating a special team of scientists that are studying the gates, trying to break the codes that someday will allow us to use the gates the way their creators did."

"Who was this human official?"

"You don't know?" She gave him a questioning look. "Even though he is not a military man or even a politician, he is one of the most powerful men in the Solar Union. I am surprised you don't know about him."

We are not military men or politicians. He remembered a man telling him that just a short while ago. "Is his name Colonel Stonewall?"

"That is the man. So, you do know him?"

"Not really, but I've met him briefly." *Another tiny sliver of knowledge nobody told me about. What else will I find out?*

She reached into the small bowl beside her and picked out something. Holding what looked like a small pebble between her thumb and forefinger, she seemed to study it. "This is the fruit of a ranga-tree. It grows only on one planet. It is an expensive delicacy only few can afford, but it is also very dangerous. Consuming a couple of these expands your mind, lets you see and understand things you can never comprehend in your normal state. Roasted the wrong way, the fruit kills you."

"Why are you telling me this? What does it have to do with the gates?"

"Nothing. It is just an example. A comparison. Few know about the fruit of the ranga-tree and its properties. Should its existence become common knowledge, too many would desire it. Falling into the wrong hands, it could be used as a weapon. So far, to the common people, the star-portals exist only in legends, in stories told by old males and dreamers. If it became known to everyone that they actually exist, criminal elements and war-like races like the Sleevers and the Snaar, to name a few, would try to find out their locations and gain control over the portals. That is the reason why the discovery of a portal on a new planet is kept a secret, and that is why it is always the military that arrives first."

"Does that mean the Anorians will also establish a military base on Cerberus?"

Even though she was from an alien species, her amused facial expression was easy to read. "Our base will be built not far from here. A builder ship will arrive within a few days, along with military personnel that will stay. We have an invested interest in this portal, just like you humans." She let out a sigh. "We've lost two troopers on a search for one agent who may or may not even be alive anymore. I'm not saying that the missing agent is not important to us. We let her join your search team to find out the location of the portal. I'm not making a secret out of that."

Turnbull suppressed a chuckle. "Speaking of secrets, my official mission here is to find out what happened to our team, but mainly it also is to locate the portal. Even that is just a part of why I came here with a battleship and a platoon of troopers. On the surface, things appear to be peaceful on the planet. Everyone gets along, but that is not so. Criminals are harassing the citizens of Freeland. Crime is rampant. The law is pretty much non-existent. Their so-called army is a joke. That will have to change. You probably don't know about the minerals being mined illegally by one of the cartels."

"I know everything about it." She smiled. "You talk about the citizens of Freeland and the changes they will have to make. There are also the Sartans and the Sleer. They have made this planet their home. They are happy with their way of life, but, sadly for them, changes are coming to Cerberus. Unwanted changes, perhaps, but they will happen. They are already happening."

"How do you know all of this?"

"I know all that and more. I am a member of the High Senate, something of which you obviously are not aware."

Her revelation came as a big surprise. "I wasn't. How can that be? You are Anorian."

She nodded. "That I am. Another fact that is not known by the masses. The human masses. Not all members of the High Senate are human. The High Senate is made up of humans, Anorians, Kraach, Accilla, and Tangari. Also a few factions from the Ventairian Empire. There are more. The High Senate was created to make sure all the different species in this galaxy live together in peace."

"All of this is new to me. It proves again that I am nothing but a chess piece moved around a giant board without knowing why. Not knowing who pulls my strings." He laughed drily. "Talking with you was quite enlightening. Right now, I feel like an ignorant fool, believing I'm somebody important."

"There is no reason for you to feel that way. You are an important piece on this giant board." Her smile was not patronizing. "Yes, I know about the game of chess. We have something quite similar, but I admit, I have taken a liking to chess, especially, when I am in an enhanced state. Right now, you wouldn't want to play with me. It wouldn't be fair—to you."

"I never learned how to play chess," he admitted. "You'd kill me with your first move." He laughed. "Or mine."

She rose to her feet with one smooth movement. "I am glad we had this little talk, Colonel Turnbull," she said, walking toward him on silent feet. Her usually slit pupils were dark, round orbs as she studied him from close. "I didn't mean to make you feel small and unimportant. The High Senate makes certain knowledge available to only a few individuals. There is a valid reason for that. Even as a military man in the higher ranks, knowledge is kept from you until there is a need for you to be informed." She paused. "There is another bit of knowledge you may be interested in. The Kraach and the Accilla will also build a base on Cerberus."

"What makes this planet so important?"

"I cannot tell you that."

"You can't or won't?"

He felt suddenly uncomfortable under the steady gaze of her golden eyes. It was difficult to guess her age, but he knew she wasn't young. This close he could see fine lines in her face, lines Ranini didn't have.

"Be satisfied with what I told you. Perhaps, in the near future, you and I will have another meeting." She stepped back, and he knew he had been dismissed.

Someone touched his arm. It was Captain Ranini. "Come."

He followed her in silence down the corridor to the exit.

Outside again, he stood looking around. He looked at the Nemesis and the Anorian battleship, wondering about the future of this planet. His talk with the Matriarch had been more than enlightening.

The sound of a ship coming in for a landing, made him lift his eyes to the sky, wondering if it would be the Anorian ship. Watching it settle down on the tarmac, he knew it didn`t belong to the Anorians. Neither did it belong to the Accilla or the Spiders. The name on the hull read: Sentinel. Clearly not a military ship. In other words, it belonged to a private company. Possibly a research vessel carrying scientist, or, most likely, either archeologists or geologists.

When the hatch finally opened and the first passenger came down the ladder, he had a feeling that trouble had just landed on Cerberus.

Two of the men from the five that jumped onto the tarmac, wore business suits. The other three men wore uniforms. They were soldiers, but it was clear from the insignia on the sleeves of their uniforms that they were not Union troopers.

[16]

ALL FIVE MEN HEADED IN TURNBULL'S DIRECTION. HE WAS CURIOUS WHO they were and what they wanted.

"Can I help you?" he asked when they stopped in front of him.

"You can help us by stating your name and rank," one of the two civilians barked.

Turnbull was taken aback by the man's obvious display of hostility. "Who wants to know?"

"My name is James Soloniak. I am a lawyer, and I represent the interests of Hyperion Mineral Explorations, the largest and most powerful company on Hyperion. We have been informed that one of our mines has been shut down illegally by a bunch of Union troopers. I am asking you again: What is your name and rank and what role did you play in this coup?"

Turnbull scratched his chin. Then he grinned. "Quite an impressive speech, Mister Soloniak. Your information is correct. One of your mines has been shut down for good. For your information, it is the first one and more closures will follow. Your statement is only partially true. It was not an illegal coup, as you put it. We acted on orders of the High Senate. The Hyperion Mineral Explorations company is on this planet illegally. The company is mining controlled minerals, in addition to robbing the people of Tsakona."

"We are not robbing anyone. We have the permission of the High Priest himself." Soloniak glared at Turnbull. "You still haven't given me your name, soldier."

"My name. Alright. I am Colonel Turnbull of the SPA. If you don't know what the letters stand for, let me enlighten you. I am a colonel with the Solar Protection Agency, and I represent the High Senate. Right now, I am the highest authority on Cerberus. My word is Law. If I tell you to get back onto your fancy ship, there is nothing you can do but follow my order. Do you understand that, Mister Soloniak?"

"We'll see about that, Colonel," Soloniak thundered. "This is preposterous. We will talk to Prime Minister Brownstone and General Mitchell about this. The High Senate does not have the right to just walk in and take over this planet. And you, Colonel! You are nothing but a puppet of the Solar Union with false visions of grandeur. Highest authority on Cerberus? Pah. I have a good mind to have you arrested by the local law enforcers and thrown in jail."

Turnbull gave Soloniak an amused look. "Good luck with that. If anyone will be arrested, it will be you and your consorts. It is in my power to confiscate your ship, arrest all of you, and have you taken to some prison planet."

"I wouldn't try that, Colonel Turnbull. That ship is heavily armed, and we have the military personnel to defend ourselves. I also want you to know that we are an affiliate of a powerful company you would not want to tangle with. It could have disastrous consequences."

"A threat, sir? Be careful what you say from now on. You are treading on dangerous grounds. And you don't want to mess with me. You mess with me, you mess with the Solar Union."

"Don't make me laugh. You suffer from an inflated ego. Nobody is that important. I can have half a dozen warships land on Cerberus within a couple of weeks. They'll flatten that small tin can of yours within the first hour of landing. You have no idea what hornet's nest you'll stir up when you act against us. We have powerful allies."

"Now you're making me laugh." Turnbull spoke almost in a conversational tone but didn't smile when he said that. "We know that the company you work for is controlled by the Vanderley Cartel. That will not stop the High Senate to act against this criminal organization. The Union will throw its might into the battle should it be warranted. There is too much at stake here. I suggest you get back into your ship and hightail it out of here as fast as you can before I lose my patience and arrest you for trespassing. I hope this is clear enough for you, Mister Soloniak?"

Soloniak struggled for words before he retorted. "How dare you talk to me that way? Obviously, you have no idea the powers I represent." He turned to the three guards and bellowed, "Arrest this pompous ass immediately!"

The three uniformed men hesitated, but then they advanced toward Turnbull.

Turnbull held his laser pistol in his hand before they got close. "One more step and it will be your last one." Then he spoke into his communicator. "Sergeant Harris, bring your squad down here on the double. Armed."

The three guards had stopped advancing. Now they looked at Soloniak for instructions. He glared at them, and then he barked. "Do what you're paid for. He is only one man. Disarm and arrest him!"

One of the soldier's hands crept toward his sidearm, but Turnbull stopped him with a sharp command. "Keep it in its holster, soldier, unless you have a death wish!"

The soldier stopped his move and took a step backward. He looked at Soloniak and shrugged. "Sorry, Sir. I'm not committing suicide. He's got the drop on me."

"You're supposed to be the best," Soloniak yelled, obviously enraged.

Turnbull kept an eye on him. He may also be armed and in his state might just do something crazy. Behind him, he heard footsteps on the tarmac. Then Harris arrived at his side. The other three troopers spread out on either side of him.

"Arrest this man," Turnbull ordered, pointing at Soloniak.

"Just him?" Harris inquired.

"So far, unless the others give us an excuse."

The three soldiers and the other man watched without interference as two of the troopers grabbed the struggling Soloniak, pulled his arms behind his back and cuffed him.

"Do something!" Soloniak screamed at the soldiers, but they didn't move.

"Throw him into the brig!" Turnbull ordered. He watched them drag the screaming lawyer to the ship until they reached the entrance. Turning to the other man who had been silent until now, he said, "How do you fit into this group?"

"My name is Isaac Sanchez. I am Mr. Soloniak's secretary." He lifted both hands in a defensive gesture. "That's my only involvement with this company. I have no opinions or interest in what goes on within the company." He smiled. "You can call me an innocent bystander."

"I'll bet," Turnbull commented, almost to himself. "Mr. Sanchez, you and the three guards are free to go. Return to your ship or go and visit the Prime Minister, I don't care. Just be mindful of what you are getting yourself involved in from now on. Hyperion Mineral Explorations has no more rights on this planet. You are only a guest here. Remember that."

Sanchez nodded. "I'll remember that. We won't create a problem, I promise."

Turnbull turned his attention to the young soldier who had disobeyed Soloniak's order. "What's your name, soldier?"

"Steven Durong, sir."

"Obviously, you are not a Union trooper. I assume, you are in the Hyperion military. Am I right?"

"You are correct, sir. Army. Special Operations."

"Let me ask you a question, Durong. Why are three professional soldiers working as personal bodyguards for a lawyer?"

"We are just following orders from our CO."

"I see." He looked at Harris. "It is obvious that HME has a lot of clout with the government of Hyperion. We can probably expect another visit either from the Hyperion military or even a ship from the Cartel. We'd better be prepared."

"I can't agree more, Colonel," Harris responded.

Turnbull turned back to Durong. "Were you drafted into the military, or did you join freely?"

"Freely, sir."

"Are you free to leave the military anytime?"

"I am."

"Then let me give you some advice, son. Leave the sinking ship as soon as you can unless you want to be swept into deep space with the rest of them. HME is going down. Things have been set into motion and there is no stopping them. Think about it."

The young soldier gave him a confused look. "Where would I go, sir?"

"Ask for asylum with the Freeland government. They'll be needing good soldiers soon. Go and talk to General Mitchell of the Freeland army. Mention my name. I am Colonel Turnbull of the Solar Protection Agency. I'm a friend of Major Wolf. You can mention that, too."

"Thank you, Colonel. I'll give it some thought."

"I'd better go and check up on my prisoner," Turnbull said with a grim smile and walked away.

As expected, Soloniak was spitting mad. When Turnbull walked into the room where Soloniak was held inside a small enclosure, the man grabbed the bars and shook them.

"You will pay for this dearly," he shouted. "You are violating my rights, and you have no right or reason to keep me prisoner. I demand you release me immediately!"

Turnbull gave him an icy stare. "On this planet you have no rights. As far as my right to keep you prisoner goes, I have every right. I am an agent of the Solar Union, and the law is on my side. If I would give the command to execute you, nobody would question my decision. Think about that, Mister Soloniak."

"I am a lawyer and shareholder of the most powerful company on Hyperion," Soloniak fumed. "I will not take this lying down. My people will come and investigate this whole charade, and you will be held accountable. You will end up on a prison planet where you will spend the rest of your miserable life, I promise you that, Mister!" Spittle ran down his mouth as he shouted those words.

"It is Colonel Turnbull. Perhaps you should write it down, so you won't forget it." Turnbull slapped his forehead with his flat hand. "Oh, I forgot. They use paper only on backwards planets. Looks like you're out of luck. Now you have to rely on your memory or your recorder if you had one." He turned and walked away, while Soloniak was still raging behind the bars.

"He sounded mad. We could hear his tirade from here," Harris remarked when Turnbull entered the mess hall. "Are you sure you want to keep him locked up? We really don't have a valid reason to keep him prisoner."

"We'll keep him over night before we let him go." Turnbull gave her a crooked smile. "Maybe I overreached a little when I had him arrested. He just rubbed me the wrong way. He's a pompous idiot with too much power, which has gone to his head. It'll do him good to cool down a little."

"He is a dangerous man, Colonel."

Turnbull waved it off. "He has no powers here on Cerberus. I wanted him to realize that. I'll deal with the fallout." He grinned. "I'm a dangerous man, too."

———

THEY MOVED INTO THE NEW BASE A WEEK LATER. IT WAS A NICE CHANGE TO have so much room. The sleeping quarters were not cramped. Each room was large enough for four bunks. The mess hall was much larger than was needed at this time, but it had been designed and built with future additions of soldiers and staff in mind. The kitchen had all the equipment needed to prepare meals, but for now, they would get their food from food converters. However, the selection of different dishes was quite generous.

The electric fence around the whole complex was also operational. There were two guard houses by the gated entrance. Also, one guard tower in every corner, controlled by warbots armed with long-range rifles. A couple of armed guard-bots watched the perimeter of the fence.

The whole complex was lit up by mini suns during the night. Overall, the base was a fortress. Nothing would get in or out without being detected. The defence system was most likely overkill on this planet, but the military never took any chances.

They detected the arrival of a big ship about a week after they settled in. It did not land at the spaceport in Greater York but about two hundred and fifty miles to the west.

From the information Turnbull received when getting ready for this mission, he knew that it was a private spaceport belonging to HME. It was also the location of a Lirsium Crystals mine. One they had planned to visit and shut down.

Turnbull did not know what to expect, but he put the base on high alert, just to be on the safe side.

Two days after the landing of the spaceship, half a dozen vehicles surrounded the base. Each vehicle sported a turret on top of its roof. All turrets were aimed at the base.

As it happened, Captain Rimini and four Anorian soldiers had come for a meeting to discuss future plans.

On the screen in the observation room, they watched one of the vehicles approaching the gate and three soldiers getting out. All three carried laser rifles openly in their hands.

"I don't believe this is a friendly visit," Harris remarked.

"Let's go and see what they want." Turnbull strapped on his belt with the laser and the stun gun. Wondering if he should also take his rifle, he decided against it. Harris and the two soldiers accompanying him would be enough. Aside from the two bots in the guard houses.

The three soldiers were standing on the other side of the closed gate. All three wore military uniforms, but one of them had a row of stripes on the front of his jacket. The hat he wore displayed a by now familiar insignia above the short shield. He sported a thick moustache with twirled ends.

"We just finished setting up this base and didn't really expect any visitors, yet. Who, may I ask, are you representing?" Turnbull watched all three of them as he spoke.

"I am Commander Francis Cornwall of Hyperion Mineral Explorations Private Special Forces. We have the backing of the Hyperion National Army of which we are an affiliate. I am here to arrest you for the damage you caused to one of our mines. We are authorized to take over this military base which you illegally erected on Cerberus. Open this gate immediately and surrender or deal with the consequences!"

"That was quite some speech with many long words, Commander Francis Cornwall," Turnbull said with a little smile. "Here is my answer: We will not open this gate. We will not surrender, and we won't let you take over this base. Tell me, what consequences are we talking about?"

"What consequences?" Cornwall pointed at the armored vehicles. "See the turrets on those six fighting machines? They shoot projectiles that will penetrate the walls of your new buildings and explode on contact, leaving nothing but complete destruction behind. We will not hesitate to use them if you do not surrender."

"A threat?" Turnbull said, his voice cold. "A hostile act committed against us is a hostile act committed against the Solar Union. Do you have any idea what those consequences would be? The Union will crush your private army like an annoying bug. If the Hyperion military dares to interfere, it will be like a rebellion against the Union, and the Union will deal with that harshly. Not only with a military strike, but also with sanctions against your planet. Complete isolation. The economy of Hyperion will collapse, and it will take a long time to recover from that."

"You certainly have a way to dramatize things. Mr. Soloniak already informed us that you are suffering from delusions of grandeur. I don't believe for one minute that you and your little fortress is so important to involve the whole Solar Union. The Union has much larger problems to deal with than being concerned with an unimportant planet like Cerberus. I'm giving you fifteen minutes to get everyone out of the buildings before we will attack. Should you try to fight us, lives will be lost. We can avoid all that if you surrender now. There will be no destruction of property and no bloodshed. It is up to you, Colonel."

Turnbull turned to Harris. "How can you best deal with a moron? Any suggestions?"

Harris shrugged. "We can let him have the first shot and then we have a legitimate excuse to destroy his little armada of fighting machines, or we shoot him right here as a warning to the others and hopefully save lives."

"Yes, we could do that, but I don't think we'll give him a chance to fire even one shot. I don't like the idea of having our brand-new buildings damaged." He faced Cornwall again. "I feel generous. I'll give you ten minutes to get back into your vehicle and get the hell away from here with your collection of fighting machines before we start shooting. The time starts now!"

Cornwall stared at him in obvious surprise. "You are a stubborn fool, Colonel Turnbull. Are you really willing to risk the destruction of your base and the lives of your people? You called me a moron. I think it is you who is the moron. You've made your choice, now you must deal with the consequences. It is on your head now. You have twenty minutes to change your mind." He hesitated. "I am sorry, Colonel, but I have my orders. I wish you will consider my offer." He turned and stalked back to his vehicle, followed by the two soldiers.

"Well, I guess they've made their choice," Turnbull stated. "Let's get back and deal with it."

Once they were back in the observation room, Turnbull got on the intercom and ordered everyone to meet in the observation room, immediately.

"As you probably all know by now, we are surrounded by half a dozen armored vehicles. Starting now, we are at war with the private army of Hyperion Mineral Explorations, but I do not wish to spill blood if I can avoid it." Then he gave the order to take out the turrets on the vehicles, a move that would cripple them. At least that is what he hoped.

They watched on the screen as the guard-bots melted the turrets into blobs of metal.

It was over in less than two minutes and quite anticlimactic.

Everyone sat waiting for something to happen. The six fighting machines sat immobile. Unless they had other weapons besides the one turret, now melted, they were useless, good only for transportation.

"It seems you took the wind out of their sails," Captain Ranini commented.

"I can't believe they were relying strictly on their armoured vehicles," Turnbull mused. "They must have something else up their sleeves."

"Maybe not," Harris speculated. "What if they assumed we would actually surrender to them and let them take over the base?"

"They can't be that stupid," Sergeant Jones said.

Suddenly, the doors of the vehicles flew open, and four soldiers jumped out of each vehicle. They spread out and ran toward the fence, brandishing long rifles.

"I hope they know the fence is electrified," Harris said.

Before the soldiers reached the fence, they stopped running, knelt, and aimed their rifles at the buildings. All twenty-four rifles fired at the same time. Twenty-four bolts of white lightening hit the walls of the base. The alarm system issued an advisory.

All walls hit by laser bolts. No damage to report.

"They've attacked us. Are we going to take defensive action, sir?" Jones asked.

"Not yet. No harm is done. All the buildings of this base are protected by an automatic shield. They have no heavy artillery left and their energy bolts are harmless."

They fired another round. The warning advisory reported the attack again.

After the third round the attackers obviously realized that their laser bolts were ineffective. They retreated back to their vehicles and climbed into them. All six vehicles lifted into the air and circled above the base.

The defense system detected energy bolts hitting the roof. Again, the protective shield held. The vehicles kept on circling.

"You are very patient, Colonel Turnbull," Ranini observed. "If we had an enemy attack our ship, we would shoot them out of the sky."

"Normally, I would also, but this base is protected, and I see no reason to kill innocent people just because I can. Those soldiers are only following orders. The only one I'm interested in is Commander Cornwall. Even he seemed reluctant to attack us. The fact that toward the end he apologized and gave us twenty minutes to change our mind, gives me reason to wonder. Like his soldiers, he is just following orders. His heart isn't in it."

"Right now, we are under siege, Colonel," Harris pointed out. "If any of us wants to go outside, we are sitting ducks. What do you suggest we do?"

"We wait. Let's give them one hour. If they haven't left by then, we'll send up one antigravity blocker as a warning. It will attach itself to one of their aircraft and neutralize the gravity generator. The craft will crash."

"Won't it crash onto your roof?" Ranini wondered.

"It will descend but won't crash onto the roof. It will bounce off the roof's energy field and slide to the ground."

"You are certain about that? We don't have any devices like that."

"At least that's what I was told by the technician." Actually, he did have some doubts, but he decided to trust the information.

It never came to the test. The six aircraft left before the hour was over. Turnbull breathed a sigh of relief. The whole incident had ended peacefully with no loss of life or even destruction of part of their new base. He hoped, this would be the end of it, but he knew it wouldn't be. Somebody else with fewer scruples than Commander Cornwall would eventually show up and things would turn ugly.

With any luck, the Union ship would soon be here and bring more troopers and military hardware to make this base the number one bastion on Cerberus. He had no doubts that once the star gate was found, the Union would build another base near that location. Along with all the ones other races would build.

"We should discuss our next move," Ranini cut into his thoughts.

He was not surprised to hear her say that. It seemed she had followed his thought process. The Anorians were gifted with the ability to read emotions and other subtle hints to give them an understanding of what was going on in somebody else's mind. It wasn't exactly reading minds but the next best thing.

"You are right," he said. "We should also be prepared to receive a visit from the Arani. They will want revenge for what we did to them at the mine."

"If they do come, it may be a good thing. We might be able to track them when they leave again."

[17]

Not much happened in the two weeks after the attack on the base, except for the arrival of the Union ship *Starlion,* bringing thirty troopers, four mechanics, three technicians, and three clerks. The hardware included another Shark and six additional corvettes. There were also huge boxes filled with uniforms and many other items. Turnbull left it to the clerks to sort out and keep stock of everything.

Expecting the additional troopers, Turnbull had hired two cooks. Also, four people to take care of the usual jobs that needed to be done around the base. The cooks were one elderly married couple, while the other four were young and unattached men. All six would live in one of the two separate buildings on the base.

With the arrival of the clerks, he stopped worrying about any other stuff. From now on, it was the responsibility of the clerks to make sure the base was running smoothly. It would be up to them to hire additional people, should it become necessary, and the purchase of supplies.

As far as he was concerned, the military base was up and running. His responsibility from now on was to take care of military matters and nothing else.

Looking around his brand-new office, he felt a sense of pride and accomplishment. The military had spared no expense to outfit this office with the latest surveillance equipment. Half a dozen screens on the walls displayed holograms of the outside world. Any ship dropping out of Over-space would automatically be detected by one of the satellites circling Cerberus and be reported. The sky was scanned on a constant basis and anything out of the ordinary was going to be registered. Several *eyes* were roaming around the countryside and checking for irregularities and suspicious activities, reporting them as soon as they were detected.

Except for the short attack by the Hyperion Mineral Explorations Private Special Forces, they did not get a real opportunity to try out the automatic defense system. However, the technicians assured him that the base was able to defend itself against the most advanced weapons without any human interference. Controlled and operated by an artificially created intelligence, it was practically fail-proof. Nonetheless, it was not omnipotent. It could be shut off if necessary. The technicians advised against meddling with the system. It should be interfered with only in extreme circumstances. Of course, shutting it down was not as easy as just flicking a switch. A certain protocol had to be followed.

When he heard the short beeping warning sound coming from one of the screens, announcing a ship dropping out of Over-space, he watched as the display grew. He recognized an Anorian builder ship. It didn't come unexpected. The matriarch had told him about their plans to establish a base on Cerberus. It wouldn't surprise him to see a ship from the Spider race appear in the not-so-distant future with plans to erect a base.

He didn't know where the Anorians planned to build their base, but according to the matriarch it wasn't going to be far away.

He had not been in contact with the Anorians since the attack on the base. Neither had there been any response from the Hyperions to their failure to take over the base. He did not believe that they would give up that easily. It was only a matter of time before they would try again, unless they were waiting for reinforcement and a bigger ship with more destructive weapons. He didn't worry too much, trusting the defence system to protect the base.

The expected attack from the Arani had not happened, either.

Things were just too quiet and peaceful and that worried him.

Then one day a vehicle arrived at the gate. The driver, a Ltd Garcia, announced that General Mitchell of the Freeland army requests to speak to the commanding officer.

Turnbull had been aware of the General's existence from his briefings, but he had not seen the need to speak to the man. Now he wondered if it was a blunder on his part. It would only have been common courtesy to at least give him a call after arriving on Cerberus. After all, he was the highest authoritative official in Freeland after the Prime minister. If he remembered correctly, he was also the Minister of Justice.

Turnbull had expected a big man, wearing a uniform decorated with medals, emanating an aura of authority. He was a bit disappointed when the man walking into his office was thin and tall, with a narrow, unimposing face. His only distinctive feature was a bushy moustache.

The young soldier with him was wearing a dark-blue uniform and a wide-brimmed hat. His face was clean-shaven except for a thin, black moustache. The holster hanging from his wide belt held a gun with a shiny grip. He looked immaculate right down to his polished high leather boots.

After walking through the door, Mitchell stopped and looked around the office. "Quite impressive," he commented. "Unlike my shabby office." He smiled, giving Turnbull a once-over. "I'm General Mitchell and this is Ltd Garcia. They told me at the gate the name of the commanding officer is Colonel Turnbull. I assume that is you?"

"You assumed right." Turnbull tried to hide his guilty feeling, even though he wondered why he should feel guilty. He had not been obligated to meet with anyone. He stepped around his desk and held out a hand. "Good to meet you, General. I must apologize for not coming to see you, but our mission was of utmost importance and took precedence over everything else. Setting up this base was also one of the priorities."

"I understand." Mitchell shook the offered hand and chuckled. "I may be a general, but I'm not really such an important personality in Freeland. Even being the Minister of Justice doesn't give me any privileges. It was Sergeant Slovinsky who reported your arrival. He spun a story that seemed a little farfetched. Apparently, you were going to take over the spaceport and the things you said about our army and the changes that were coming. You scared the hell out of the poor man. I admit I was a bit disappointed that you didn't introduce yourself, especially since Major Wolf came to see me after his ship landed. By the way, how is Major Wolf? He said he would visit me again, but I've never heard from him again."

Turnbull gave him a look of surprise. "You don't know?"

"Know what?"

"He is one of the reasons we are here. Major Wolf and his team were abducted by the alien invaders. We came to find them, and we will stop those aliens."

Mitchell's reaction was one of genuine shock. "I know nothing about that." He turned to his lieutenant. "Did you know?"

Garcia shook his head. "It's news to me."

Turnbull took the opportunity to address the young lieutenant. "I didn't mean to ignore you, Ltd Garcia." He wondered if he should salute or just offer his hand. He decided to shake the young soldier's hand.

Garcia shook his hand with a solid grip, surprising Turnbull, who had expected a limp handshake. He didn't know why. Possibly because of the negative things he'd heard about the Freeland army.

"Is that the reason the Solar Union has built this fortress?" Mitchell broke into Turnbull's thoughts.

Turnbull looked at the General with pity in his eyes. The poor man had no clue of what was going to happen to his country. "This fortress, as you call it, is only the beginning. The Union will send more ships and troopers. You may have noticed the presence of the Anorians. They are building a base not far from here. There will be others, like the Spiders for instance. Changes are coming to your world, General Mitchell. Prepare yourself for that."

Mitchell walked to one of the chairs and sat down. "I must admit it doesn't really come as a great surprise, but I'm still struggling with accepting it. Major Wolf already told me that changes were inevitable. He said Freeland was in a mess and it would be up to the Union to fix it."

"That's about sums it up," Turnbull said.

"There is something else. The Prime minister came to see me. He was not happy. He told me that a man by the name of Sanchez came to his residence complaining about the treatment he received from you. He wasn't just mad; he was fuming and wanted justice. Apparently, he was representing Hyperion Mineral Explorations, and he threatened to take action if nothing was done about you. He never said what kind of action."

Turnbull couldn't help but chuckle. "Just the threats a rat uses when cornered. For your information, that company has a ship sitting at their private spaceport where they are mining Lirsium Crystals; illegally, I might add. We've closed down one of their mines and we will close down this one and any other mines they may have. You might also be interested in this next bit of info. HME has either partnered with the Arani, or the Arani have infiltrated, even taken over, that company. We don't know any details yet."

Mitchell didn't comment right away. When he did, he seemed shaken. "That is not good news. What is the Union going to do about that?"

"For one thing, we will not only shut down the mines; we will also take apart HME and investigate the Vanderley Cartel. You may not be familiar with that one, but it is one of the most influential and ruthless criminal organizations in the Galaxy. The High Senate has shied away from tackling them, but we can't allow criminals to have free rein. They need to be stopped before they get too powerful. It may already be too late." Turnbull knew he sounded angry, but criminals were a thorn in his side. They were like cockroaches that seemed to exist on every planet. It was his duty as a lawman to exterminate them.

"Is that just you talking or is the Solar Union actually going to do something about them?" The doubt was not to be missed in Mitchell's comment.

"It will happen, believe it. By the way, the ship they have sitting by that mine is a war vessel. They attacked our base, trying to take over. The coup was unsuccessful. They limped back to their ship. They may try again, even though we've melted the cannons they had mounted on their tanks into useless blobs. Maybe they have something up their sleeve. We don't know what they are waiting for. Perhaps for reinforcement." Turnbull smiled grimly. "Next time we won't be so merciful. We'll destroy them completely, including their warship."

"It'll mean war." Mitchell shuddered. "We are not used to such violence."

"From what I heard, your society is riddled with crime and violence. To clean that up is another part of our mission. Soon a ship will come, bringing special investigators and peacekeepers trained in domestic violence. We'll make Freeland a peaceful nation. Your people will be much happier."

Mitchell wasn't convinced. It was plain to see in his face. "It is not as bad as you make it sound. We have an understanding with those that are creating unrest. We all try to get along."

Turnbull's laugh was anything but cheerful. "We don't make deals with criminals, General. It won't be long before they take over. No, you have to get control over them before it is too late."

"I'm not sure if all this should cheer me up." Mitchell didn't look happy. "I have a feeling we will be moving into a violent future, and it will be a long time before things will return to normal."

"I'm afraid so, but the way I see it, it was inevitable. Eventually, the upstanding citizens of Freeland will be forced to make a stand. How? I don't know. Your police force is corrupt, and you don't even have an army. Two thousand baton swirling and dancing uniformed men and women are useless when it comes to defending a nation."

"There is something else I am wondering about. What caused this sudden attraction to our planet? Why is the Union setting up a permanent base? Why are the Anorians doing the same thing? Why are the Spiders interested in our planet?"

Turnbull hesitated answering. What should he tell the General? The truth? Wasn't the existence of the star-portal supposed to be a secret? What difference will it make if he confides in the General? There was really not much of a choice. He deserved to know the truth. It would come out eventually.

"Have you ever wondered where these invaders come from?"

"Do you mean what planet?" Mitchell looked puzzled.

"Not exactly. Let me rephrase the question. By what means did they arrive on Cerberus?"

"Spaceship, I assume. Is there any other way?"

"The answer may shock you. It opens up more questions. Have you ever heard legends and stories about an ancient race of intelligent beings that populated this Galaxy long before the many different species arrived on the scene? Apparently, they were nearly omnipotent beings that actually created all the different races by traveling from one planetary system to another and seed them with different DNAs?"

The expression on Mitchell's face was one of confusion. He clearly didn't know what Turnbull was talking about. "I must admit I haven't. Remember, we have very little contact with other planets, which means gossip and speculative stories don't reach us."

"There are plenty of speculative stories told on every planet. The legend about a vanished ancient race is one of them, except it isn't a legend anymore. We have evidence and proof that this ancient race actually existed. Instead of traveling through space in spaceships they moved from one planet to another through portals or star-gates. It was instant travel. We know of a few star-gates on different planets. One of those star-gates is here on Cerberus. Our mission is to locate that gate."

"I don't understand how that works. You mean it is like a door you step through here on Cerberus and you come out on another planet?"

Turnbull gave him a nod of confirmation. "That's how it is, except it isn't a door. It is more like a huge building with machines inside. To be honest, I have never seen one. I've learned about these gates only just recently myself. The different governments are keeping the existence of the gates a secret. For security reasons, apparently."

Mitchell sat in his seat with that look of disbelief still on his face. He twirled his moustache between his thumbs and forefingers "This is difficult to digest. Are you telling me that the invaders came here through one of those gates?"

"That's what we believe, because they look like Anorians, but nobody has ever heard of Anorian males being the dominant gender. Also, their technology is different from ours and any of the other races. From the report Major Wolf left us, the Arani, as they call their race, admitted that they came to Cerberus from the 'other side'." Turnbull paused to let it sink in before continuing. "The Sartans are also presenting us with a fair share of puzzlement. They arrived on this planet about two thousand years ago, but they have no knowledge of their origin. In fact, they consider themselves native to this planet, which they are not. They have no technology, live under primitive conditions. They haven't progressed during those two thousand years. We suspect they also came here through the gate."

"I admit, we've been wondering about them also, but it never occurred to us that they may have come to Cerberus by other means than a space-ship," Mitchell pondered.

Turnbull lifted a hand. "We have no proof they did come here through the gate. It is only speculation, but, just like the Arani, we don't know their home planet. We could assume their ancestors arrived here in a spaceship and they've lost all technological knowledge and reverted back to a primitive stage, but that is highly unlikely. There should be some evidence of that. Ruins and relics, and other telltales of some kind of technology. There is none."

Mitchell bent forward. "Everything you tell me sounds logical, but you don't know this planet and the people living here. You haven't been here long enough. Where does your knowledge come from?"

"You have a right to ask," Turnbull agreed. "My knowledge does not come from my own experience, obviously. It comes from the reports I've read. The Union has extensive records of the history of Cerberus since the first settlers arrived here nine hundred standard years ago. We have the report from Major Wolf and plenty of information from the Scouts, in addition to reports from ship captains and other travelers. Cerberus may seem like a forgotten world, but it isn't. If humans would have arrived here two thousand years ago, there would be some records somewhere."

"You're saying the Sartans are not humans?"

"Not at all. They aren't Earth-humans, but we don't question their right to be called human. The reports I've read stated that sexual unions between Earth-humans and Sartans result in offspring that are no different from children of pure Earth-humans. They have the same DNA."

"Interesting," Mitchell said. "Even though we get along with the Sartans, there are many among us that consider them sub-humans. Mainly because of their primitive society. It seems we are wrong about them."

"It does look that way." Turnbull walked over to the window and looked at the corvettes and the two Sharks parked in the yard. Something needed to happen soon. Even the troopers were getting restless, itching for action. He turned back to face Mitchell.

As of reading his thoughts, Mitchell said, "I've noticed a number of aircraft sitting there seemingly idle. They don't look very large. For what exactly are they used?"

"We call them corvettes. Built for two people, one pilot and one gunner. They are fast and easy to maneuver." Turnbull's smile was cynical. "They don't make an easy target, but if one should be shot down, we lose only one craft with a minimum number of casualties."

"Typical military talk," Mitchell commented. "Statistics. Numbers. With no regard for the human lives lost."

"I am only quoting from the book. Every member in my team is important to me and I will never send them on a mission that is guaranteed to fail. However, there are no guaranties. All of us are soldiers and we knew the risks when we joined the military. We face death every time we go into combat, knowing we may not survive. That is the only guaranty we ever get."

"It makes me wonder why anyone joins the military," Mitchell's smile was not a happy one. "I brought you something that may cheer you up." He turned to his lieutenant. "Ltd Garcia, please, give me your backpack."

Garcia complied. Mitchell took the pack and opened it. He removed a couple of bottles, which he put onto Turnbull's desk. "Our ancestors brought with them many plants that originated on Earth. Grapes were among them. The soil on Cerberus and the temperature in some regions is perfect for growing different varieties of grapes. Quite a few farmers have vineyards that produce exceptional sweet grapes. Our wines are excellent, and I can assure you they will rival anything you have ever tasted. Aside from wine, they also make great different kinds of spirits. I brought a bottle of our finest wines and a bottle of brandy. I hope, you will like both."

Turnbull didn't have to pretend when he said, "I appreciate wine and other types of alcoholic beverages. I don't always get a chance to enjoy either." He reached for one of the bottles and held it against the light. The rays of the alien sun made the liquid inside sparkle. "Thank you, General. I appreciate this gesture, and I will enjoy both these bottles."

The sounding of an alarm made him look up and scan the screens. A cold computer-generated voice announced the detection of a number of unknown vessels approaching the base from the north. Moments later the same voice advised that the base was under attack.

His desk communicator lit up and a human voice shouted, "We are being bombarded by hundreds of drones!"

At the same time the cold voice of the defence system informed him that a number of small missiles had penetrated the defense screen and caused considerable damage in the west wing of the base.

His desk communicator lit up again and another human voice shouted, "The defense system is not holding!"

"How the hell is that possible?" Turnbull barked. "We're supposed to be able to defend the base against the most advanced weapons!"

"There are too many drones, sir." He recognized the voice belonging to one of the technicians. "We did not count on that."

Turnbull scanned the screens again. Three of them displayed different angles of the attack. He counted ten large aircraft hovering some distance away. Another screen displayed a cloud of drones buzzing around in the sky like a swarm of angry giant insects.

The door to Turnbull's office opened and Sergeant Harris entered. "What are your orders, sir?"

Turnbull pointed at the screen that displayed the large aircraft. "They are keeping their distance. We have to take the battle to them. Take all twelve corvettes and give those bastards hell."

Harris saluted. "Aye, aye, sir."

"What is happening?" General Mitchell inquired.

"War, General," Turnbull said louder than intended. "This is what war is like."

"Who are they?"

"Arani."

Ten minutes later, he watched the three-dimensional image displayed in the large video sphere as the corvettes shot into the air, heading for the enemy aircraft a few miles away. They reached their target within minutes. Turnbull glanced at General Mitchel and wasn't surprised the see the man watch with fascination as the corvettes began attacking the much larger aircraft of the Arani.

It took only moments for one of the enemy vessels to explode under the onslaught of the corvettes.

"One down and only nine more to go," Turnbull commented with satisfaction.

It didn't take long for the Arani to react. Until now, all their aircraft had been stationary, but after the destruction of the first vessel, they began to move, but not fast enough. The corvettes managed to blow up a second one, but after that they tried without success to get close to the other ones.

The enemy was fighting back. Blinding beams of light flashed toward the corvettes from the Arani craft. Only the small size and speed of the corvettes saved them from being hit. They separated and scattered like a swarm of birds being threatened by a large predator. They didn't stay away for long. Instead of attacking one enemy craft as one unit, they each chose one, therefore presenting smaller targets.

Turnbull's confidence in his fighting force did not disappoint him. It didn't take more than two hours before all the enemy vessels had been destroyed. In many ways they didn't have a chance against the small and superfast corvettes.

But the battle didn't end without losses. Two of the corvettes were hit and went down in a blazing ball of fire.

Turnbull didn't want to think about the four troopers that lost their lives.

The swarm of drones still filled the sky around the base, but it didn't look as crowded as before. The automatic defense system of the base had been shooting them down systematically. How many of them had managed to penetrate the defense net was still unknown to Turnbull, but the reports of hits had stopped some time ago.

At one point during the battle, one of the defense screens issued an advisory, warning about the presence of half a dozen aircraft approaching from the east. They never came close, just hovered in the sky.

Turnbull looked at the screen and noticed that they were gone.

"It seems the battle is over," Mitchell said. "You've won."

Turnbull expelled air through his pursed lips. "It is over for now. Hopefully, it isn't just a short victory. Our work has just begun. We must locate their headquarters, but most of all we must discover where they come from."

[18]

THE DAMAGE TO THE BASE HAD NOT BEEN AS EXTENSIVE AS HE FEARED. WITH the help of the four workers he had hired, the technicians and mechanics managed to repair most of the damage. He put in a request to send a repair ship and restore the base to what it had been before the attack.

The Anorians had decided to build their base about five miles to the east. From videos taken by spy-eyes he watched as the base came to completion. The buildings looked different from the buildings in the Solar Union base.

A couple of weeks after the battle, Captain Ranini paid them a visit. She and one of her troopers arrived shortly after noon.

When she walked into his office, she looked around with obvious interest. "Humans enjoy certain luxuries that we Anorians do without," she commented.

"We do, I admit that," Turnbull told her with a little smile. "However, don't be fooled. I don't always live in such luxurious surroundings. I have a feeling that whoever comes here to replace me will be some soft politician or some other military brass somebody wants to get out of the way. This luxury is supposed to keep them from complaining."

She chuckled. "In that case, don't get too complacent. Luxury like this will make you soft." Her expression became serious. "You probably noticed that we watched the battle from a safe distance. We would have come to your assistance had you requested it."

"I appreciate that, but we managed. Next time we may not be so lucky. We need all the friends we can get."

"You can always count on us. We Anorians never had a quarrel with you humans, and we want to keep it that way. There are plenty of hostile races out there."

"I couldn't help but notice that your base is finished. Your builder ship has left," Turnbull commented.

"Just in time," she told him. "We are expecting a ship bringing more soldiers and other personnel within a few days. They will also bring additional aircraft and weapons."

He felt his eyes narrow when he looked at her. "Are you making plans for a battle?"

"We believe in being prepared. None of us knows what the future will bring. It seems the Anari are digging in. They won't leave voluntarily; that is clear. We anticipate being here for a long time. Aren't you?"

"Yes, we are, but part of our mission here is to bring order to Freeland. There are seven million humans and three million Sartans living on Cerberus. After all, this is a human colony."

She gave him a contemptuous smile. "That may be so, but with the presence of a gate, Cerberus becomes a planet of great interest. Humans will have to share it with other races, like it or not. You must realize that."

Turnbull became aware of his fingers drumming his desktop. He stopped doing it and gave Ranini a thoughtful look. "I realize that. I also realize there is nothing we can do about it short of starting a war with every race in the Galaxy. That, of course, would be absurd, downright stupid, aside from committing racial suicide. Nobody wants that. Besides, it wouldn't surprise me if one of these days, a Sleer ship, carrying a load of new colonists, lands at the spaceport, therefore staking their claim on Cerberus."

"It would be within their rights," Ranini agreed. "You are probably wondering why I'm here."

"The thought occurred to me. I don't think it is because you missed my charming company," he said with a little chuckle.

She smiled. "If this were a social visit, I would have come alone wearing only my boots and bringing a flask full of Anorian wine."

"I didn't know Anorians drink wine, never mind making it."

"Now you know one of our little secrets. There are many planets in the Anorian Empire with diverse societies. Not unlike the Human Empire. Some of us make wine and other alcoholic spirits, and we also drink it."

He smirked. "Since you are wearing a uniform and aren't carrying a flask of wine, I gather this is not a social call."

"Perhaps another time." Her smile teased him for short moment but then faded away, and her expression became more sombre. "We managed to break through the barrier our prisoner had built around his mind. Don't ask what we had to do, but we did get a few coordinates from him. It could be the location of their base here on Cerberus. Unfortunately, the information is quite sketchy. We are planning to check it out, and we are willing to share the location with you. Would you be interested in accompanying us? We are expecting it to be a dangerous mission, and we will have to be prepared to fight. It would be good to have you by our side."

"Of course, we will be part of that mission. We want to find the site of their base as much as you do, with the ultimate goal being the discovery of the star-gate's location."

"Which, obviously, is also our goal."

Turnbull got up and walked over to a cabinet and removed the bottle of wine General Mitchell gave him, deciding this occasion was as good as any to open it. Mitchell had been thoughtful enough to include a corkscrew. He also took out the only two glasses he had. Carefully filling the two glasses, he walked back to his desk and handed one glass to Ranini. "This bottle was a gift, and I have no idea what the wine tastes like." His smile was almost apologetic. "I hope we both will still be friends after this." He lifted the glass. "Cheers, Captain Ranini."

She sniffed the golden liquid. "It does have a pleasant aroma," she commented and took a small sip. After taking another sip, she smiled and said, "You may have to arrange for a few bottles to be sent to our base. I believe it will put me in great favour with the matriarch." Then she emptied the glass.

Turnbull had to admit that Mitchell had not exaggerated when he claimed this wine to be as good as any he ever tasted. "You are right. This is good stuff. It wouldn't hurt to get in contact with the producers and purchase a few cases."

———

It was a week after Turnbull's meeting with Ranini when one Anorian aircraft and one of the Sharks rose into the cloudy sky. Accompanying the Anorian craft were two bullet-shaped scout ships, similar to the corvettes. Turnbull had decided to have only five corvettes escort them. He couldn't leave the base without protection. Should it somehow become necessary to have more corvettes, it wouldn't take long for them to come to their assistance.

The Anorian craft carried eight soldiers, so did the Shark. Sergeant Harris and Specialist Beverly Thompson were among the crew of the Shark.

Two of his original crew were flying one corvette. The other four corvettes were manned by eight of the newly arrived troopers.

Once in the air, the Anorian craft and the Shark split. The corvettes spread out also. It was important to cover as much territory as possible to increase the chance of locating the Arani base. Even though they had the approximate location of the enemy base, they did not have the exact coordinates. Of course, there was a good chance their small fleet would be detected by the Arani's aerial defence before either the humans or the Anorians were aware of the enemy base.

It didn't take long before they left Freeland airspace and entered Sartan airspace. Surely, the Sartans would be aware of the aircraft flying overhead. They might even expect a raid, not knowing that the objects in the sky were not enemies but friends.

As the landscape unfolded beneath them, Turnbull was reminded of the primitive society the Sartans represented. He had been briefed about them, but it still came as a surprise. They flew over small farms and small towns with buildings no higher than two stories. The streets were either packed soil or cobble stones in the towns. People traveled with animal-drawn carts and wagons, or they walked. The only objects in the air were small and large birds. Even some of them looked primitive. Once, a small flock of giant birds with long beaks and leathery wings, looking oddly enough like pterodactyls, flew high above them.

They flew over one large city. The buildings didn't appear as simple and primitive as the ones in the towns. Zooming in on one particular large collection of buildings, Turnbull realized it was obviously a place of worship. He saw one building that could not be mistaken for anything else but a temple. In a large courtyard, a group of warriors wearing leather armour and helmets, practiced with primitive weapons. There were also priests dressed in long robes walking in a garden behind the temple.

"Everything looks so peaceful," Sergeant Harris remarked beside Turnbull.

"It does, doesn't it? From what I've learned, that is probably a deception. Even Tsakona isn't as peaceful as it appears. The Priesthood has a firm grip on the Sartan citizens. The warriors you see practicing in the courtyard are collecting taxes from the average citizens. Apparently, the warriors are brutal and merciless."

"I am not a history buff, but what I still remember from my basic education classes, feudal societies are like that. They use brutal force to suck out the last piece of gold or silver from their citizens," Harris added to Turnbull's observation.

"That is so true, but it isn't only the Priesthood that collects taxes. There still are the Kings. They also demand their share of the tribute." Turnbull chuckled. "That's what they call it. It still is taxes, just a different name."

"That makes it so much easier to bear." Harris shook her head. "I'm surely glad I am not living in a society like that. They are nothing but slaves."

Turnbull threw her a sidelong glance. "Some people might argue with you. I've been called a slave to my profession. In many ways that person was right. Don't you think so?"

"It is all a matter of perspective." She didn't answer the question, and Turnbull didn't blame her. Since he outranked her, she would never tell him what her thoughts were on that subject.

After about an hour, they left Tsakona behind. The terrain had changed from flat to mountainous. Some of the taller mountains were covered with a layer of snow, but the valleys between them were green and lush-looking.

"There are still a lot of unexplored areas to discover," Harris said, as she watched the large screen that displayed the vast forests and flat prairie-like land below them. "I haven't seen any signs indicating that anyone lives down there."

"This is a large planet with a population of ten million humans and a small number of Sleer. There is plenty of room for more people. Eventually, the day will come when it becomes overcrowded, like all the other colonies."

She looked at him. "You sound like a doomsday prophet."

"Just an observation. Cerberus might have had a good chance to stay an idyllic planet because of its location, but with the presence of a stargate, that chance went out the window. The gate will attract not only humans. Every race in the Galaxy will want a piece of the planet and the gate."

"Didn't you say that Freeland is not as peaceful as it appears? It is corrupted and run by gangs. That doesn't sound very idyllic to me."

"Unfortunately, that is true," he said grimly. "The future of Freeland does not look rosy. Without interference, there will be civil war. The honest people will finally get fed up and take matters into their own hands. They will fight back against the criminals. Many will die and there is no guarantee that good will win over evil. Either way, there will be nothing but chaos without any laws, or it will end up as a dictatorship. Goodbye freedom, either way."

She chuckled. "Thanks for these cheery thoughts. I hope you are wrong."

"It was just a possible scenario. The Union won't let it happen. I'm sure the Department of Colony Developments is already putting together a team of peacekeepers and organizers to straighten out this mess. Things will change, that is for certain, but whatever happens isn't our problem. We have to concentrate on our final mission, which is to find the stargate."

"Or at least the location of the Arani camp," Harris added.

They were flying over another mountain range, when the screen lit up and the three-dimensional image of Captain Ranini from the Anorian ship materialized. "One of our scout ships has detected an irregularity on the other side of the mountain ridge," she informed them. "We think it might be the Arani base. I suggest we land and work out a strategy on what to do next."

"Good idea," Turnbull agreed. "Find a suitable spot."

"There is a plateau ahead. It is large enough for all our craft to land and park."

"We have it on screen," he told her.

After the image of Ranini faded away, Turnbull contacted the five corvettes. "We will land for a discussion. Follow us."

It took another half hour until all aircraft had landed safely. The plateau was a perfect landing place; flat and even as if some giant had taken a saw and cut off the tip of the mountain. Small boulders dotted the area with enough empty space between them to allow all the craft to be parked without a problem.

The five corvettes were parked beside the Shark. Not far from them, rested the two Anorian scout craft. The large Anorian vessel squatted on the ground like a shiny predatory giant insect, ready to take to the air again.

Turnbull took the opportunity to stretch his legs and walk around a little. He told the crew to do the same if they wanted to.

The air was crisp and clean. He didn't see any trees or other plants, only boulders and millions of small stones. He bent down and picked up a shiny, blue rock and studied it.

"That looks like a precious stone," somebody said.

It was Sergeant Harris who had come out of the Shark to join him.

"I believe it is a sapphire." Turnbull turned the stone around in his hand to inspect it from all sides. "This could be worth a small fortune on some planets."

Harris bent down to pick another stone. "I disagree." She laughed. "There are enough of them here to buy a whole planet."

He took a closer look around. "I'm not a professional and I don't know much about rock collecting, but I know what a sapphire looks like. I have a feeling this is a special find. Places like this with such an abundance of precious stones must be rare."

"I'm sure it is." Harris picked up another one, larger than the others. "These stones will still be here in a thousand years. Nobody will ever come up here unless they fly over with an aircraft. However, there really is nothing here to see from the air to entice anyone to land on this dead piece of rock."

Turnbull chuckled. "Maybe you and I should quit the military and become prospectors. We could keep this place a secret and pick as many stones as we want. We'd be rich beyond imagination. We could buy a small planet and create a kingdom of our own. I'd be the king and you the queen."

Her blue eyes sparkled with mischief but also with a certain curiosity. "We'd have to be a couple if we want to rule as king and queen. I mean, we'd have to be married to gain the respect of the people in our kingdom."

"We'd have to be examples of what is proper." With a shrug, he said, "Then again, with our great wealth we could afford not to care what anyone thinks." He put the sapphire into his pocket. "A trinket," he explained. "Something to make me dream of things that will never happen."

"It could," she insisted. "Would it be so bad to move to some obscure planet, wealthy and married to each other, with no worries about the future? Spending our time lying on a sandy beach, sunning our already tanned bodies, go fishing and hunting whenever we feel like it. Does that sound so bad?"

"We'd be bored out of our minds in a few years, probably killing each other," he said.

Their conversation was interrupted by the arrival of an Anorian soldier. "Captain Ranini wants to meet with you," she said. She spoke Inglis with a slight lisp, the way most Anorians spoke. The only Anorian he ever met that didn't speak with a lisp was Captain Ranini.

"Where does she want to meet?"

"She invites you to come to our craft."

"Alone?"

"You can bring one trooper."

"Tell her I'll be there shortly." He watched the Anorian soldier walking back to her craft. With one last look at the mountains and the valley between them, he turned to Harris. "It was nice to dream, but it is time to get back to reality. I want you with me, Sergeant."

"Of course, Colonel."

When Turnbull and Harris entered the alien craft, he took a quick look around. He took note of a few things.

The Anorian ship was larger than the Shark. The interior was designed differently as well. The pilot's chair and the gunner's seat faced the screens in the front of the craft, just like in the Shark. Then there was an area with an open center and with seats lining the outside walls. Behind this area were five seats on either side for the crew. Those seats could be made into cots for sleeping. Cargo space was in the rear of the craft.

Aside from Ranini and one other soldier the rest of the soldiers had also left the ship. She indicated for Turnbull and Harris to take a seat on one side. She and her aid sat across from them.

"I suggest we spend the night here," Ranini started the discussion. "I hope you agree."

"I won't have a problem with it," Turnbull told her. "What exactly have your scouts discovered?"

"I'll show you."

One of the screens in the front came to life. Turnbull stared at the display. "That looks suspiciously like an army camp," he commented.

"Not just a camp. Those buildings are permanent structures. They are planning to make this their home. I count at least fifteen craft. Not all appear to be warcraft. Some are for transportation."

"There is one thing I don't understand. If they want to stay on Cerberus, why would they cause so much destruction in Tsakona and in Freeland?" Turnbull wondered. "I don't think anyone would have objected to their plan to create a home for themselves here."

"There is more of a mystery here," Ranini said. "Watch the screen and pay close attention to the building on the bottom left of the screen."

Turnbull realized that the images on the screen were not just screenshots. They were actually moving.

He saw figures coming out of the building Ranini had indicated. The display suddenly became larger as the watcher zoomed in on it.

"What the hell!" Turnbull cursed. "Am I seeing correctly? I mean is this real?"

"It is real," Ranini assured him.

Turnbull turned to Harris. "What do you make of this?"

"Probably as much or as little as you, sir."

"Harris. Those are Spiders, for heaven's sake. Spiders! What are they doing here?"

"You call them Spiders. We call them by their proper name. Kraach," Ranini said softly. "It seems the Kraach are behind all of this. We are facing a completely different threat."

"If the Spiders, Kraach, are involved, we have a huge problem on our hands. I am surprised we haven't seen at least one of their ships landing on Cerberus, yet." Turnbull scratched his head and stared at the display.

There were a number of Spiders standing in front of the building they had come out of. Turnbull had, of course, seen members of their race before, but never had dealings with them. They called their race Kraach, but humans had dubbed them 'Spiders' because they looked like giant spiders. Their approximately three-foot oval bodies were covered with black hair. Six long, multi-jointed legs supported those bodies. Their two short front limbs ended in long, bony fingers and their sharp mandibles could take off a human hand without any problems.

"I suspect these particular Kraach came through the gate to this planet," Ranini voiced her opinion. "I studied Captain Gorini's report in every detail. When she and Major Wolf captured those seven male Arani, the prisoners told them that the Overlords are giving them orders to plunder the towns. The Overlords call themselves T'Par. According to the description the prisoners gave them, the T'Par on the other side are the Kraach on our side."

"That would explain the presence of these Spiders," Turnbull mused. "What we see here are the T'Par. In many ways, I am relieved to hear that, because we don't want a war with the Spiders." He grimaced. "I mean, the Kraach. The word Spiders flows easier across my lips."

"It doesn't matter what you call them. I agree with you when you say that a war with the Kraach is not something any of us want. They are the oldest of all races existing currently in the Galaxy, and their technology is superior in every way to weapons we command. Nobody knows what kind of weapons they possess."

"I cannot agree more," Turnbull said. "One question. How did you manage to get this close to their base to record these pictures?"

Ranini smiled. "You are not the only ones with miniscule spy-bots."

"Yours are probably superior to ours. Let's face it; the Anorians possessed space travel long before humans developed it. Our ancestors were probably still bashing each other's brains out with animal jawbones and wooden clubs when yours were already colonizing other planets."

"That is true, and yet, our species is also one of the younger races to conquer space." She gave Turnbull a speculative look. "Even though humans are probably the youngest species to acquire space travel, we and many other races do not underestimate you. You evolved much faster than many others. Humans are aggressive and ruthless. Your numbers increase at an alarming speed, which worries many of the older races. Many fear you."

"I wasn't aware of that."

"It isn't something we broadcast, but you are watched. That is one of the reasons humans will never be allowed to control the star-gates. When news got out that Cerberus may be a planet with a star-gate, warning bells went off. We may be the only race so far to establish a presence here, the others will follow."

"We know and we are prepared to deal with that," Turnbull told her. "However, it seems that right now we are facing a much larger problem. If the T'Par are as advanced as the Kraach and as warlike, the small battle we fought with the Arani was just a prelude of worse things to come." He looked back at the display on the screen. "Do you have any suggestions how to proceed from here?"

[19]

THE DECISION WAS TAKEN OUT OF THEIR HANDS. IT WAS NEAR SUNDOWN when a huge, black aircraft rose up behind the mountain ridge.

Turnbull barked a command into his communicator. The crews of the five corvettes scrambled to take their places in the small warcraft. Within moments they rose into the sky. The gunners in the Shark also got ready to defend the aircraft. There were two missile launchers in the front and three laser cannons in the rear.

There was a flurry of movement outside the Anorian craft, also. The two scout ships took to the air at the same time the corvettes did.

The enemy ship came closer at an alarming speed. It was not a thing of beauty, and its sheer size was menacing and intimidating, but the humans and Anorians were ready.

To everyone's surprise, the expected attack did not come. The alien ship suddenly stopped advancing; instead, it hovered some distance away. It hung in the sky like a giant predatory insect.

One of the small screens in the front lit up, but the only thing it displayed were colorful lines that moved on the screen in an intricate pattern. Then a voice spoke in perfect Inglis, "Solar Union ship. Do not attack. We repeat. Do not attack. We are not the enemy. We come in peace. Please, relay this message to the Anorian ship's crew in case they do not receive our message. We repeat. Do not attack. If you do, we must retaliate and destroy you. We have superior weapons, but we prefer not to use them. We will send a small craft. Do not attack the craft. It is not armed. Two negotiators will come to your ship to talk."

The voice stopped abruptly.

Turnbull looked at Harris. "What do you make of that?"

She stayed silent for a moment. Then she said, "Those words did not come from a human throat. It could be a trick."

"Control," he addressed the brain of the ship. "Connect me with the Anorian vessel."

Ranini answered immediately. "We were contacted also," she said. "What do you want to do?"

"I think it is genuine. We should wait for their craft and see what happens."

"I agree."

They watched on the screen how an oval object dropped like an egg out of the bottom of the alien ship and headed for them. It landed near the corvettes. A crack appeared in its side and first one and then another Spider crawled out. They stood and waited.

"I believe we should welcome them," Turner remarked. "Specialist Thompson. Go. Be careful, but don't show any aggression. I don't think you are in any danger. They won't do anything stupid. Ask what they want and bring them into the ship."

Then he gave instructions to the gunners and the pilots of the corvettes, "Do not act unless I give you the order!"

They followed Thompson on the screen. She walked slowly toward the alien ship, arms spread and her hands open.

"I am unarmed." Her voice over the speakers sounded loud in the silence of the control room. "Welcome. I am inviting you to come aboard our ship if that is what you wish. Colonel Turnbull is anxious to meet with you."

"We are also looking forward to meeting with the Colonel. We would like to speak with the Anorian Captain, too. Is she on board your ship?" The voice sounded mechanical. The Spiders undoubtedly used a translating device to communicate.

"She is not, but we can arrange to have her at the meeting."

"Good. Then let us proceed."

The two Spiders followed Thompson as she headed back toward the ship.

Turnbull had never seen members of the Spider race up close. When these two entered the control room, he realized how large their long, hairy legs made them appear. He knew it was an illusion, because their oval bodies were only about three feet in diameter, but with their long legs, they towered over the humans.

"Greetings," one of them said with a mechanical voice. "We are here to display our good will toward humans and the Anorians. We are the T'Par and do not seek conflict but peace."

"We seek no conflict, either, but your servants are the ones coming to this planet, committing destruction and plunder; mining resources they have no permission to mine."

"It is not us who are committing those deeds."

"Are the Arani not your servants?" Turnbull spoke louder than intended. "They told us that the Overlords ordered them to come to this world. Are you who call themselves the T'Par, not the Overlords?"

"There is truth in what you say but also lies."

That monotonous voice was grating on Turnbull's nerves. "Clarify that, please."

"We are the T'Par, and they are the Arani. That is true. We did not order them to plunder this world. They lie. We strive to live in peace, even though it is true, among the T'Par there are splinter groups that are not honorable. Some Arani are honorable, and some are not. These are not. They are renegades."

Turnbull took a moment to digest what the T'Par said. "The base that lies on the other side of the mountains, the one we saw, does it belong to you?"

"It does not."

"Does it belong to the Arani?"

"It does."

"Why would they tell us that they were ordered by the Overlords to plunder this planet?"

"The ones they call Overlords belong to a different faction. They are more warlike than us."

"What is going to happen now?" It was Ranini asking the question.

"We need to stop the group of T'Par that has created this problem from using the portal. The Arani must also be stopped. However, for now we would like to start negotiations with the authorities of this planet about sharing resources."

"Are you talking about mining certain minerals?" Turnbull asked.

"That is correct."

"We don't have the authority to do that, but we will forward the request to the appropriate powers. That is all we can promise. You can tell your superiors that."

"They already know. Everything that transpires here is being transmitted to our ship as it happens."

Turnbull allowed himself a little chuckle. "I guess you don't trust us."

"You are wrong. We do trust you, as you will have to trust us. There is something we want to tell you, but you must come with us to our ship. You and the Anorian."

"Can't you tell us now?"

"No. Not only tell but also show. It can only be done on our ship."

Turnbull looked at Ranini. "What is your opinion? Can we risk going with them?"

"I am not convinced we should, but at the same time I am curious." She smiled. "One of my weaknesses. I am curious by nature. It has gotten me in trouble before, but..." she shrugged. "I am a slow learner."

"I guess we'll go then." Turnbull addressed the T'Par. "You heard. When did you want us to come?"

"As soon as we leave here. You will accompany us."

Turnbull wished he could discover some emotion in the mechanical voice, but that was just wishful thinking. There was no way to read anything into artificially created vocal sounds.

He turned to Harris. "You'll be in charge, Sergeant. Be alert but don't take any action that might jeopardize the safety of the crew. If you're attacked, defend the ship with everything you've got."

Harris saluted. "Understood, Sir."

"Your ship and crew won't be in any danger from us," one of the T'Par said.

"Glad to hear that. I'm not sure if that makes me feel much safer. I have no choice but to trust you. I've never had any personal dealings with members of the Spider race and therefor have little knowledge about them. We humans get along fine with the Spiders. Many of our people trade with them."

"You talk about Spiders. We know nothing about a race called Spiders on this side of the portal."

"My apologies. We humans call them Spiders. They call their race Kraach."

"Why do you call them Spiders?"

"When humans ran into them for the first time, they dubbed them that, and the name stuck." He shrugged. "We humans are like that." He had no intention of telling them the reason humans had named the Kraach Spiders.

"Interesting," the T'Par commented, but because of the flat sounding voice Turnbull wondered if the T'Par did indeed find it so. "We will leave now. Follow us to our ship." Both T'Par turned at the same time and headed for the exit.

Turnbull looked at Ranini. "Might as well go."

She just nodded.

Turnbull wondered how all four of them would fit into the alien ship. There were no seats, only soft, round cushions. He and Ranini climbed inside and squatted on the cushions in the back. When the T'Par entered, they folded their legs under them as they lowered their bodies into the cushions. Suddenly, they looked small and less threatening.

The small vessel rose into the sky and headed for the mothership, closing the gap between both in mere minutes. As the distance shrunk and the mothership came closer, its size became even more apparent. It loomed over the little ship like a small planet. An opening appeared in its belly, swallowing them like a giant fish snapping up a tasty morsel.

They found themselves in what seemed like an underground garage. There were at least a dozen craft like the one they came in already parked there.

"Quite impressive," Turnbull whispered just loud enough for Ranini to hear.

She didn't answer but nodded.

They all got out. "You are in no danger," one of the T'Par assured them. "Just come with us."

The cold mechanical voice did nothing to ease Turnbull's anxiety. His nerves were as taut as the strings of a violin. He and Ranini were at the mercy of their hosts. Neither of them was armed. He felt like a lamb who inadvertently had wandered into the cave of a hungry predator.

They had to walk briskly to keep up with the two T'Par on their six long legs. After just a short walk, they stopped at a big round pillar. A door opened in the pillar, revealing a room that turned out to be an elevator.

"Please, enter," one of the T'Par told them. "Our job is done."

Turnbull hesitated.

"Nothing will happen to you," the T'Par reassured him. "If we wanted to cause you harm we would have done so already."

Ranini entered first. Turnbull followed her, albeit reluctantly.

There was a barely noticeable humming sound as the elevator began to rise. It stopped again after a few moments. When the door whooshed open, Turnbull and Ranini stepped out of it. Instead of entering an empty, large chamber, they stood in a small room with round circles on the walls.

"What now?" Turnbull wondered aloud.

"They look like doors," Ranini guessed.

No sooner had she finished talking, the inside of one of the circles lit up and began to dissolve, revealing a gaping hole. Before they decided how to proceed, a tall humanoid figure stepped out of the hole.

Dressed in a flowing robe, it was impossible to tell if it was male or female. The figure was humanoid but not human, its ancestors most likely carnivorous felines. Two yellow cat's eyes over a flat nose and a wide mouth added to that assumption.

It spoke a few words in a guttural language, but Turnbull's translator needed more than a few words to translate.

"Where are you taking us?" he asked.

The creature gave him a vacant stare and then spoke again, but it still wasn't enough. It turned and stepped through the door it had used to come into the room.

"We might as well follow," Turnbull said to Ranini.

The room they entered was fairly large. It wasn't empty. Turnbull was surprised to see desks on a T'Par ship. However, what alarmed him were the ones sitting behind the desks.

Anorians. Female Anorians.

Their fingers moved rapidly across the flat screens floating in front of them.

Ranini was, obviously, as surprised as he was. Possibly even more so. A few steps took her to one of the desks. The female behind it looked up and stared at Ranini. "What is an Anorian doing on a T'Par ship?" Ranini asked with a demanding voice.

The female looked at her with the same blank look the cat-creature had given them. Then she said, "I don't understand the question."

To Turnbull's surprise he understood what she said. Then he noticed that all the females were dressed in the same flowing robes as the cat-creature.

Realizing they were not Anorians but Arani, he questioned their presence on a T'Par ship. He also realized why he understood the female. The language of the Arani was already in his translator. It had learned from the males.

Ranini must have come to the same conclusion because she came back to Turnbull. "Those are not Anorians," she stated. "I am beginning to wonder what is going on. I wish I had a weapon."

A few of the other females were now looking at Turnbull and Ranini. One of them asked, "Who are you?"

"My name is Ranini. I am an Anorian," Ranini told them. "I am from this side of the portal. You and I may look the same, but we are not the same."

"You speak our language."

"I don't. I have a translator chip in my head. It does it for me." Ranini looked at the cat-creature. "It doesn't work with this one. Is it male or female?"

"Male."

"Tell him to say a few complete sentences so my translator can learn."

The Arani female spoke to the male in the same guttural language it had used unsuccessfully to communicate with Turnbull and Ranini. He nodded and looked at them. Then it spoke. At first, nothing much happened, but then a few words made sense.

"Baranda," the male said and pointed at his chest. "Baranda. My identity." Unintelligible and then, "Come me." Garbled again. Then, "You meet guider." He spoke more rapidly now and then the language became clearer. "You come with me to meet the Mentors. They will explain." Two short, white incisors gleamed dully in his exposed teeth as he gave them a smile, confirming his carnivore ancestry, but also giving him a feral appearance.

Ranini turned to the Arani female that has spoken to them. "Who are the Mentors?"

"You will find out." She turned away, back to the screen on her desk.

Baranda led them to another door. Stepping through it, they found themselves in another elevator. It began to move but stopped almost immediately. Turnbull assumed they had moved up only one floor.

The room they entered, was different from the one below. Scanning the room, Turnbull felt adrenaline shooting through his body with alarm bells going off. He counted seven Arani males either sitting on chairs or standing in front of large screens. On one side of the room, on a web that stretched from one wall to another, sat five T'Par, with their long legs folded under their bodies.

"Why do I suddenly have this ominous feeling?" Turnbull asked Ranini.

"Something isn't right," she stated. "More than ever do I wish I had a weapon."

Their guide led them to the T'Par on the web. He stood rigid for a moment. Then he bowed, turned, and walked away, leaving Turnbull and Ranini wondering what was going to happen next.

One of the T'Par moved while the other four sat as rigid as before. "We are the Mentors," a mechanical voice said. "We sense your uneasiness. There is no need for that. You will not be harmed."

"I feel relieved to hear that," Turnbull said it but for some reason he didn't feel relaxed. "I am Colonel Turnbull of the Solar Union military. My partner is Captain Ranini with the Anorian military. We are here on a mission to find one of our teams that has been taken prisoner by a group of Arani renegades. The two T'Par that brought us to your ship told us you will explain everything, and you will help us."

None of the T'Par moved, even the one in the center. Then one of them spoke. "You have not been told the whole truth. Our apologies. We are not a military vessel but a scientific research ship."

Turnbull threw a quick glance at Ranini to see her reaction to this revelation. He almost felt like laughing. "You threatened to destroy us with your mighty weapons."

"It was a bluff to make sure you don't attack us. We are a peaceful ship. Everyone on board is a scientist in some way. We are very much interested in establishing a relationship with the races on this side of the portal. This planet is unique in many ways. It is one of the very few that has a portal large enough to let a ship of this size transfer across. The portal must not be controlled by outlaws." The mechanical voice stopped.

Turnbull tried to digest what he just heard. This news was completely unexpected. "This is not what we expected to hear from you," he finally said. "Let me ask you a question. Do you have any knowledge about the team we are looking for?"

"Your team is held prisoner in the camp you see in the valley on the other side of the mountain ridge."

"How do you know this?"

"We captured one of the renegade Arani. We learned your language from his translating device. From him we also gained knowledge about the conditions on this side of the portal."

Turnbull looked at Ranini. "What is your opinion? Do you believe this? It all seems so unreal."

"Probably because it is the truth. Sometimes the most unbelievable stories are facts. I don't get any negative vibes from them, but I don't know how much I can trust my intuition in this case. They, like the Kraach, are so different from us humanoids." She lifted her shoulders as if to say, 'Your guess is as good as mine.'

He turned his attention back to the T'Par. "Where is the captured Arani now?"

"He is our prisoner."

"Is he on the ship? Can I talk to him?"

"We will have him brought."

Turnbull nodded. Finally, it looked like they were making progress. It seemed that Wolf and the others were still alive and almost within grasp. If this whole thing wasn't some elaborate scheme things might actually come to a satisfying conclusion. Their mission might just be successful in every way.

He watched as a few moments later three Arani came through a door. The one in the middle looked subdued. When they stopped in front of Turnbull, he noticed that he had a collar around his neck.

Turnbull stepped up to him. "What is your name?"

The prisoner gave him a sullen look. "What do you care?"

"I don't really care, but by exchanging names we might be able to put our differences aside and behave like civilized beings. My name is Turnbull. I am a soldier in the Solar Union military. Are you a soldier?"

The Arani shook his head. "No."

"What should I call you?"

"Raamur. I am known as Raamur."

"Raamur. Answer me one question. What are you doing on this planet?"

"I could ask you the same. What are *you* doing on this planet?" Raamur's look was defiant.

Turnbull smiled grimly. "I'm here to stop you and your friends from plundering this world and to remove you if necessary."

"Why?"

"Because you came uninvited, and you are robbing the people that populate this world. You and your friends have destroyed property, committed murder, and are illegally mining this planet's valuable resources. Need I go on?"

Raamur avoided looking at Turnbull when he said, "I am doing nothing wrong. I only follow orders."

"Who gives you these orders?"

"The Overlords."

Turnbull pointed at the T'Par, wondering what the prisoner was going to say. "Are they the Overlords?"

Raamur shook his head. "No. Not these."

"Do they look like these?"

Raamur just nodded.

"Okay. We're making some headway here. You say that the Overlords are ordering you to plunder this world. Are you and your people slaves of the Overlords?"

He nodded again.

"Would you like to be free?"

This time Raamur looked at Turnbull. "What does that mean? Things are the way they've always been. We can't change that. The Overlords have ruled us for as long as I can remember. Only they are free."

"You can be free if you want to be. Let's ask the two that are holding you about their status." Turnbull addressed one of the two Arani. "Are you slaves of the T'Par?"

The Arani smiled. "No. We are all equals here on the ship. I'm an engineer. Roonndar is a geologist. The T'Par are our mentors and advisors. They are not our masters."

"Did you hear that, Raamur? They are free. They are here of their own free will. You could be like them. Would you like to be free of the Overlords?"

Raamur didn't answer, but there was something in his facial expression that gave Turnbull hope. "What do you know about the five people you are holding prisoner in that camp of yours? Four human males and one female Anorian." He pointed at Ranini. "Like her."

"Do you mean the ones we captured by the mine?"

"Yes. They are the ones. Do you know where in the camp they are kept?"

"I do. I was there when they were captured and brought there."

Turnbull took a deep breath. His gaze lingered on Raamur, wondering if he could break through his mind's automatic defence. "I'm giving you a chance to gain your freedom. You can throw off the shackles that keep you prisoner of the Overlords. All you have to do is help us free our friends."

Raamur stared at Turnbull. "How can I help you with that? That base is a fortress."

"All you have to do is show us the layout of the base, the number of the personnel, your defence system, the weapons you have, and the location where the prisoners are held."

"Is that all?" The sarcasms in his voice could not be missed.

"I ask you very little compared to what I'm offering. You have nothing to lose but everything to gain. Freedom is a precious thing."

"What would I do with my freedom? I couldn't go home. There is no place for me anywhere."

"I asked you before if you are a soldier. You told me you weren't. What exactly is your role or job?"

Raamur stared at the floor. "I have no special skills. I do many different things."

"That is not necessarily a bad thing. It means you have many talents. It also means you can learn." Turnbull thought of something else to say to make his mind more receptive to the idea of being free. "Let's find out what you face if you are not cooperating with us." He turned to the five T'Par. They sat silent and rigid, showing no emotion. "Tell Raamur what is going to happen to him if we find he is useless to us. Will he be put to death?"

"We don't kill for the sake of killing. He will be released in the mountains to give him a chance to survive, but there is no guarantee he will."

"Thank you. I would not be so merciful. He and his kind have imprisoned four humans and one Anorian. They wantonly destroyed property and murdered many of my people. I am willing to forget all that and give him his freedom for information. That is a good deal." He looked again at Raamur. "You heard. What will it be—freedom or certain death?"

"I'm as good as dead already. Where will I go? Tell me." Turnbull detected the sudden panic in Raamur's voice. He seemed to realize he didn't have any choice at all.

"Can I make a suggestion?" one of the two Arani spoke up.

"Go ahead," Turnbull told him.

"He could move to one of the planets where our species is not

241

controlled by the renegade T'Par. If he is willing, he can learn a trade or use his skills to work for one of the large companies."

Turnbull looked over to the T'Par on the web. "Will you allow him to stay on this ship until you get back to the other side of the portal? I'm sure you'll find something for him to do to earn his place on your ship."

"If he helps to rescue your friends, he is welcome to stay," one of them said in his emotionless voice. "We are also willing to assist him in finding a suitable planet."

"You heard," Turnbull said to the prisoner. "You are getting a chance to turn your life around. Don't reject it."

"How can I trust any of you?"

"You take us on faith, which we will have to do with the information you give us."

Raamur heaved a sigh. He seemed suddenly more relaxed. "I will help you."

"Good." Turnbull felt like sighing also, but not like relaxing. The most difficult task was still ahead. The information Raamur was going to provide would be of great help. Just knowing where the missing team was being held was an important piece of what lay ahead, but getting into the enemy base was not going to be easy. Would the scientists on this vessel be able to render help was still a question. They were scientists not soldiers. The way it appeared, it would be up to the humans and the Anorians to launch the rescue mission.

[20]

ONE OF THE PROBLEMS THEY FACED WAS GETTING CLOSE TO THE ENEMY BASE without being detected. Turnbull wished they had a cloaking device like the Spiders, but until now, that was one scientific marvel they had not been able to develop. The Spiders didn't want to share.

The T'Par did not have a cloaking device, either.

Raamur had kept his word and provided them with a detailed plan of the base and the location where Wolf and the others were being held. When asked what kind of detection net the base had, he wasn't quite sure, but according to him, it was not very sophisticated. Apparently, nobody had seen the need for an elaborate defence system. The base was hidden deep in the mountains. Air traffic was non-existent on this planet. They did not worry about being discovered or attacked by anyone from the air. If it were to happen, whoever made it across the mountains would be on foot. And even that was something they wouldn't expect.

This was going to be a huge advantage for Turnbull and his force. The assault would come unexpected and sudden.

After discussing the situation with Captain Ranini, they made the decision to use the five corvettes and the two Anorian scout ships to move the soldiers as close as possible to the base. The combined assault by humans and Anorians would take place during the night.

It would take two trips to move all the soldiers.

Before the attack, Turnbull sent out a seeker to find a suitable landing spot for the corvettes. It had to be far enough from the base not to attract any attention but close enough for the soldiers to travel safely on foot in the darkness. The seeker also mapped out the safest path to take to the enemy base.

The planning and the preparations took three days.

Turnbull was, of course, in the first transport.

The night was dark with just a few stars in the sky. Only a quarter of the satellite was visible, which created perfect conditions for their mission. While waiting for the second wave to arrive, Turnbull perused the area. The ground was covered with short grasses and the odd small shrub. None of them presented any obstacles to prevent the corvettes from landing.

As soon as the second group of troopers arrived, Turnbull gathered everyone around. "You've all been briefed on the layout of the enemy base, and each group knows what to do. There are five separate buildings. Team Alpha One will head for the first building where the prisoners are kept. Once we secure the area, I will give the signal for the coordinated attack. Team Alpha Two is responsible for destroying the ships. You will be in the first wave. You will attach the explosive devices. As soon as all the explosives are set, Teams Bravo One, Bravo Two, and Bravo Three will begin the main wave of the attack. You all have your designated targets. If you face opposition, shoot to kill, but try to take prisoners if possible. The moment everyone is inside their assigned building, Alpha Two will trigger the explosives that destroy the ships. Alright. Let's get moving."

He pulled the night-goggles over his eyes and began the walk. According to the survey, it shouldn't take longer than thirty minutes to reach the enemy base.

Even though the seeker had mapped the route, the walk was not smooth. A few times Turnbull almost took a tumble when his foot caught on an exposed root from one of the small shrubs or the occasional stunted tree. Slippery rocks covered with moss were another obstacle to watch out for. He noticed he wasn't the only one struggling.

They reached their target within the allotted time.

The troopers crouched behind small shrubbery or lay hidden in the grass. The base lay in darkness and in silence. Turnbull looked through his binoculars. The screen showed no movement. As assumed, the personnel on the base felt secure and safe inside their fortress. He doubted that they had posted any guards or set up an electronic surveillance system.

However, he did not allow himself to relax. Appearances could be deceiving. He would not be lulled into false security. Once the base was awake, things would turn from lazy into an inferno of violence and chaos.

"Alright," he said quietly into his communicator, "Team Alpha One with me. Team Alpha Two, move out."

He rose from his crouching position and headed for the building that was supposed to hold the prisoners. Sergeant Miller, Specialists Thompson, and Wong were close behind him. He didn't have to check if Team Alpha Two had left to take care of the ships. With Sergeant Harris leading the team, he knew he didn't have to worry. The other members of the team were Specialists Whang, Sargoni, and Krushnov. Sargoni had special training in explosives, the reason he had chosen him to be with Team Alpha Two.

The night was unusually silent. He noticed the absence of the usual sounds of the night creatures that lived in the forests and in the grasslands. It seemed the vegetation in the valley this high in the mountains was not a desirable environment for wildlife, but that didn't mean they were not there. Some predators are silent and deadly. You don't see them until it is too late.

'That's what we are. Silent predators. Death disguised as human beings. I hope we'll find Wolf and the others before the enemy knows we are here.'

Humans did not design the buildings, but, basically, they weren't much different from structures built by humans. Or even the Anorians.

They entered the building through a small side door. It was locked. A few bursts from a laser melted the lock, and the door slid open. It was dark inside, but with their night-goggles they had no problem seeing everything clearly. Finding themselves in a narrow corridor, they searched for a door. It was at the end of the corridor. They entered a larger room. It was filled with what appeared to be parts of various appliances. This was obviously a storage room. The next room was much larger. Turnbull was the first one through the door. The light in the room seemed bright. He pushed up his goggles and found the light to be dim but bright enough. Immediately after entering the room, Turnbull flattened himself against a wall. About halfway down, stood one Arani. Obviously, a sentry. He had his back to Turnbull. It was not clear if he was armed.

"Stay back," Turnbull whispered. Then he advanced slowly and silently. The Arani turned just before Turnbull reached him, but he didn't have enough time to react. Turnbull smashed the stock of his rifle into his throat. The sentry staggered from the impact, stumbled around gasping for air, and then he fell. Holding both hands to his throat, he lay convulsing on the floor; his feet kicked until his movements became feebler, and then he lay still.

After searching the body for weapons and discovering none on him, Turnbull felt a stab of regret for killing an unarmed being in cold blood without a valid reason. He could have been taken prisoner. At the very least, they could have interrogated him to find out the exact location where Wolf's team was held prisoner.

In the meantime, the rest of his team had joined him. Miller seemed to study the dead body with interest. "So that's what a male Anorian looks like. Until now, I've only seen females."

"They call their race Arani," Turnbull informed him. "The males are the dominant gender, unlike with the Anorians where the females run the place. The Anorian males are doing the domestic chores. Most never leave their home world. That's why you don't see any."

"I like that arrangement." Beverley Thompson chuckled. "I wish we'd have more females in the military. Maybe things wouldn't get screwed up so badly."

"Careful what you say, girl," Wong said. "You're in the minority here."

"Leave it for later," Turnbull said sharply. "Let's find the prisoners."

"Sorry, sir. I meant no disrespect in my statement." Thompson pointed. "I see an outline in the wall. It could be a door."

It was. There was no visible lock to open the door, but when Wong touched a faint looking circle with his flat hand, the door began to hum and then it slid open. He was the first one to enter the room on the other side. He lifted his left arm and then he said, "All clear."

The room lay in semi-darkness. At first, Turnbull saw only pieces of what looked like furniture. The designs were different but still recognisable as tables and chairs. He pulled down his night-goggles again and everything became clearer.

He saw five narrow beds. Each bed was occupied. Holding up his arm to keep the others from advancing, he slowly walked toward one of the beds. He didn't want to startle whoever lay there.

Bending over the sleeping figure, he saw it was a man. He lay on his side and his face was partially covered by his right arm. However, Turnbull saw enough to notice the man's hair was disheveled and his face unshaven. He moved and turned onto his back while Turnbull was looking at him.

Then he opened his eyes.

His right arm shot up and his fingers grabbed Turnbull's throat. The move was unexpected. Turnbull slapped the man's arm away and stepped back.

The man rolled from his bed and dropped into a defensive stance. The thin blanket that had covered his body slipped to the ground, revealing his nakedness.

"Who are you?" The words came out in a harsh, gravelly voice.

"Ethan?" Turnbull asked, realizing that it was his friend.

"Who wants to know?" Obviously, Wolf didn't recognize him in the semi-darkness behind the goggles and dressed in his combat uniform.

In the meantime, the other sleepers woke up. Somebody attacked Turnbull from behind, and he found himself in a stranglehold, unable to speak. Then the room was flooded with a bright light when one of his team switched on their headlamp.

"We are the rescue team," a voice shouted.

Turnbull recognized Beverly Thompson's voice.

The person holding Turnbull in the stranglehold let go. "I am Colonel Turnbull," he said, more for the benefit of the others, and then, looking at Wolf. "It's me. Harry. We came to take you home."

Wolf stood motionless for a moment. "Harry?" he asked. "Is it really you?"

Turnbull removed his goggles and walked up to his friend. "In the flesh."

"What took you so long?" Wolf gave him a weak grin. Looking down on himself, he said, "Sorry, I'm not dressed for the occasion. Those bastards took away our clothing and the rest of our stuff." He rubbed his unshaven chin. "Even my shaving cream. I must look like a wild man."

Turnbull laughed. "You can borrow mine. I'll even lend you my comb." He turned to look around. "Who took me into that stranglehold?" Not far away from him stood an Anorian female. Also naked. "You must be Captain Gorini. Your people will be happy to find you in good health."

"Not so healthy anymore," she said with a little smile. "I feel a little weak these days. The food in this place left something to be desired."

"You could have fooled me. I thought you'd choke me to death."

Another person came up to him and slapped him on the back. "Glad to see you, Turnbull. I hope somebody missed me."

Turnbull turned to look at the big man. "Alfred Swann. Major Alfred Swann, the man of mystery. I have a message for you from Colonel Stonewall."

"You've met Colonel Stonewall?"

"I have. He told me all about you."

"What's the message?"

"He said not to lie to your friends."

Swann gave him a startled look. "He said that?"

Turnbull smirked. "No, he didn't. Those are my words."

"I never lied to any of you, my friend. I just didn't tell you. The existence of Scouts Security is not common knowledge. It is not shared, especially not with military people. I'm sorry you feel betrayed."

"Not betrayed. Disappointed. Nothing to worry about. Obviously, you had your reasons. The secret is out. I'm just glad you are okay."

Swann rubbed his stubbly face. Then he smiled, took a step forward, and gave Turnbull a bearhug. "Don't act so nonchalant, my old friend. Admit, you worried about me and Ethan. That's what friends do."

Embarrassed by Swann's show of affection, Turnbull gave the big man a gentle shove. "Not so close. Did you forget you're naked?"

With a loud laugh, Swann let go of Turnbull. "I'm getting so used to being naked, I sometimes forget. You didn't by any chance bring some clothing for us?"

Turnbull shook his head. "Sorry. We had no idea we'd find you naked. We may have to strip a couple of the Arani."

Swann was suddenly serious. "What are your plans? This is a large complex with many Arani. In addition to several T'Par. They are living in the last building. How did you get here, and how will you get away? Are there only five of you?"

"There are seventeen troopers in my team and nine Anorians."

"Where are they?"

"Waiting for my command to launch the attack." Turnbull turned away and spoke into his communicator. "Team Alpha Two. What is your status?

The answer came immediately. "All explosives are in place. Ready for the next phase."

It was time to initiate Phase Two. "All teams. Mount the attack—now!" He waved to Miller. "Sergeant Miller and Wong. Sweep this building. Kill anyone you find. Bring some clothing."

"Understood, sir." Miller tipped his helmet. Both men left the room.

Turnbull finally paid attention to the other two men that had been with Wolf and Swann. "I'm sorry," he said to the one who was sitting on his bed. "I have two more names. Ikeda and Randor. Which one are you?"

"I am Scout Brian Ikeda." He pointed to the last man. "That is Randor."

Turnbull looked at Randor. "I was told you are Sartan."

"He may be Sartan, but he is one of us," Wolf said. "We don't make a distinction."

"I wasn't," Turnbull stated. "Merely making an observation."

"That's alright." Wolf sat down on his bed. "You wouldn't by chance have any water or some food?"

Turnbull looked at Beverly Thompson. "Thompson. You carry water and food in your backpack. Look after them. I'm going to join Miller and Wong. Stay vigilant and keep an eye on the entrance."

He stalked to the door and went outside. Pulling down his goggles, he stepped into the darkness of the corridor. He had a feeling of apprehension. The missing team was safe, but the battle was just now beginning. He had to find Miller and Wong. "Sergeant Miller. What's your status?"

"We ran into some opposition. We're pinned down."

"I will find you." He activated the location finder on his wristband. A virtual cube materialized on his wrist. "Find Miller and Wong." Three points of light pulsed inside the cube. Two red and one green. An arrow pointed from the green light to the red ones. He began following the arrow. When he came to an empty room, he found two corridors leading out of it. The arrow pointed to one exit. He had no intention of taking that one.

"Show alternate route."

The head of the arrow moved. He was hoping it would lead him around the altercation, giving him an advantage. Moving as fast as he could, he traveled down a series of corridors. He passed a few doors, but the arrow didn't stop at any of them. Finally, it did. Carefully opening the door, he saw several Arani kneeling behind what looked like beds. He realized he was looking into sleeping quarters. The Arani soldiers were armed with rifles.

Looking past the Arani, he saw a large piece of furniture turned onto its side. He figured Miller and Wong were hiding behind it. He lifted his laser rifle, feeling like a butcher. The Arani had no idea they were about to be slaughtered by an unseen assassin.

It was over in less than one minute. Death had come to them on the silent wings of a night hunter.

"Safe to come out," he told Miller and Wong.

They left their hiding place and walked cautiously into the room.

"Did you come across any other opposition?"

"Yes. We killed three of the enemy. This building is safe now," Miller said.

"We'll have to strip them and take their clothing."

They began the unpleasant job of removing the uniforms from the dead Arani. They even took the boots they had standing beside their beds.

"Let's head back."

They had almost reached the room where Wolf and the others had been held, when Turnbull's communicator came to life. It was the voice of Sergeant Harris.

"We've secured buildings four and five. The Arani have not reported back. They are in buildings two and three. We're going in. What are your orders concerning the ships?"

"Blow them up. Now. The element of surprise has passed."

The sound of explosions could be heard a few moments later.

"Wong, you take these clothes to the rescued team. Sergeant, you and I will go and help the others."

The night was lit up by the fires that were consuming the ships. Any escape route for the enemy was cut off. They had no option but to surrender if they wanted to live.

Buildings two and three were the largest buildings. If they could trust the information Raamur gave them, building three was the one the T'Par occupied. When Turnbull and Miller approached building three, they were met by silence. Lasers didn't make any loud sounds, only the soft, barely audible hissing when a laser was discharged.

When they entered the building, they stepped into a different world. High above them, giant spider nets crisscrossed the huge room from one wall to another. The area under the nets was divided by walls to create smaller rooms.

An object lying in the jungle of nets drew Turnbull's attention. He realized it was the body of one of the T'Par. It didn't move and was presumably dead. Turnbull pushed up his goggles. They were not needed, because the room was bright from the flashes of lasers being discharged. Cautiously, they advanced to one of the rooms. It was empty except for the body of one of the Arani. Moving on to the next room, a laser beam barely missed them.. They took cover behind a large bale of some kind of material, joining two Anorian soldiers. One of them lay on the ground. She was pressing a hand against her shoulder.

"How bad is it?"

"Just grazed," she said. "But it hurts."

"How many are we facing?"

The unharmed Anorian shrugged. "Probably only one."

"T'Par?"

She nodded. "She is fast and alert. She's had us pinned down for a long time."

"Perhaps, she will listen to reason. "Turnbull stood up without exposing his body. "T'Par soldier. I am Major Turnbull. We are in control of this base. Surrender and we can end this peacefully. Time is running out. Your ships have been destroyed, and you have no place to go. There is no need for anyone to die."

There was no answer, and then a mechanical voice said, "How can I trust you?"

"I give you my word of honor. I am a soldier, and I have sworn not to take a life wantonly. If you surrender peacefully, we will not kill you. I promise."

There was another pause. "I have decided to trust you. I am coming out without my weapon if you meet without yours."

"Be careful, Major," Miller warned. "It could be a trick."

"I'll take that chance." Turnbull walked from behind the bale with his arms spread. "I trust you, also."

The T'Par had already come out from its hiding place. It stood on its six legs, watching him warily. "I am injured."

"We will help you if we can," Turnbull promised.

The others came out from their hiding place behind the bale of cloth.

"What do you want to do about this one?" Miller asked.

Before Turnbull could answer, two Anorians came rushing out of the next room. When they saw the T'Par both brought up their weapons.

"Don't shoot!" Turnbull shouted.

They lowered their lasers. "Everything under control?" one of them asked, looking at the Anorian beside Turnbull.

"Yes, it is. Ramdini has been wounded. She may need to be treated."

"I am fine," Ramdini said. "It can wait. What is happening?"

"We have two prisoners. We came to see how you are doing."

"One prisoner, as you can see."

252

"Bring those two into this room. Ramdini, are you well enough to guard them?"

"I can," Ramdini assured her.

Turnbull turned when he heard voices coming from the entrance. He saw Sergeant Harris and her team coming into the building.

"Building Two secured," Harris reported.

"Good," Turnbull said. "This is the last building. Let's check out what is happening in the other rooms." He thought of something and addressed the T'Par. "How many of your people are still out there?"

"Three, if they are alive."

"Can you communicate with them?"

"Yes, I can. Why?"

"Tell them to give themselves up. There is no more need for anyone to die. They are outnumbered. Their chances of surviving are slim."

The T'Par was silent for a moment, and then it said, "They will lay down their weapons if their survival is guaranteed."

"It is guaranteed. Give the word and I will order my soldiers to stop fighting."

"Let it be then."

"Good." Turnbull relaxed. It was over. The base was in their hands. "Attention all units. This is Colonel Turnbull. The T'Par have agreed to lay down their weapons. Stop fighting immediately. I repeat. Stop fighting immediately."

Looking again at their prisoner. "Tell your people to gather in this room. They will be treated fairly."

———

THE ALIEN SUN WAS RISING INTO THE MORNING SKY. IT LOOKED LIKE IT WAS going to be a clear and sunny day. The troopers and the Anorian soldiers were assembled in the yard outside. The humans had suffered two casualties. Carl Becker and Oman Albar were dead. One of the Anorians had been killed and one wounded.

It was different with the prisoners. Only one of the T'Par was dead. Two were wounded, but at last count sixteen Arani had been killed.

Three had sustained nonthreatening wounds. Twenty-three had survived.

All the prisoners were either standing or sitting in front of building four.

Wolf and his four companions had decided not to come out yet. They felt too weak to stand for long or even walk around outside.

There wasn't much left of the ships but melted plastic and twisted metal.

"What are we going to do about the prisoners?" Turnbull said to Captain Ranini.

The Anorian was still studying the rubble that had once been several aircraft. "Too bad we had to destroy all those ships. They may have come in handy."

Turnbull nodded. "I agree, but we couldn't take the chance of any of them escaping. They may have brought support. We could never have faced a warship. Not without our corvettes."

"You are right. You are wondering what we should do with the prisoners. I'm not sure. We can't kill them. Not after you guaranteed them they would be safe. It is a problem. There are too many of them to take with us."

Captain Harris, who was standing beside Turnbull, suddenly burst out, "The decision may have been taken out of our hands." She pointed east.

Turnbull and Ranini turned at the same time to look east.

A cold shudder ran down Turnbull's back. There, above the mountain, a ship had appeared.

It was huge and ugly looking. A giant oval monstrosity, and it came in fast. There was no time to seek cover. The troopers and the Anorian soldiers went down on one knee, their laser rifles aimed at the new threat.

When the ship neared the ground, six short struts appeared on the underside. They unfolded, became six long legs, giving the ship the appearance of a giant spider.

There was no denying to whom this ship belonged.

A hole appeared in the belly of the ship, and two Spiders floated to the ground. And then two more.

Turnbull corrected himself.

They were not Spiders. The design of this ship was similar in design to the Spider ships, but only similar.

These were T'Par. The enemy.

"Do not fire," he ordered the troopers. "Nobody act until I give the order."

The four T'Par seemed to wait for something. Then to Turnbull's surprise, two Arani floated to the ground. They began walking away from the ship but then stopped.

Nothing happened for awhile.

"I think they are waiting for us to make the next move," Turnbull said. "I am going to meet them."

"Are you sure that is wise?" Harris cautioned.

"It may not be, but I'll see what they want." He handed Harris his laser rifle and then began the walk toward the ship.

"I'll come with you," a voice said beside him. It was Ranini. "I think I should, because those two are Arani. My kind."

The two Arani watched Turnbull and Ranini coming closer. Turnbull's senses were on alert. He was watching for any aggressive moves, but the Arani stood immobile, only their eyes seemed alive.

He still had his sidearm, just in case.

He and Ranini stopped about ten feet in front of the two Arani. Neither one said anything. All four kept studying each other.

"Greetings," Turnbull finally said.

One of the two Arani gave them a nod. Then he said, "Greetings to you also. We are the T'Par. We did not come to start a conflict."

"That is good to know," Turnbull commented. "Unfortunately, your people and your Overlords, the T'Par, have done a lot of damage to the people living on this planet. You have plundered their lands, destroyed property, and murdered innocent people. You have removed minerals without permission. That is why we have taken over this outpost. You and the Arani are not welcomed anymore."

"You have spoken truth, but you are also mistaken. We have not done those things you are accusing us of. The ones who did those things are renegades. Outlaws. We have come to make peace with the inhabitants of this planet. We are the T'Par."

"So you've stated already. I am Colonel Turnbull. I am a human. This is Captain Ranini. She is an Anorian female. She may look like you, but she is not Arani."

"We are not Arani. We are T'Par."

"I don't understand."

"These bodies were grown artificially. Our brains were removed from damaged T'Par and transplanted into these bodies."

Stunned for a moment by this revelation, Turnbull didn't comment.

"If what you say is true, what is your real reason for being here?" Ranini said.

"To punish the outlaws and to stop them from doing what they have done. Also, we want to trade with the different races living on this side of the Gate. We have much to offer."

"We are willing to do that. I think I can speak for the humans when I say so are they." She glanced at Turnbull.

"She is correct," Turnbull agreed with her. "However, there is much to discuss. We have prisoners and are wondering what to do with them." He pointed at the assembled captives.

"They are renegades and will be dealt with," the T'Par in the form of an Arani said. "They will be punished."

"Will you kill them?" Turnbull was concerned about that.

"No, but they will become servants."

"In a way I am glad to hear that. Not all of them may be evil. Some of them might be cooks and some are responsible for other chores." Turnbull felt relieved. As a soldier, he was used to violence and death, but he didn't condone cold-blooded murder and the committing of senseless atrocities.

"Are you empowered to discuss the exchange of trade goods or to make decisions on other matters?"

"I'm afraid not. I am a soldier, and I am responsible for the upholding of laws and to make peace when possible. I can let my superiors know of your intentions, and they will organize meetings with your people and those that are dealing with those matters."

"We will take possession of this base and make it our headquarters on this planet. Any future discussions can take place on this base. Will that be to your satisfaction?"

Turnbull turned to Ranini. "Do you agree with that suggestion?"

Ranini shrugged. "Like you I don't have any powers beyond what I am required to do in my capacity as a soldier. I have no objections to this proposal. It is up to both our governments to make other arrangements."

"You heard," Turnbull said to the T'Par. "That will be alright until it is decided otherwise."

"Good. We are satisfied." Both T'Par turned and walked back to their ship.

This did not surprise Turnbull. The Spiders were not known for great conversations, why would the T'Par be any different?

EPILOGUE

THEY CALLED IT THE GOLDEN FORK. IT WAS THE CLOSEST TAVERN NEXT TO the spaceport. Until now, the only customers had been locals, but ever since the first private spaceship carrying a group of fortune hunters landed on the small spaceport, things had changed. It hadn't taken long for the word to get out that Cerberus was rich with precious stones, and it didn't take much effort to locate and mine them.

Changes were coming to Greater York, the capital city of Freeland. The few hotels near the spaceport were filled to capacity. There are always men that recognize an opportunity, and a few such men with foresight had begun repairing old, run-down houses and changing them into rooms for rent.

Talks between representatives from the Solar Union's Trading Commission and the T'Par had begun. The Trading Commission represented not only humans, but also the Anorian Empire.

The Spiders had expressed an interest in talking to the T'Par about exchanging trade goods. Since Cerberus was a planet mainly occupied by humans, the Solar Union was reluctant to give permission to other species.

Turnbull lifted his tankard and took a long swallow. Putting it back onto the table, he wiped the foam from his mouth and sighed. "I will miss this place. This is the best ale I've drank for quite some time. They still brew it in family-run breweries from natural ingredients, unlike that artificially produced stuff they serve on some of the more advanced planets."

Wolf nodded in agreement. "I can't argue with you there. Do you have an idea when you'll be sent on another assignment?"

"Not yet, but I'm expecting my replacement any day now. After that, it will be just a matter of time before I'll get my marching orders. How about you?"

Wolf smiled. "I'm still on recovery-leave. I just got back from Windy Lake where I stayed with Ambassador Amsterdam. He lost his job with Hyperion Mineral Explorations after you shut down the mines, but he did have the foresight to plan for such an eventual event and bought a house in Windy Lake years ago."

"Smart man. He wasn't really an ambassador, was he?"

"He was but not for the Union. He was an ambassador for Hyperion. Everyone assumed the Union had an embassy here on Cerberus, which, of course, was not the case."

"How is Swann doing? I haven't talked to him since we came back."

"Alfred? He's staying at Scouts Base in Windy Lake. He's fine."

Turnbull chuckled. "What a surprise to find out he's a Major with Scout's Security. Righthand man of Colonel Stonewall, the most powerful man in the Solar Union."

"You've met Stonewall. What's he like?"

Turnbull pursed his lips. "There is something about him that commands respect, and yet, he seems humble in many ways. A down-to-Earth attitude. His position has not gone to his head."

"According to his reputation, he is incorruptible and cannot be bought, something Admiral Swenson doubts. He believes that everyone has his price." Wolf lifted his tankard. "Here's to our mystery friend Major Alfred Swann."

"I'll drink to that."

THE END

———

Available Spring 2026
Operation Stargate #6:
Artemis, Shattered Sanctuary

THANK YOU FOR READING

Did you enjoy this book?

We invite you to leave a review at the website of your choice, such as Goodreads, Amazon, Barnes & Noble, etc.

DID YOU KNOW THAT LEAVING A REVIEW...

- Helps other readers find books they may enjoy.
- Gives you a chance to let your voice be heard.
- Gives authors recognition for their hard work.
- Doesn't have to be long. A sentence or two about why you liked the book will do.

ABOUT THE AUTHOR

Herbert Grosshans is a Canadian writer. He lives near Winnipeg, Canada. Already as a young boy, he was a voracious reader. He loved the old legends about Nordic gods and immortals. Thor with his war-hammer was his favorite. Stories about Kings and knights and Vikings, giants and dwarfs, wizards and witches fascinated him. When he was fourteen, he was introduced to Science Fiction. He was hooked after reading his first story. However, he also loved Westerns and Crime novels. He pretty much read everything, no matter what genre, but Science Fiction and Fantasy became his favorite. It wasn't long before he began writing his own short stories. He also tried writing a novel. When he completed his first full-length novel 'The Galactics' he knew he could do it. That novel is still hiding inside an envelope in a closet and will probably never be seen or read by anyone else.

Later on in life, he concentrated mostly on writing and didn't read as much as he used to. He wrote his stories during his lunch hour into a scribbler. At home, he pounded away on his old manual typewriter. He didn't care too much about spelling and proper sentences. As long as the story in his head was written and put on paper.

That all changed with the arrival of computers. Suddenly, it became much easier to make changes and correct mistakes. It also created more opportunities to become published.

He published his first novel 'Daughter of the Dark' in 2006 with Midnight Showcase. It was the first book in his series The Xandra. The series has since grown to eight books.

So far, he has published over thirty books. The majority are, of course,

Science Fiction, but a few are Detective stories and Thrillers. No Westerns —yet. Most of his stories contain Erotica.

He also published one non-fiction book with Amazon under the title 'The Published Writer', a guide on how to get published.

His books are available from his publisher Melange Books, LLC. To find out more about Herbert's books, please, visit his blog.

Website: www.fictitioustales.weebly.com
Blog: hegro.blogspot.com
Blog: hergros.blogspot.com
Email: hegro@shaw.ca

ALSO BY HERBERT GROSSHANS

OPERATION STARGATE SERIES

Codename Salamander

Savanna

The Aregon Files Volume 1

The Aregon Files Volume 2

Mission Aurora

Cerberus

MYSTERY NOVELS

Bullet of Revenge

A Matter of Justice

Mark of the Cobra

SCI-FI NOVELS

Orola

Orion

SWORD AND SORCERY

Clouds Over Maridaan

SEEDS OF CHAOS DUOLOGY

Eden's Gate

Hell's Gate

STARDOGS DUOLOGY

Return to Redsky

Redemption

STARS IN CHAINS DUOLOGY

Slave

Liberator

A STONEWALL CHRONICLES NOVEL

Outpost Epsilon

A New Dawn

Epsion City

Raptor's Tooth

WEB OF CONSPIRACY TRILOGY

Death of a Hero

Traitors and Patriots

Tarnished Valor

THE XANDRA SERIES

Daughter of the Dark

Mother of Light

Goddess of Life

Lure of Seduction

Escape from Paradise

Iceworld

Alien World

Dark World

SHORT STORY COLLECTIONS

Dual Visions

Tapestry of Dreams

Time Flares

www.ingramcontent.com/pod-product-compliance
Lightning Source LLC
Chambersburg PA
CBHW020611260626
47157CB00003B/953